Twisting Hercules

ALSO BY KIM MALAJ

Ember in Time Series
Castle of Teskom
Recover or Yield
Protectors of Time
Guide Time Inside

Who Is Maggie
Twisting Hercules

The Old Untold
Failed Book Cover Journals (A-Z)

Twisting Hercules

Kim Malaj

Twisting Hercules

ISBN: 9781958502174 Paperback
       9781958502051 Paperback
       9781958502266 Hardcover
       9781958502112 Hardcover

Copyright © 2023 Kim Malaj

All rights reserved. Except for any review, the reproduction or utilization of this work in whole or in part in any form by any electronic, mechanical or other means now known or invented, including xerography, photocopying, and recording, or in any information storage or retrieval system, is forbidden without the written permission of the author.

Kim Malaj
Haxhaj Nd. 19
Bajze, Albania 4306
www.kimmalaj.com

This is a work of fiction. Names, characters, places, and incidents are either the product of the author's imagination or are used fictitiously, and any resemblance to actual business establishments, events, locations, or persons, living or dead, is entirely coincidental.

First Edition: May 1, 2023

To my readers near and dear to my hometown of Lawson. This book is my chance to tip my hat to youth and growing up small. Where everyone knew everybody and there was never a stranger behind any door.

Cheers!

1

Silvey brakes hard screeching to a stop outside of the missile bunker. She climbs out of her truck and slides her bag out from the second row.

"Go to college do something with your life," she mutters, checking the battery life on her voltage meters. "Electrician is a man's field."

She slams the truck door, wishing she had slammed the front door of her mother's house on her way out this morning.

"Dre, she's never going to accept that I love this job and that I am so much like my father. It eats her up at night."

"Silvey," Andrea says, "she's just bitter that your father has moved on and is taking it out on you."

Silvey checks the parking lot. A small car and a white truck are parked parallel to her. "Ha, maybe. But I've got to run. I think the inspector is here."

"Ok, but remember I have plans for us later and yes it requires your attendance."

"Uh, about that."

"Silvey Rhoades, don't you dare bail on me!"

"I promise I'll try to make it," Silvey says, tapping her phone to look at the invite in a new text message from Andrea. The same invite she's sent three times in the last two days. "It's semi-formal?"

"For the eight hundredth time, yes!"

"I'm just teasing," Silvey says. "I laid out my dress and heels this morning. See you around six?"

"Girl, you'll cause my first grey hair. I swear!"

"Ha, life goals! Later, Dre." Silvey taps her headphone and pockets it before stepping inside the old silo. She grins and admires her progress as she starts the walk down the winding ramp to the fifth level.

The steel grates under her boots no longer clang. She inspects the new rubber mats cushioning her weight. *They feel like a cloud, but when were they installed?* She sticks her head over the railing and finds two men below laying out a roll of the rubber mats between tanks on the next level.

"Hey," Silvey says, her voice echoes around the silo. "What time did you guys start?"

One man looks around. He finally looks up and waves.

Silvey laughs. "Midge?"

"Hey now, no one calls me that anymore!" Micah says. "Are you the lone wolf I've been hearing about?"

Silvey smiles. "Lone wolf. Hmm, I like the sound of that." She taps light fixtures hanging above the seed trays. "If you mean these, then yes. Each one accommodates the owners' custom specifications for each plant. They're calculated to grow fresh greens, various herbs, strawberries, cherry tomatoes, and peppers so far."

"Cool," Micah says, pulling the adhesive strip off the back of the next mat. "It's the first vertical farming project we had the chance to bid on."

"Same," Silvey says. "After years of working alongside other union electricians, this was my first attempt to leave the old man's club and snub behind."

Micah laughs. "Do you remember the Lewis twins?"

Silvey smiles. "Of course, you've heard I out bid them for this project." She laughs and shakes her head as she winds her way through the tanks.

2

"Lawson is a small town," Micah says, laying down the next mat. "How many weeks do you have left here?"

"Three weeks left on the permit," Silvey says, joining Micah on his level. "Is this your only contribution?" She points to the mats.

"We have similar mats and shelving going into the office and distribution lines next door after this install."

"Nice!" Silvey says, bouncing on her heels. "They feel like a cloud."

"It's my best-selling product." Micah whirls his finger around. "The sound must have been deafening in here before. Everything echoes."

She nods. "The lack of sound under my step is what caught my attention."

The other man stands and turns towards Silvey.

She takes a step back, bumping into a tank. He's a head over her in height, but his smile stops her heart for a brief second. *Damn.*

Micah catches her reddening cheeks and grins. "Silvey Rhoades, meet Baxton Auburn."

"Hi," Baxton says, "it's nice to meet you, but you can call me Bax." He tips the bill his blue KC cap to her.

Micah coughs.

"Nice to meet you, too," Silvey says, adjusting her bag. She hesitantly walks towards Bax and shrinks in his shadow as she passes. She tilts her head down, her blonde hair shields her rosy cheeks from his view. "I'll be on level five if you need anything." She tries to walk casually ahead fighting every impulse to rush forward. As she rounds the first curve, she glances back over and catches Bax watching her. He looks away immediately.

So, it's not just me. Silvey focuses on not tripping and stops when she reaches her last install. She sits her bag down. She assesses the next set of lights and pulls out her tools to finish the wiring she laid out yesterday.

"Hey Silvey," Micah calls out.

"Yea?" Silvey says, looking up to find Micah. He's leaning over the edge of the railing pointing up to the tinted glass overhead.

"Was it raining when you came in?"

"No, but there were some clouds coming in from the west."

"Crap," Micah says, patting his pockets. He pulls out his phone. "I better get the rest of the mats inside."

"Can you double check my windows are rolled up?" Silvey asks.

"Of course." Micah jogs up the ramp.

Silvey turns her attention back towards the next light fixture.

Two minutes later, she hears Micah return. "Windows are good."

"Thanks Midge," Silvey says, "I mean Micah!" She shakes her head. *He's going to kill me if I keep calling him that.*

Ten years ago, Micah came trapesing into her freshman algebra class wearing a bright, neon green soccer jersey with the name Midge and the number three on the back. He was new at the end of their eighth-grade year. Silvey couldn't recall his first name and she took to calling him Midge from that day forward—and it stuck until graduation.

Micah stood on top of a cooler at a house party and declared he wanted his nickname to die at graduation. Giving everyone a two-week warning.

Silvey crossed paths with Micah, maybe a dozen times since they graduated, and she fails to remember his actual name every time.

"Hey, we got a real green looking sky," Micah shouts, sitting down another roll of mats. "Do either of you have a storm warning on your phone?"

Silvey pulls out her phone—zero bars and no messages on her lock screen. "No signal down here."

"Same," Bax says. "I'll come up and help you get the rest of them out of the truck."

Silvey sets her meter down. "I can come up!"

"Thanks, but there's only four left," Micah says. "We've got it!"

The wind whistles down to Silvey when they open the door. She watches the men vanish from sight and turns her attention back to her task.

Right, just our ever-changing weather—not a bad storm.

Growing up in tornado alley, Silvey is accustomed to the storms, but her mom is terrified. She goes in full panic mode anytime there is a hint of a storm heading their direction. Silvey, on the other hand could sit for hours on the porch watching the storms roll in.

I hope mom made it to work before the clouds rolled in. Silvey replays the argument with her mom this morning while connecting the wiring for the newest light fixture.

"Dre's right," Silvey mutters to herself, "I need to give mom a pass. She's just pissed off at dad." She tests the switch and the light flickers on. "Let there be light." She chuckles at her dad's sense of humor trickling out.

Silvey checks the schematics for the light settings and vegetable seedlings assigned to this tank. "Radish, who picks those up and says yes I'll make that for dinner?"

"What was that?" Bax shouts down.

Silvey looks up and Bax is staring down at her. He's soaked from head to toe, leaving his once semi tight shirt clinging to every ripple of muscle. "I take it you didn't make it in before the rain?"

"I needed a second shower." He smiles and takes off his hat—auburn curls spring out. He shakes his chin length hair and droplets fly out. He twists his hat, making his biceps flex, and more water falls to the floor.

"Whoa," Silvey whispers, looking down to hide her grin and reddening cheeks.

"Hey Silvey!" Micah shouts down over the thrum of the pouring rain hitting the glass. "We may have more than just a storm rolling in. Do you know if the tornado sirens work out this way?" He pulls on the door against the blustering wind and rain.

"I think so," Silvey says. "Does it look that bad?"

BANG

Silvey ducks and holds her hands over her ears as the sound ricochets. "What was that?"

"The door," Bax says, running towards the door. "Micah?"

"Ugh," Micah says, sliding down the wall and resting on the floor.

"Silvey, is there a first aid kit in here?" Bax asks, kneeling next to Micah.

"How bad is it?" Silvey leans over the rail.

"Smashed his nose," Bax says, assessing Micah. "Does it hurt anywhere else?"

"No," Micah says, squeezing his eyes closed and tilting his head back.

"It looks like he caught the door with his nose when it slammed closed."

"Check the small office up there," Silvey says, running down the circular ramp. "I'll check the office at the bottom."

"Hold your tongue up over your front teeth." Bax shows Micah. "Applying pressure can reduce the bleeding."

"Ouch," Micah groans. "I think I may have a loose tooth."

Bax ducks into the small office. He opens the drawers to the small dusty desk, finds only a small pencil and notepad, but otherwise empty. He checks behind the door and beside the small fridge. "Nothing." He steps out and leans over the railing. "Any luck?"

Silvey jiggles the handle for the corner office at the bottom of the ramp. "The office is locked down here." She jogs back up the ramp. "I'll check my work bag."

Micah grunts and tries to stand.

Bax presses Micah's shoulder. "Not quite yet. Keep your head back until the bleeding slows. I think you're right about your tooth. Your top lip is swelling pretty fast."

"How's the nose?" Micah asks.

"Swollen but straight," Bax says. "I'll grab a water bottle to wash the blood off your face and neck."

Silvey unzips every pouch and digs through every pocket until she finds a small white plastic case. "Bingo!" She pops it open and finds three Band-Aids, two antiseptic wipes and a tampon. "Got just the thing!" She sprints up the ramp and the lights flicker as a rumble of thunder shakes the glass panels.

6

"The silo is off grid, right?" Bax asks, looking up at the green glass panels overhead.

"It will be, but not yet," Silvey says, kneeling next to Bax. She pops open the case and pulls out the tampon. "Ta da!"

Micah frowns. "What in the hell Silvey?"

"The oldest trick in the book," Silvey says, taking the tampon out of the plastic wrapping and popping it out of the applicator.

Micah squirms.

"I always wondered why they were so long," Bax says, winking at Micah.

Silvey slides out the utility knife from her pocket, clicks the blade up, and splits the tampon in half. She holds up the two ends.

"Rinse him off once more," Silvey says, glancing at Bax. He nods and dumps the remaining water over Micah's face and neck. "Great, now lean your head all the way back."

"Why?" Micah asks. His eyes dart from the tampon to Bax. "What are you going to do with that?"

"Stop the bleeding," Silvey says, inching closer.

Micah closes his eyes and tilts his head back.

"In you go," Silvey says, shoving the ends of the tampon up each nostril. "All done buddy."

Bax opens a second bottle of water and tilts it forward, giving Silvey a stream to wash her hands.

"Thanks," Silvey says, standing and pocketing her knife. She rolls to her toes to peek out the small round window. "Guys, we may want to head down to the very bottom."

Bax helps Micah to his feet. "Is it a…"

"A big one!" Silvey steps back away from the window.

Bax leans down to look out the window. "Son of a…"

"It's not like we haven't seen one before," Micah says, nudging Bax aside.

A dark funnel cloud is dancing over the grazing field and heading straight towards them. All that's in its way is a tree line and the parking lot.

"It's as wide as a trailer house," Micah whispers.

"Right," Silvey says, motioning down the ramp. "I know we are relatively safe underground, but I overheard the welder saying he wanted to install some additional anchors to balance the weight of the tanks. I don't want to risk it up here," she points to the window, "if it decides to suck the air out of here." She points to the sides of the silo. "There are emergency ladders from the bottom. If anything happens to the ramps, we still have a safe route up and out."

Micah turns eyes wide. "It's already moving my truck."

"Let's go," Bax says, nudging him forward.

Silvey drops the old metal lock on the door and rushes after them.

The roar of the tornado makes them pause and stare up at the metal and glass roof as it lifts and falls.

"That may not hold!" Silvey yells. "Run!"

2

Andrea opens the basement door and steps into what used to be her kitchen. A few cabinet doors scattered on the floor and the stove are all that's left. She sniffs the air. "Oh, that's gas!" She searches for a valve behind the stove, but that part of the wall is missing. The valve is missing from the buried line. "Where was the main shut off?"

She spots her neighbor Norma stepping over the debris of what used to be her bedroom.

"Hey Norma!" Andrea says, waving both hands over her head. "Are you ok?"

"I think so," Norma says, "but I see that our houses are not so great."

Andrea nods, stepping outside. "Do you know where the gas main shut off is for our homes?" She points to the back of her stove. "It's leaking pretty bad."

"Oh dear," Norma says, "Red always took care of that stuff, but my son would know." She opens her red flip phone and presses one. "It's ringing."

Andrea paces the length of the kitchen looking for any exterior valves.

"Hi, yes, yes I'm fine, but the house is well…" Norma sighs. "Son, I need to ask you something. Can you stop with the twenty questions?"

Andrea pauses and turns towards Norma. Her petite frame looks even smaller next to the missing walls of her house.

Norma winks at Andrea. "Where are the gas and water main shut offs for our homes?" She nods. "I'll call you back in a few." She snaps the phone shut. "Gas valve is by the gas meter on the north side of the house, and water main are by the mailboxes."

"Thanks," Andrea says, "I'll get mine and yours turned off. Just in case."

"Can you check on Vernon's too?" Norma says, pointing to the blue house on the other side of Andrea's home. "He's still in the nursing home recovering from his stroke."

"Yes, ma'am." Andrea circles the house and finds the north side of her home remarkably untouched, and the meter still intact. She turns the valve to the right and watches the dial on the meter slow to a stop. "Whew, one crisis adverted." She turns to assess the damage to Vernon's home and rapidly blinks. "No, no, it can't be… where's his house?"

Andrea circles to the front of her home and looks up and down the street. She counts—only six out of seventeen homes are still standing. She chokes back a sob and covers her mouth to muffle her scream.

"Focus Andrea." She slaps her cheeks and rushes to where the mailbox once stood. She spots the metal cover, kneels, pops it off, and twists the valve to the right. She races over to Norma's mailbox, but only finds a splintered post. She shuts off her water and finds Norma's gas meter. She turns off the gas and jogs back. "Norma?"

"I'm here," Norma says, assessing her tub. "I believe a remodel may be in order. My son wanted me to have one of those fancy walk-in tubs and he may get his wish."

"Question?" Andrea asks, stepping up and over the remaining bits of Norma's exterior bathroom wall. "I need to

10

run down and start house checks. Do you know who would most likely have been home this morning?"

"Well, let's see," Norma says, turning to orientate herself in the direction of the street. "Start with old Bert down the street. He didn't have a basement, and neither did the young couple across the street from him."

Andrea swallows and blinks back a tear. "Ok, I'll start that direction and work my way back. Stay inside for now and avoid the front porch. Not sure how well it held up." *Lord, please don't let her look out front.*

"No worries," Norma says, patting Andrea's cheek. "My fridge is blocking the hallway. My only exit is basically where you're standing."

Andrea turns and looks out over the field behind them. "I can hear the sirens in the distance. Help is coming. I'll be back in ten minutes tops."

"Be careful and watch out for any nails, glass or down power lines," Norma says, wagging her finger.

"Yes, ma'am." Andrea carefully climbs back over the wall and hits the ground at a sprint. She spots movement ahead. A woman is standing in the middle of a yard staring at a home with no roof and two whole sides missing. "Are you hurt?"

The woman turns her tear-streaked face towards Andrea and shakes her head. "I made it to the basement just in time."

Andrea checks the woman over. She's in house slippers and a fuzzy orange robe. "Stay put. You can't be walking around here in those." She points to the woman's feet.

"I was in the shower when the siren went off," the woman says, patting her still damp hair.

"I need to check on the patio homes," Andrea says, pointing down the street.

"Oh, they're gone!" The woman points a shaking finger towards the end of the street.

There is only one house still standing on the street past the woman and Andrea. The other homes look like piles of wood stacked for a fire on the foundations.

"Wave any emergency service vehicles this way," Andrea says over her shoulder. "Just in case!" She runs towards Bert's driveway.

Andrea's panting and holding her side as she slows to pick her way over the rubble. She spots a toilet in the far corner. "Bert? Are you here?" She hears a faint cough from the direction of the bathroom. "Help is coming!" She looks for an accessible path over but ultimately decides to go around.

A blare of horns and sirens coming from town sound closer.

"You hear that, Bert?" Andrea asks, stepping up on the tiles next to the toilet. "They're getting closer. Can you hear me?" She pushes aside a piece of sheetrock and a support beam laying over the bathtub. She finds layers of blankets underneath. "Are you alone?"

"Help," Bert whispers.

"I've got you!" Andrea says, tossing blankets and pillows out of the tub until she uncovers Bert's face and arm. "You're going to be ok."

Bert stares at Andrea. "What's happening?"

"We got hit by a tornado," Andrea says, tossing the rest of the pillows out and assessing his entire body, *no blood.* "Are you hurt?"

"I don't know," Bert says, reaching up for Andrea's hand.

She nods and takes his hand. "You did great with the layers of blankets and pillows. Let's sit you up slowly." He nods and his head emerges above the rim of the tub.

"My goodness," Bert says. His bottom lip wobbles.

"It's ok," she says, supporting his position. "We will rebuild."

He blinks back tears and nods. "Right."

Flashing lights divert Andrea's attention. "And look the calvary has arrived."

Three men and a woman dressed in various states of gear pile out of the firetruck.

Andrea waves one over. "Thanks for coming so quick!"

"What do you got?" the man asks, stepping up beside Andrea.

"Bert was quick and got in the tub with a lot of pillows and blankets." She points to the piles around the tub and debris. "I've only helped him sit up. If you've got this, I need to check on the house across the street. These two were the only ones on the street without basements."

"You live here?" the man asks, taking a pin light out of his pocket.

"Yes, down the street."

"Take Danny with you," he gestures to a fireman with a medic bag. "Bert, were you alone?"

"Yes sir," Bert says.

Andrea carefully exits the rubble and jogs to the man scanning the street. "Danny?"

"Yea," Danny says.

"With me," Andrea says, jogging across the street. "These two homes are the only ones without basements on the street."

Danny audibly sighs.

Andrea glances back.

"Sorry, but when we pulled on this street," Danny says, "my mind plunged into the increasing number of fatalities the further we went."

Andrea nods. "Let's work fast. There is a young couple that lives here."

"Do you know their names?" Danny asks, adjusting his bag across his body. He follows Andrea moving along the side of the house.

"Afraid not," Andrea says. "Is anyone there? Can you hear me?" She looks back at Danny. "Do you see any remnants of a bathroom?"

"Not yet," Danny says, testing his weight. He steps up on a fallen beam to get a better look. "I think it's in that corner." He points to the opposite corner.

Andrea jogs in that direction. "Can you hear me?"

Danny stumbles over the debris and snags his pants on a bed frame. He struggles to get his pant leg free.

"What the hell, Danny?" an older man shouts, jogging up to the house.

Danny freezes and turns. "Hey dad."

"We may have a young couple in here."

"You idiot, are you trying to crush them?" Danny's dad points below his son. "Head back to the truck and stay out of the debris!"

Danny breaks free and carefully makes it back where he started.

"Ma'am, sorry about my son. My name is Gene."

Andrea nods. "I'm Andrea Meyer." She points over towards Danny. "He was just trying to help."

Gene shakes his head. "I understand this home and the one across the street didn't have a shelter or basement." Andrea nods. "Do you know the people that live here?"

"Not by name, only in passing."

Gene nods. "You found Bert?"

"Thanks to Norma," Andrea says.

"Aunt Norma," Gene says, pushing a few pieces of furniture aside to reach the tub. "Always watching out for others."

Andrea smiles and helps him move a large beam aside. "Is everyone in this town related to Norma?"

"Almost," Gene says, pointing down to the empty tub. "Do you know if there are two bathrooms in this layout?"

"Maybe," Andrea says, "but I think the hall bathroom had a walk-in shower."

"Can anyone hear me?" Gene yells. "Fire and rescue teams are here!"

Andrea looks around. "Hopefully, they're both at work."

"I'll mark this house as a follow-up until we can locate the homeowners." Gene presses his call button on his radio. "Four to dispatch."

The radio crackles. "Four, go ahead."

"Do we have names and phone numbers for the residents on Sam Phil yet?"

"Yes sir, I'll send it to the trucks and team onsite. And sir, we received a distressed call from Evelyn Rhoades. Her daughter Silvey was out at the old nike base."

"Shit!" Andrea mutters.

Gene glances at Andrea. "I'll send Danny out to do a wellness check."

Dispatch calls, "Ten four."

"Ten four." Gene faces Andrea. "You're friends with Silvey?"

"Yes," Andrea says. "We spoke this morning. She's the electrician working on the vertical farm there at the base."

Gene nods. "I heard about that." He glances over his shoulder. "The tornado's path touched down between here and Park Lane Circle. It tore up your neighborhood before heading east through the baseball fields towards the old base."

"And?" Andrea asks.

"I posted crews here and Park Lane Circle. It's mostly fields between here and the base. I planned to send another unit out to canvas the area between here and the base once the rigs arrive from Cameron and Richmond."

Andrea nods. "Can I go with Danny?"

"Absolutely. She's likely safe considering she was working inside the silo plus… someone needs to keep an eye on my idiot son." Gene hands her a set of keys. "Take the small white truck and don't let him inside any of the structures. If you need to enter the buildings, call dispatch from the radio inside the truck."

"Thank you," Andrea says, shaking the keys. "I promise we won't go in. And my house is the red brick one with no kitchen next to Norma." She points down the street. "My husband is overseas at the moment, and I was working remotely today. Otherwise, I would've been in the city."

"I'll mark it down," Gene says. "Danny, escort this kind lady out to the old nike base for a wellness check on a resident. Stay out of the structures and take my truck."

3

Dark? Why is it so dark?

Bax reaches out until his hand finds a solid surface. He drags his fingers along the rough texture. *Concrete block?* He finds another block, then another until he finds a switch. He flips it up and a light flickers on. He blinks until his eyes adjust.

A single bulb hangs in the middle of the small room with a desk, chair, and a small window that slides open.

Bax leans forward to peer out the window. His eyes fall on a chain linked fence and he leans closer, spotting the coiled barbed wire along the top.

"What in the hell?" Bax asks, stepping away from the window and bumping his hip into a doorknob. He rubs his hip and opens the door.

A cool night breeze chills his nose and ears instantly. He pulls on his sleeves and notices the tan color. He glances down at a military uniform. "What am I wearing?"

He tilts up the name badge attached to his tan uniform. "B. Auburn. What's happening?"

Headlights appear in the distance, pulling his attention away from the badge. He scans his surroundings. He spots the outline of three buildings about a hundred yards away. He follows the lit single drive from the buildings back to a gate. He looks back at the small office. *It looks like a guard shack.*

Bright headlights illuminate the gate.

Bax hesitantly steps towards the gate.

An old, armored truck rolls to a stop. A uniformed man emerges from the driver's side. His fair skin glows against the dark sky.

Bax stiffens after spotting the sidearm on the man's hip.

"Are you going to open the gate or just stand there all night?" the man shouts.

Bax blinks. "Yes, sir." He inspects the gate. *Don't panic, but how do I open it?* He spots a track with wheels at the top. *It slides open, but all or part?* He pulls on the section closest to him and the gate opens, gliding to the far side.

"Don't leave it open!" the man shouts, getting back in the truck. *That guy sounds funny.*

Bax nods and waits for the truck to speed through. He slides the gate closed. He marches back into the small office and spots a calendar on the wall near the door. "April." He flips the calendar over. "1962!" He rips it off the wall and turns towards the desk. "What is happening!"

He goes through the desk drawers and finds a few pencils—and a newspaper. "Lawson Review… April 12, 1962?" He flips the paper over. *It looks new, but how?* He reads a few headlines. "Seattle's World Fair… do we even have world fairs now?"

The ground rumbles and rattles the desk.

WOOOOOOOOOOONG

Bax steps out of the shack and turns towards the shouting. He strains to make out the commands coming from the buildings but spots a few flashes of light.

POP, POP

Is somebody firing at me?

POP

Bax ducks behind the shack and crouches covering his head as more shots are fired and the shouts creep closer.

"This is a nightmare. Wake up!"

Bax's eyes fly open. He struggles to recognize his surroundings until his eyes land on a section of the ramp hovering over him. *I'm back inside the silo.*

"Silvey! Micah!" Bax yells, pushing a piece of the steel grate off his legs. He wiggles his toes inside his boots. *I can feel them!* "Guys!" He twists around spotting a hand and a boot under a blue fiberglass hydroponic container.

"I'm coming!" Bax yells, rolling to all fours and his left arm gives out under his weight. He assesses the blood dripping down his arm and rolls back his sleeve to inspect the source. A gash about three inches long starts mid bicep down to his elbow. He undoes his rachet belt, pulls it out of his pant loops, wraps the belt above the gash and pulls it as tight as he can manage. He rachets it closed. The blood flow slows.

"Micah! Silvey!" Bax climbs over a twisted section of the ramp.

REEEEE

Bax pauses and looks up. A section of the ramp still anchored to the wall is rattling under the weight of the fallen sections above it. "If that falls, the rest is coming down!" He scrambles over the scattered fallen debris until he's next to the boot. "We need to move, and quickly!"

He gently lifts and pushes the empty container off to one side, revealing Micah.

"No!"

Micah is face down with a piece of the railing poking through his back and a pool of blood surrounds him.

Bax steps back and bends over, losing all remnants of his breakfast. He wipes his mouth with his shirt and returns to Micah. He kneels next to him and places two fingers on his neck and waits. "Come on, buddy!" He moves his fingers again and waits.

No pulse.

Tears drip off Bax's chin and plop in the red pool below.

18

"Silvey!" He fishes out his phone. The screen crumbles under his thumb. "Please! Anyone!"

The steel overhead groans, and a tethered anchor falls loose. The supporting section of the ramp drops a foot.

Bax picks his way over the dirt slick grates, railing, and containers towards the smashed office in the corner.

"Silvey! Brace yourself!"

He pulls one of the fiberglass containers close and slides down the wall. He curls as tight as he can and uses the container to cover most of his tall frame.

POP

Bax cowers and covers his ears as the clatter of steel slams to the surface. He feels a whoosh of air and chunks of debris slam against the container shielding his face.

"Silvey!" Bax shouts, slowly lowering the container and assessing the additional damage.

All but one section of the twelve levels of ramps are resting in a heap in the center of the silo.

Bax stands and screams, "SILVEY!"

4

"Silvey Lynn," a woman says. "It's time to put that cigarette out and come back down. We need you and your notepad down with the doctor."

Silvey looks at the ember end of a cigarette in her hand. "I don't smoke." She looks the woman up and down noticing her beehive hair and her red fit and flare dress falling just below her knees. "Do I know you?"

"Ha," the woman says, cocking her hip out to the side and hitting her temple with the heel of her hand. "Did you fall and hit your head or something?"

Silvey shakes her head and drops the cigarette. She steps on the lit end and twists her… *red pumps?* Her eyes follow the length of her leg to a flare of a bright blue dress.

"Why in the hell am I wearing a dress?" Silvey asks, glaring at the woman's deep frown.

"Silvey Lynn, what else would you wear to work?"

"This is a genuine nightmare!" She tugs on the tight sleeves. "It's suffocating and don't get me started on the shoes. Did Dre put you up to this?"

The woman shakes her head. "I don't know whom Dre is, but you're almost late and the boss hates it when you doddle." She lightly swats Silvey on the bum towards a tan door.

I've seen this door. Silvey opens the door and steps inside.

A man wearing a dark khaki uniform glances up from a clipboard and smiles. "Going down?"

"Midge, what in the hell?" Silvey takes a step back and bumps into the door.

"You look a little surprised." The officer presses a green button. The gears overhead start to turn and a metal cage big enough for two people rises from the bottom. "It's the only way down to the control rooms."

Silvey narrows her eyes and closely inspects the details of his military-like uniform with a black armband with the letters MP in white. "Midge, this isn't funny!"

"Ma'am?" The officer opens the gate to the lift.

"Seriously?" Silvey asks, glaring at him.

The officer raises a single eyebrow and frowns. "I'm sorry. Did I upset you?"

"Micah, tell me right now. What in the holy trippy world is happening?"

"Ma'am?"

"You say 'ma'am' one more time. I will kick you where it counts."

The officer takes a step back and holds the clipboard below his belt. "I am the MP on duty. At this station, I supervise the entrance as workers come in and out, plus I secure and operate the lift." He points to an identification card pinned to Silvey's left lapel. "Another officer is waiting to escort you to the office for the doctor requesting your service." He points down and shrugs. "That's all I know and all I am cleared to tell you."

Silvey shakes her head and reaches for the door handle. "I don't know what kind of prank you and Dre have put together, but I'm done!" She twists the handle and pushes against the door, but it doesn't open. She pulls and stumbles back bumping into the officer. "Shit!"

"Ms. Rhoades!" a man shouts from below. "Stop flirting with the officer and get down here!"

Silvey glances at the grated bottom of the lift and the officer tapping his foot impatiently below. She assesses the two pieces of wood in the center. She looks back at the officer.

"Please step on the wooden planks in the center," the MP says, offering his hand. She hesitates. He sighs. "The wood is to protect your heels. We don't want them to fall through the small gaps."

"Hmph!" Silvey straightens her posture and slaps his hand away. "You'll pay for this!" She hastily steps into the middle of the lift.

The officer frowns and secures the opening. He starts the lift.

Silvey scans the walls as she descends and focuses on the rebar ladder on the far wall. *Odd, it's set between two rail tracks.* She follows the tracks down to a mechanical lift. "OH MY GOD! That's a freaking missile!"

She looks back up. *Midge is gone.*

"Wake up!"

Silvey stirs. *I can't breathe.* She pushes against the weight pressing against her chest. Her eyes fly open when her fingers press against something damp.

"What the… grass?" She blinks. "Why am I lying face down on grass?"

You're useless if you panic.

She shakes her head and takes a long, deep breath and slowly exhales. *Five, four, three, two, one. See Silvey, you are in control. You can breathe.*

Silvey laughs at her mental pep talk and attempts to roll over, but her hips and chest are pinned. She looks back at the muddy metal box.

Where have I seen that before? The truck in the parking lot!

"MICAH! BAX!"

Silvey scans the surrounding ground. A line of trees to her right and an open pasture straight ahead and to her left. The box is blocking her view of everything behind her.

She squeezes her eyes shut. *What in the hell happened!*

She recalls the sound of cracking glass and her hand reaching for the handrail. The pops and screeching of twisting steel as the structure shakes. Bax and Micah falling!

"I let go, but I didn't fall!" Silvey laughs, the sound a mix of scream and horror. "It's just a bad dream. Wake up, Silvey!" Her right eye begins to twitch as her heart escalates. *I was inside the silo. Now outside. I didn't walk out. I didn't fall. How did I wind up in a field?*

"Help! Can anyone hear me?"

The only answer to her call is a distant siren.

Silvey closes her eyes and takes in another long, deep breath and slowly exhales. *Five, four, three, two…*

Ding

Silvey opens her eyes wide. "No freaking way!" She stretches her arm until her fingers find the edge of her pocket. "Ugh!" She places her elbows under her shoulders and pushes up and pulls her weight forward. She shimmies her hips a few inches and tries for her phone again snagging the corner. She tightens her grip and pulls out her phone.

"Please work!" Silvey taps the screen, and her lock screen flares to life. "Sweet heavens!" She slides the sequence to open her phone. And watches as nine missed call notifications fill the screen all from her mom and the last from Dre.

She immediately dials Dre and rests it against her head. It rings once.

"SILVEY!" Andrea shouts.

Silvey moves the phone away from her ear. "Hey Dre, about tonight…"

"Silvey Lynn Rhoades," Andrea says, cutting her off. "I can't do sarcasm. Where are you?"

"Are you ok?" Silvey asks, fighting a wave of nausea.

"I don't know how to answer that," Andrea says, stepping out of the truck at the entry to the old nike base. It is littered with hundreds of pieces of steel, roofing, blue vinyl siding matching her neighbor's house, and wood splintered like toothpicks sticking straight up out of the ground. "Where are you?"

"Don't freak out," Silvey says.

"Way pass that!" Andrea says.

"I'm face down in some grass… it looks like a pasture."

"A pasture?" Andrea puts her phone on speaker.

Danny jogs around the truck and comes to her side.

"I'm pinned under a toolbox from a truck," Silvey says.

"But where?" Andrea asks.

"I'll send you my location. But Dre…"

"No buts, send it now!"

Silvey texts her location to Dre. "Sent! But I'm serious. You need to get somebody out to check the silo. Micah and Bax are inside. They were falling when I was…"

"You were what Silvey?"

"I flew up…"

"Jesus!" Andrea yells.

"Silvey," Danny says.

"Who's that?" Silvey asks.

"Danny with the fire department," Andrea says.

"Are you bleeding?" Danny asks.

"I don't think there's any blood, but I can't see my legs or back."

"That's good, right?" Andrea asks Danny. He nods. "Silvey, your mom…"

"Is she ok?" Silvey asks.

"Yes," Andrea says. "It hit my side of town."

"Oh Dre your new house… how bad?" Silvey asks.

"I will need a new kitchen, but one of the six houses still standing."

"Woah," Silvey whispers.

"According to the coordinates," Danny says, "you're nearly a mile away from the base closer to Vibbard."

24

"You're kidding?" Silvey pulls up the map on her phone and zooms into her location. "Son of a…"

"What's your battery situation?" Danny asks, tapping his phone to dial his father.

"Um, twenty-two percent," Silvey says.

"We're on our way!" Danny says. "Try not to move at all." He opens the truck door for Andrea. "I'll call a crew to come look for the two men in the silo."

"Thank you!" Silvey says, resting the phone on the ground. "Hey Dre, can you tell me why I was in a blue dress and red heels?"

Andrea hops back into the truck and watches Danny shout on the phone as he runs back to the driver's side. "You in a dress and heels without me twisting your arm. Hell has truly frozen over."

Silvey chuckles. "It was a strange dream. I thought it was a prank until I saw the missiles."

"You saw missiles in your dream?" Andrea asks, glancing at Danny. He shakes his head.

"Yep," Silvey says. "What happened on your end of town?"

"The sirens went off when I was in a meeting with my California clients," Andrea says. "I wrapped up the call early after I promised to send an all clear. Which reminds me, I haven't done that yet."

"We've called in the jaws team and the Richmond unit is heading in this direction," Danny says, sliding into and firing up the truck.

"Jaws?" Andrea asks.

"Jaws of life, typically used to extract people from cars."

"Silvey, did you hear all of that?" Andrea asks.

"Yes," Silvey says, "thank you!"

"Continue?" Andrea asks.

"Yes, please," Silvey says. Her teeth chatter.

"I made it to the basement just before the storm went quiet and then the lights went out. I hunkered down in the tub with hubbies gaming beanbag over me. I waited there while the storm roared overhead."

"Does Scott know?" Silvey asks.

"I sent the fool a heads-up message," Andrea says, bracing against the dash as Danny makes a hard left onto the road barely missing a tree limb. "His response… I'll give you one guess."

"K," Silvey whispers.

"Exactly!" Andrea reaches up for the handle over the door. "Slow down! There is stuff all over the road."

Danny pumps the brakes, barely missing a large piece of twisted metal siding in the middle of the road. "Sorry."

"Are… arrrre you…. ok?" Silvey asks, shivering.

"Silvey, we're fine," Andrea says, glancing at Danny. He mouths the word shock. "Are you?"

"Cold, so cold."

"Silvey, you may be going into shock. Tell me who Micah and Bax are?"

"Midge…"

"No! His wife is due soon."

Silvey's heavy eyes pop open. "Oh, you're right! Jessica and Midge. She calls him Mike."

"I know, it's weird," Andrea says, pointing out another piece of siding on the road.

Danny slows as another car pops over the hill. It slams into the piece of siding sending it straight towards the truck.

"Ah!" Andrea screams and ducks below the dashboard.

Danny slams on the brakes.

5

Bax stumbles over the fallen steel. He shoves the pieces of framing and hydroponic containers away from Micah's body.

He slowly moves a large section of a ramp inch by inch, straining under the weight on his good arm. "To slow!" He looks around and spots a container and a piece of the railing. He positions the railing under the ramp, using the container as leverage, and presses down. The ramp lifts. He kicks another container under it, and it holds the weight of the steel ramp. He lets go, shoving the rest of the debris off Micah. He squats down. "I'm going to get us out of here. I promise."

"Silvey," Bax whispers breathlessly and wipes his brow with his still damp shirt. "Where are you?" He looks over the pile of steel and up at the large opening.

He carefully steps his way over to the wall of the silo. "Silvey, can you hear me?" He slowly works his way around, stopping every few feet to look through the piles.

He's made it around the entire circle. "Come on, Silvey!" He kicks a piece of the railing and clatters off the side of the wall.

The clouds shift and a bit of sunlight hits Bax's tear-streaked face. He tilts his chin up, soaks in the sun for a breath, before wiping the tears from his face. "Get it together!" He gently slaps his cheeks and blinks away the remaining tears. "I need to find help!" He walks around until he finds rebar protruding from the wall in staggered formation up to the top.

"Of course, Silvey mentioned a ladder." Bax tightens the belt around his arm and stares up at the old, rusted rungs. *One rung at a time.* He reaches up and tests his weight on the first rung. He adjusts his grip, uses his feet as leverage as he reaches for the second rung. His injured arm aches under the strain. He climbs up five more rungs and looks down. He spots Micah's prone body.

I'm getting help! I'm not leaving you behind.

He scans the pile for any sign of Silvey's blonde hair or tan pants.

What are the chances you didn't fall down?

He shakes his head and climbs up about ten more rungs and takes a second look down. He wobbles and closes his eyes. He inhales and holds his breath as he slowly opens his eyes again. His knees soften and he tightens his grip to keep himself from falling.

"Oh, hell no!" He squeezes his eyes shut. *Since when did I become scared of heights?*

Bax climbs up to the top without another glance at the bottom. The silo's roof opening is level with the ground. He rolls out and lays flat on his back. After catching his breath, he sits up.

Bax gets to his feet and turns in a slow circle. The parking lot is void of any cars, trucks, or pavement. The landscape around the silo has been ripped off.

Holy hell.

The width of the path clearly evident by the missing trees and raw ground along the edge of the property from the northwest. He shakes his head.

It's wider than the length of a football field.

He turns towards the west and can see the white farmhouse on the hill, still intact, about a half mile away.

Maybe they can call for help!

He glances to the south and east. An utter chaos of debris from what looks like metal siding, furniture, cars, and wood splintering the land. It continues over the next rise.

He turns back to the north. "It hit Lawson before coming here!"

Bax swallows back a sob of sheer terror. "Silvey!" He scans the grounds and spots a bit of blonde hair. He rushes forward and drops to his knees.

A baby doll with a bright pink dress now splattered with mud stares up at him. But the hair—so similar to Silvey. He picks up the doll and gets back to his feet.

He starts towards the road, scanning the ground. "Silvey! Can you hear me?" He picks up his pace and jogs towards the road but ducks when the clatter of steel-on-steel sings through the air.

The siding bounces off the hood of Danny's truck and smashes into the windshield, cracking the glass.

Danny throws the truck in park, hops out, tosses the siding off the truck, and runs to the other car.

A woman is staring straight ahead with her hands frozen on the wheel.

Danny taps on the window. "Ma'am, are you ok?"

She doesn't blink or respond.

Smoke hisses out of the front of her car.

Danny tries the door handle, but it's locked. He pounds on the window until she finally blinks.

"Ah!" the woman screams, noticing Danny for the first time.

Danny steps back and bumps into Andrea.

"You didn't have to scare her like that!" Andrea says, pushing him aside and going for the woman's door, but she freezes. "Damn, it's Jessica. Call an ambulance right now!"

"Is she hurt?" Danny asks, stepping closer.

"Very pregnant and I believe in labor!" Andrea says, looking in the window.

"Shit!" Danny says, rushing back to the truck.

"Jessica," Andrea says, softly tapping on the window. "It's me, Andrea. I think you might be in labor."

Jessica blinks and nods. "Mike he's… he's not answering."

Andrea nods and points to the lock. "Let's get you out of the car."

Jessica presses unlock and releases the door. "He's just over the next hill."

Andrea swallows. "Danny is calling an ambulance. We need to get you checked out first." Jessica shakes her head. "We've already got people on their way to Micah and Bax."

"People… wait, why?" Jessica asks, waddling towards the hill. "Is he ok?"

"I'm sure he's just fine," Andrea says, redirecting her towards the truck.

"A Richmond fire and rescue crew are about five minutes out," Danny says, grabbing a few flares from the back of the truck. "I need to set these up around her car. Take the truck and the medic bag. We are losing daylight and Silvey may already be in shock."

"Silvey!" Andrea yells. "Where the hell is my phone?"

Jessica groans and braces against the truck for support.

Andrea runs around the truck to the passenger side and yanks open the door. "Silvey! Can you hear me?" She pats the seat down and squats, blindly patting under the seat. *Come on!*

"How close are your contractions?" Danny yells, jogging back to Jessica.

"Two minutes apart," Jessica says.

"A little help here!" Andrea says. "Do these seats fold forward? I can't find the phone!"

Danny opens the door and releases the latch to the bench seat. It angles forward. He spots it immediately and grabs the phone. "It's off." He tosses it towards her.

"No!" Andrea cries, tapping on the screen and power button. "Please tell me you have a charger!"

Danny presses the seat back down and checks the cord hanging from the dash. "Android or apple?"

"Apple!" Andrea says, reaching for the cord.

Danny shakes his head. "Sorry, no luck. Jessica, do you have an apple charger in your car?"

"There's a charger for the tablet in my hospital bag. I'm not sure if it's the same."

Danny runs to her car's driver's side.

"In the trunk!" Jessica yells over the sirens now wailing close enough they can see their lights.

Danny pops the trunk and sprints across the road with her bag. He holds it up so she can search through a side pocket.

"This is all I got," Jessica says, pulling out a new cord. "It was a birthday gift from my sister. I haven't even plugged it in yet."

Andrea tests the connection, and it fits. "Tell your sister I will buy her drinks for a year!" She kisses Jessica on the cheek. "I've got to go find Silvey. Get to the hospital, don't worry about Midge."

Jessica frowns. "Find?"

"Danny can explain," Andrea says, guiding her away from the truck. "I'll stop by to visit you and the baby with Silvey. I promise."

Jessica nods.

A fire engine rolls to a stop near Danny. He looks over at Andrea. "Forward Silvey's location to 911 with her first and last name."

"Ok," Andrea says. She starts the truck, plugs in her phone, and powers it on.

Danny opens the driver's side door. "They can handle Jessica and the silo!"

"Let's go," Andrea says, "I'm driving."

Danny frowns but doesn't argue and runs to the other side.

Andrea forwards the location then dials Silvey. She shifts the truck in drive. It rings twice and then goes straight to voicemail. She hands Danny the phone. "Keep calling her!"

Danny dials again, it repeats the two rings and then straight to voicemail. He pulls up the location history and taps the last spot. "I think we're going to have to hike through a tree line to a field up here on the right. I'm texting that we may need a medivac on standby. And sending the location to myself, since your phone will probably die the second we have to walk."

"Save her phone number," Andrea says, scanning the road ahead. "She may pick up." She slows down and points to a cattle gate on the right just ahead. "The Wright's won't mind, right?"

"You know who own's this land?"

"Correction, I used to know." Andrea shrugs. "I'm not sure if they still do, but I can pull that card if push comes to shove." She pulls onto a small gravel drive and throws the truck in park. She hops out of the truck, pulls a metal pin out of the gate's lock, and pushes it open. *Some things never change. She smiles recalling the old bonfire days in this very field.*

Danny slides over and takes the wheel. He drives the truck through the gate and waits for Andrea to close it. He waits for her to climb back in, but she doesn't. He pokes his head out the window. "Burning daylight!"

She shakes her head, picks up something, and jogs to the passenger side of the truck. "I'm pretty sure this is somebody's family album and an urn. It was just lying in the ditch."

Danny glances at the items she sits on the floorboard. "Seriously?"

"Afraid so," Andrea says. "I think it's the older couple up the street. Their son died last year while working out on one of those oil rigs in the gulf and they had him cremated."

"I remember my dad saying something about that last year," Danny says, turning the truck towards the tree line. He turns the map towards her. "I think we can cut through most of this field to the trees. What do you think?"

"There was an old pond just over this next rise," Andrea says, sitting on the edge of the seat. I can't see through the cracks on this side. "Turn on your high beams. It will at least catch the glint of metal or water before we run into either."

Danny slows as they take the next rise and rolls to a stop. A white twisted truck is blocking their path. He throws their truck in park and dials the station.

"It's Danny," he says when they pick up. "I need to run a plate. Alpha, three, bravo, tango, tango, charlie."

Andrea grabs the medical case and bag from the back of the truck. She surveys the scene and her bottom lip trembles. *Are we too late?*

The field is littered with furniture, cars, more vinyl siding, roof shingles, and more splintered wood. She glances up spotting a flash of red. A cardinal flag is tangled in the branches near the top of one of the large oak trees.

"It's Micah's truck," Danny says, ending the call and checking around the truck. "Silvey thought the thing pinning her down was a toolbox, right?"

"Right," Andrea says, pulling her attention towards the destroyed truck.

"Half of his is missing," Danny says, pointing to the bed of Micah's truck.

"Call the chopper! An ambulance won't make it very far."

Danny scans the field for the first time. "It's a freaking mine field!"

"She can't be more than a few hundred yards," Andrea says. "Keep an eye out for anything big and white. Oh, and if there's cattle, an electric fence is probably on the property somewhere."

Danny nods, taking the bag and case from Andrea. "I've got these. Keep your eye on that dot." He points to his phone.

Andrea navigates around various bumpers, cushions, and random pieces of wood until they get to the tree line. She spots a piece of white fabric tied to a line about thigh height. "Electric fence. I'll go under and then you can hand me the equipment."

"Are we still on the right path?" Danny asks, handing her the bag and then the case.

"Yes," Andrea says, handing him the gear back. She cuts through the woods and slows as she nears the next field. She scans the perimeter for another wire.

The sun has dropped below the woods.

"Do you see another line?" Andrea says, looking back. "Danny?" *Where in the hell did he go?*

6

"Help!" Bax yells, waving the doll over his head. "I need help!"

The firetruck flicks on a high beam and scans the road ahead until it finds Bax's tall figure standing near the road up the hill.

Bax waves again. "Over here!"

The light blinks and the truck rolls forward.

"Silvey," Bax whispers, "I promise I will find you."

The truck stops and two firemen hop out. "Are you Micah?"

"No, Baxton Auburn, but Micah is still inside the silo." He points over his shoulder. "And I haven't found Silvey."

"I'm Rob and this is Wyatt." Rob points to the chopper inbound. "They've located Silvey."

"They found her?" Bax says and he wobbles to the side as his knees give out. "Is she…"

"Whoa," Rob says, catching Bax's elbow noticing his injury. "Let's patch you up. Can you tell Wyatt exactly where Micah is and if you know of any injuries?"

Bax shakes his head. "Micah's at the bottom of the silo. He's… dead."

"Are you sure?" Wyatt says, waving over the second truck.

"Yes," Bax says, releasing his belt around his arm. "I found him under a pile of steel with a piece of the handrail…" He points to his stomach and then to his back. "He had no pulse and there was a large pool of blood."

"Understand, I'm sorry to hear that about your friend." Rob cuts away Bax's sleeve. "You will definitely need stitches. How recent was your last tetanus shot?"

"About two months ago," Bax says, pointing to his calf.

Rob raises an eyebrow.

"I walked into a jagged hitch of an old truck and had to get stitches."

"Can you tell us what happened here?" Wyatt asks.

Bax looks around. "I thought that was pretty obvious?"

Wyatt chuckles. "No, I mean how you seem to be relatively well, your friend Micah at the bottom of the silo dead, and the girl in a field a mile south of here."

"Wyatt," Rob scolds.

"Nah, I get it," Bax says. "I've been replaying it over and over." He points over his shoulder. "An old missile silo seems like the safest place to be in a storm, right?"

Wyatt nods.

"Turns out that a tornado can tear a missile hatch off an old silo." Bax shakes his head. "And we were running down the spiral ramp when the roof flew off. The last time I saw Silvey she was holding on to one of the handrails before the ramp under Micah and I gave out." He closes his eyes and takes in a breath. "I woke up under a pile of fiberglass tanks and steel grates from the ramp."

"How high up were you?" Rob asks, assessing his pupils with a pin light.

"Maybe level four," Bax says.

"Do think you hit your head?"

"Probably," Bax says, leaning away from his light.

"How many levels?" Wyatt asks.

"There were twelve," Bax says. "The tornado tore up a few levels, but the rest were damaged. It collapsed after I uncovered Micah. I had to uncover him a second time."

"Damn," Rob whispers, sitting back. "And you thought the girl was under the wreckage?"

Bax nods. "I looked, and I couldn't find her."

"What's with the doll?" Wyatt asks, pointing to Bax's lap.

"I saw the hair. I thought it was Silvey—she's blonde too."

"Hmm," Wyatt says, "and how did you make it up twelve stories?"

"The silo has an old rebar ladder on the wall."

"Rob, is he patched up enough to show us how to get down?" Wyatt asks.

"Yep, but he's getting a ride to the hospital for a full workup and sutures."

"Thanks, but I'm fine," Bax says. "Micah's family will need to be notified and I want to be there."

"No, is not an option post tornado and fall," Rob says, shaking his head. "Plus, we just sent his wife off in an ambulance."

"Jessica was here?" Bax asks.

"She came looking for her husband when he didn't return her calls," Rob says. "She was in labor when we arrived. She'll probably deliver later tonight."

Bax hangs his head. "He's going to miss everything."

"The least we can do for him is get him out of the silo." Rob offers Bax a hand.

Bax takes his hand and stands.

Wyatt clicks on the flashlight. The remaining dusk fades to night as they reach the edge of the silo.

Bax points out the ladder. "May I?" He reaches for the flashlight.

Wyatt hands it over.

Bax shines the light below and holds the beam over Micah's prone form. He passes the flashlight to Rob and steps back from the edge when his vision blurs.

"Are you ok?" Rob asks Bax as he teeters back and falls.

7

"Danny, stop messing around!" Andrea yells into the fading light. "Where are you?"

"Over here!" Danny shouts. "I've got a body, no pulse."

Andrea staggers over towards him. "Is it…"

Danny stands blocking her view. "It's male. There's nothing I can do for him. Let's keep moving."

Andrea attempts to look past him, but he moves into her line of sight. She glares at him.

"Trust me," Danny says.

Andrea notices his ruby red nose and glistening cheeks for the first time. "Bad?"

"Nightmare for life," Danny whispers, turning her towards the field ahead. "We should be close enough to see her."

Andrea hesitates. "What if she's…"

"We can't afford to think like that," Danny says. "Come on. I don't see another line or fence. You?"

Andrea shakes her head.

"Let's go," Danny says, opening the map. "She should be right over the rise."

Andrea finds her legs again and marches beside Danny, matching his long stride up the small hill.

"There!" Andrea spots the mud splattered white toolbox. "Silvey!" She runs towards the prone body. "It's her!" She slides to a stop.

Silvey's blonde hair is splayed out in tangled clumps.

"Help me!" Andrea says, squatting next to the side of the toolbox.

Danny drops the bag and his case. He matches her stance. "On three. One, two, three."

"Ah," Andrea grunts. Her biceps burn and back pulls as they slowly move it away from Silvey's body.

Danny checks their progress. "Let go! We're clear!"

Andrea releases her grip and heaves in a long breath. "Silvey!"

The toolbox dents the ground.

Andrea falls to her knees near Silvey's head. "We're here Silvey." She pushes the hair away from Silvey's face. "We found you."

Danny drags his bag and case to Silvey's side. He checks her neck and wrist. "She's got a pulse." He does a quick assessment of her breath sounds with a stethoscope. "Breathing is steady, but her right lung sounds muffled." He lifts her shirt to examine her back and abdomen. "She has some internal bleeding. I'm calling in the medivac."

He quickly sends the stats and the location to the team on standby. He checks the field for the best clearance of trees and debris before igniting four flares in a square about a hundred feet from Silvey.

Danny returns and opens the case. He pulls out a hard neck brace sliding in a cushion after assessing Silvey's neck. He unfolds and presses the locks down on a backboard with two blocks. "I need to immobilize her neck and spine before I can roll her over."

"What can I do?" Andrea asks.

"Go to her feet," Danny says. "I'll have you hold her ankles against the board."

Andrea leans forward. "Just keep breathing!" She sits back and crawls around to her feet.

Danny works quickly, securing Silvey's neck brace and laying out the backboard across her spine with the two foam blocks on either side of the brace around her neck. He secures the board to Silvey's thighs and then sits back on his heels. He motions his hands to the left. "I am going to roll her to the left, your right."

"Got it," Andrea says, reaching under the backboard and holding her ankles steady.

"On three," Danny says. Andrea nods. "One, two, three."

They did it. Silvey is face up on the backboard.

"Dress," Silvey groans.

Andrea scrambles up towards Silvey's face. "Silvey, I'm here!"

"Midge," Silvey whispers. "Pain…"

"We've got a chopper coming," Andrea says. "You're hurt pretty bad but stubborn enough to survive a damn tornado."

One of Silvey's eyes opens slightly. "Missile…"

"We met a unit heading to the silo," Andrea says. "They're looking for them now."

Danny finishes strapping the rest of her to the board. He leans over and presses the stethoscope to her lungs and abdomen.

Silvey winces.

"It hurts here?" Danny asks, leaning away from Silvey.

"Everywhere," Silvey whispers.

"Her lips are turning blue," Andrea says. "What's happening?"

Danny tosses Andrea a foil square. "It's a warming blanket." He pulls a sharpie out. "Do you know if she has any allergies and her date of birth?"

"Penicillin." Andrea quickly unfolds the blanket. "April 18, 1994." She drapes the blanket over Silvey and sits back on her heels.

Danny writes her name, allergies, and date of birth on Silvey's right arm with a black sharpie. He pulls out a bag-valve mask and places it over Silvey's nose and mouth.

"Is she ok?" Andrea asks, watching the slow rise of Silvey's chest.

"She will be," Danny says, squeezing the bag. "Can you find the pulse oximeter and place it over her finger? It's blue and white, about two inches long. It should be in the outside pocket."

Andrea digs through the pocket and pulls out the device. She turns it over. "How do I turn it on?"

"It has a sensor to conserve battery life."

Andrea gently removes Silvey's hand from under the blanket. "Her hands ice cold." She gently places Silvey's finger inside the monitor. "That can't be normal."

"Her blood is pumping to keep her vital organs alive at the moment," Danny says, looking overhead. "I think I hear the chopper coming in from the south."

Andrea searches the dusk lit sky. She hears the thump of the blades before she spots the aircraft.

The yellow chopper flies over them, but then it circles back and positions itself over the flaring marks.

"Can I go with her?" Andrea shouts over the noise.

"Depends on the weight and number of crew," Danny yells back.

Andrea nods, turning her back to the helicopter and uses her body to shield Silvey from the wind and dirt.

"What do we got?" a man yells, running from the chopper towards Danny.

"Crush injury from that," Danny says, pointing to the white toolbox. "After being sucked up in a tornado about a mile away from here at the old nike base. She was conscious for a few minutes, breathing diminished and pulse growing weaker. She has notable signs of internal bleeding in her abdomen and pooling near the spleen."

"We've got her," the man says.

Two other uniformed crewmembers arrive with a stretcher and quickly but carefully move Silvey on to the stretcher and carry her back to the chopper.

"Do you have room for one more?" Danny shouts.

"Bird's full," the man shouts. "We're taking her straight to the trauma center. We have a team ready and waiting."

"Thank you!" Andrea shouts as the crew returns to the aircraft.

8

Red twirling lights illuminate the wall-to-wall cement hallway.

"What's happening?" Silvey demands, standing in an open doorway.

Seven men wearing tan uniforms look up from their green screen monitors. The man closest to the door stands quickly and blocks Silvey's view of the room.

She takes a hesitant step back into the hallway.

The man slams the door in her face.

"What in the hell!" Silvey shouts. "So rude!"

"Ma'am?"

Silvey turns and spots another man, wearing a similar tan uniform, walking towards her.

"What's going on?" Silvey points up to the twirling red light.

"Who are you and more importantly, how did you get down here?" The man stops a foot away from Silvey.

She leans forward to read his name on his badge. "Mr. Wilson, my name is Silvey Rhoades."

"Captain Wilson."

Silvey tilts her head to the side. "Army?"

"Army Air Defense. You haven't answered my second question."

"I took the lift down. A man wearing a similar uniform escorted me to a room down the hall." Silvey twirls her finger. "Is this some kind of drill or something?"

He shakes his head. "That's classified."

"Great!" Silvey points to her badge. "What secret level am I?"

"You're a civilian and should've never been admitted entry onto the base… let alone down here."

"Amazing! Please, show me the way out of this nightmare."

The walls and floor vibrate.

WOOOOOOOOONG

Silvey covers her ears and shouts over the blaring siren. "Can we go now?"

"No ma'am," he says and turns. He quickly walks away.

"Wait!" Silvey shouts, running after him. She wobbles and pauses for a second to kick off the red heels. "Where am I supposed to go?"

Captain Wilson turns a corner without looking back.

"Wait!" Silvey turns the corner. The red twirling lights and siren stop. Leaving her alone and in the pitch dark. "No, no, no!"

9

"Baxton!" Gage says, pulling back the curtain.

"Hey cousin," Bax says, pulling up a blanket over his skimpy hospital gown. "Sorry to put you two through a long drive over here."

Rozanne walks in ahead of Gage. Her signature long brown hair is pulled up in a ponytail.

"Don't you dare apologize," Rozanne says, shaking her head.

Gage bats away the wave of her hair.

Bax spots Gage's dramatic waving and smiles.

"We're just happy you're breathing." Her eyes linger on the IV tube running to a bag over his head. "They said something about surgery?"

"Apparently, I busted a kidney and possibly my spleen."

"How?" Gage asks, looking Bax over from head to toe.

"Short story. I fell about seven stories on a pile of steel and concrete."

"I'll need the longer story after surgery," Gage says.

"Well, you have a room ready at our house." Rozanne runs a finger over the faint scar near her cheek. "Gage is an excellent nurse."

"Ha," Gage laughs. "Very funny."

"It's true," Rozanne says, poking Gage in the side.

"Alright, you two," Bax says. "I'll call you in the morning. According to the surgeon, it could be a long wait for an operating room. And another few hours once I am in."

Rozanne shakes her head. "Nonsense. Monroe has the pharmacy covered tomorrow, Dusty has the shop covered, and we booked a room across the street. One of us will be in the waiting room throughout the night."

"Seriously guys, I'm fine."

"I promised your mother," Gage says, "and I prefer to keep my word."

"You called my mother?" Bax asks.

"Bax, you were injured in a major tornado that is all over the news," Gage says. "She would have had my hide if I didn't call her. Why didn't you?"

Bax sighs. "I didn't want her to worry and to be honest, minus the cut on my arm I didn't know I had any injuries."

A nurse pulls back the curtain. "Mr. Auburn, they're ready for you." They nod to Rozanne and Gage. "We'll update the family in the waiting room once we've completed."

"Thank you," Rozanne says, grasping Bax's hand. "See you on the other side."

Gage tousles Bax's curls. "Give them hell."

Bax swats his hand away. "Seriously, dude."

"Love ya," Gage says, taking Rozanne's hand. He nods to the nurse. "Take care of my cousin."

The nurse winks at Gage. "He's in great hands."

10

"It's been three hours," Evelyn says, folding her hands. "I just want an update on how my daughter, Silvey, is doing."

The nurse sighs. "She's still in surgery. Once they reach a point where it's safe to step out, they will come directly to the family, I promise."

Evelyn shakes her head. "She was in surgery when I arrived, and no one has been able to share any information. Like, why she needed surgery and who gave consent?"

"Trauma patients don't require consent when the next of kin is unavailable and the risk of waiting outweighs the survival of the patient. I'm sure they are doing everything they can to save your daughter." The nurse looks over their shoulder and leans across the nursing station. They whisper, "And the trauma team working tonight is the only team I would let touch my own family members. They are the best of the best."

Evelyn wipes away a falling tear. "That's some comfort."

"There's a chaplain on call tonight. Would you like me to page him and have him wait with you until your other family arrives?"

"Her father is pacing the lobby," Evelyn says, rolling her eyes. "He hates hospitals and that's as far as he will go. Can you believe that? His only daughter and he can't come up one floor."

The nurse nods. "It's a pretty common fear."

"Common or not, he can push past this just once for Silvey."

"I understand your frustration," the nurse says. "Maybe I'll send the chaplain down to your husband and see if he can work a miracle this evening."

"Ha! Ex-husband." Evelyn snorts. "By all means." She waves her hand.

"What's his first name?" the nurse asks.

"His name is Tom, but he answers to Buzz."

The nurse smiles. "That's unique. I'll send the page now. Is there anything else I can help you with?"

"No, thank you," Evelyn says. She lingers in the hallway outside of the waiting room.

There is only one seat open, next to an old man slumped forward in his chair, snoring.

The television in the corner is tuned into the local news.

An announcer says, "We've just received an update from Lawson and Vibbard town officials."

Evelyn steps inside the waiting room. Her eyes fixed on the screen.

"They're reporting ten known fatalities, seven residents are missing, and the injury list from minor to severe has reached fifty-five. Red Cross arrived this evening to help the residents affected by the tornado with food and shelter. They are also working with city officials and local police to establish search parties at first light. The missing residents range from a two-year-old child to a seventy-five-year-old man all believed to be home when the tornado touched down. Volunteers will gather at Southwest Elementary just before dawn."

"She's not missing," Evelyn whispers.

"The national weather service confirmed it was an EF5 tornado. The sustained winds were clocked at two hundred miles per hour. The latest models show it was on the ground for a total of seventeen minutes." The announcer pauses and looks visibly shaken. "The destruction of personal property, lives and livelihoods all took a tremendous hit today for our neighbors in these small communities. Our station will keep the viewers updated from the Red Cross shelter tomorrow morning. Stay safe, Kansas City."

Andrea runs into the waiting room. "Has anyone seen a woman about this tall?" She holds a hand to her shoulder. "Blonde hair in her mid-fifties."

A brown-haired man nods. "There was a woman in a pink shirt that could fit that description. She answered a phone call and stepped out about five minutes ago."

"Did you see which direction she went?" Andrea asks.

"Left, I think," he says, looking at the woman to his right.

"I was texting Mary, sorry," she says.

"It's ok," Andrea says, "thanks."

Andrea steps out into the hall and takes a left. "Please let me find her." She rushes past the nurse's station and spots a flash of pink up ahead.

"Evelyn," Andrea whisper shouts. She picks up her pace.

A nurse, backing out of a room, steps into Andrea's path.

"Oof," Andrea says, holding up her hands.

"What's on fire?" the nurse asks, watching Andrea catch her balance.

"Sorry," Andrea says, dancing around the nurse, pulling a computer on wheels out of the room. "So sorry."

Evelyn looks over her shoulder. "Andrea?"

"Yes!" Andrea rushes towards Evelyn. "I've been looking for you."

"Silvey?" Evelyn asks, dropping her phone.

It smacks the floor with a deafening thwack.

"No!" Andrea says, bending to retrieve Evelyn's phone. "Buzz collapsed in the main lobby. They've taken him to the emergency room."

"What! When?"

"Just now," Andrea says, handing her phone back. "Do you want to go down or stay up here?"

"How bad is he?" Evelyn asks, walking back towards the waiting room.

"They were doing chest compressions when I walked in," Andrea says.

Evelyn stops and does an about face for the elevator. "Stay here and if anyone comes looking for me. Call me immediately!"

"Of course, but Evelyn fair warning, she's down there too!"

The elevator door opens.

Evelyn steps inside. "Who?"

"His girlfriend, Sheila."

Evelyn sticks her chin out and straightens her posture. "Just great!"

The elevator door closes.

"Is there a problem?" a nurse asks, stepping beside Andrea.

"Her ex-husband collapsed in the lobby and his girlfriend is down there with him," Andrea says. "The term bitter does not begin to express how she feels about the 'other' woman. I would say warn the staff, but I am sure they are used to family fireworks in the ER."

"Ah, I see," the nurse says. "Checking her tablet. You're here for…"

"Silvey Rhoades."

"We should have an update in the next half hour or so."

"Thanks, I'll be in the waiting room."

The nurse holds up a finger. "Have you signed in?"

"No, not yet."

The nurse hands Andrea a clipboard and pen. "Patient's name, your name, relationship to patient, and your phone number."

Andrea quickly fills in her information and glances at her phone. *Two percent, shit.* "Any chance you have a spare charger I can use?"

"Wireless charging is set up on all side tables. You should be fine."

Andrea sighs and smiles. "Thanks." She hands back the clipboard and pen.

"No problem," the nurse says.

"Did you find her?" the man asks, watching Andrea place her phone on the table.

"Yes, thanks," Andrea says, taking a seat across from them. "Are you two from Lawson?"

"Excelsior," the man says. "I'm Gage. This is my wife, Roz." He winks at his wife. "I mean Rozanne."

"Nice to meet you. I'm Andrea."

"Are you from Lawson?" Rozanne asks, setting her phone down.

"Yes, it's been an eventful day."

"Were you hit by the…" Gage asks.

"Yes, but not as bad as most of my neighbors." Andrea sighs and frowns. "Eleven homes were leveled on my street."

"That's awful," Rozanne says. "Are you here waiting on family?"

"My best friend, Silvey, is in surgery and her father just collapsed in the lobby."

"Oh geez," Rozanne says. "And the woman you were looking for?"

"Silvey's mom."

"Simply awful." Rozanne takes Gage's hand and squeezes.

"Are you here for family or a friend?" Andrea asks.

Rozanne gestures to Gage. "His cousin Bax was injured out at the old nike base."

"Bax and Micah!" Andrea shouts.

Rozanne flinches.

"Sorry I didn't mean to shout."

"It's fine." Rozanne glances at Gage. "Was that his boss's name?"

"Yes," Gage says. "You know Bax?"

"No, my friend Silvey was working with them this morning when the storm hit." Andrea moves to a chair closer to Rozanne. "She was sucked out of the silo when the roof came off."

"Oh!" Rozanne covers her mouth.

"We found her in a field nearly a mile away from the base."

"Whoa," Gage whispers.

"And she mentioned Micah and Bax before…" Andrea says, glancing at her lap. "They life flighted her here."

Gage frowns. "And all Bax mentioned was his fall. I knew I should have insisted on the longer story."

"Do you know how Micah is doing?" Rozanne asks.

"We met his wife Jessica on the road while looking for Silvey," Andrea says. "She's up in labor and delivery at the moment. I'm not sure on Micah's status." She glances around the waiting room. "Any idea who they are waiting for?" She nods towards an old man with his head tilted forward, softly snoring, and the woman sitting to his right.

Rozanne whispers, "I heard the nurse mention something about a heart attack and an open-heart surgery."

"Well, I don't think Midge would be here for that," Andrea says.

"Midge?" Gage asks.

"Crap! It's Micah's nickname from high school. Silvey called him by that earlier."

"Ah," Gage says. "I think Dusty, my mechanic at the shop, and him are friends." He shrugs. "Any chance your friend Silvey is an electrician?"

"Actually, yes, why?" Andrea asks, raising an eyebrow.

"Dusty had a major crush on that girl," Gage says.

Rozanne elbows Gage in the side.

"What was that for?" Gage asks, rubbing his ribs.

"You didn't like it when our business was being tossed around for town gossip and now you're blabbing on about Dusty?"

Andrea laughs. "Silvey knew all about Dusty."

"See," Gage says, pointing at Rozanne. "Not gossip, if it's true."

Rozanne rolls her eyes. "Regardless, it's none of our business."

"Seriously," Andrea says, "my lips are sealed. Silvey is—she's Miss Independent—times a thousand."

Gage chuckles. "Poor Dusty. He never had a chance."

Andrea scrunches her brow. "You know, I don't think he ever had the balls to actually ask her out."

"You're saying he has a shot?" Gage asks.

Andrea smiles. "He'll never know until he pulls the trigger."

A nurse steps into the waiting room.

The three of them quiet and focus their attention on the nurse.

"I'm looking for the family of Ms. Rhoades."

Andrea stands and quickly retrieves her phone. "Her mother just stepped out to check on her husband in the emergency room." She follows the nurse out of the room and dials Evelyn.

"A resident stepped out of the operating room to give the family a quick update." She gestures to a man pacing the width of the hallway. He's dressed in light blue scrubs and a surgical cap covering most of his red hair.

"Andrea!" Evelyn answers.

"I'm putting you on speaker," Andrea says, tapping her phone. "We're about to get an update."

The resident pauses and frowns at the phone.

"Silvey's mother, Evelyn," Andrea says, holding the phone towards the resident, "is with Silvey's dad down in the emergency room."

The resident glances at the nurse. They nod and open the door to a small room with four chairs.

"My name is Dr. Zinterman," he says, extending his arm towards a chair.

"I'm Andrea," she says nervously taking a seat.

"My attending asked me to step out and give an update on Ms. Rhoades." He clears his throat. "She arrived with extensive internal bleeding, several fractures to her pelvic bone, lumbar spine, and her right femur."

"Oh, God!" Evelyn cries over the phone. "My baby."

"Hang on, Evelyn," Andrea says, wiping away her own tears. "We need to hear the rest."

"Ok," Evelyn whimpers.

Andrea nods to Dr. Zinterman.

"We've removed her appendix, spleen, parts of her small intestine and one ovary. All were damaged beyond repair. We're actively working on the bleeding in her abdomen and pelvic regions. We have administered several blood transfusions, but…" He pauses to look at the nurse. They nod. "She's crashed twice on the table."

Andrea covers her mouth and tightens her grip around her phone.

"What do you mean crashed?" Evelyn asks.

"Her heart stopped, and we had to resuscitate her."

"No!" Evelyn wails.

"Evelyn," Andrea says, holding the phone close to her chin and letting the tears fall. "He's not done."

"Our scans also indicated a closed head injury that we are closely monitoring. She will be transferred into the intensive care unit and placed in a medically induced coma. We'll run additional labs, tests, and perform a neurological exam to assess the extent of her head injury."

"Is the coma necessary?" Andrea asks.

"This will give her body time to recover from the trauma. We'll have a clearer picture of her recovery once the labs and neuro exam come back."

"You think she'll recover?" Andrea blurts out.

"The road will be very long," the doctor says, "but yes."

"Did you hear that, Evelyn?" Andrea asks. "Silvey's going to make it!"

11

Silvey blindly feels her way down the hall until she finds an open door.

"Hello!"

The echo of her own voice returns.

Return to where I started? Or stay in one place until the lights are back on?

A cool breeze slides across her bare legs. She shakes off the chill gliding up her spine.

Definitely back the way I came.

Silvey makes it three steps before stubbing her toe on something solid. "What the…" She hops on one foot, holding her injured toe until the throbbing subsides.

Why is this happening?

She reaches her hand out and finds a cool, solid surface.

Brilliant, Silvey. You're walking into walls now.

She keeps her hand on the rough cement wall and starts to hobble forward until her hands find a cold, smooth surface. She pats the surface down until she finds a handle. She twists and turns, but it doesn't budge.

"Hello! Anyone!"

Silvey bangs on the door until her fists go numb. Shaking out her hands she puts her ear to the door—hearing only the low hum of a fan.

Find the way up, don't panic.

She uses her hand to anchor her path and creeps forward.

Silvey spots a small dot of light ahead. "Hello! Andrea?"

"Who's there?" a man whispers.

"Silvey. Silvey Rhoades."

The light bounces up and down in rhythm with the heavy footsteps.

Silvey backs up against the wall. The light falls on her face, and she lifts her hand to shield her eyes.

"Who are you?" Silvey asks.

"Bax," he says, holding the light up to his face.

"Bax!" Silvey throws her arms around him.

"How did you get down here?" Bax says, awkwardly patting the top of her head.

Silvey steps away from him. "Midge put me on the lift and sent me down here!"

Bax shakes his head. "No! He couldn't have."

"Seriously!" Silvey says. "Look!" She grabs the flashlight and waves it down over her bright blue dress. "I didn't arrive for work wearing this?"

Bax coughs. "Whoa!"

"See, I'm not lying!"

"I think I would remember that dress, but Micah is…"

"Is he here?" Silvey asks, cutting him off. "Is this payback for using his old nickname?" She pans the light down the hall.

Bax leans his face level with Silvey. "Micah's dead."

Silvey shoves the flashlight into Bax's chest. "Not funny, none of this is!"

"Trust me, none of this is a joke." Bax shines the light over his tan uniform. "I just climbed down a ladder to avoid gunfire."

"Are you serious?"

"Yes," Bax says.

Silvey shakes her head. "But you're wearing the same uniform Midge was wearing."

"Silvey," Bax says, reaching for her hand. "What is the last thing you remember from this morning?"

Silvey steps out of his reach. She bites her bottom lip and closes her eyes. "The tampon string hanging out of Micah's nose." She snickers. "And then we were running down the ramp."

"Before the tornado tore the roof off the silo," Bax says.

Silvey opens her eyes and meets his watery eyes looking down at her.

"You and Micah falling."

Bax nods. "We did." He wipes the corners of his eye with a knuckle. "Micah's gone… he's dead."

"No," Silvey whispers.

Bax swallows. "I saw him…"

Silvey pushes past him. "Midge, come out now. This is not funny!"

Bax turns his light and follows Silvey a few feet, but then she whirls and points her finger hard on his chest.

"Why are you doing this?"

"I am not doing anything!" Bax says. "But I know the last thing I remember before waking up in this uniform." He frowns. "It was a mask over my nose and mouth."

"What?" Silvey asks.

"I swear!" Bax says, holding a hand over his heart. "Silvey."

Silvey lowers her hand and balls her fists.

"Do you remember anything else?" Bax asks, looking down at her.

She steps back and glares up at him. "I told you that already!"

"Before being here?" He waves his arm around.

Silvey takes another step back. "Grass."

"Grass?"

"I remember grass sticking to my face and neck," she says, touching her cheek and neck. "Then darkness… before standing outside the silo holding a lit cigarette."

"You smoke?"

"No!" Silvey sighs. "A lady I've never seen before was outside telling me I was late and needed to get down here to take notes."

"Back up," Bax says. "And you believed the woman?"

"No, but she swatted me in here and then there's the badge, plus what I was wearing." She holds up the badge and her barefoot.

"Ok…" Bax stares at her feet.

"I was wearing high heels! Which I never do unless I'm strong armed by Dre to wear to some formal charity event."

"Dre is your…"

"My best friend, Andrea," Silvey says.

Bax smirks and clears his throat. "So, the silo, grass, darkness, and then here wearing a dress and heels?"

"Right," Silvey says, nodding, "that sounds nuts too."

"True, but at least we aren't alone in our crazy," Bax says, waving his flashlight around.

"That's something," Silvey says, folding her arms across her chest.

"Was it always this dark down here?" Bax asks, pointing the flashlight up towards the ceiling.

"No, the hallway had working lights."

"Did you hear a siren?" Bax asks.

"Yes," Silvey says, "a very long, loud one."

"When did the lights go out?" Bax asks, moving across the width of the hallway.

"Right after the siren. Maybe twenty minutes ago." Silvey holds up her bare wrists in front of his flashlight. "I don't exactly have a way to tell time."

"Did you see anything or anyone?"

"Yes," Silvey says, taking Bax's hand in one hand and his light in the other. She leads him to a solid steel door. "There's a bunch of men dressed like you in what I can only describe as a control room."

"Why do you think it was a control room?" Bax asks, leaning his ear to the door.

"It looked like the ones in old movies about mission control stations." Silvey uses her hands like she's typing on a keyboard.

"A bunch of green screens on old monitors laid out in a few rows. And one wall of screens. I counted seven men."

"Did they explain what was happening?"

Silvey shrugs. "No, when I asked what was going on, a man slammed the door in my face."

"Rude," Bax says, pushing and then pulling on the door handle. "Come on!" He pounds on the door.

"The door looked solid, like a vault door. I doubt they can hear you."

"And the lights when out after they shut the door?"

"No, after I spoke to Captain Wilson,"

Bax stops pounding. "Like a military officer?"

"Yeah," Silvey says. "He said I didn't have clearance and shouldn't be down here."

"Why didn't he show you the exit?"

"That's when the siren started." She points over Bax's shoulder. "He turned and quickly walked away. I went after him, but then the lights went out."

Bax kneels, placing his cheek to the floor, and looks under the door. "I can't see anything." Silvey hands him the flashlight. He shines the light under the door. "Nothing!" He stands and turns the light towards the hallway. "And the lift you took down was where?"

"In the direction you came from," Silvey says, aiming his light down the hall to their left. "I walked by a huge missile and then down a long hallway."

"A missile?"

Silvey shrugs. "Pretty sure."

"1962…"

"What?" Silvey asks.

"I saw a paper and calendar up there from 1962."

"What year was the base built?" Silvey asks.

"Micah mentioned it was around the late fifties," Bax says.

Silvey snorts. "Are you—joking?"

"No," Bax says. "But if we have to go back the way I came down… we may need to run. Do you want to find your shoes?" He points the light towards her bare feet.

"Hell no," Silvey says, rolling up onto her toes. "I can't run in those. Let's go!"

Bax pans the light back and forth as they work their way down the dark hallway. He pauses the light on a ladder anchored to the wall. "This is where I climbed down."

"What's up there?" Silvey asks.

"A space barely big enough for an old desk, chair and a sliding window." Bax walks ahead. "I found the hatch covering the ladder by accident while hiding from the gunfire just outside the shack."

"Bax!"

"What?" he asks, moving the light over her face. "Did you hear something?"

"No, explain why somebody was shooting," Silvey says.

Bax lifts a shoulder. "I can't."

"Do you know who was shooting?"

"Not exactly," Bax says. "I was ordered to let a truck in and a few minutes later the ground trembled, then a bunch of men were shouting. It was dark, I couldn't see anyone, and then there were shots ringing out. A few bullets were pinging off the fence near the shack." He pats his utility belt. "I wasn't armed with anything but a flashlight, so I hid."

"Ha!" Silvey scoffs.

"It was an air defense base, right?" Bax asks.

"I believe that's what Captain Wilson said."

"But it shut down a long time ago," Bax says.

Silvey nods.

"What if that newspaper isn't old?" Bax asks.

Silvey laughs. "That's not possible… right?" She tugs at the collar of her dress and her heart drums a bit harder. "You think we time traveled to 1962?"

"Maybe?" Bax says, shining the light over his uniform. "Pretty sure I don't own anything like this, nor would I consciously let somebody dress me in this uniform." He waves the light up and down Silvey's petite figure. "And you said yourself that isn't a wardrobe choice you would make."

"Well, true," Silvey says, chewing on the inside of her cheek. "But there's a logical explanation for that, right?"

"Explain the logic while we find an exit," Bax says.

"Ok," Silvey says, falling into step beside Bax.

12

"Why isn't he waking up?" Gage asks, pacing between Bax's hospital bed and the window. "It's been hours."

"Two hours." The doctor swipes up and scans Baxton's chart. "We've ruled out any neurological causes. His brain activity and scans were all normal. And we've double checked the medication administered since he was admitted—ruling out any pharmacokinetic or pharmacodynamic related issues for the delayed emergence. Only things we are waiting on is his post-op labs and a pathology report from surgery."

"And that would indicate what?" Gage asks, wishing Rozanne was back from the hotel.

"Ruling out any metabolic alterations that could impair his emergence from the sedation administered for the surgery."

"What exactly did you do?"

"We managed to repair his kidney and expect it to heal without any complications. But we did decide to remove his spleen once we saw the damage."

"Can you live without a spleen?" Gage asks, looking Bax over.

"Yes, but a common infection like a cold may take him longer to recover." The surgeon taps the tablet. "His vitals remain strong, with no red flags. I expect he'll wake up on his own soon."

The nurse nudges the surgeon. "His heart rate just spiked."

Bax's chest jolts up.

"What was that!" Gage yells, stepping away from the bedside.

The nurse moves in front of Gage.

The vital display flickers.

"Did that just shock him?" Gage asks, looking at the leads from the device to Bax.

"No, that's not possible." The nurse disconnects the leads. "But we'll take this one out and bring a new one in."

"But why would his chest jump up like that?" Gage asks, staring at the surgeon.

The surgeon opens their mouth but then closes it again. "I wish I had a plausible explanation. We'll get a new set of vitals before we hook him back up."

Gage watches the nurse wrap a blood pressure cuff around Bax's arm. "What do you really think is going on?"

"I think he'll wake up without any complications." The surgeon glances over at Gage holding Bax's eyelid open and pockets his penlight. "His pupils are reactive."

"Blood pressure is normal," the nurse says, pushing the vital monitor cart around the bed. "I'll step out and get a thermometer."

"A delayed emergence from anesthesia is rare but not unheard of, and your cousin looks like a strong, healthy young man. If he was older and frail, I would be more concerned."

The nurse returns with the thermometer and a new vital monitor. They swipe the red glowing end of the thermometer across Bax's forehead and behind his ear. They show the surgeon the temperature before wiping the device with an alcohol swab.

"He is running a low-grade temperature," the surgeon says, checking the tablet again. "Again, all normal after a major surgery. We'll keep a close eye on that and adjust the antibiotics as needed. I'll round again after his labs come back and hopefully chat with both of you."

Gage nods. "Thanks."

The nurse turns on the monitor and tests the lead on themself before placing the lead on Bax.

"Ok," the nurse says, stepping back from the bed. "Here is the call light." They hand the white cord with a red button to Gage. "If he starts to wake up or you notice anything like you saw before, don't hesitate to press the button. I'll send a tech down to sit with you shortly."

"Can he hear me?" Gage asks, before the nurse reaches the door.

"Most likely, so be kind."

13

Andrea steps into the elevator. "Four please."

A man with bright white hair turns with a wink and smiles. "Us too." He points with his thumb at a petite woman to his right.

The woman smiles. "Are you visiting family?"

"No, ma'am, my best friend." Andrea tries to smile, but she feels it fall before it reaches her cheeks. "You two?"

"A young man about your age caught in that terrible tornado," the woman says.

Andrea nods. "It was… terrible."

The elevator dings and the doors open.

The man holds his arm out for the woman and Andrea to exit.

"Thanks," Andrea says. She heads to the desk and signs in on a clipboard. She hands the pen to the woman and nods to the older man. "Sign in and the nurse will check if the patient is ready for visitors."

"Thank you," the woman says, taking the clipboard.

"Andrea?"

Andrea looks over her shoulder. "Oh, hi Rozanne. How's Bax doing?"

"Still a wait and see scenario," Rozanne says, hugging the woman from the elevator. "This is Silvey's friend Andrea." She gestures to the woman. "And this is Mary and her husband, Monroe."

"Silvey," Mary says, "was she the young woman that was working with Bax?"

"Yes," Andrea says.

"How's she doing?" Rozanne asks.

"Still medically sedated," Andrea says. "But her brain activity is off the charts. Which is promising, according to her medical team."

"Interesting," Rozanne says. "The doctor mentioned something very similar about Bax this morning."

Monroe chuckles. "Maybe they're inside chatting."

Mary points at Monroe. "What are you talking about?"

"A documentary I saw a few months ago," Monroe says. "They interviewed twelve people that spent time in an extended coma. And all but two of them recalled detailed experiences and conversations. Two of them were strangers injured in a bus crash and when they woke up, they knew details about the other person that they learned while on the other side."

Mary rolls her eyes. "And you, Mr. Science, believed them?"

Monroe shrugs. "The brain is powerful, and we are still learning about it every day."

"Well, let's hope they are finding a way out and not some bright light," Andrea says.

"Very true," Rozanne says. "Did Silvey's dad recover?"

"Kind of," Andrea says, pointing at the ceiling. "He's up one floor. Minor stroke and needs a stent or two. He's waiting on the surgeon now."

"I'll add her dad to our prayer group," Mary says, nodding at Andrea. "Silvey and Bax are already on it. Do you know his name?"

"Buzz Rhoades," Andrea says.

Monroe chuckles. "I know that young man."

Andrea laughs. "That is not how I would ever describe Buzz."

Monroe laughs. "He's our son's age and I think they played ball together way back in the day."

Andrea smiles.

The unit door opens, and a nurse pokes their head out. "Andrea?"

"It was nice meeting you," Andrea says, waving to the nurse. "Tell Gage hi for me."

"Will do," Rozanne says.

Andrea walks in behind the nurse and the door clicks closed.

Andrea stops at the sink and washes her hands.

"I see it's not your first visit." The nurse sets the clipboard on the desk and picks up a tablet. "I have some news."

Andrea dries her hands and drops the paper towel in the trash bin. "Good, I hope?"

"Our latest labs indicate that her blood counts have stabilized."

"Translation?" Andrea asks.

"A second surgery to stop any bleeding doesn't look necessary."

Andrea nods. "That is great news." She looks over the nurse's shoulder. "May I sit with her?"

"Yes," the nurse says, walking with Andrea to the sliding glass door. "She's a bit restless, so you might notice some spikes in her heart rate."

"Is that normal?" Andrea asks, looking over the many tubes and leads connected to Silvey's petite still body under a pile of blankets.

"It's not abnormal," the nurse says, sliding open the door. "She's on her own path to recovery."

Andrea scoots the chair closer to the bed and sits. She lifts the blankets and finds Silvey's hand.

It's cold.

Andrea takes Silvey's hand in hers. "Silvey, I don't know if you can hear me, but I'll give you the latest run down." She glances at the monitor over the bed. Her heart rate stays between seventy-two and seventy-five. "Your dad is heading into surgery. And your mom is losing her mind. Between you and Buzz, I don't think she's slept since you were admitted."

Silvey's heart monitor beeps louder.

"I've tried to get her to rest, trust me." Andrea laughs. "I believe she's running on spite and coffee at the moment. And your dad's other half couldn't take the drama. She bailed after the doctor said surgery was required."

Silvey's lips curl up on one side.

Andrea leans forward. "Silvey Lynn, did you just smile?"

Silvey's mouth twitches again.

"You can hear me!" Andrea squeezes her hand. "Great, wake up and get your butt home!"

Silvey's mouth twitches a third time.

"Well," Andrea says. "Scott officially freaked out when he saw footage of our street. He's on his way home via red eye from Istanbul." She looks up at the ceiling to slow the tears forming. "Speaking of home… Silvey. They found six of the missing people from my street." She sniffles. "All dead—none of them had a chance."

"Dre! Can you hear me? I'm not dead!" Silvey yells into the darkness. Her voice echoes back… *"dead, dead, dead."*

Silvey's heart rate doubles on the display. An alarm blares loudly and Andrea flinches.

Silvey shouts, *"I'm here!"*

Andrea lets go of Silvey's hand. "What's happening?" She stands and waves in a passing nurse.

The nurse steps in and glances at the display. "She's agitated. I'll check with her nurse and see when she's due for another round of pain medication."

Andrea nods and wipes away the falling tears.

A second nurse walks in and checks one of the monitors. "She should settle back down in a few minutes." The nurse presses a button silencing the alarm. "Her mother called down to check on her a minute ago. They've cleared her father for surgery."

Andrea nods. "And Silvey's ok?"

"She's fine. Her pain medication was due." They point to the monitor. "Her heart rate and blood pressure are returning to normal." They pat the chair. "You can stay a bit longer."

66

"Thanks," Andrea says, sitting down and resting her hand over Silvey's hand.

The nurse slides the door closed.

"I'll stick to good news," Andrea whispers, watching Silvey's face. "Jessica had a baby girl early this morning." She glances at the monitors and continues. "She and the baby are doing great. I plan to stop by their room before I pick up Scott from the airport."

"And my neighbor, Norma, is watching over the house. Her son along with some volunteers got the back side of the house boarded up and the front window covered to prevent anyone or the rain from coming inside. We've got more storms coming in today and tomorrow."

Andrea sits back and sighs. "I finally responded to my client's calls, texts, and emails after I left them hanging mid tornado warning. I sent them a picture of my street before and after." She shakes her head. "I know it sounds dramatic, but I wanted their understanding on why I won't be returning messages or working for at least a week or two." She leans forward. "Yes, I, workaholic Andrea, have put down the laptop and removed my work email app from my phone."

Andrea's phone dings. She takes her phone out of her pocket and swipes up. "Not work, it's your mom." She quickly types back *almost done*. She pockets her phone. "Silvey, they are wheeling Buzz into surgery in a few minutes. He's grumpy but otherwise fine. Your mom is coming down to visit."

Andrea leans over Silvey and kisses her forehead. "I'll give Jessica your congrats and then head to pick up Scott. I'll come back tomorrow."

"Andrea!" Silvey shouts again, creeping forward and feeling her way through the dark. *"Wait! Take me with you!"*

14

The heart rate monitor connected to Baxton starts a rapid, loud beep.

Rozanne stands and checks the display. "His heart rate is over a hundred. Get the nurse!"

Gage runs out of the hospital room.

"Bax, if you can hear me," Rozanne says. "Think calm and happy thoughts. Gage is getting a nurse."

The monitor beeping escalates.

Rozanne hears footsteps racing towards the door. She steps away from the bed.

A nurse enters ahead of Gage. They silence the alarm and turn to them. "Can you two step out in the hall?"

"Of course," Rozanne says, taking Gage's hand.

The nurse presses the call button. "Page the doctor."

Gage pauses at the door. "Is he waking up?"

The nurse looks up. "Hopefully."

Rozanne tugs on his hand. "Let's give them a chance to assess Bax."

Gage walks down the hall to the elevators. He presses the down arrow. "I need some air and could use another coffee."

"I'll let the nurse know we aren't wandering far." Rozanne steps back to the desk.

The elevator door opens.

Gage holds an arm over the threshold and glances inside. "Oh hey, Andrea. One second Roz is at the desk."

"No problem," Andrea says, pocketing her phone. "How's Baxton?"

"Agitated, his heart rate just doubled," Gage says, motioning for Rozanne to hurry.

Rozanne rushes inside and Gage steps in releasing the door.

"Hey, that's odd." Andrea raises an eyebrow. "Silvey's heart rate caused her monitor to alarm, too."

Rozanne glances between Gage and Andrea.

"Do you think what Monroe suggested could be true?" Rozanne asks.

"Roz told me what Monroe suggested." Gage chuckles. "You think they are enjoying some kind of coma rave party?"

Andrea smiles. "Maybe, but who knows? Silvey is medically sedated. She could be tripping on whatever they are giving her to keep her under."

"It's the exact opposite for Bax," Gage says. "He's got a drip for hydration. And an antibiotic injection twice a day, but no meds to keep him under."

The elevator door opens to the quiet lobby.

"Hmm, I've got to go and pick up my husband from the airport," Andrea says, pointing towards the exit to the parking garage. "I'll swing by tomorrow and check on Baxton."

"Thanks, we'll check on Silvey while you're gone," Rozanne says.

"Thank you!" Andrea says, rushing towards the exit.

15

Silvey and Bax walk a few paces.

"I feel alive." Silvey pokes Bax.

He turns the light towards Silvey. "Very alive."

"I've heard enough to know that this is not reality. We are hallucinating."

Bax nods. "It's one hell of a trip."

"I'm finding a way up and out of here," Silvey says, taking his flashlight.

Bax loses her silhouette to the darkness almost instantly. The bouncing beam of the flashlight dances far ahead. *Damn, she's fast for someone so short!*

"I'm coming," Bax says, jogging towards the light. He blinks and is back in total darkness. "Silvey? Where are you?"

"You, you, you, you…" his voice echoes back.

What in the hell? Bax spins in a slow circle. His eyes adjust to the darkness, and he makes out a long cone-shaped object ahead.

"Not funny! Silvey, where did you go?"

"Go, go, go, go…"

The echo sends a chill up his spine.

"Hello, earth to Silvey!" Bax keeps his eyes on the long shape ahead and inches forward. "Hello?"

A flash of light hits Bax's face, and he jerks up, flailing his arms and his fists connects with something hard.

"Bax!" Gage yells. "Calm down, buddy!"

Bax blinks, and a few very worried faces come into focus. "What's happening?"

"You're in the hospital," Gage says, waving his hand around.

"But Silvey," Bax says, taking in the pale blue walls and the monitors next to a bed with rails. He pulls on the blue gown covering his chest. "I don't understand."

Rozanne steps beside Gage. "You were working at the old nike base when a big tornado hit the area. Do you recall any of that?"

Bax looks from Rozanne's forced smile to a nurse standing across from her. "I had surgery?"

The nurse nods. "They repaired your damaged left kidney and removed your spleen."

Bax lays back. "Is a spleen important?"

"Its primary function is to fight off infections," the nurse says. "Not vital to your day-to-day health, but a common cold may take you longer to recover than it used to." They hold up a dark blue cuff. "May I check your blood pressure?"

Bax nods.

"Are you in pain?" the nurse asks, sliding the cuff up Bax's uninjured arm.

Bax stares at the ceiling and feels something damp on his ribs. "Pain, no, but I think I may have busted a stitch."

The nurse pulls back the blanket and gown. "Your correct." They poke a dark red spot above the sutures.

Bax winces.

"That hurts?" the nurse asks, assessing the wound.

"A bit tender," Bax says, shaking his head. "I did smack my ribs on something right before…"

"Before what?" Gage asks, standing over Bax.

Bax glances at the nurse placing the stethoscope and then winks at Gage.

Gage nods.

The nurse releases the air out of the blood pressure cuff. "The doctor will be by in a bit, and I'll be back in with a suture kit and a new bandage."

Gage and Bax watch the nurse leave and close the door.

Rozanne steps on the other side of the bed. "What is going on with you two?"

Gage quirks up the corner of his mouth and folds his arms across his chest. "Bax was about to explain what happened before he woke up."

Bax rolls his eyes. "I don't think either of you will believe me."

"Try us," Rozanne says. "We've dealt with our fair share of odd experiences."

Bax raises an eyebrow. "You're referencing the missing girl mystery you two unfolded?"

Rozanne smiles. "Sure." She winks at Gage recalling a mysterious journal that uncovered a century old cold case leading back to her great-grandparent's adoption of what was once considered a missing girl.

"Well, what I experienced was real—but impossible." Bax shifts to his right side to take the pressure off the wound. "I met Silvey. She's the electrician working out at the vertical farm."

Gage and Rozanne nod.

"We've met a friend of hers in the waiting room," Gage says. "Silvey's in the intensive care unit."

Bax blinks. "She's here in the hospital?"

"Yes," Rozanne says, "on this floor."

"But how?" Bax whispers.

"Her friend Andrea said they life flighted her here from a field about a mile away from the base," Gage says.

"I don't think that is what he's confused about," Rozanne says, studying Bax's furrowed brow. "Is it Bax?"

"No." Bax glances at the door. "Silvey was with me."

16

"Bax!" Silvey yells, panning the light over the hallway. "Where are you?" The light dims and she shakes the flashlight, but the light dims even more. "Bax, the flashlight is dying! Where did you go?"

She feels the air around her charge and the hair on her head lifts away from her scalp. She pans the beam over the walls and pauses on a small electrical box. She pops it open.

"These are ancient," Silvey mumbles, holding the flashlight over the red and blue round fuses. She unscrews one of the fuses. "These look brand new. No visible damage." She screws it back in and checks the labels. "Lab, chamber, and corridor."

"Bax, I found something," Silvey says, waving the light, but it goes dim and dies. She shakes the flashlight again. "And we're back in the dark."

The charge in the air happens again and she steps away from the electrical box.

All the lights return at once.

Silvey blinks as her eyes adjust and she looks for Bax, but she's alone in a sterile white space. She can't find the end of the wall with the ceiling or the floor. She feels a slight disorientation and kneels to touch the floor. *How big is this space?* She slowly inches forward until she finds the wall and stands again. Leaving her hand anchored to the wall she starts to walk the perimeter. "The only thing of any color visible beyond the white on white is me and this damn dress."

"Bax, can you hear me?" Silvey calls out and jumps when a person comes into view. She laughs at the frightened look on her own face as she assesses her appearance for the first time. Her hair was tied back in a ponytail, but several pieces have fallen framing her face. "I look absolutely ridiculous." She twirls and checks the back of her dress. "No zipper?" She pulls out the tag and holds it up towards the mirror. "Sears? Andrea would be impressed." She turns and taps the mirror until she finds a gap. "Bax, I'm leaving here with or without you."

Silvey steps through the gap and enters a room full of giant fuses and wires leading to the walls of the white room. "What is this thing?"

She carefully walks through the maze of equipment, cables, water lines, and wires surrounding one large piece in the middle. Metal tags, engraved with Property of the US Government, are stuck on nearly every surface, but not on the one device in the center.

Silvey walks close enough to read it, *Scylla II*. "Where have I seen that before?"

She stands back and examines the whole structure and gasps. "This is a nuclear fusion reactor or something like it. Dang, I wish I would have paid more attention in physics."

The labels on the fuse box… lab, chamber, corridor. "This isn't just an Army Air Defense base!" She rushes around to the control panel opposite of the reactor. There is a stack of papers. She flips through several pages and her hands tremble. "It's research. They're researching nuclear fusion. Holy…"

17

Bax lays back on the bed. "That's everything."

Gage and Rozanne exchange a look before turning their focus back to Bax.

"I know," Bax says, watching their exchange. "It's nuts."

"You've just explained a traumatic experience with the tornado and Micah's death," Gage says, sitting on the edge of the bed.

Bax averts his eyes down to his hands.

"Add major surgery and concern for Silvey," Rozanne says. "It's not that farfetched to have such an encounter while you were unconscious."

"Encounter?" Bax whispers, risking a look up at Rozanne.

She nods towards the door. "Plus, Silvey is still sedated."

Bax lifts an eyebrow.

Rozanne winks. "So whatever plane of the cosmic world you traveled to while under… it's possible."

Bax laughs, and then abruptly frowns, holding his left side.

"Pain?" Gage asks.

"A bit. You never told me Roz was funny."

Gage smiles at Rozanne. "It's one of her many hidden talents."

"So many," Rozanne says, holding up two fingers.

Gage laughs and pulls out his phone. "We should call your mom. She's been calling every hour and asking for an update."

"Oh," Bax says, scanning the room for a clock. "What time is it there?"

"Early, but I know she hasn't slept much," Gage says.

Bax leans to the right. "She doesn't need to know about my little adventure with Silvey."

"I'm definitely not going down that road with her," Gage says, pressing the phone into Bax's hand. "We'll step out and give you a moment."

Rozanne follows Gage out into the hall.

"Do you think it's ok to leave him alone?" Rozanne asks, hovering near the door. "He's only been awake for about thirty minutes and the doctor has not cleared him."

"I don't plan on leaving, but wanted to be out of earshot," Gage whispers. "Do you actually believe him?"

Rozanne shrugs. "He's been through something very traumatic, and the mind can see things that others can't."

"Oh, you would know all about that." Gage pats her on the shoulder. "Have you seen Maggie lately?"

Rozanne rolls her eyes, recalling her encounter with a red-headed young lady a few years ago. Said red head just happens to be not of this world. "I see a ghost a few times and now you think I'm like the ghost whisperer on the old tv show?"

"You both have long brown hair," Gage says, tugging on her ponytail.

Rozanne bumps Gage's shoulder with hers. "Ha!"

"I guess we won't know until Silvey is awake and talking." Gage looks down the hall.

Rozanne pulls out her phone and taps the phrase: *World Fair 1962* into the search box. "Bingo!"

"What is it?" Gage asks, peeking over her shoulder and reading the first result, *Seattle World Fair.*

"The newspaper headline about the fair is accurate," Rozanne says. "And the chances of Bax knowing about the years and locations of the World Fairs seems pretty unlikely, right?"

"He's off the phone," Gage says, peeking inside the room. "Let's ask." He walks in and Bax hands Gage his phone. "How happy was she to hear your voice?"

Bax smiles. "I've just made her birthday, Christmas and New Year's dreams come true."

"She's been really worried." Rozanne clicks on the first result and turns the phone towards Bax.

Bax takes the phone and reads the first few lines. "I'm not crazy?"

"Not unless you've been studying the history of the World Fair," Gage says, lifting an eyebrow.

Bax looks up from the phone. "Ha, ha. I've never been good with dates or history."

Rozanne claps. "Congrats! Your first trip to another timeline!"

"Whoa," Bax says, shaking his head. "Let's not celebrate this trippy experience. It could still be a side effect or…"

"A rogue artificial intelligence," Gage says, pointing at Bax. "Wasn't that a plotline of that movie with Keanu Reeves?"

Rozanne and Bax laugh.

Knock, knock

A young, slender man pokes his head into the room. "Hi, I'm Dr. Godley."

"Are you here to assess the miracle boy?" Gage asks, pointing his thumb at Bax.

Bax shakes his head. "Come in. My cousin and his wife were just stepping out to find me some food." He pats his stomach. "Something hearty."

Gage salutes Bax. "Doc, any dietary restrictions?"

"Let's stick with a soft diet until we get him up and moving," Dr. Godley says, checking the tablet.

Bax groans.

"Got it," Rozanne says. "We'll be back soon."

Dr. Godley stands at the foot of Baxton's hospital bed, tapping on his tablet. "I'm just looking over your chart and your medical history. Have you had any previous surgeries?"

"Does the last one count?" Bax asks.

"No," he says, placing the tablet on the edge of the bed. "I'm going to run through a few tests here with you."

Bax nods. "Then I can go home?"

"Maybe tomorrow," he says, pulling out a pin light from his pocket. "I've ordered a new set of bloodwork and scans to be completed."

18

Silvey reads the research, flipping page after page until her eyes dry out. "I can't believe they just left this down here." She folds up a copy of one of the schematics for the reactor and checks her dress for a pocket. She sighs and stuffs it down the very tight top of her dress.

"Time to get the hell out of here," Silvey says, looking for an exit. She finds a door beyond another mirror and listens for a beat. *Silence is good, right?* She twists the handle and the door creaks open. She peeks in and gasps.

Seven men turn from their monitors and look her over.

"Hey fellas," Silvey says with a wave. "Can you tell me how to get out of here? I'm a bit turned around."

"How did you get in there?" a man asks rushing towards her.

"One of your men slammed a door in my face and then the lights went out," Silvey says, searching for said rude guy. She points to a man standing off to the right. "Ask him why I was left alone with no idea where to go in the dark." She feels a jab to her arm. She twists her arm and looks down at the glint of metal poking out of her arm. Her eyes fall heavy, and she falls.

"I'm getting the nurse," Evelyn says, watching Silvey's hand ball into a fist.

Evelyn leaves the room and waves to a nurse behind the desk. "Can you come check on my daughter?"

"Sure," the nurse says, walking around the desk. "What's the problem?"

"She's moving a lot for someone that is supposed to be sedated," Evelyn says.

The nurse steps into the room and finds Silvey motionless.

"I swear," Evelyn says. "Her knees bent and then she balled her hand in a fist." She mimics the action with her hand going from limp to a fist.

"I'll check her vitals and medications," the nurse says, walking over to the monitors and a tablet on the table next to the bed. She taps the screen and drags her finger over the chart. "She's not due for any additional medication for another hour." She taps on the screen a few more times. "Her vitals appear strong, but I do see a slight elevation of her heart and respiratory rate a few minutes ago. The doctor should be rounding soon. If she appears agitated or you notice any additional movement in the next few minutes, let me know. I'll note the event on her chart."

"How long will they keep her like this?" Evelyn asks, pointing to all the tubes and wires leading to the monitors.

"The team that assessed her this morning wanted another few days of medical sedation to give her time to rest before we start the process of weening her off the ventilator to allow her to breathe on her own."

Evelyn nods and wipes away a falling tear. "A few days."

"She's doing really well," the nurse says, turning to Silvey. "Her list of injuries may be long, but her little body will bounce back."

Evelyn sniffles. "I need her."

The nurse nods and gives Evelyn a pat on her shoulder. "She'll need you."

Evelyn sits back down and takes Silvey's hand. "You hear that baby girl. You'll bounce back!"

19

Baxton rubs his hands together as Rozanne and Gage walk back into his hospital room. "Please tell me you brought a feast!"

"Well," Rozanne says, sitting a bag on the side table. "I learned the best way to fill up on a soft diet." She taps the faint scar on her cheek. "And I had six long weeks to experience the joys of all soft food."

Gage laughs. "Let's just say she hooked you up."

Rozanne opens the bag, pulls out four large dishes.

"Jackpot!" Baxton says, removing the lids of the steamed white rice, queso, guacamole and shredded chicken. "Thank you!"

"Did the doctor give you an estimated time of departure?" Gage asks, taking the bag from Rozanne and handing Bax a set of plastic utensils.

"Waiting on another round of scans to come back and a few labs." Bax holds the plastic fork over the chicken. "And if they're clear, I'm good to go."

"That's great news," Rozanne says, sitting a cup with a straw next to the open dishes.

"What's this?" Bax asks, looking inside the cup. "No way! It's a root beer float!"

Gage winks at Rozanne. "It's the little things."

She smiles. "Enjoy your meal." She nods towards the door. "I'll step down the hall and see if I can get any update on Silvey."

Bax nods and covers his full mouth. "Thanks!"

Rozanne nods to the volunteer in a bright pink vest behind the desk. "Hi, my name is Rozanne Auburn. My husband's cousin, Baxton, was working with your patient, Silvey Rhoades, the morning of the tornado."

The volunteer nods. "I heard he's awake. That's great news. How can I help you?"

"Is there any family or friends of Silvey's here?" Rozanne asks, glancing at the clipboard on the corner of the counter. "Baxton would like an update on Silvey."

"Her mother is inside with her now," the volunteer says. "I'll let her know Baxton is awake, if that's ok and that his family would like to speak with her."

"Yes, please. Thank you."

The volunteer picks up the phone and passes the message along. A few minutes later, the door to the unit swings open and a petite blonde woman steps out.

"Hi, are you Silvey's mom?" Rozanne asks.

"Yes, my name is Evelyn."

"I'm Rozanne," she says, gesturing to a few chairs in the hall. "My husband's cousin Baxton Auburn was working with Micah and Silvey."

Evelyn nods. "Andrea mentioned how kind you've been asking after Silvey."

Rozanne smiles. "How's Silvey doing?"

"According to the nurse, her vitals are strong and the latest test show progress but…" Evelyn sighs. "… she's not out of the woods."

84

"Is she still in a coma?" Rozanne asks.

"Yes," Evelyn says, "another two days of this and then maybe we can start the process of weening her off the vent."

Rozanne nods. "That's good."

"I'm sorry, my manners," Evelyn says. "How is Baxton?"

"Oh no worries," Rozanne says, nodding towards Baxton's room. "Baxton is awake and eating right now. If the last round of tests come back all clear, he'll be discharged soon."

"That's wonderful to hear," Evelyn says, nodding towards the desk. "If Baxton would like to see Silvey before he goes home, I will put him on the list."

Rozanne nods. "I think he would, thank you. How is Silvey's dad doing?"

Evelyn frowns. "He's a giant pain in the… sorry again my manners." She points up. "He's up one floor. I believe they're talking about discharging him tomorrow."

Rozanne smiles. "That's good news."

Evelyn pats Rozanne on the arm. "I hope that's all I hear over the next few days."

"Roz," Gage says.

Rozanne turns and finds Gage walking towards her. "Hey Gage, this is Evelyn, Silvey's mom. Evelyn, this is my husband and Baxton's cousin."

Evelyn stands and shakes his hand. "It is nice to meet you."

Gage shakes her hand. "You too." He extends his hand to Rozanne. "The nurse said the doctor was on their way down to talk to Baxton and they wanted us in the room."

"Bad news or discharge?" Rozanne asks, taking his hand and standing next to Evelyn.

"They wouldn't say," Gage says. He turns to Evelyn. "I'm sorry to cut your visit short."

"I understand," Evelyn says, glancing down the hallway. "Please tell Baxton he's welcome to visit Silvey."

"Will do," Rozanne says. She leans over and hugs Evelyn. "Stay strong and rest up."

Evelyn nods and releases Rozanne. "Go on."

Gage and Rozanne hurry down the hall.

"What's happening?" Rozanne whispers.

Gage squeezes her hand. "I wish I knew."

Baxton stands next to the bed wearing only a pair of shorts. He tosses the hospital gown on the bed and reaches for the shirt Gage left for him. He twists and flexes his arms. "I wonder how much muscle I've lost?"

Gage swings open the door and then immediately blocks Rozanne. "Sorry man."

"No worries," Baxton says, sliding on the shirt. "I'm covered up."

"Should have knocked!" Gage says, looking over his shoulder.

Bax shrugs. "Nothing to see here. I'm pretty sure I've lost some muscle definition in my arms, though."

Rozanne chuckles. "Men take notice of their physique, but not their dirty socks on the floor."

Bax looks down around his feet. "Was I wearing socks?"

Gage laughs. "Nah, just a jab at my pride from my beautiful bride."

Bax looks up at Rozanne. "You had me there for a moment."

Rozanne shakes her head. "Sorry I couldn't help it."

"Hi folks," a woman says from the open door. "I'm Dr. Harving." She taps on a tablet. "Who's Baxton Auburn?"

Baxton raises his hand and sits on the hospital bed. "Are you here to set me free?"

"Maybe, but we have a few questions that we need to answer before we can begin that process," Dr. Harving says, looking over at Gage and Rozanne. "And you two are family?"

"Gage, his cousin," Gage says, pointing to Baxton and then to Rozanne. "And my wife Rozanne."

"Are you two going to be in charge of Baxton's discharge care?" Dr. Harving asks.

"Whoa," Baxton says, raising his hands. "I don't need anyone to care for me. I'm fine."

Dr. Harving glances down at the chart. "Mr. Auburn."

Baxton holds up his hand. "Bax is fine."

"Bax, you've survived a EF5 tornado, fallen at least seven stories, witness the death of a coworker, had major surgery, and spent two days in a coma."

Bax nods. "True, but I'm fine, really."

"My concern is not about your physical health."

Bax leans forward to get a closer look at Dr. Harving's badge. "You're a shrink?"

"Psychiatrist," Dr. Harving says. "And I specialize in post-trauma recovery."

Bax leans back and looks over at Rozanne and Gage. "Please tell her I'm fine."

"Bax," Rozanne says, "she's right. I know you feel fine now, but you've been through a lot. Trust me, a traumatic experience can have sneaky repercussions."

Gage nods. "She's not wrong buddy. What is your recommendation Dr. Harving?"

"It says in your chart you live alone," Dr. Harving says, looking at Bax. "Is that correct?"

"Yes," Bax says.

"My recommendation would be that you are not alone for the first week post discharge and that you follow up with your primary care provider and a counselor or psychologist." She pulls out a pamphlet from her pocket. "This is information about a post trauma and survivors support group. They have meetings all over the Kansas City area, including the northland."

"I really don't think that's necessary," Bax says, looking at the cover.

"Bax, just take the pamphlet," Gage says. Bax squints his eyes and shakes his head at Gage. "She's not dragging you to the meetings."

"Fine," Bax says, taking the pamphlet. "But seriously, I'm telling you it's all good up here." He taps his temple. "Is that it? Can I go now?"

"Not quite," Dr. Harving says. "The wife of your coworker is out in the hallway. She's asked for a few minutes of your time to discuss the morning of the tornado, but only if you were ready and able. Thoughts?"

Bax straightens. "Jessica? She's here?"

"Yes, with her newborn," Dr. Harving says. "She's on her way home, but didn't want to leave the hospital until after she spoke to you."

"Please let her in," Bax says.

"Of course," Dr. Harving says. She steps into the hallway and pushes in a wheelchair with Jessica holding her daughter wrapped in a soft purple blanket.

"We'll give you the room," Rozanne says, taking Gage's hand.

"Actually, I would really like you to stay," Jessica says, glancing over at Bax. "The questions I have may be difficult to answer and I want you to have the same support I've had over the last few days."

Bax nods. "Thanks Jess. This is my cousin Gage and his wife, Rozanne." He reaches for the baby. "May I?"

Jessica leans forward and places the infant in his hands. She smiles. "She looks so tiny in your hands."

"She?" Bax asks, staring at the tiny fingers reaching out of the blanket.

"Yes, meet Lola Micah Hutchins."

"Hi Lola," Bax whispers. He looks up. "She's perfect."

Jessica nods. "She is."

"I'm real sor…" Bax says.

"No," Jessica says, cutting him off. "I can't take any more apologies. Please."

Bax nods. "How can I help?"

"Tell me about Mike's morning before…" Jessica says, looking down at her hands. "… the damn tornado."

"It was a busy morning, installing the industrial mats," Bax says. "It was just the two of us until eight. Silvey, I believe you two know each other." Jessica nods. He continues. "She came in to work on a few levels below us." He grins. "She may have let the cat out of the bag. I learned about his old high school nickname."

Jessica shakes her head. "She's the one that made it stick to him like glue."

Bax smiles. "Pretty sure she's still sticking with it after all these years."

"Not surprised," Jessica says.

"If it's any consolation," Bax says, "she kept correcting herself."

Jessica shrugs. "Effort counts."

Bax nods and continues to explain their trips to the truck to bring in the last of the mats, the storm rolling in, and the door smacking Micah in the face.

Jessica holds up her hand. "According to the medical examiner he had cotton up both nostrils and I couldn't for the life of me figure out how or why!"

Bax laughs, and Lola squirms. "Oops sorry," he whispers into Lola's hair. "He had a bloody nose and the only supplies we had to stop it was a tampon, courtesy of Silvey."

Jessica's mouth falls open.

Rozanne snorts. Gage laughs and points at Rozanne. She shoves him in the shoulder and they both clamp a hand over their mouths.

Jessica shakes her head. "You mean to tell me that my husband died with a tampon shoved up his nose?"

"Afraid so," Bax says.

"Oh, he will haunt her for that," Jessica says smiling.

Bax smiles. "I'm pretty sure he has already."

Jessica's smile falls.

Bax glances at Dr. Harving and over at Gage and Rozanne.

"What do you mean?" Jessica says.

"Long story for another day," Bax says.

Dr. Harving straightens. "Is it related to Micah?"

"Not really," Bax says, avoiding eye contact with Dr. Harving.

"So, after the tampon incident, what happened?" Jessica asks.

"We ran for cover," Bax says, "but the glass cover shattered." He swallows hard. "Are you sure you want to hear the next part?"

Jessica nods. "Did he suffer?"

"I don't think so," Bax says. "When I found him, he was already gone."

Jessica looks him over. "But you're fine?"

"I know, it's not fair," Bax says, meeting her watery eyes. "He should be here, not me."

"No, Baxton," Jessica says, wiping away her tears. "I don't wish you harm…" She swallows. "… I didn't mean that I want him instead of you. I just want you and Silvey to live! And to have no one else feel this way." She sobs and covers her face. "I'm sorry, so sorry."

Bax reaches his hand over to Jessica. "I'm here, Silvey's here. We're here."

◊

Bax watches Dr. Harving push Jessica and Lola out of the room. "I hope they'll be ok."

Gage walks over to Baxton's bedside. "You gave her some closure. That's all you can do right now."

Bax hangs his head and lets his tears fall.

20

Why is it so dark? Silvey blinks, but the darkness remains. *Why can't I see anything?*

"Hello…" Silvey says.

"Oh good," a man says. "You're awake!"

Silvey turns to look for the man speaking, but can't make out anything in the dark.

"What is your real name?"

"Who's asking?" Silvey asks. "And more importantly why am I blind at the moment?"

The man chuckles. "The fact that you're in the dark is a courtesy—you've trespassed on government property, young lady."

"I did no such thing," Silvey says.

"Do you know what the penalty is for aiding a spy?" the man asks.

Silvey flinches. "What in the hell are you talking about?"

"You were seen with a man suspected of treason."

"Bull shit!" Silvey says.

"Language!" the man scolds. "Who do you work for?"

"Myself!" Silvey says.

"Ha!" the man says. His breath wafts over her face.

Silvey wrinkles her nose. *Cigarettes and butterscotch?*

"We believe that you and your friend are the reason four of my men were shot and killed."

"Look, man, I'm sorry for your loss, but I've been stuck down here for hours."

"Stuck? You mean snuck?"

"No!" Silvey shouts. "S-T-U-C-K."

"Bull shit!"

Silvey nods. "That man and I were trying to find a way out of here."

"So, you did know that you were trespassing?" the man says.

"Captain Wilson mentioned something about my clearance, but then he walked away without showing me out!"

"You spoke to Captain Wilson?" the man whispers.

"Yep! Right after, some guy in the control room slammed a door in my face."

"That's not possible!" the man shouts.

Silvey laughs. "Wilson, or that your men are rude?"

"Both!" the man says.

A bright light hits Silvey's face. She rears her head back and squeezes her eyes shut.

Baxton eases down into a wheelchair. "Is this really necessary?" His knees are nearly level with his shoulders.

The nurse pats him on the shoulder. "It's hospital protocol."

"Her room is just down the hall," Baxton says, pointing towards the door.

"I'm aware," the nurse says, pushing the chair out of the room. "Just a warning. Ms. Rhoades is still sedated and has a lot of tubes and leads hooked up."

Bax nods. "Got it." He closes his eyes, picturing Silvey's smile as she holds up a tampon and teases Micah.

"Hi," the nurse says, stopping at a desk.

Baxton's eyes fly open. He jumps a bit and winces. He wraps his arm across his ribs. He turns to look up at the nurse.

"This is Baxton Auburn," the nurse says. "He would like to visit Silvey Rhoades."

The volunteer behind the desk looks over at Baxton. They nod and check their tablet. "Ah, yes. Let me check on her status at the moment." They pick up the phone and turn their back to the nurse and Baxton.

The nurse leans down to Baxton. "You good?"

Baxton nods and fidgets with the hem of his shirt.

The volunteer behind the desk hangs up the phone. "We're good. I can wheel him back to the room." They walk around the counter.

Baxton's nurse nods and steps in front of him. "Baxton, I'm off in twenty minutes. Your evening nurse will be Mistina. She'll take care of the remaining discharge paperwork."

"Thanks," Baxton says. "I won't be long."

The unit door opens. A rhythmic beeping fills the quiet space between the volunteer and Baxton. They stop in front of the third glass door. The nurse slides open the door and pushes him to Silvey's bedside.

"Her nurse is Beth," the volunteer says, engaging the brakes on the wheelchair. "When you're ready to leave, just let her know."

"Got it," Baxton whispers. "Can she hear me?"

"Absolutely," the volunteer says before sliding the door closed.

"Hey Silvey," Baxton says, leaning forward. "Can you hear me?"

"Bax?" Silvey slowly opens her eyes. The blinding light consumes her vision. "I can't see!"

The man laughs. "That's the point!"

The vital alarm near Silvey's bed loudly beeps.

Silvey jerks her head back.

Bax looks from Silvey to the door and back to her. "You can hear me?"

"Bax!" Silvey shouts.

Silvey's chest lifts and falls from the bed.

A second alarm starts beeping.

"Something is wrong!" Bax shouts towards the door. A scuffle of footsteps outside the room grows louder. "They're coming!"

"Who's coming?" Silvey asks.

The man laughs again. "No one is coming for you!"

Silvey feels a speck of spit fall on her face. She throws her head forward but misses the man.

A nurse wheels Bax's chair away from the bed. "She's fighting the vent. Please roll outside!" The nurse reaches over and silences one of the alarms.

"Feisty!" the man taunts.

Silvey twists her head around to look for the man, but she's still blind.

"Sir!" the nurse shouts.

Bax shakes his head. "Sorry." He slowly backs the wheelchair out of the room and watches Silvey's body writhe.

Another nurse steps into the room and pulls a curtain across the glass, blocking Bax's view. He leans forward to stand, but a hand presses on his shoulder. He turns to find a man in a similar chair to his left.

"What did you say to upset my daughter?" the man asks.

Bax's mouth falls open.

The man reaches forward and places a finger under Bax's chin. "Speechless?"

"I'm sorry," Bax asks, pulling his head away from the man. "Who are you?"

The man holds up his wrist adorned with an orange and white hospital logo patient band. "Buzz Rhoades."

"You're Silvey's dad?" Bax asks, glancing towards the commotion behind the curtain.

"For another few years," Buzz says, tapping his chest. "At least."

Bax studies Buzz's thick, white hair, grey-blue eyes, salt and pepper shadow of a new beard below his red cheeks. "You're no older than my mom. Surely a few years is a bit low, right?"

"According to the doc," Buzz says, focusing on the door to Silvey's room. "My heart has a few good years left."

Bax looks away from Buzz. "That's rough. She's going to need your help."

"May I ask who you are?" Buzz asks.

"Baxton Auburn."

"And how do you know my daughter?"

"Work," Bax says, keeping his eyes on the curtain.

"You're an electrician too?" Buzz asks, lifting an eyebrow. "I thought I knew all the youngsters."

"No sir," Bax says. "I'm an installer for Hutchins."

"I've heard about Micah," Buzz says. "I'm really sorry he didn't make it."

The color drains from Bax's face. He whispers, "It was quick."

"How long have you known Silvey?" Buzz asks.

"I only met her a few hours before it happened."

"She's tough," Buzz says, nodding towards Silvey.

Bax nods.

"So," Buzz says, leaning forward. "What did you say to her? It looks like it set off every alarm in there."

Bax shakes his head. "Hey Silvey, can you hear me?"

Buzz scratches the stubble on his chin. "That's it?"

"Yep," Bax says. "They are discharging me this evening. I didn't want to leave without…"

"Without what?" Buzz asks.

"I don't know exactly," Bax says, frowning. "I just needed to know that she was here and breathing."

Buzz frowns. "Here as opposed to where?"

Bax audibly swallows. "Not stuck inside the silo."

Buzz's eyes widen. "I had a weird dream about Silvey while I was in surgery. She was lost in the dark and I couldn't find her."

"Wait," Bax says. "You were there inside the silo too?"

Buzz shakes his head. "Physically, no." He taps his head. "But it felt real."

A nurse steps out of Silvey's room. "We're going to page the doctor."

"Is she ok?" Buzz and Bax ask in unison.

"Yes, I believe that this may be a sign she's ready to breathe on her own," the nurse says.

"That's good news?" Buzz asks.

"Yes, but I'm sorry for the timing," the nurse says, pointing towards the door. "We have a team coming down to assist and can't have visitors on the unit." She holds up a cordless phone. "I've called an aid from your units to come down and take you back to your rooms."

Buzz and Bax nod.

"Can you call my room when it's done?" Buzz asks. His eyes glass over.

"Yes, sir," the nurse says. "And Mr. Auburn?"

"I'm being discharged in an hour or so, thanks," Bax says.

The nurse nods as the unit doors open. She waves over the two aids.

Buzz reaches over to Bax's chair. "Give me your number."

"Sir," Bax says.

"I'll call you when I know something," Buzz says.

Bax frowns. "My phone didn't survive…"

"No worries," Buzz says, "I'll give you my number."

One of the aids pulls out a pen and a neon green sticky note pad from their scrub top. "Here."

"Thanks," Buzz says, scribbling down his number. He peels off the note and hands it to Bax.

Bax takes the sticky note. "Thank you."

Buzz nods. "She's going to make it out of the dark."

Bax nods. "I hope so."

21

Silvey tries to open her mouth but ends up gasping for a breath.

"Silvey," a woman says. "I'm taking out a tube."

Silvey gasps and her throat burns. She coughs.

"It's out," a woman says, tapping the monitor and removing an oxygen mask from her mouth. "Her respiration and oxygen levels are stable. Silvey, can you hear me?"

"Yes," Silvey whispers.

"You are in the hospital," a woman says. "We've just taken you off the vent that was breathing for you. Your throat may feel a bit raw."

"Can't see," Silvey whispers. She reaches up towards her face but feels a hand on hers. A soft cloth slides over her eyes and she pries her eyes open. A face comes into focus. "Water?"

"Sure," the woman says, moving away from the bed. "I'm Beth, your nurse for the evening." She returns to Silvey's bedside with a cup and a straw. "Slow sip from the straw."

Silvey sips and swallows the icy water. "Thanks." She looks around the room. "Is the man gone?"

"We sent your visitor away," Beth says, pointing towards the door.

"Visitor?" Silvey asks.

"Baxton Auburn," Beth says. "Is he a friend of yours?"

"Bax?" Silvey asks. "He was here?"

"Yes," Beth says, checking the monitors next to Silvey.

Silvey whispers, "He made it out?"

Beth tilts her head to the side and watches Silvey's reaction. "We sent him and your dad back to their rooms just before we removed the vent."

"My dad?" Silvey tries to sit forward but groans. "Ugh."

"Easy," Beth says, placing a hand on Silvey's shoulder and gently presses her back towards the bed. "He's ok."

"What happened to my dad?" Silvey asks, searching the room.

"He can tell you all about it soon," Beth says, looking towards the door. "I need to ask you a few questions."

"Sure," Silvey says, assessing her discomfort.

Beth picks up the tablet and taps the screen. "What is your full name?"

"Silvey Lynn Rhoades."

"What year is it?"

"2022, I hope."

Beth looks up from the tablet. "Correct."

"Where do you live?"

"Lawson."

"Are you in any pain?" Beth asks.

Silvey looks down at the blankets covering her body. "I don't think pain is the word for it. Maybe a bit sore."

"On a scale of 1, no pain, to 10, need the emergency room stat?"

"A four," Silvey says.

Beth nods and taps the tablet a few more times. "Do you recall why you are in the hospital?"

Silvey chews on the corner of her bottom lip. "To be honest, that's a bit fuzzy."

"What's the last thing you recall?" Beth asks, placing the tablet on the side table.

Silvey closes her eyes. "Darkness. A man was questioning me in the dark about why I was trespassing with Bax." She opens her eyes and sighs.

"Silvey," Beth says, picking up the tablet. "Do you know who the man was questioning you?"

"No, he never shared his name," Silvey says, frowning. "Do you know how Bax escaped?"

Beth glances up at Silvey's eyes searching her face for an explanation. "Silvey, I'm not sure what I can share about Mr. Auburn." She looks down at the tablet. "I have your emergency contacts as Evelyn and Buzz Rhoades, your parents, correct?"

"Yes," Silvey says.

"I would like to share your status with your parents."

Silvey lifts an eyebrow. "What is my status?"

Beth smiles. "Currently off the vent, vitals steady, breathing unassisted, awake, and talking."

"How long have I've been here?"

"Four days," Beth says.

Silvey shakes her head. "Four days… here in this bed?"

"Yes," Beth says. "I would like to review your injuries when you have a family member here."

"That bad?" Silvey asks, looking under the blankets.

"It's a long list…"

Silvey wiggles her toes but doesn't feel anything. "Am I paralyzed?"

"No, it's nothing you can't recover from," Beth says. "Do you mind if I step out and make the call to your parents?"

"Only if you call my best friend Andrea first," Silvey says, smiling. "Do you have her information?"

Beth taps her tablet again. "Yes, I have Mrs. Andrea Meyer."

Silvey frowns. "Meyer?"

"Is that correct?" Beth asks, hovering her finger over the tablet.

"Not unless she's gotten married and changed her name in the last four days," Silvey says.

"She mentioned she had to leave to pick up her husband," Beth says. "Same Andrea or different?"

"Dre married Scott Meyer?" Silvey asks, shaking her head. "I can't believe it." She taps her fingers on the side of the bed. "Is the number listed 816–555–7695?"

"Yes," Beth says. "Do you still want her to be the first call?"

Silvey nods. "Yes, Dre's presence is required as a buffer when dealing with my mother."

Beth smiles. "Here's a call button." She hands her a red button. "If you need anything, press here." She points to the top. "I'll be less than six feet away."

Silvey nods. "Thanks."

Beth steps out of the room and gently closes the glass door. She sighs.

A nurse behind the desk stands. "Is she…" they tap their head. "All there?"

Beth frowns. "To be determined. Did neuro call back?"

"Yes, about two minutes ago," the nurse says, handing Beth a stack of messages. "Her mother called twice, and a lady named Jessica called to ask about Silvey's status."

Beth nods. "Did neuro mention when they could assess her?"

"Within the hour," the nurse says, shrugging. "So maybe before midnight."

Beth smiles. "True." She nods towards the door. "I need to call her people. Can you keep an eye on her vitals?"

"Sure, no problem."

Beth pulls out the cordless phone and dials the contact number for Andrea and waits. It rings once.

"Hi, Andrea speaking," she says. "Is Silvey ok?"

"Hi Andrea," Beth says. "My name is Beth, I'm Silvey's nurse. Are you here in the hospital?"

"Not at the moment," Andrea says, pulling her car off the road. "Is she…"

"She's awake…"

"Awake!" Andrea shouts, looking over her shoulder to merge back onto the road. "I'll be there in an hour, tops. I'm already on the road."

"I'll call Evelyn," Beth says. "Drive safe."

"Thank you!" Andrea says, merging on the road. "See you soon."

Beth hangs up the phone and dials Evelyn's number. It rings twice.

"Hello," Evelyn says.

"Hi is this, Evelyn Rhoades?" Beth asks.

"Yes," Evelyn says.

"I'm Beth, Silvey's nurse."

"Oh no, what's happened?" Evelyn asks.

"Silvey's awake and talking," Beth says.

"Oh, my goodness, really?" Evelyn asks.

"Yes, are you here in the hospital?"

"Across the street at the hotel," Evelyn says. "I can be there in ten minutes."

"No rush," Beth says. "We must run a few tests. Can you stop by in an hour?"

"Yes," Evelyn says. "I'll call Buzz."

"Thanks, see you soon." Beth sets the phone on the counter. She taps the screen of the tablet and charts the communication with Evelyn and Andrea. She also writes a side note to inquire about Andrea's marital status.

"Hey Beth," the nurse says, leaving Silvey's room. "She's asking about a man named Micah. Her heart rate spiked when she was talking about him."

Beth nods. "I believe that is one of the men that was working with Silvey the morning of the tornado." She taps the tablet and scrolls through the history given by her mother. She shows the nurse the line about the morning of the tornado. "It looks like Baxton and Micah were working with Silvey."

"Well, we know that Baxton made it," the nurse says, pointing to the visitor log on the counter. "But what about Micah?"

Beth shrugs. "I'm not sure. I know some names have been posted publicly after the families were notified." She pulls out her personal phone and types in Micah and Lawson into the search bar. A picture of a young man with thick black hair, hazel eyes, and a warm smile stares up at her. *He's about Silvey's age.* "He didn't make it." She shows the nurse the photo and the caption below: *Micah Hutchins, 26, resident of Lawson, Missouri and owner of Hutchins & Co. was one of the twenty-two fatalities of the devastating tornado that struck Lawson and Vibbard.*

"They're so young," the nurse says, tapping the phone. "Oh, look." They point to the next line of the caption: *His wife Jessica and newborn daughter Lola.* "I spoke to a woman named Jessica earlier. Do you still have that message?"

Beth pulls out the messages and finds the one with Jessica's name. "Jessica Hutchins." She turns the note towards the nurse.

The nurse shakes their head.

"We'll wait for the family," Beth says, pocketing the phone and picking up the tablet. "I'll sit with her until neuro shows up."

Beth slowly enters the room and finds Silvey's head below the blanket.

"Silvey," Beth says.

"How many stitches do I have?" Silvey asks. Her voice muffled under the blankets. "Like a hundred?"

"That's probably close," Beth says.

Silvey extricates her head from under the covers and looks up. "I was joking."

"I'm afraid that may be on the low end," Beth says.

"Is there reason I am so numb?" Silvey asks, poking her abdomen.

"The medication," Beth says, pointing to an IV line. "We've tried to keep you comfortable during the last few days. Your body needed time to rest and recover."

"Any chance we can ween that down a bit?" Silvey asks. "I feel like I am in a tub of ice."

"Soon," Beth says. "You'll meet with your medical team to discuss the next steps once your family arrives. I spoke to Andrea and Evelyn. Both will be here in an hour."

"And my dad?" Silvey asks.

"Evelyn stated she would call him," Beth says.

Silvey rolls her eyes. "You know that they're divorced, right?"

"Oh," Beth says. "Will she actually call him?"

102

Silvey shakes her head. "When hell freezes over, maybe."

Beth nods. "I'll call to double check."

"Thanks," Silvey says. "Any chance you can bring back some food?"

"You're hungry?" Beth asks, hesitating at the door.

"Not really, but I like to snack during stressful conversations."

Beth smiles. "I'll see what flavors of jello we have on hand."

Silvey frowns. "Ugh, I was hoping for something salty."

"Sorry, not quite to that stage," Beth says. "Any flavors I should avoid?"

"Nothing green in the jello or pudding category is ever good."

Beth nods. "Agree, I'll check and be right back."

Silvey watches Beth slide the door closed and glances over at the machines next to her bed. "Four machines. How much energy are they consuming?" She chuckles. "Oh, if my mother could hear me now… asking about the kilowatts keeping me numb. She would have them put me back to sleep."

Silvey lays back and stares up at the ceiling tiles. *How did I wind up in a dress?*

The door slides open, and Beth holds up a red jello cup. "Cherry?" She waves a spoon towards Silvey.

Silvey glances over at Beth. "Sure… only if it has rum inside?"

"Ha," Beth says, sitting the cup and spoon on the side table. "If only. I do have a resident and doctor here to see you."

"Can they clear me for a real meal?" Silvey asks, inspecting the jello cup.

"Not quite," Beth says. She waves the man wearing a white coat over blue scrubs into the room and a young woman wearing a nearly identical outfit follows him in.

Beth nods to the man. "Silvey this is Dr. Landon Knipp and Dr. Sarah Marvin."

Silvey tilts her head to the side. "Sarah 'The Brain' Marvin!"

Dr. Knipp glances at Sarah's slack jaw and back to Silvey. "Have you two met already?"

"Does preschool count?" Silvey asks, grinning from ear to ear.

"Well, well," Dr. Knipp says, looking at Sarah. "You failed to mention your relationship with the patient when you eagerly asked to consult on this case."

"Sorry, sir," Sarah says. "It's been hard the last few days with residents from my hometown flooding our trauma center." She gestures to Silvey. "When I saw Silvey's name on the list this morning I only wanted the best possible doctors to look after her."

"And you are the best?" Dr. Knipp asks.

Sarah straightens her posture. "You're the best neurologist in this hospital and I want to learn from the best. Plus, Silvey's brain has always fascinated me." She winks at Silvey.

Silvey laughs. "She was the smartest in our class by a landslide. I trust her opinion."

"Dr. Marvin can stay and take notes," Dr. Knipp says, passing the tablet to Sarah.

"I'll step out," Beth says. "Let me know if you have any questions." She slides the door closed.

Dr. Knipp nods. "I am going to do a physical examination and then we can talk about how you ended up here."

22

Dr. Knipp pockets his reflex hammer and pulls up the chair next to Silvey's bed. He sits down. "Other than a few weak reflex responses, I don't have any physical concerns at this time. I'll test again after they've weened you off the pain medications." He looks over his shoulder at Dr. Marvin. "And your long-term memory is great considering your recognition of Dr. Marvin and her interesting choice of a nickname. But I would like to ask a few additional questions."

"The brain is fitting considering your chosen line of medicine," Silvey says, nodding at Dr. Marvin's reddening cheeks. "Ask away."

"Can you tell me your date of birth?" Dr. Knipp asks.

"April 18, 1994," Silvey says.

"Your middle name," Dr. Knipp says.

"Lynn."

"What year is it?"

"2022."

"What is three times four?"

Silvey rolls her eyes. "Twelve."

"Your best friend Andrea's last name," Dr. Knipp says.

"Loveland," Silvey says.

Sarah shakes her head and frowns.

"What's wrong?" Silvey asks. "Did Andrea really marry Scott?"

Dr. Knipp looks over at Sarah's frown and nods.

"Four or five years ago," Sarah says. "And you were the maid of honor."

"No shit," Silvey whispers. "Why don't I recall that?"

"Let's fixate on what you do remember," Dr. Knipp says. "Tell me the last meal you ate."

Silvey scrunches her brow creasing her forehead. She stares at the ceiling. "Um, maybe cereal."

"What kind of work do you do?" Dr. Knipp asks.

"I'm an electrician."

"And what were you working on?"

"An old missile silo conversion to a vertical farm."

"What do you recall about the base?"

"Darkness." Silvey closes her eyes. "A man's breath in my face that smelled like smoke and butterscotch."

"This man was with you working at the base?"

"No," Silvey says, shaking her head. "I never saw his face."

Dr. Knipp looks over at Dr. Marvin. She shakes her head.

"Silvey," Dr. Knipp says. "Can you walk me through what you remember?"

Silvey opens her eyes and looks at Dr. Knipp. "I can, but it won't make any sense."

"Try me," Dr. Knipp says.

"I remember working at the silo with Bax and Midge…"

"Baxton and Micah," Sarah says.

"Yea, yea," Silvey says.

"Is Midge another nickname?" Dr. Knipp asks.

"Yes," Silvey and Sarah answer in unison.

"Please continue," Dr. Knipp says.

"But the one I can't shake or remember clearly…" Silvey holds up her hand with two fingers raised. "I was standing outside the silo with a lit cigarette. And I don't smoke. Never have, never will." She points to Sarah. "She can back me up."

106

Sarah nods. "True, she gave her friends hell for smoking in high school."

"And I was wearing a dress with freaking high heels."

Sarah laughs. "Bull shit!"

"Dr. Marvin!" Dr. Knipp says.

"Sorry doc," Sarah says, covering her wide smile. "But she would never in a million years be caught in a dress and heels at work."

Dr. Knipp glances at Silvey. "I'm sorry my resident has not remained professional."

"Nah, she's just confirmed what I remember about this whole thing is insane."

"Walk me through what you recall, and I promise Dr. Marvin will not interrupt or comment." Dr. Knipp looks at Sarah. She presses her lips together in a firm line and nods. "Great, go ahead."

Silvey spends the next thirty minutes explaining her encounter with a guard that looked like Midge, the lift, the missiles, the control room, red flashing lights, a loud siren, her encounter with Captain Wilson, Bax, the white room, lab, and the jab in the arm.

Dr. Knipp and Dr. Marvin exchange a quick glance.

"See, you think I am nuts," Silvey says, pointing at Sarah. "You know that I am not one for tall tales, right?"

Sarah audibly swallows. "Silvey, I know what you experienced while sedated seems very real and it's not that uncommon. There are loads of case studies that have documented experiences of patients that were in comas."

"Dr. Marvin's right," Dr. Knipp says, standing and pushing the chair back. "We'll schedule a consult with our psych department…"

"What?" Silvey shouts. "No!"

"It's not because we think you're crazy, Silvey," Sarah says, reaching a hand over to Silvey's shoulder. "It's a lot of traumas to process. Therapy for your mind and body will be an important part of your recovery moving forward."

Silvey wrinkles her nose. "It smells a bit fishy."

Sarah laughs. "We are not putting you in some looney bin and throwing away the key."

Silvey holds up her pinky. "Pinky swear it!"

Sarah rolls her eyes. "Seriously?"

"Come on," Silvey says, gesturing to her covered body. "Not exactly going anywhere. Just give me some peace of mind."

"I, Dr. Sarah The Brain Marvin, swear that you are not going to a looney bin," Sarah says, wrapping her pinky around Silvey's finger.

Dr. Knipp laughs. "I may not swear to keep that nickname in this room."

Sarah glares at him. "Oh, we'll see Doctor Nerdro."

Silvey laughs. "Nerdro!"

"Kill me now," Dr. Knipp says, sliding open the door. "We're done here."

"Silvey," Sarah scolds. "What the hell dude? He's not going to forgive and forget this when he writes my recommendation for my fellowship."

Silvey holds up her hands. "I'm sorry I got you in trouble."

Sarah shakes her head. "More like instigated. I better catch up with him. Stay out of trouble. I'll check back with you tomorrow."

Silvey salutes Sarah. "Pinky out!"

Sarah steps out of the room laughing.

"Sarah," Andrea says, walking towards her.

"Hey Dre," Sarah says, hugging her. "Silvey still has me in stitches. Some things never change."

"She's, ok?" Andrea asks, releasing Sarah.

"I'll let you see for yourself," Sarah says, nodding towards the door. "I've got to catch up with my attending. See you later."

Andrea nods. "See you later."

"Evelyn and Buzz are at the door," Beth says, walking past Andrea. "Go on in. I'll grab an extra chair and be there shortly."

Andrea pokes her head in the room. "Silvey Lynn!"

Silvey smiles. "Oh, good you're here."

"You're, ok?" Andrea asks, coming to her side.

"Extremely numb, but right as rain."

"Your mom and dad are here too," Andrea says, scooting the chair close to the bed. "I saw Sarah on the way in."

"I may have let her old nickname out of the bag," Silvey says, giggling.

"You didn't!" Andrea cups her mouth to squash her laughter.

"Pretty sure 'The Brain' is not too happy about it."

"Silvey," Evelyn says from the open door.

"Hi mom," Silvey says, lifting a hand. Her eyes fall on a man in a hospital gown sitting in a wheelchair. "Dad? What the hell happened to you?"

"Hey kid," Buzz says. "I'm good just had to have a minor repair." He taps his chest. "Ticker is ticking good now."

"You had heart surgery?" Silvey asks. The monitor over her head starts beeping.

Beth steps into the room. "Hey Silvey. Let's take a few long breaths and get that heart rate down."

Evelyn swats Buzz on the shoulder. "I told you this would be too much."

"She's tough," Buzz says, glaring at Evelyn. "And keep your hands to yourself."

Silvey shakes her head. "Seriously! Can you two not bicker for once in my life?"

Andrea blocks Silvey's view of her parents. "They are here to support you."

Beth silences the alarm. "I need Silvey to remain as calm as possible while we discuss her current status and the list of her injuries." She looks from Evelyn to Buzz. "Are we good?"

"Of course," Evelyn says.

Buzz nods.

Andrea sits back in her chair.

"Silvey?" Beth asks. "Are you good?"

"Yes," Silvey says, kneading a fistful of the blankets.

Beth holds up her tablet and swipes her finger across the screen. "You were transported to the hospital via helicopter four days ago."

"From where?"

"A field about a mile away from the nike base," Andrea says.

"How did I end up in a field?" Silvey asks.

"A tornado," Andrea whispers.

"I was Dorothy'd?" Silvey asks.

"Well, it's not the wonderful world of Oz, but yes," Andrea says. "Do you remember any of it?"

"Not really," Silvey says. "I remember working with Bax and Midge inside the silo and then my conversation with them later, but it's all muddy." She looks over at her parents. "How bad was the tornado?"

Andrea glances at Beth.

Beth nods. "You can tell her."

"Tell me what?" Silvey asks, shifting her attention to Andrea.

"It was bad," Andrea says. "It leveled more than a dozen homes, including most of my neighborhood."

"Oh God," Silvey whispers.

Andrea eyes well over. "And Micah didn't make it."

"No," Silvey says, shaking her head. "I saw him."

"Baxton found Micah under the debris inside the silo, but it was too late."

"Midge is really gone?" Silvey asks. Her tears fall fast and drip off her chin.

"Yes," Andrea says, resting her hand over Silvey's fist. "But I have some good news." Silvey takes Andrea's hand. "Jessica delivered a healthy baby girl. We have a piece of Micah's legacy through little miss Lola."

Silvey nods and wipes her cheeks with her free hand. "Lola."

"Jessica has called to check on you," Beth says. "If you want to call her later, we can make that happen."

"Yes," Silvey says. "I also need to speak with Baxton."

"He's without a phone at the moment," Buzz says.

"How do you know that?" Evelyn asks, glaring at Buzz.

"I spoke to the young man," Buzz says, ignoring Evelyn's glare. "He took my number down and said he would call first thing in the morning to check on you."

Silvey nods.

"Are you ok if I continue?" Beth asks.

Silvey nods again.

Beth taps the tablet. "You went from the helipad directly to the operating room upon arrival to stop extensive internal bleeding. You've received four blood transfusions. And they removed your appendix, spleen, parts of your small intestine and one ovary. All were damaged beyond repair."

"What does a spleen do?" Silvey asks, looking down at her covered abdomen.

"It helps filter your blood," Beth says.

"And without it?" Silvey asks, glancing up at Beth.

"Common illnesses like a cold or the flu may wipe you out a bit longer than most."

"And I had two ovaries," Silvey says, glancing at Evelyn's tear-streaked face.

"Yes," Beth says. "We'll schedule a consult with a gynecologist to discuss your reproductive health before you are discharged."

Evelyn gasps.

"Mom," Silvey says. "It's not like I was planning to have kids tomorrow."

"You can conceive with one ovary," Beth says.

"She's not sterile?" Evelyn asks.

"No," Beth says.

"Whew," Evelyn says.

"Jesus," Buzz whispers, "always the drama queen."

"Dad," Silvey says, watching her mom's fist ball up. "It's fine. Beth, please continue."

"After the internal bleeding was mended," Beth says. "We put you through a series of scans. They found several fractures to your ribs, pelvic bone, lumbar spine, and right femur."

"But you said I wasn't paralyzed," Silvey says, pointing towards her toes.

"Dr. Knipp believes that there is no evidence of a spinal cord injury." Beth taps the tablet. "They've ordered a new set of scans for tomorrow morning. The orthopedic surgeon will decide if additional surgeries will be required to repair your pelvic bone and femur."

"That is a long list," Silvey says. "I'm glad I know, but damn."

Beth holds up a finger. "The scans also indicate a closed head injury."

Silvey sighs. "Define closed."

"It means your hard head held your brains inside," Buzz says. "I've had a few of those during my motorcycle era."

Evelyn rolls her eyes. "Oh, just another thing you two have in common."

"Evelyn," Andrea says, raising a single eyebrow. "Let's stay focused."

Buzz and Silvey share matching smirks.

"Silvey, you may experience confusion, a shortened attention span, memory problems, problem-solving deficits, problems with judgment, or loss of time and space. Just to name a few."

"That explains my memory void of Scott and Andrea," Silvey says.

"What are you talking about?" Andrea asks.

"I forgot that you married Scott," Silvey says.

"You were my maid of honor," Andrea says, turning towards Beth. "Is selective memory loss possible?"

Beth frowns. "What do you mean?"

"Silvey hated everything about my wedding," Andrea says. "Between her dress, the four-inch heels and the forced proximity to her ex-boyfriend for the entire weekend."

"Ew!" Silvey scrunches her nose up and frowns. "Justin was there?"

"He was Scott's best man."

"Sorry Dre," Silvey says. "But maybe that is something we don't revisit."

"We'll be doing additional testing to evaluate the extent of the possible memory loss," Beth says. "How long ago was the wedding?"

"Four years ago, next month," Andrea says, looking down at her ring. "It was the same year she received her master electrician license."

Silvey tilts her head to the side. "But I'm an electrical contractor now, right?"

Buzz nods. "And the youngest female electrical contractor in the Kansas City area."

Silvey smiles. "You don't actually know that as a fact."

Buzz shrugs. "Maybe not, but it's still a hell of an accomplishment."

"Beth," Evelyn says, waving her hand. "Can you give us an idea of how long Silvey will be here?"

"Here in the intensive care unit for tonight," Beth says. "I'll know more after the scans are back and the doc's finish their exams. We'll have a multi-disciplinary team meeting tomorrow to discuss the next steps of surgery and rehab."

"Are we talking weeks or months of rehab?" Silvey asks.

"Let's answer that after the meeting with the docs," Beth says. "But I'm hopeful that she can be transferred to the orthopedic step-down floor after we ween her off most of the medication."

"I'm getting discharged tomorrow," Buzz says. "And I have strict orders of no work, lifting, drinking or smoking, so I'll just camp out here with Silvey."

"Like hell," Evelyn says.

"Mom," Silvey says, waving her hands in the air. "He's better off here than at home. And I know you have to work. We'll be fine."

"I see," Evelyn says, standing and slinging her purse over her shoulder. "Well, if I am no longer needed, I'll just leave."

"Evelyn Velva Rhoades sit your rear down," Andrea says.

Evelyn slumps back into the chair.

"Silvey will need you," Andrea says. "And Buzz isn't exactly in full form quite yet. We will take turns keeping Silvey company. Isn't that right, Silvey?"

Silvey nods. She bites the inside of her cheek as she takes in the doe eyes and open mouths set on her parents' faces.

Andrea turns towards Silvey and grins. "Well now, that is settled. I'll work on a meal plan for you and your parents while you are here."

"Don't you have enough going on with work?" Silvey asks. "Plus, your house. How bad is it?"

"Off work for six weeks," Andrea says. "And the house will need a new kitchen and deck, but Scott is off, too. He can handle the contractors."

"Six weeks," Silvey says. "No way, you'll go insane."

"That is precisely why I will handle the meals and rehab schedule for you and the family." Andrea sticks her hand out. "Deal?"

Silvey shakes her hand.

Andrea turns to Evelyn and Buzz.

"Deal," they say in unison.

Beth nods. "If only all my patients had an Andrea."

"You say that now," Silvey mutters.

"Hey I heard that," Andrea says.

"Sorry," Silvey says sheepishly grinning and tapping her head. "Problems with judgement."

Buzz laughs.

Andrea cuts Buzz a look that makes him laugh harder.

Beth loses her composure and laughs too. She snorts and covers her mouth.

Andrea breaks her firm look, laughing along with Buzz and now Silvey.

Evelyn rolls her eyes. "You two are the worst."

23

Silvey counts the tiny grey spots on the ceiling for the hundredth time. *I'm not crazy… just not tired.* She taps the side of the bed and looks at the clock. *Only five more hours until morning.* The hum of the machines next to her bed increases her restlessness. She pats the covers and hits the red call button.

The door to her room slides open, and a head pokes around the curtain.

Silvey waves.

"Oh, you're awake?" a man says, stepping into the room.

Silvey squints at his backlit figure.

"Are you in pain?" the man asks, checking the IV and vital monitors.

"Nope," Silvey says, "still numb." She gestures from her chest down towards her feet.

"What can I do for you?"

"I don't suppose the ICU has a TV, tablet, or even a newspaper I can borrow to entertain myself for the next few hours?" Silvey asks.

"Um," the man says, fidgeting his weight from foot to foot. "I can check. It's only my third shift on this floor and most of my patients aren't conscious."

Silvey spots his shiny badge attached to the red and gold lanyard. "Well Geoff, I'm Silvey and extremely bored." She points to the ceiling tile over her bed. "There are 8,297 grey spots."

Geoff looks up at the ceiling tile. "Damn, that's beyond bored!"

Silvey laughs. "See what I mean. Can you please hook me up?"

Geoff laughs. "Of course. Let's see what I can find." He walks towards the door.

"Seriously, not picky," Silvey says as he starts to close the door.

"I'll figure something out," Geoff says.

Geoff returns a few minutes later and waves a newspaper in one hand and holds up a deck of cards in the other hand. "How's your solitaire game?"

"Legendary," Silvey says, reaching for the cards. "Is the paper recent?"

Geoff examines the front page. "Yesterday's paper. Do you want me to leave it?"

"Sure," Silvey says, sliding the cards out of the box. She mixes the deck and tilts her head towards the side table. "Can you pull that closer?"

Geoff slides the table over and sits the paper on the table. He taps the photo on the front page. "There are a few photos of that town hit by the tornado."

Silvey glances down at the paper. "Oh, shit!" She tosses the cards on the table and picks up the paper.

"Wait were you there?" Geoff asks.

Silvey gestures to her body under the covers. "Duh!"

"I'm so sorry," Geoff says. "I'm a call light away if you need anything." He backs out of the room and slides the door closed.

Silvey studies the aerial shots blown up on the front page. "That's Dre's street." She traces the outline of Andrea's house.

"How did anyone survive that?" She unfolds the paper. A black-and-white photo of a soldier is located on the bottom half of the paper. She studies the man's face and gasps. "No way!"

The headline next to the image *MISSING SOLDIER FOUND.*

"Missing?" Silvey whispers. She places the paper on the table and smooths the crease. And begins to read.

Missing Army Air Defense Captain Wilson was found wandering in a field a half mile from the Nike Air Base south of Lawson, Missouri during the search for missing residents affected by the devastating tornado. The search lead, Herman Paulson, mistook him for a member of the search party, but his uniform lead to a conversation that left the men speechless.

"I asked if he had lost his reflector vest," Herman says. "We gave every search volunteer a vest, but he was wearing a clean, pressed khaki uniform. The man just shook his head and stared at me. I noticed his name on the uniform and addressed him. Mr. Wilson, I'm Herman, are you lost?"

Herman states the man's response really left him baffled. "It's Captain Wilson and I'm not lost. Did we do it? Did we win?"

Herman stated he radio the station leading the search and after a few exchanges they discovered the man he claimed to be had been missing for over sixty years. Captain Wilson's case was left cold with no new leads after his disappearance on April 6, 1962, from a night shift at the Nike Base. He's spoken with investigators but has not released a public statement at this time.

Silvey rereads the article until her eyes fall heavy. She leans her head back on the pillow and closes her eyes.

24

A bright light flickers and hovers over Silvey's face.

Silvey squeezes her eyes shut. "What's going on?"

"You're back!" a man growls.

Silvey jerks her head back as his smelly breath floats over her face. She slowly opens her eyes and squints through the glare. A man hovers in and out of focus. "Where am I?"

"Where you shouldn't be!" His menacing tone sends a ripple of shivers down Silvey's spine. She tries to move but feels restrained.

"Enough with the games," Silvey hisses. "Release me and explain what the hell you want!"

"I want you to tell me who the man was with you!"

"Release me!" Silvey spats.

"After you tell me who he is!"

"No one you need to know!" Silvey says, struggling to break her arm away from a chair. A cool metal digs into her forearm. "Why am I handcuffed to this chair?"

"You are a national security threat," a woman says.

Silvey spots a petite woman in the corner. *She's the woman that pushed me inside!* "It was you that pushed me into the building on a fool's errand. You did this!"

The man clicks off the light blinding Silvey and the room falls dark again.

"Seriously! What the hell is going on?" Silvey closes her eyes and tries to steady her breathing. But a beeping noise only makes her panic escalate. "Get me out of here!"

"Silvey!" a man shouts and hands shake her shoulders. "Wake up!"

Silvey opens her eyes and the man's face comes into focus. "Geoff?"

He nods and releases her shoulders. "You were yelling in your sleep. I couldn't wake you for a while."

Silvey lifts her hands and examines her wrists. "I'm free."

"Silvey, are you ok?" Geoff asks, checking the monitors. "Your heart rate was off the charts a minute ago."

"I am now," Silvey whispers.

Geoff pulls up a chair and sits. "Do you want to talk about it?"

"I'm not sure," Silvey says, looking him over. "It was all very real but also not possible at the same time."

"Do you know where you are right now?" Geoff asks.

Silvey rolls her eyes. "I'm in the hospital and you are my nurse."

"Great," Geoff says. "You were shouting about a woman pushing you into a building."

Silvey frowns. "She's part of this whole thing. I just don't know how or why." She taps the paper. "But I met him."

Geoff turns the paper towards him and reads the article next to the photo. "Captain Wilson?"

Silvey nods. "Yes. He was there in the hallway before everything went dark."

"What hallway?" Geoff asks.

"That's where it gets weird," Silvey says. She spends the next twenty minutes going over everything she recalls starting with the encounter with the woman outside and the same woman in the corner of the room.

Geoff sits back in his chair. "Whoa."

"Right," Silvey says. "I can't be in two places at once."

Geoff rubs a hand over his face and stands. "You didn't leave your bed." He pulls the long echocardiogram paper over to her. She glances at one continuous line etched in various wave patterns across the strip. "Your heart tells the story here." He extends the length of the paper and studies the waves. "Oh, wait a second."

"What is it?" Silvey asks, watching all the color drain from his face.

"There's a gap," Geoff whispers. "This is not possible!"

Silvey furrows her brow. "Are you trying to be funny?"

Geoff holds up a section where there are no waves, just one flat line through the center.

"Hmm," Silvey says, looking up from the paper. "I take it a flat line is abnormal?"

Geoff nods and drops the strip of paper. He abruptly turns and leaves the room. He returns with a tablet in his hand and is frantically scrolling.

"What are you looking for?" Silvey says, trying to see the screen.

"An explanation," Geoff says. His hand freezes and he turns the device towards Silvey.

Silvey studies the grid of numbers and shrugs. "What am I supposed to see?"

"The monitors are directly linked to your chart," Geoff says, pointing to the monitor. "Every vital sign captured is charted automatically."

"And?" Silvey asks.

"The gap from the paper read out matches the gap in the vitals record in your chart."

"Ok," Silvey says. "Technical error?"

"Or—" Geoff says, leaning close, "you really are a time traveler."

Silvey laughs. "And her little dog, too."

Geoff leans back and frowns.

"Not a Wizard of Oz fan?" Silvey asks.

Geoff snaps and points at Silvey. "Because you're like Dorothy and the tornado."

Silvey nods. "And they say millennials aren't hip."

Geoff smirks.

"What time is it?" Silvey asks.

"Nearly five," Geoff says.

25

"Bax, are you decent?" Rozanne says, knocking lightly on the bedroom door.

Bax rolls over and spots the old alarm clock on the nightstand. "It's after ten, geez." He pulls the covers back. "Just a minute." He slides on the shirt he tossed on the floor the night before and adjusts his shorts. The wood floors creak under his steps as he walks to and opens the door.

Rozanne smiles at the sheet line indention across Bax's cheek. "I've got food in the fridge and dinner in the crock pot. Help yourself. I've got to run a few errands for Monroe and Gage. I should be home before the crock pot gets done. Any questions?"

"No ma'am," Baxton says.

"Good," Rozanne says, holding up a bottle of water and a small white paper cup. "Your antibiotic is the yellow and green pill and the one for pain is the small white tab."

"I don't want any pain meds," Bax says, taking the antibiotic and the bottle of water. He places the pill in his mouth and swallows a swig of water. "I'll put the pain pill back in the bottle. That is where?"

"Kitchen counter," Rozanne says. "Do you need anything while I am out?"

"Do you have a house phone?" Baxton asks. "I need to make a few calls and start the insurance claim on my car and phone."

"Mary picked up a new phone for you this morning," Rozanne says, pointing at Baxton's slack jaw. "She's nothing short of amazing. She also dropped off a few casseroles."

Baxton closes his mouth and shakes his head. "I knew she was helpful, but that's next level."

"It gets better," Rozanne says, walking towards the kitchen. "She persuaded the sales guy to transfer your old number and contacts to the new phone. So, unless there was something you didn't save to the cloud it should be ready to go."

"How did she manage that?" Baxton asks, following her into the antique but spacious kitchen. He drops the tablet in the full pill bottle left on the counter.

"It is her superpower," Rozanne says, handing Baxton the brand new phone. "It's charged and ready to go."

"Wow," Baxton says, tapping the screen. "I've missed twenty-eight calls and have about sixty messages."

"Your name was released to the media last night," Rozanne says. "Most of the calls are likely requests for interviews."

"Why?" Baxton asks, looking up from the phone.

"Baxton, you survived the tornado," Rozanne says. "And the people need a champion in the wake of such tragedy."

Baxton takes a step back. "I'm not… a champion."

Rozanne frowns. "I get it." She picks up her purse. "It's your call on whom you give your time to." She pats his shoulder and walks towards the front door. "See you later. Call if you think of anything you need."

"See ya," Baxton says, pulling out a chair from the kitchen table. He thumbs through the missed calls and stops. "Hutchins & Company." He hovers his thumb over the contact. "Who's in the office today?" He presses the call icon and waits.

"Hutchins and Company, Monica speaking."

"Hi, Monica, it's Bax. Did you call me this morning?"

"Hey Bax. Yes, I did. Jessica called late last night and wanted me to call all of our employees and contractors attached to the project at the nike base. The workers comp insurance will pick up all costs from the hospital and payment for time off while you recover."

"She doesn't need to worry about us," Bax says. "She's got enough on her plate."

"Trust me, I know. I started our call with that lecture, but she cut me off."

Bax chuckles. "She's persistent. That's for sure."

"And running on zero sleep," Monica says. "And we've received at least a hundred calls from the media in the last few hours."

"I have several missed calls from numbers I don't recognize," Bax says. "I'm guessing most are media as well."

"I've prepared a statement from the company, but you are free to speak to them. I've warned each outlet that if they even attempted to contact Jessica, I would hunt them down one by one."

"Ha," Bax laughs. "How did they take your threat?"

"A long pause followed by 'I see' or a 'yes ma'am.'"

"I'll avoid them for as long as possible. Public speaking is not my thing. I definitely don't want to be on camera if they ask me about Micah."

"I know what you mean," Monica says. "Are you going to be able to attend the services?"

"Yes," Bax says, tapping the table. "Did the owners of the vertical farm reach out?"

"They called that evening. They have a person onsite to assess the damages. An insurance inspector has been sniffing around for a possible fault on the welder's union to cover their insurance claims with a little more padding."

"Vultures," Bax mutters. "It was a big ass tornado! It wouldn't have made any difference what size anchors or rebar they installed. The outcome would still be the same."

"Micah's death?" Monica whispers.

"No, a giant pile of steel twisted and mangled in a heap at the bottom of the silo." Bax sighs. "I don't know how I made it out alive."

"Can I ask you one question?" Monica asks.

"Sure," Bax says.

"Did you have any warning?" Monica asks.

"Not much," Bax says. "We saw it from a small window from the top. Micah and I had just rushed the materials inside from the rain." He glances out the screen door. The sun is high spotlighting the edge of the pond. "I'd say less than five minutes before it hit."

"Geez," Monica says. "I'm so sorry."

"It's really no one's fault but mother nature."

"True, hey sorry I have to run. My other line is ringing."

"No worries, talk to you later." Bax ends the call and sits the phone on the table. He finishes the bottle of water and his stomach growls. "Right, food."

He rummages through the fridge and picks out two covered dishes and places them on the counter. Reheating instructions are written in perfect penmanship on a yellow sticky note. "Microwave single serving on a plate covered for two minutes or place the entire casserole in a preheated oven at 350 for eight minutes."

Bax peels off the lid and inspects the dish. "Pasta with beef and cheese, yes, please." He opens a few drawers and cabinets until he locates a plate, knife, and fork. He cuts a giant serving and plops it on a plate before covering the dish with a paper towel. He opens the microwave and slides the plate in before closing the door. He studies the instructions and decides to go with three minutes considering the massive portion size. He returns to the table and scrolls through the missed messages.

Hi Baxton Auburn, my name is Nita Dreven, a reporter with channel four....

"Delete!" Baxton says, pressing the trash icon on the message. He deletes ten similar messages before the microwave dings.

"Eat first, delete later," Bax says. He takes the hot plate out of the microwave and juggles the dish until he places it on the table.

"Three minutes was way too long." He blows on his red fingertips and sits down.

He picks up his fork and his phone rings. "Seriously." He sits the fork down and picks up the phone. "Unknown caller. Yea decline." He presses the red decline button, picks up his fork, and scoops up a piece of pasta. He blows on the bite and has it just to his mouth when his phone rings again. "Damn.''

He drops his fork and stares at the screen. "Why would someone from the US Government call me?"

"Answer and find out," a man says.

Baxton whirls around and stares at a man dressed in a navy uniform standing on the other side of the screen door.

"Who the hell are you?" Bax asks.

"Special Agent Neil Carlton with the FBI," the man says, holding up a badge.

Bax steps closer to the door. "Why are you here?"

"We have a few questions about the incident at the nike base."

"Why would the FBI have questions about private property that was hit by a tornado?"

"All very great questions, but it's more about what was uncovered at the base post tornado that has brought me to your door." He gestures to the porch. "We can sit outside if that will make you feel less cornered."

"I don't feel cornered," Bax says.

The agent points to Bax's hand. "I believe you, but maybe let's put that back on the table."

Bax looks down at his white knuckles wrapped around a butter knife. He turns and places the knife back on the table. "Sorry, it was an honest reflex."

"No need for apologies," agent Carlton says. "I'll be on the porch when you're ready."

Bax looks down at the steaming pasta and then to his phone. He opens the notes app and presses record before he pockets his phone.

"Can I get you something to drink?" Bax asks, hesitating at the door.

"I'm good, thanks," agent Carlton says.

Bax swings the door open and steps out on the porch.

The agent is sitting on the large porch swing.

"It's a beautiful piece of property," agent Carlton says, without turning his gaze away from the pond.

"It is," Bax says, choosing a chair away from the agent. He sits down facing the pond. "Can we skip the small talk?"

"Absolutely," agent Carlton says. He turns towards Baxton. "The reason I'm here is classified, but I have some questions related to events you can recall after the tornado hit the silo."

Baxton nods.

"Did you see anyone onsite after the tornado?"

"Alive or dead?" Baxton asks, keeping his eyes fixed on the pond.

"Let's start with alive," agent Carlton says.

"The two firemen I waved down."

Agent Carlton checks his notepad. "Do you recall their names?"

"No."

"And dead?" agent Carlton asks.

"Micah Hutchins."

"Your former boss?"

"Yes," Bax says, looking down at his lap.

"I see," agent Carlton says. "Did you find any passages inside the silo?"

Bax looks up at the agent, meeting his green eyes set below bushy black eyebrows. "Sir, have you seen the site?"

"Yes."

Bax shakes his head. "Then why are you here asking me questions you already know the answer to?"

"We found a ladder."

Bax looks at his hands and holds them up with his palms facing the agent. "I had to climb the ladder to get out of the silo and find help."

"Where was the ladder you used?" agent Carlton says, standing.

Bax stands and towers over the agent by nearly a foot. "On the wall of the silo. It was staggered rebar."

Agent Carlton shakes his head. "Hm."

Bax takes a step back. "You don't believe me?"

"I believe that you think that is true."

"Don't patronize me," Bax says, tapping his head. "I remember that climb very well. Apparently, I have a small phobia of heights."

"And when you reached the top?"

"I walked towards the road to find help."

"I've spoken with the two firemen," agent Carlton says. "They agreed that you were pretty shaken up when they arrived on scene and that you were holding a doll."

"The doll's hair was the same color," Baxton says, closing his eyes, "as her."

"As her?"

Bax sighs and looks him over. "Silvey Rhoades."

Agent Carlton shakes his head.

"I thought she had fallen along with Micah and I," Bax says. "But I couldn't find her. She was hanging onto the handrailing when the roof blew off, but then she was gone."

"And when you didn't find her inside," agent Carlton says, pointing up. "You assumed she was sucked out of the silo."

"Well yeah," Bax says.

Agent Carlton folds his arms across his chest. "Why do you think that?"

"Her friend said they found her in a field a mile away from the base," Bax says.

"What friend?" agent Carlton asks.

"Andrea," Bax says.

"Hmm," agent Carlton says, smiling. "You believe that a woman sucked up into an EF5 tornado could survive?"

Bax shrugs. "I didn't have to. I saw Silvey in the ICU before I was discharged."

"She's awake," agent Carlton asks.

"That's none of your business," Bax says, folding his arms across his chest. "What do you think happened?"

"I believe you and Ms. Rhoades may have seen something at the base and are using the wreckage of the tornado to cover it up?"

Bax bends so their faces are level. "Are you tripping on something?"

Agent Carlton widens his eyes.

Bax continues. "Because that is the most insane theory I've ever heard?" He holds his stare until the agent blinks. "And that, sir, is where we end things today. I'm hungry, and I have zero tolerance for your wild theories." He turns his back to the agent and walks to the door.

"One last question?"

Bax opens the door and looks over his shoulder.

Agent Carlton locks eyes with Bax. "Does the year 1962 mean anything to you?"

Bax doesn't flinch. "No, sir." He steps inside and lets the screen door slam behind him. He closes the main door and engages the deadbolt. He pulls out his phone and stops the recording. *What the hell was that?*

Bax looks out the window and watches the agent back out of the drive and turn to exit the property. "I need to talk to Silvey." He ignores the food on the table and walks down the hall to his temporary bedroom. He snatches the note with Buzz's phone number and dials the number. He paces the length of the bed until it starts ringing.

"If this is a reporter!" Buzz yells.

"It's Baxton Auburn," Bax says.

"Boy, you're lucky," Buzz says. "My phone has been ringing off the hook all morning."

"Mine too," Bax says. "How are you doing?"

"Fit as I can be," Buzz says. "I am being discharged this morning."

"That's great to hear," Bax says, walking out of the bedroom back towards the kitchen. "Were you able to see Silvey?"

"Yep," Buzz says. "She was awake and talking last night."

"How is she doing?"

"Physically pretty banged up," Buzz says. "But they are keeping her well medicated. She's a bit spotty memory wise. They think that could be related to her head injury."

"Does she remember the tornado?" Bax asks.

"Not really," Buzz says. "She did mention Micah and you inside the silo."

"Oh, yeah?" Bax asks, trying to keep his voice level.

"But nothing concrete," Buzz says. "I am heading down to see her in a few. Can I give her this number?"

"Yes, please," Bax says.

"Great," Buzz says. "I'll see you at Micah's service, right?"

"Yes, sir."

"Good," Buzz says. "See you soon."

26

Silvey lays back after a fourth doctor finishes their exam. "What's the verdict? Do I get to bust out of here or what?"

"We are meeting in a few minutes to discuss the next steps," Beth says, sliding the door closed behind the doctor. Her navy-blue scrubs look new with the word 'nurse' embroidered across the pocket. "They were the last doctor on the list this morning."

"Awesome, does we include me in this meeting?" Silvey asks, watching Beth check the IVs.

Beth turns to face Silvey. "We will bring the conclusion of the meeting to you for a final decision."

Silvey rolls her eyes. "Great."

"I know it's frustrating," Beth says. "But the fact that you're able to contribute is a miracle."

"You've seen my scans," Silvey says, meeting Beth's glistening eyes.

Beth nods. "I did take a look."

Silvey shifts her covers up. "How bad is it?"

"It's…" Beth says, but the door slides open. She turns away from Silvey and wipes her cheek. "May I help you?"

Silvey tries to see around Beth, but she's blocking her view.

A woman dressed in all black flips open a badge. "My name is Agent Michelle Vickers, FBI."

"Ok," Beth says, gesturing for the woman to step out of the room.

"I need a few moments with Ms. Rhoades," agent Vickers says.

Beth turns her back on the agent and stares at Silvey's wide eyes. "What do you think?"

Silvey blinks. "Uh, sure?"

Beth hands Silvey the call light. "Just in case." She turns towards the agent. "Please don't take too long. We have a team of doctors waiting to discuss her care."

"I only need a few minutes," agent Vickers says, stepping aside to allow room for Beth to pass. She walks towards Silvey with her badge still open. "Ms. Rhoades."

"Agent Michelle Vickers," Silvey says, inspecting the identification.

"May I ask you a few questions about the events at the base?" agent Vickers asks, pocketing her badge and pulling out a small notebook.

"Sure," Silvey says, folding her hands together and hiding the call light.

"Can you tell me what you discovered in the silo?" agent Vickers asks.

"Discovered?" Silvey asks, shaking her head. "Ma'am, I am, or should say was the electrician for the vertical farm."

Agent Vickers shakes her head. "I believe that we both know that's not the whole story."

Silvey frowns. "You may want to check with the owners. I believe they have a signed contract that says otherwise."

"We found evidence Ms. Rhoades. We know that you were down there."

Silvey laughs. "Is this a joke?"

Agent Vickers frowns. "It's a matter of national security."

"Seriously?" Silvey narrows her eyes and matches the agent's steely expression. "What do you want from me?"

"The truth."

Silvey tilts her head to the side. "My name is Silvey Rhoades. I'm here in the hospital and I'm an electrician."

"And your relationship to Baxton Auburn?" agent Vickers asks.

"I met him a few hours before the tornado," Silvey says.

"And Captain Wilson?" agent Vickers asks, lifting an eyebrow.

Silvey shrugs. "Only what I read in the article."

"What article?"

"The one on the front page of the paper." Silvey points to the paper sitting on the side table. "See for yourself."

Agent Vickers picks up the paper. She mumbles a curse and sits the paper back down. "You've never seen this man before?" She taps the image of the soldier.

Silvey winks at the agent. "In my lifetime, no."

Agent Vickers leans forward staring Silvey down. "I know you've met the captain."

"Times up," Beth says from the doorway. "You'll have to come back later if you want to speak to Ms. Rhoades."

"Or never," Silvey says under her breath.

"Ms. Rhoades, our conversation is not over," agent Vickers says.

"It is now," Silvey says, smiling at her dad's grin as he enters the room.

The agent glares at Silvey.

Silvey keeps her eyes pinned on her father until the agent leaves. She sighs.

"What was that?" Buzz asks, taking the seat next to Silvey's bed.

"FBI," Silvey whispers. Three more people dressed in scrubs enter her room followed by Andrea and her mom.

"Silvey," Beth says, pointing to a lady in bright pink scrubs and auburn hair. "This is Francie. She's your designated care coordinator. Next to her is Dr. Sabry and Dr. Nu."

The two men raise their hands.

Silvey looks Dr. Sabry up and down for a minute. "Were you in the room during my first surgery?"

He nods. "I was part of the trauma team when you arrived."

"You recognize him?" Andrea asks.

"I don't know," Silvey says, looking at the other man and shrugging. "Well, let's not piddle paddle around it. Give me the bad news first."

Andrea rolls her eyes. "She's nothing if not blunt."

Buzz grins and pokes Silvey's shoulder.

"Ms. Rhoades," Francie says.

"Please, just call me Silvey," Silvey says, pointing her thumb at her mom. "That's Ms. Rhoades."

Francie nods. "We've reviewed the latest labs, scans and gathered the notes from the physical exams and have determined the next recommended course of treatment will be surgery." She nods to Dr. Nu.

"Silvey, we need to surgically repair two vertebras in your lumbar spine, the pelvic and femur fractures," Dr. Nu says. "We've planned to do this in one surgery with a designated break if it becomes to taxing."

"That's the bad news?" Silvey asks.

Andrea frowns. "Spinal surgery is not a walk in the park."

"Ok sure," Silvey says. "But I will walk in the park again, right?"

"Right," Dr. Nu answers.

"The hardest part will be the recovery," Francie says. "It will require extensive hours of therapy."

Silvey nods. "I'll do the work."

"Great," Francie says. "Dr. Sabry will go over some of the risks."

"Silvey," Dr. Sabry says. "Surgery risks include infection, blood clots, dural tear, leakage of cerebrospinal fluid, nerve injury, paralysis or death."

"And without the surgery," Silvey says.

"Pretty much the same list," Dr. Sabry says. "We believe that the injury to your lumbar spine is within a millimeter of your spinal cord. Dr. Knipp will be overseeing this portion of the surgery." He winks at Silvey. "Including Dr. Marvin."

Silvey grins.

Silvey's mom, Evelyn, catches their exchange. "Dr. Marvin?"

"The Brain," Silvey and Andrea say in unison.

Buzz laughs.

Beth and Dr. Sabry cover their mouths to muffle their laughter.

Francie and Dr. Nu exchange a glance and they shrug.

"Dr. Sarah 'The Brain' Marvin," Silvey says, looking from Francie to Dr. Nu. "An old nickname."

Francie nods. "Got it. Silvey, do we have your consent?"

"Yes ma'am," Silvey says. "When do you slice and dice?"

Evelyn gasps. "Silvey Lynn."

"Mom," Silvey says. "I need my sense of humor to keep my sanity from cracking. Please, just roll with the punch lines for once."

"This evening around seven," Francie says. "If you consent."

"I consent," Silvey says. "Where do I sign?"

Francie holds up a tablet and stylus pen. "Here you go."

Beth takes the tablet and shows Silvey the line to sign.

Silvey hovers the pen over the tablet as she scans the consent form. "One question." She looks up from the tablet. "If I don't make it, can you make sure my organs are donated?"

Buzz holds up his hand. "I get dibs on your heart."

"Jesus," Evelyn says, leaving the room.

Andrea smiles. "I'll go fetch."

"I'll show you where we can update your wishes after you sign the consent form," Beth says.

Silvey signs and hands the stylus pen back to Beth.

Beth passes the tablet back to Francie.

"If you don't have any further questions," Dr. Nu says. "We'll see you at seven."

"All good," Silvey says.

"I'll be back with my tablet to update your wishes," Beth says, waiting for the others to file out.

"Thanks," Silvey says, turning towards Buzz. "How mad do you think she is?"

Buzz chuckles. "I'm sure Andrea has her hands full."

"Oops," Silvey says.

"Here," Buzz says, handing her a phone.

"What's up?" Silvey asks, looking at the dark screen.

"Andrea found your phone, but it was in pretty bad shape. You can borrow mine until we get it replaced."

"Thanks," Silvey says.

"Baxton Auburn called me," Buzz says, tapping the screen. "And I saved his number. He really wants to speak to you."

"Good," Silvey says. "I need to speak with him, too."

"Are you going to explain who that woman was staring you down when I arrived?" Buzz asks.

"FBI," Silvey says. She points to the paper. "She was asking questions about Captain Wilson and the base."

Buzz lifts an eyebrow and stares at the man's picture. "Odd."

"Right," Silvey says, shrugging.

"Silvey," Buzz says, lowering his brow. "It's all very suspicious. Especially if the FBI is poking around."

"I know," Silvey says. "Maybe Bax saw something?"

"Maybe," Buzz says, standing. "I'm going home this afternoon to pack a few things. I'll be back before you go in for surgery. Keep the phone, call the boy."

27

Bax sighs and stares at the missed call notifications. He clicks clear all and sits the phone on the table next to his plate. He scoops up a bite of the cooled pasta.

"Hmm," Bax moans over a full mouth. He finishes the plate in less than two minutes. "Oh, that just opened the bottomless pit of my stomach." He eyes the casserole on the counter. *Baxton show some self-control.*

"Dude," Gage says from the kitchen doorway.

Baxton jumps. "When did you get here?"

"About two bites into the pasta you just inhaled," Gage says.

"I didn't hear you come in," Bax says, looking at the open front door.

"Noted," Gage says, walking into the kitchen and inspecting the casserole dish on the counter. "How was the pasta?"

"Amazing," Bax says, scooping up another helping.

"Nice," Gage says, taking out a plate. "How's the pain?"

"None," Bax says, glancing at the bottles on the counter. "I don't plan on taking the pain pills."

"I understand," Gage says, placing his plate in the microwave. "Have you returned any calls yet?"

"You know about the phone?" Bax asks, nodding towards the table.

"Roz stopped by the shop and mentioned that Mary dropped it off this morning," Gage says, opening a bottle of water. "She also said it was blowing up the second it was turned on."

"Understatement," Bax says. "I'm not returning any calls or texts to the media. That's a hard no."

Gage laughs. "I get it. When Roz went through all that court stuff with the damn stalker and kidnapping, we were flooded with media requests. We were under a gag order until the trials were over, and they still called."

"Ugh," Bax says, shaking his head. "And then the FBI showed up here today."

"Wait what?" Gage asks, taking his plate out of the microwave.

Bax walks to the table, pulls up the recording, and presses play.

Gage listens to the recording while he eats. Bax joins him at the table with his second serving.

"1962," Gage says, leaving the table and walks to the living room. He walks back into the kitchen waving a newspaper. "Look at this." He unrolls the paper and points to the article on the bottom half of the front page.

Bax's eyes land on the aerial pictures of the neighborhood. He shakes his head and looks where Gage is pointing. He reads the article about Captain Wilson. "No shit."

"Bax?" Gage asks.

"Silvey mentioned a run in with Captain Wilson before I found her," Bax says. "Is there any more about this?" He pulls open the paper and scans the headlines.

"Not in there," Gage says, pulling out his phone. "One of the volunteers on the search party was recording and caught the interaction with the man claiming to be Captain Wilson." He taps the screen a few times and shows the video of a man in a bright orange vest approaching a second man in his mid-forties dressed in a khaki-colored uniform.

Bax takes the phone and pauses it. "Gage, it's the same uniform I remember wearing." He turns the paused image towards Gage. "Down to the buttons on the top."

Gage picks up his plate and walks towards the sink. "It's all very bizarre. I had a customer from Vibbard stop by the shop. Her car had some minor dents from flying debris, but she found a newspaper from April 1962 stuck to her windshield." He turns on the water, washes the plate and fork before placing it in the drying rack. He turns towards Bax.

"Are you good, man?" Gage asks, walking over and waving a hand in front of Bax's face.

Bax blinks. "Um, not sure."

Gage glances at the orange pill bottles on the counter. "Is there anything you are taking that may make you sweaty?"

"No," Bax says, wiping his brow. "Any chance you have a spare car?"

"Of course, but you aren't supposed to be alone for a bit."

Bax glares at Gage.

Gage holds up his hands. "Doctor's orders."

"Is that why you came home for lunch?" Bax asks, taking his plate to the sink and washing his dirty plate, knife and fork. He turns to look at Gage. "Dude?"

Gage is looking at Bax's phone. "You just received a text from Silvey's dad."

Bax drops the plate in the drying rack. "Really?"

"Buzz, right?" Gage asks.

Bax picks up his phone and opens the message. "It's Silvey. She wants to video chat."

"You might want to change your shirt," Gage says.

Bax looks down at the red stain on the front of his shirt. "Did you happen to grab any clothes from my place?"

"Roz packed and placed it all in the dresser," Gage says, shaking his keys. "I need to get back and relieve Dusty. You good?"

Bax waves Gage towards the door. "I'll be fine, go."

28

Bax throws on a clean grey shirt. He closes the dresser drawer and the mirror rattles. He looks at his reflection and pulls up his auburn curls. He searches for a hair tie on the bedside table. "Come on!"

He ducks out of the bedroom and into the hall bathroom. He snags a black hair band from the counter and ties his hair up into a messy man bun. A few curls fall out and he tucks them behind his ears.

"It's just a conversation," Bax says to the mirror. He wipes his sweaty palms off on his shirt and walks back to the kitchen. He picks up his phone and hits the video icon next to Buzz's name.

He stares at his face until Silvey's freckled nose fills the screen.

"Hi, sorry," Silvey says, jostling the phone. "Dad's phone has everything magnetized for his old ass eyes." She moves the phone away until her whole face is visible.

"Hi," Bax says. "How are you doing?"

"Conscious," Silvey says smiling. "Despite all mother nature threw at me."

Bax smiles. "It's unreal."

"How are you doing?" Silvey asks.

"I'm alive," Bax says. "And home at my cousin's house. The doctor insisted I should have supervision during the first few nights at home."

Silvey nods. "Home sounds amazing right now."

"What's the status for you?" Bax asks.

"Heading in for another surgery this evening," Silvey says. "Then hopefully a rehab floor, so I can get the hell out of here."

"Not a fan of hospitals, either?" Bax asks.

"More like not a fan of debt," Silvey says. "I have insurance, but without income during this stretch it will be hard to see the silver lining anytime soon."

Bax frowns. "I believe we have that in common."

"Do you know what else we have in common?" Silvey asks.

Bax shakes his head. "What's that?"

"1962."

Bax's jaw falls open and Silvey points at the phone.

"I knew it was real!"

"You were there in the dark?" Bax whispers.

Silvey nods. "I was, and did you see the newspaper?"

"Yes!" Bax stands and starts pacing the length of the kitchen. "But how is any of it possible?"

"I haven't exactly worked that out," Silvey says. "But how did you disappear?"

"One minute, I was following you and the next I was awake in a hospital room." Bax stops pacing. "What happened… after?"

"The lights came back on and I was in a white chamber attached to a research lab," Silvey says, pointing to her arm. "I got jabbed in the arm with something after trying to exit the lab. I wound up in that control room with the guys and old monitors." She shakes her head. "I woke up handcuffed to a chair in a dark room."

"Shit," Bax mutters. "I'm sorry."

Silvey frowns. "For what?"

"I should have helped you," Bax says.

"How?" Silvey asks. "We weren't actually there, right?"

"According to the FBI…" Bax says.

"Wait, what?" Silvey interrupts him. "They came to see you too?"

"About an hour ago," Bax says. "You?"

"Same," Silvey says. She leans close to the phone. "Did you tell them or anyone else?"

Bax chuckles. "That you and I were there?"

Silvey nods.

"Not to the fed," Bax says.

"Phew," Silvey says. "I had a female agent, and she was super sketchy."

"I didn't trust a word the agent said, and that was before I saw the article. But I did explain it all to my cousin and his wife. I was very confused when I woke up."

Silvey frowns. "Did they believe you?"

"Rozanne, my cousin's wife didn't invalidate my experience and Gage, my cousin was skeptical." Bax pushes an escaped curl back behind his ear. "What about you?"

"A nurse, neuro doc, and a resident, which just happened to be a grade school friend." Silvey checks the door. "I haven't had time to tell the full story to Dre yet."

"Silvey," Bax says, "what do you think really happened that night?"

"The guy questioning me in the dark," Silvey says, "kept saying you were wanted for treason."

"Treason?" Bax pulls out a chair, slumps down, and holds the phone in his shaking hands. "Do you really think we committed some kind of crime?"

"I highly doubt it!" Silvey says and smiles. "If that's really the case… we have perfect alibis."

Bax laughs. "Um, well from that perspective, so true!"

"Here's the thing I don't get," Silvey says. "The lab I found had research notes for what looked like a nuclear fusion reactor."

"Whoa," Bax whispers. "I wonder if that was public knowledge?"

"I'm guessing the missiles were just a cover for the research," Silvey says. "It was something called Scylla II."

"And you think Captain Wilson knew about the lab?" Bax asks.

"It was on the same level," Silvey says. "I never did find steps or an actual exit."

"That's interesting," Bax says.

"Any other theory?" Silvey asks.

"Low level conspiracy theory," Bax says. "Wilson thought the alarms were an actual attack and locked himself inside a bunker."

"For sixty years?" Silvey asks, shaking her head.

"Why else would he ask 'did we win' after they found him?" Bax asks.

"Win what?" Silvey asks.

"The base was built to defend against German and Russian missiles, so…" Bax says, lifting a hand and shrugging. "Or nuclear energy?"

"Oh, that has legs," Silvey says, tapping her chin.

Bax nods. "Do you have a theory?"

"Not a theory," Silvey says. "But very glad I am not alone in my very real hallucination."

Bax smiles. "Not alone."

"And Midge," Silvey says. "He was there before I saw you."

Bax's smile falls. "You mentioned that he was there, but I had already seen him under the…"

"Stop!" Silvey says. "I can't hear those details. I have a very vivid imagination."

"Sorry," Bax says, shaking his head. "It's an image I would love to forget."

Silvey nods. "I believe you."

"What do we do with this um… experience?" Bax asks.

"Well, in a few hours they are putting me under again," Silvey says. "I guess I'll let you know tomorrow."

"You think you'll go back?" Bax asks.

"I did this morning when I fell asleep," Silvey says.

"Whoa," Bax whispers.

Silvey turns the camera towards the IV monitors. "My guess… it is the drugs." She turns her phone back to herself.

Bax glances at the counter. "I've only taken an antibiotic since I woke up from the coma."

Silvey shrugs. "It's the only theory I have."

Bax sighs. "It may have some weight to it."

"Who knows?" Silvey smiles and holds up one finger. "Can you dig into some research?"

Bax nods. "I don't think I could obsess about anything else. I was going to start with April 1962."

"If there was a breach," Silvey says. "I'm pretty sure that would be kept out of the public records. Do you have any friends in the military?"

"A few actually," Bax says. "I'll see what I can dig up."

"Thanks," Silvey says, fighting a yawn. "I appreciate it."

"Get some rest," Bax says, "and try to stay in our timeline if you can."

Silvey smirks. "Our timeline seems to be split, traitor."

Bax laughs hard. He holds his side to stop the pull of the stitches. "I meant the here and now, not 1962."

"Later Bax," Silvey says.

The call ends before he can respond. He stares at the dark screen. "Damn, she's beautiful."

29

"Silvey," Beth says from the open door.

"Hey," Silvey says, waving her in. "Sorry I was on the phone a little longer than expected."

"Did the conversation go well?" Beth asks, hanging a new bag of fluids.

"It confirms that my internal psyche is still intact," Silvey says.

Beth lifts an eyebrow. "Oh?"

"It's real," Silvey says. "I'm a time traveler."

Beth laughs and drops the empty deflated bag. She bends to pick it up, smacking her head on the side of Silvey's bed. "Oh!" She straightens and holds her hand over her left eye.

"Are you ok?" Silvey asks, searching for her call light.

"I think so," Beth says, pulling her hand away and blood runs down the side of her face. "Uh oh."

"Not ok!" Silvey says. "We need help in here!"

The door slides open. A tall man in dark scrubs bolts in the room.

"Beth needs help," Silvey says.

"What did you do?" the man asks, assessing Beth's blood-streaked face. He glares at Silvey.

Silvey holds her hands up. "She smacked her face on the bed when she bent to pick that up." She points to the bag on the floor.

He doesn't move.

Silvey shakes her head. "Help her!"

Beth waves her clean hand. "I'll be fine. Don't worry." She pushes past the man who's eyes are fixed on Silvey.

"I am not exactly in swinging form," Silvey says, gesturing to the lines and tubes attached to her arms.

"Hmm," the man says, turning his back to her and follows Beth.

"What the hell?" Silvey mutters, glaring at the man. Her phone pings. A text notification pops up on the screen. She slides her finger across the screen to open a new video message.

Andrea's face fills the screen. She's sitting in her car. "Scott and I are meeting with a contractor this afternoon. If I don't make it back before seven, I'll be there when you get out of surgery." She starts the car. "The FBI just called me. I gave him a play-by-play of finding you in the field. Is there anything I should know?"

Silvey texts her back. *Him?*

Andrea's response appears immediately. *Agent Carlton.*

"Interesting." Silvey types back. *It's odd they are asking questions about tornado victims. Good luck with the contractor and have my dad run the numbers on the electrical… if you can't wait for me.*

The phone dings again. *Just focus on your health.*

Ha, ha. Silvey smiles and responds. *I'm trapped in a bed tethered to machines. Not like I can cut and run.*

Andrea's next message comes with a knock on the door. *True, but fair warning your mom is on her way back up.*

Silvey glances up at her mother's drawn expression. "What's wrong?"

"Your nurse, Beth… her face," Evelyn says.

"Ah," Silvey says, turning the phone over. "She smacked her face on my bed."

"Silvey Lynn!" Evelyn says.

146

"What?" Silvey asks. "Why does everyone think it's somehow my fault?"

"Well, was it?" Evelyn asks.

"No," Silvey says. "Seriously, mom."

"Sorry," Evelyn says, pulling a chair closer.

Silvey rolls her eyes. "I can't believe that I am confined to a bed and my own mother is accusing me of assault."

Evelyn sits in the chair. "You are your father's daughter."

"Dad doesn't go around punching people," Silvey says.

"Now maybe," Evelyn mutters.

"You're ridiculous," Silvey says. "Why are you here?"

Evelyn flinches. "You are about to have a major surgery and I want us to talk."

"Talk?" Silvey asks. Her face flushes red hot. "You came in swinging accusations, so tell me what's on your mind?"

"Silvey," Evelyn says. "I'm sorry that I thought you could hurt your nurse. And I am here to amend for our argument the morning before… all of this happened."

"The argument you started about the profession I chose and have worked really hard for?"

Evelyn nods. "You are my one and only child. And I only want what is best for you."

Silvey opens her mouth, but Evelyn holds up her hand.

"Please let me finish," Evelyn says.

Silvey closes her mouth in a firm line and bites the inside of her cheek.

"Yes," Evelyn says, "your profession aligns with your father. And yes, that does bother me."

Silvey rolls her eyes.

Evelyn holds up a finger. "But I also know the kind of crew he has worked with over the years, and I worry about your safety."

Silvey follows Evelyn's gaze over the blankets and up to the monitors.

"It's not like the crew did this to me," Silvey says.

Evelyn frowns. "The agent with the FBI…"

"Mom!" Silvey says, throwing up her hands. "What are you even talking about?"

Evelyn averts her eyes to her lap. "They seem to think that you're involved in a massive cover up with that other boy, Baxton."

"And you believe them?" Silvey asks.

"Silvey, please," Evelyn says, reaching for her hand.

Silvey moves her hand out of reach. "Just go. I can't deal with your drama today."

BEEP BEEP

Evelyn and Silvey jump.

Silvey looks at the red flashing light on one of the IV monitors.

Evelyn blinks back tears and stands with her purse. "I'll get the nurse."

The tall male nurse slides open the door. "Please step out."

"I'll be right back," Evelyn says at the door.

Silvey ignores her and focuses on the male nurse. "How's Beth?"

"Three stitches and will have a nasty black eye," he says, silencing the alarm. "I'm Warren. Beth said she would stop by your room tomorrow, but she's on her way home."

"Dang," Silvey says. "Warren, I promise I didn't do anything."

"I apologize for my initial reaction," Warren says, resetting the monitor. "We get some rowdy patients and I'm a float nurse. My last shift included a brawl in the ER between two women."

"Oh," Silvey says, pointing to the door. "Was it my mother and my father's new woman?"

Warren glances at Evelyn pacing outside the room. "She's a few decades too old for that brawl." He taps the monitor. "I don't think Beth finished setting up the IV before her encounter with your bed. You may feel a bit fuzzy when it kicks in."

"Great, can you tell my mom I'm too tired for a visit?" Silvey asks and leans back resting her head on the pillow.

"I can," Warren says. "Is there anything else you need?"

"Is there a reason it's so dim in here all the time?" Silvey asks.

"Patient comfort mostly."

"Hmm," Silvey says, fighting the heaviness, pushing her eyelids down.

"Welcome back," the man says.

Silvey blinks until her eyes focus on a man. His dark parted hair is slicked down to his head and he's wearing round wire-frame glasses. A woman sitting next to him shifts in her chair drawing her attention away from the man.

"What's going on?" She takes in the cinderblock walls and concrete floor.

"You've been avoiding the truth," the woman says.

Silvey stares at the woman's beehive hairdo. *It's her.* "You again!"

"How about we even the playing field?" the man asks, drawing Silvey's attention away from the woman. "I'll ask one question; you answer and vice versa."

"Fine." Silvey says, folding her free arms across her chest.

"What did Captain Wilson say to you?"

"His name, rank, and then ran away after the siren started." Silvey leans forward. "Who are you?"

"John and Jane," the man says.

"Bull shit!" Silvey says. "And your last name is Doe?"

Jane shakes her head. "Ms. Rhoades, tread lightly."

Silvey glares at the woman. "I never told you my name."

Jane flips over a piece of paper. "Did you take this?"

Silvey glances at the paper. It's the drawing of the schematic for the reactor. She studies the image and squints at the writing in the margin. "Fancy drawing but I can't even read what that says."

"Try again," Jane says, pushing the paper closer.

"This isn't English, and I barely passed Spanish, which was my only foreign language credit." She shrugs. "Where is this bunker located?"

"Missouri," John says. "When did you meet him?"

"I met Captain Wilson in the hall after a man in the control room slammed the door in my face," Silvey says. "Where in Missouri are we?"

"Near the base," John says. "Where did you meet the other man you were fleeing with?"

"Met him here," Silvey says. "What base?"

"Ms. Rhoades," Jane says. "Don't be smart with us."

"Fine, I'll play dumb," Silvey says, tugging on her blonde hair. "Suits me, right?"

Jane scoffs. "This is going nowhere."

John holds up a hand. "Ok, let's start over."

Silvey folds her arms across her chest. "Please, enlighten me."

John picks up the paper. "We found this paper, along with your badge inside the control room."

"And," Silvey says.

"Why were you in the control room?" Jane asks.

"You should know," Silvey says, pointing at Jane. "It was you that sent me inside in the first place. I was escorted to a small conference room with a notepad and pencil. I sat there alone until the swirling red light illuminated the hallway. The door to a control room was open when I approached."

"The door was open?" John asks, glancing again at Jane.

Jane shrugs. "And you saw what inside?"

"Seven men in tan uniforms sitting at black and green monitors," Silvey says.

"And?" Jane asks.

"Darkness," Silvey says, pointing to her arm. "I got jabbed in the arm before I wound up in here. Are we done?"

"No," Jane says, slamming her hand on the table.

Silvey blinks but doesn't startle. She just stares Jane down. Silvey asks Jane, "Are you done acting out?"

John smirks and Silvey catches his amusement out of the corner of her eye.

Silvey patiently waits for Jane to answer.

The moment of silence ends with John's sigh.

"Take her back to the holding room," John says. A door behind Silvey opens and two men in matching uniforms walk in. "We're not done Ms. Rhoades."

One of the men reaches for Silvey's arm.

"Touch me and I will punch you in the balls," Silvey says, leaning away.

The man holds up his hand and takes a step back.

Silvey stands and glares at Jane. "By the way, beehives are making a comeback. Bravo."

Jane raises a hand up towards her hair.

Silvey smirks.

"Follow me," the uniform man says.

"Ms. Rhoades," John says as Silvey reaches the threshold.

Silvey turns to look back.

John is walking towards her. He's maybe an inch taller than her. "Your time in the holding cell will be as long as we like, so think long and hard about your cooperation."

"Threaten me again, John," Silvey says. "And the only thing you will get is a fat lawsuit for unlawful detainment. I expect that the list of charges is already quite lengthy." She holds up her red wrists, raw from the handcuffs. "Your funeral."

John nods to the men with her. "Make sure someone stays at her door."

"You'll regret this," Silvey says.

30

Evelyn stands as Buzz walks into the waiting room. "Have you heard?"

"Heard what?" Buzz asks, looking around the room at the vacant, floral padded chairs. "I just got here."

"Silvey slipped back into a coma," Evelyn says. "The doctors are considering postponing the surgery."

"What?" Buzz asks. "She was fine when I left. What the hell happened?"

"She fell asleep," Evelyn says. "And they can't wake her."

"Shit," Buzz says, sitting down on the padded chair. "She seemed great before I left."

Evelyn wipes a tear and sits across from him. "Did the FBI call you?"

"No," Buzz says. "I left my phone with Silvey. Why would the FBI call?"

Evelyn sighs. "They claim that Silvey and the Baxton boy are mixed in some kind of coverup."

Buzz laughs. "And you believed them?"

Evelyn huffs.

"Why are you so quick to throw Silvey under the bus?" Buzz asks. "It's like you're always cheering for the opposing team with our daughter."

"I do not," Evelyn says. "And how dare you question my parenting? At least I show up."

"What the hell is that supposed to mean?" Buzz shouts.

"Whoa," Andrea says from the doorway. "Go to your corners."

Evelyn glares at Andrea.

"Buzz, you can't let her get to you," Andrea says, tapping her chest. "The doctor gave you strict instructions about avoiding stressful situations."

"Of course," Evelyn says, "you will side with him. Just like Silvey."

"Evelyn," Andrea says, stepping into the room. "You know I am here for Silvey. Not to take sides. And I would appreciate it if you two can fill me in on why Silvey can't have visitors."

"She's in a coma," Evelyn says.

"On purpose?" Andrea asks, sitting next to Evelyn.

"No, they are running a few tests now to determine the why," Evelyn says. "And discussing postponing the surgery."

"She was texting me less than two hours ago," Andrea says, pulling out her phone. "How did this happen?"

Evelyn throws up her hands. "I guess you are blaming me?"

"Whoa, why would I do that?" Andrea asks.

"Because I was the last one in to see her," Evelyn says.

"And why would your visit with Silvey put her in a coma?" Buzz asks.

Evelyn stands and walks to the window looking out to the hallway. "They believe Silvey is part of something, and I asked her some questions."

"They who?" Andrea asks, looking at Buzz. He shakes his head.

"The FBI."

"Evelyn," Andrea says. "How could you?"

Evelyn straightens her petite frame to her full height and turns towards them. "They have evidence."

"I was there," Andrea says. "I saw the path of destruction the tornado left in the field that led to Silvey. The only evidence I need is a memory I wish I could forget. People did not survive and your daughter did. Take that for evidence!"

Evelyn turns her back to Andrea and Buzz. "I know but…"

"But nothing," Buzz says, interrupting Evelyn. "She's a victim of a freaking natural disaster."

Evelyn sniffles and walks out of the waiting room.

"Well," Buzz says. "How's my ticker supposed to survive that tornado?" He points to Evelyn retreating to the hall.

"Buzz," Andrea whispers. "I think she's hit a new level of spite."

Buzz laughs.

"I'm going to try to track down Sarah," Andrea says. "Maybe the brain can tell us where Silvey's gone to."

Buzz nods. "I'll be here."

Andrea walks to the counter outside of the ICU. "Hi."

A white-haired volunteer wearing a bright pink vest looks up. "Hi darlin."

"Can you page Dr. Sarah Marvin?" Andrea asks.

"Um, let me check with the operator."

Andrea watches her pick up the desk phone and dials zero.

"Hi, it's Jan, a volunteer. I have a visitor asking to page a Dr. Sarah Marvin." She looks up at Andrea and winks. "Uh huh, sure. Ma'am what's your name?"

"Andrea Meyer."

Jan repeats her name to the operator and hangs up. "The operator has paged Dr. Marvin."

"Thank you," Andrea says. "Where will she return the call?"

"Here at the desk," Jan says, "I can transfer the call to the waiting room across the hall if that's ok?"

Andrea nods. "Thanks again." She walks back into the waiting room.

Buzz is flipping channels on the TV in the corner.

"Any luck?" Buzz asks, watching Andrea sit next to a small table with a phone.

"Hope so," Andrea says. "They paged Sarah and will transfer the call to this phone if she answers."

"Good," Buzz says, leaving the TV on the local news. "Have you seen this?" He points to the TV. A photo of the recovered soldier next to his missing flyer with his photo. "He's barely aged a day. What do you make of that?"

Andrea focuses on the news segment. She shakes her head. "Is this a hoax?"

Buzz shrugs. "It's bizarre. I remember seeing those old flyers around town, but they were eventually lost to the weather."

"Strange," Andrea says.

"We bring you the original news clip from our station." The segment rolls grainy black and white footage of the base from outside a guarded gate and the camera pans to a young reporter. "I'm Roger Finch, live outside the Nike Base where Captain Darryl Wilson was last seen April 5th at a Boy Scout banquet held on the base. He was first reported missing by his wife when he failed to return home after a twenty-four-hour shift. His commanding officer states Captain Wilson is believed to be still on the base and a thorough search of the entire base is underway."

The segment changes to the teary eyes of a woman with her arm around a young boy. A man asks, "Your husband has been missing for six months. And the military has claimed Captain Wilson is officially AWOL. What are your thoughts?"

"My husband is a good man. He loves his job and his country. The idea of him going AWOL is absurd despite what the military says. I know my husband. He would never jeopardize his career or leave us."

Ring

Andrea jumps and picks up the receiver. "Hi! Sarah?"

Buzz mutes the TV.

"Andrea?" Sarah asks.

"Yes, have you heard about Silvey?" Andrea asks, watching the waiting room door swing open.

Evelyn walks into the waiting room.

"Yes," Sarah says. "I am consulting with the team of physicians in about ten minutes to discuss her surgery. How's the family holding up?"

"We would like some clarity on why she was speaking and now in a coma," Andrea says, gesturing to Evelyn to a chair across from her. "I'm going to put you on speaker. One second." She clicks the speaker button on the phone and sits the receiver down. "Alright Sarah, Buzz and Evelyn are here with me."

"Hi," Sarah says. "In Silvey's case we knew that she suffered from a closed head injury and that the swelling had receded during her medically induced coma. We believe that her time awake may have been too much too soon."

"Can a stressful conversation make the brain swell?" Buzz asks, glaring at Evelyn's red puffy eyes.

"The body has a way of protecting itself," Sarah says, "and I have to believe that Silvey's brain just may have needed a little time out."

"What does this mean for her surgery?" Andrea asks.

"Her coma doesn't add any risks to the surgery we proposed this morning and she's already provided consent. But we are running a few tests now to rule out any other cause of her sudden coma."

"Thanks Sarah," Andrea says. "We are here in the waiting room. Please, just let us know when you do."

"I'll stop by and give you and the family the decision in less than an hour," Sarah says.

156

31

Baxton paces the porch going over the details from the library archives on his phone. Captain Wilson's disappearance was a headline for six months, until the government pulled the rug out and said he left on his own. Only one article offered a different opinion from an anonymous writer in a letter to the editor.

Dear Editor,

I believe the military is covering up the disappearance of Captain Wilson and a possible connection to an imposter intercepted on the evening of the scout banquet. I overheard Captain Wilson and another uniformed man discussing a suspicious man that arrived late with a young man not wearing a scout uniform. And later watched two men escort the suspicious man away with Captain Wilson. But they failed to report that the man in question was found dead in an old, abandoned car near Crooked Creek. I recognized the sketch of the man printed in this paper a week after the banquet.

The Ray County Sherriff's department were asking for the public's help to identify the man. I called to report what I saw and overheard the night of the banquet, but I never saw anything until last week. The body was identified as Hans Gobert, a brother of a Nazi officer tried and executed for his crimes. Hans had been suspected of spying on other bases across the country before he was found dead near Elmira. So, I ask you kind, lovely readers. The night one of our own goes missing is the night that a man suspected of spying with ties back to Nazi Germany is last seen with Captain Wilson. Coincidence?

Sincerely,
Anonymous

Baxton searches for the name Hans Gobert in the archives and finds one sentence in an article from the Ray County Coroner. *The remains of the unknown man found in an abandon car south of Elmira near the Crooked Creek was identified as Hans Gobert.* He searches for the terms 'Ray County Sherriff' and the word 'help' for the month of April in 1962 and finds the sketch of the man in the third result.

"It's him," Bax whispers, pacing the length of the porch.

Gage pulls up to the house and hops out of the truck.

"The man at the gate…" Bax immediately dials Silvey, but it goes straight to voicemail.

"Are you wearing the stain off the porch?" Gage asks, stepping up on the porch.

Baxton stops and turns towards Gage. He lowers his phone. "Hey."

"Dude, you don't look so good," Gage says, rushing towards Baxton. "What's happened?"

Baxton swipes the screen on his phone and holds up the black and white sketch. "I saw him."

"Let's go inside and talk," Gage says, assessing Baxton. "Your face is ghost white and sweaty."

Baxton nods and follows Gage inside.

"Gage?" Rozanne calls after the screen door slams shut behind Baxton. "I thought I heard your truck."

"Yes, ma'am," Gage says, hanging his keys on the wall just inside the front door.

"Did you convince Bax to come inside?" Rozanne asks, emerging from the hallway.

"Here," Baxton says, holding up a hand.

"Good," Rozanne says. "Andrea called and there is news about Silvey."

Baxton drops his phone. It thwacks against the hardwood floor. "What?"

Gage bends and scoops up Baxton's phone. He assesses the crack free screen and hands it back to Baxton. "Lucky it's intact."

"Have a seat," Rozanne says, gesturing towards the couch.

Baxton rounds the couch and sits on the edge. His knee bounces as he watches Gage kiss Rozanne on the cheek before he sits on the other end of the couch opposite of Baxton.

Rozanne sits her phone down on the dark wood coffee table. "Andrea wanted Bax to know that Silvey slipped into a coma this afternoon."

"No," Baxton says, shaking his head. He stands. "She's trapped there. I know it."

"What are you talking about?" Gage asks.

"She remembered everything I told you about. She was there. I believe that she could be in serious danger."

"But she's still in the ICU, right?" Gage asks, turning towards Rozanne.

"Yes, and they are still proceeding with the surgery this evening," Rozanne says. "The injury to her lower spine needs immediate intervention."

"No, it's not safe," Bax says, walking towards the kitchen.

"Slow down," Gage says, following Bax. "Can you explain what you mean?"

Bax picks up the pain pills and opens the bottle. "Silvey and I were there. It's real. And the sketch of the man proves it."

"What sketch?" Rozanne asks, wrapping her arm around Gage.

"Hans Gobert was there," Baxton says, tipping out four pills. "He was driving the truck."

Rozanne steps forward and places her hand over the pills. "What are you doing with these?"

"Silvey thinks that drugs have an effect on our time there," Baxton says. "I haven't taken anything for pain since I've been home. I have to try!"

Rozanne shakes her head. "Bax, take a breath."

"And tell us about the Hans fellow," Gage says.

Baxton sighs. "I've been researching that time period since my conversation with Silvey. And there was an incident with Hans the night Captain Wilson went missing."

"Backup, the Captain Wilson they found in the field?" Gage asks, turning towards the table and picking up the newspaper. He hands it to Rozanne and points to the picture of Captain Wilson.

"Yes, and the same man Silvey spoke to before the siren went off," Baxton says. "He was last seen escorting Hans away from a boy scout banquet that they held on the base."

"Ok," Rozanne says. "But the captain is alive and well now, so why is Silvey in danger?"

"After I vanished the lights came back on and she found a research lab for a nuclear fusion reactor," Baxton says. "And they took Silvey."

"But she's not really there," Rozanne says. "She's safe at the hospital."

"You don't get it," Bax says. "She's jumping every time she's unconscious."

"Whoa," Gage says. "You think she's leaping what... time?"

"How else do we explain everything that happened?" Bax asks, throwing back his hand full of pills.

"Wait!" Rozanne says, dropping the paper and lunging towards Bax.

He steps to the side barely missing Rozanne. He picks up a bottle of water from the counter and chugs.

"You idiot," Gage says. "Do we need to take him to the ER and have his stomach pumped?"

"No," Bax says, glaring at Gage. "I'll be in bed until I find her."

Baxton charges past Rozanne and Gage. He slams the door to the room a second later, taps the back of his head to the door, and slides to the floor. *What the hell did I just do?* He crawls over to the bed and climbs on top of the covers. *Rozanne's going to kick my ass in the morning.*

"Shit," Gage says. "What do we do now?"

"Pray that idiot wakes up in six to eight hours," Rozanne says.

"Is it safe?" Gage asks as Rozanne picks up the bottle and inspects the label.

"He basically took a dose that will tranquilize him," Rozanne says, capping the bottle and hiding it in a cabinet behind a can of peas. "But we aren't letting him do that again. I'll take them with me to work tomorrow morning and have Monroe dispose of them."

"Do you think we should call Monroe?" Gage asks.

"No, I'll check on Bax in a few hours and make sure he is still breathing and has a pulse."

"What do you make of all of this?" Gage asks, pointing to the newspaper.

"Bax seems very sure that he was there with Silvey," Rozanne says, shrugging. "And I can't judge him after my own paranormal experience."

32

Evelyn stands up when Sarah, dressed in green scrubs, walks into the waiting room.

"We've got Silvey prepped for surgery," Sarah says, holding up her hands. "I'll scrub out and give you guys an update in about four hours."

"And your team thinks this is safe?" Evelyn asks.

Sarah nods. "We have every confidence that moving forward to protect Silvey's spine is the next step to her recovery."

"If she wakes up," Evelyn mutters.

"Your negative attitude is not helping," Buzz says.

Andrea stands. "I'll walk Sarah out." She mouths the words *simmer down* to Buzz.

He shrugs and turns his back away from Evelyn.

"Damn," Sarah whispers, closing the door to the waiting room. "They really don't like each other."

"Understatement of the century," Andrea says. "Ringleader in this fight is not a pleasant task, either. I get why Silvey complained so much about her mother now."

Sarah chuckles. "Well, the good news, Silvey's brain appears strong and we have a great team assigned to her case."

Andrea hugs Sarah. "Thank you!"

"Best of luck with those two," Sarah says, releasing her.

"I'm about to call Scott and have him bring me wine," Andrea says.

"Be sure to disguise it in something other than a bottle," Sarah says, winking and walking away. "I'd hate to break hospital policy."

Andrea salutes Sarah. "Good to know." She slowly opens the door to the waiting room. "Are you two good here for a while?"

Buzz nods.

Evelyn looks up from her phone. "I'm fine."

"I'm heading down to my car to fetch my bag and call Scott," Andrea says. "He's heading this way in about an hour. Is there anything you need?"

"Not unless he can sneak in a cold six pack," Buzz says.

"Seriously!" Evelyn spats.

"Evelyn," Andrea says. "What about you?"

Evelyn flares her nostrils. "I'm fine."

"Noted. Be back in twenty." Andrea closes the door and walks to the counter. A new volunteer in a pink vest looks up. Andrea spots her name tag. "Hi Doris, if you hear any shouting in there I would advise to um, let it play out and not try to intervene."

"Oh?" Doris asks, raising an eyebrow. "Do I need to call security?"

Andrea laughs. "Not unless they are a magical marriage counselor or priest."

Doris frowns.

"Silvey's parents had a recent and very bitter divorce. They do not do well in the presence of one another."

Doris nods. "Got it. Thanks for the warning."

"I'll be back in less than thirty minutes," Andrea says, tapping the desk and walking towards the elevator. She presses the down arrow and checks her phone. "Five minutes to seven, so eleven before we hear anything."

The elevator door opens.

A man steps to the side. "Going down?"

Andrea nods and steps inside. "Lobby please."

The man presses the 'L' button and reaches a hand inside his jacket. He pulls out a billfold and unfolds it.

Andrea catches the shiny glint of a badge. She looks the man over from head to toe. He's wearing all black and has a military high and tight buzz cut.

The elevator slows on level two and stops. The doors don't open.

The man turns to Andrea and holds up his badge. "Mrs. Meyer, we spoke earlier. I'm Agent Carlton with the FBI. We need to ask you a few more questions about your relationship with Ms. Rhoades."

"Hell no," Andrea says, stepping around him and pressing the open door button. "I'm not being cornered in a damn elevator for this conversation."

The doors slide open, and a woman blocks Andrea's exit.

"Excuse me," Andrea says, attempting to walk past her, but she steps in her path. The woman holds up a badge. "Do you have any idea what unlawful detainment is?"

"Let's go, Mrs. Meyer," agent Carlton says, grabbing Andrea's arm just above her elbow.

"Get your hands off of me!" Andrea shouts.

The agent releases his grip and gestures to the open elevator door. "We have a room down the hall. We only need a few minutes of your time."

"Not unless I have my lawyer present," Andrea says.

"It's not that kind of conversation," agent Carlton says.

"You're detaining me without cause and without my permission," Andrea says, folding her arms across her chest. "Tell me what kind of conversation makes you trap a person inside an elevator?"

"Opportunistic," the female agent says.

"Who do you think you are?" Andrea says, pointing her finger in the woman's face.

The woman holds up her badge level with Andrea's face. "Agent Michelle Vickers."

Andrea glares at Agent Vickers.

"We have new information," agent Carlton says. "We just need to confirm a few details."

The elevator door is beeping. A man wearing a hospital badge approaches the elevator.

"Sir, I am being harassed by these two people," Andrea says, widening her eyes. "Can you please escort me down to the lobby?"

The man pushes by Agent Vickers.

Vickers glares at Andrea.

"You two can take the stairs," the man says, gesturing Agent Carlton to the hallway.

Agent Carlton steps out into the hall next to Agent Vickers as the door slides shut.

"Thank you!" Andrea says. "You have no idea how long I was stuck there."

"I'm sorry," the man says, touching his badge. "I'm Donnie Connors, a hospital administrator. I'll be sure to have those two escorted out by security. We have a zero-tolerance policy for that kind of behavior."

"I appreciate it, Donnie," Andrea says.

The door dings and the elevator doors slide open.

"Have a great evening," Donnie says, holding his arm across the threshold as Andrea exits.

"You too," Andrea says, crossing the lobby in long strides. She pushes open the door and sighs. The evening air is muggy but comforting after her icy encounter with the agents. She walks over to the parking garage and opts for the stairs. She dials Scott clearing the last step.

"Hey hun," Scott answers.

"Hey, how are you?" Andrea asks, stopping at the trunk of her car.

"Almost got the overnight bag packed," Scott says. "I was just about to call to make sure you had everything you needed."

Andrea pops her trunk and reaches inside for her tote but pauses when she catches sight of a person walking towards her. She slams the trunk closed and walks to her passenger side, opens the door, slides in, shuts, and locks the door.

"Are you there?" Scott asks.

"Um something odd is going on." Andrea checks her mirrors for any sign of the person passing her car. "I was just accosted in an elevator by two FBI agents with questions about Silvey."

"What? Why?"

"From what I've pieced together," Andrea says, turning to look at a car pulling through. "They are convinced that Silvey has something to do with the appearance of that soldier they found after the tornado."

"That's absurd," Scott says.

A minivan parks in the spot across from Andrea. "I know. They have Evelyn convinced that Silvey's injuries couldn't be from the tornado and that she was staged in the field."

"Evil Evelyn," Scott mutters.

"Scott, we agreed to forget that nickname." Andrea smiles watching a man attempt to unfold a stroller.

"Sorry," Scott says. "Do you think there's any substance to their claim?"

"Absolutely not," Andrea says, unlocking her doors. "Can you bring my water bottle? I think I left it on the dresser."

"Got it," Scott says. "And what else?"

"Fill said water bottle with wine," Andrea says.

"Andrea," Scott says.

"Red please, there should be a bottle from the Albanian vineyard."

"You're serious?" Scott asks.

"Very," Andrea says. "The passive aggression in that room has quickly moved past passive and I need some liquid courage to sit front row to that drama shit show."

"Ah, ok."

"And feel free to go heavy on the snacks," Andrea says, stepping out of the car. She looks up and down the row as the family across from her ambles out of their van and the man clicks a car seat into the stroller. She smiles and gives a thumb up to the man wiping away sweat from his brow.

He shakes his head. "It's never easy."

Andrea pops the trunk and shoulders her tote. "True."

"True, what?" Scott asks.

"Oh nothing," Andrea says. "Are you ready to go now?"

"Um, not unless you have a corkscrew hidden in the wine cellar."

"The kitchen's gone," Andrea says, thumping the heel of her hand to her forehead.

"Yea," Scott says.

"Can you pick one up with the snacks?" Andrea says, taking the steps.

"I want snacks!" a kid yells.

"Shit," Andrea whispers.

"What's wrong?" Scott asks.

"I mentioned the word snack a little too close to a small family waiting for the elevator. One of the kids is now begging his dad for a snack."

"Smooth," Scott says. "Stick to the stairs. I'll see you in an hour."

"Drive safe," Andrea says, poking her head out the exit. She looks left and right before she emerges from the parking garage. "Love you."

"Love you too," Scott says.

33

Silvey slumps onto a hard metal cot. "What could they possibly think I did to deserve a tiny room that smells like wet feet?"

She hears the officer outside the door cough to hide a laugh.

"Don't worry I'm here all night at this rate," Silvey says. She's met with a wall of silence. "What's green but smells like red paint?"

Silvey taps the side of the cot. "Oh, come on… green paint."

The officer laughs.

"Why did the donkey say hee haw?" Silvey asks, inspecting the bare walls. "Because he's haw-ngry."

The officer clears their throat.

"Ah, I see, not into farm jokes." She stands and moves closer to the door. "Why aren't there any insects on an Army base?" She taps on the door. "I can hear the wheel spinning."

"Because it's a no-fly zone," the officer says.

Silvey laughs. "Bravo!"

The officer laughs. "You're terrible at comedy. Don't quit your day job."

"Would you believe me if I said I was an electrical contractor and have my own business?" Silvey asks, flicking on and off the light switch.

The officer laughs harder. "Ok, ok, maybe you are a comedian."

Silvey sighs. "Why did you join the army?"

"I didn't," the officer says. "I am part of the Secret Service."

"Why would a secret service officer be assigned guard duty for a civilian?" Silvey asks.

"You still deny your involvement with the traitor?" the officer asks.

"I don't believe he is a traitor. You and your team have a serious case of misinformation."

"Hmm," the officer says. "I seriously doubt that."

"Oh yea?" Silvey asks. "Why do you think two civilians randomly appeared in a section of the base that requires special clearance?"

"My theory," the officer says. "You were the Patsy to distract the captain while the Nazi got away."

"Nazi?" Silvey steps away from the door. "You're joking, right?"

"I would never joke about that," the officer says.

"Well, it's wrong," Silvey says. "All of this is wrong."

"If you say so," the officer says.

Silvey paces the three steps from the cot to the wall and back. "Can I ask you one more bizarre question?"

"Maybe," the officer says, fighting a yawn.

"What month and year is it?" Silvey asks.

"April 1962."

"Interesting."

"Jones!" a man shouts.

"Yes, sir!" the officer says.

"Are you speaking to the witness?"

"No, sir," the officer says.

Silvey steps closer to the door. She whispers, "Liar."

The officer kicks the door. "She's running her mouth, sir."

"You realize your voice echoes down here," the man says.

"Sorry sir! It won't happen again."

Silvey laughs. "Now who's the one in trouble."

The door rattles with another kick.

Silvey knocks on the door. "Knock, knock."

"Zip it," the officer whispers.

"Are you going to play along?" Silvey asks.

"I said be quiet," the officer says.

"Who's there?" Silvey asks, lowering her tone to match the officer. "Tank."

She puts her hands on her hips and puffs out her chest. "Tank who?" she asks, mimicking him again.

"You're welcome." Silvey chuckles.

The light overhead brightens and then pops bathing her in darkness. The light under the door goes dark.

"Did we lose power?" Silvey asks, trying the switch again. "It looked like a power surge." She bangs on the door. "Hello!" She presses her ear to the door. *Don't panic.*

Woo-woo-woo-woo-woo

Silvey covers her ears with both hands and backs away from the door. *What is happening!* She lifts one hand and sighs when the only sound she can hear is her own breath.

"Is anyone out there?" Silvey asks, feeling her way to the door.

"Silvey?" a man asks.

"Yes," Silvey answers, "who are you?"

"Bax."

"No, no, no," Silvey says. "I'm hallucinating."

"No," Bax says, opening the door.

Silvey steps away from the door. She assesses the tall dark outline filling the doorframe. "You're really physically here?"

"Yes," Bax says, reaching a hand towards her. "But blind as a bat."

Silvey sidesteps his hand. "I can't see you. How do I know it's really you?"

"Midge," Bax whispers.

Silvey reaches her hand out towards his hand. The connection pops with a charge of static. "But how?"

"Drugs," Bax says.

"What?" Silvey whispers.

"Andrea called," Bax says. "And told Roz you fell back into a coma. I didn't want you to be back here alone."

"Bax, you took drugs to find me?" Silvey asks.

"Uh, yes," Bax says. "I know it sounds nuts…"

"Nuts dude… that's insane," Silvey says. "How did you even know it would work?"

"I didn't," Bax says. "But after I found out that it was all real…"

"Wait what?" Silvey asks, squeezing his hand.

"The man I let on this base was Hans Gobert," Bax says. "I found his sketch in the newspaper archives after the date on the paper I found inside the guard shack."

"It's real?" Silvey whispers.

"It was very real and Gobert had ties back to Nazi Germany."

"Shut up!" Silvey says, releasing his hand.

"There's more," Bax says.

"Do you think it's safe to talk about this here?" Silvey asks.

"I think we're alone," Bax says, looking over his shoulder. "I still can't see a thing, but I didn't pass anyone in the hallway."

"There was a man guarding this door right before the lights and the siren went off," Silvey says. "Did you hear the siren?"

"No," Bax says, reaching for her hand again.

She grasps his hand.

"Let's see if we can find a way out."

"That didn't end so well last time," Silvey says. "Maybe we should just wait and hide."

"Silvey," Bax says, leaning close to her. "The last time anyone saw Captain Wilson before he was declared missing, he had an encounter with Gobert." He takes a breath and rushes his next sentence. "And Gobert was found dead in a car up near the Crooked Creek."

"Hold up," Silvey says. "Do you think that Captain Wilson had something to do with his death?"

"I can't say I know enough to make that assumption," Bax says.

"The two people interrogating me were surprised I had a run in with Captain Wilson," Silvey says. "Like it wasn't possible."

"You think he was already declared missing?" Bax asks.

"Maybe?" Silvey taps her finger against his palm. "Let's assume the captain was missing before we arrived."

"The timeline adds up because Gobert was definitely not questioned after I saw him at the gate," Bax says. "The shots started right after his arrival, so it couldn't be the same night with Captain Wilson."

"Exactly," Silvey says.

Bax chuckles. "Conspiracy theory number two. Hans Gobert was a spy and his first appearance on base was a scouting mission to get a lay of the land."

"But Captain Wilson could identify him," Silvey says. "And we know for sure he was down here the same night. So was Gobert the distraction while the Captain took something of value? Maybe from the lab?"

"A good theory," Bax says. "But why show up sixty years later?"

Silvey sighs. She taps Bax's chest. "Why us?"

Bax shakes his head. "I still haven't figured out why we are connected to this place and time?"

"Did you research anything about a time paradox?" Silvey asks. "Or the Scylla thing?"

"Time paradox, no," Bax says. "But the reactor was real, but I found nothing to connect it to the base or the military."

"The FBI thinks we are involved in our time," Silvey says, "and they think we are involved in this time. What do they have that ties us to this?"

Bax places something plastic in her hand. "I know you can't see this, but we're wearing laminated name badges."

"But they've met both of us," Silvey says. "They can obviously see we weren't born before 1962."

"Silvey, our names are now tied to the Nike Base because of the tornado, and maybe this tripped a red flag?"

"That's a stretch," Silvey says.

"Do you remember a movie where a nuclear alarm goes off and a family locks themselves in a bunker?" Bax asks.

"The guy from the mummy was in it, right?" Silvey asks.

"Yes!" Bax says. "What if Wilson locked himself inside a bunker and the tornado impacted the locks?"

"Oh, that's interesting." Silvey smiles. "What if it's not a bunker... the reactor was tethered to that white room." Silvey snaps. "What if it's a time traveling chamber?"

Bax whistles. "Are we high?"

"Probably," Silvey says. "What do we do now?"

A red flashing light whirls in the hallway, and the siren starts again.

Woo-woo-woo-woo-woo

Bax steps behind the door leaving it open just a crack.

Silvey holds her hands over her ears and watches the red-light flash over Bax's curly hair.

Bax turns to look at Silvey and his mouth falls open.

"What?" Silvey asks, dropping her hands.

The siren stopped.

He points at her face. "You're fading."

Silvey looks down. The blue dress she'd been wearing has been replaced with a blue checkered hospital gown. She peeks under the gown and hugs her chest. *Why am I naked!*

"What the..." Silvey whispers, holding the gown closed in the back.

Bax shrugs.

Beep, beep, beep

"Do you hear that?" Silvey asks, looking past Bax into the hall.

"Hear what?" Bax asks.

"A soft beeping sound," Silvey says.

"No," Bax says. "But now that we can see." He points to the red flashing light in the hall. "Let's make a run for it."

"In this?" Silvey pinches the thin fabric.

Bax looks down at his long sleeve shirt and quickly takes it off.

Silvey's mouth instantly dries out and she gulps a little too loud. Bax grins and tosses her the shirt, blinding her view of his long, lean bare torso and sculpted arms. Silvey slides on his shirt over her gown, and it falls to her mid-thigh.

Bax laughs.

"Thanks." Silvey waves the floppy end of the long sleeve hanging several inches past her hand. "How tall are you?"

"Just over six five."

"That checks," Silvey says, rolling up the sleeves to free her hands.

"Are you good barefoot?" Bax asks.

"Yes," Silvey says, inspecting her bare feet. "Ready?"

Bax nods and checks the hall. "Do you know which way you came from?"

"From the right," Silvey says, following him out of the room and into the hall.

"Let's hope the left is the right decision," Bax says.

34

Andrea stands when Scott enters the waiting room.

"Hi, I've got snacks," Scott says, handing the bag of snacks to Buzz and the water bottle to Andrea. He winks.

Andrea sighs and takes a long sip.

Scott chuckles. "All good? Any word?"

Andrea shakes her head. "We should get an update in about an hour or so."

Scott rests his laptop bag on a chair and looks around the room. "Is it just us three?"

"Evelyn stepped out to use the restroom and another family just left."

Scott nods. "Buzz, how are you doing?"

"Better now, without the cloud of suffocation hovering over us and you brought hot tamales."

Evelyn clears her throat. "Isn't he lovely?"

Buzz smirks and turns his attention towards the box of candy.

"Hi, Evelyn," Scott says.

"Hi," Evelyn answers.

Andrea picks up the bag. "Scott brought us snacks. Take a look."

Evelyn shakes her head. "No, thank you. Zero appetite when I am stressed."

"Well, I come with community news," Scott says.

"Oh?" Evelyn asks.

"The Red Cross volunteers are pulling out tomorrow since everyone affected by the tornado have safe accommodations and the missing were located and identified." Scott nods to the television in the corner. "And there is a piece about the missing soldier they found on the news tonight. They were talking about a news anchor they flew in from New York City at the Dollar General."

"You mean our little town is about to make national headlines?" Buzz asks.

"Where have you been?" Evelyn scoffs. "It's been national news all week."

Buzz glares at her.

Andrea takes another long sip.

"Did they say what channel?" Buzz asks, holding up the remote.

"Channel five I think," Scott says.

Buzz flips the channel to five and turns up the volume. An old rerun of Big Bang Theory plays on mute. "All set." Buzz places the remote on the small table beside him. "I'm going to go get my recommended steps in."

Evelyn rolls her eyes.

"See you in a bit," Andrea says, opening a bag of chips.

Scott opens his bag and hands Andrea a stack of papers. "I printed off the bids. Do you want to go over them while we wait?"

"Sure," Andrea says after swallowing a chip. "Did you like the contractor this afternoon?"

"He seems pretty reasonable, but I am concerned about the distance. His crew and him live in Stanberry or near there, and that's a long drive to make every day."

"True, but I liked that they had almost every trade under one company so minimal sub-contracting will be required. And their work has some excellent reviews from all over the KC

176

metro area and even a few in Omaha. They work a long distance from home pretty often. I don't think we should exclude them because of the distance."

"I have a client that drives down from Stanberry every six weeks," Evelyn says. "I can give her a call if you want a local's opinion."

Andrea smiles. "Thanks Evelyn, I'll let you know."

"Happy to help somebody for a change," Evelyn says.

Scott smiles. "Does your client mind the drive?"

"I don't think so," Evelyn says. "She works down at the Elm's a few days a week. She makes the trip this way pretty often."

"Ah, it can't be too bad, right?" Andrea asks, looking over at Scott.

"I'll put them at the top of the list," Scott says. "We have one more bid from some freelance guys from the city."

Andrea goes over each line item and pauses over one item. "Why is there a tub install listed on page two?"

"You said you wanted a longer tub and if we are already going to have people there working," Scott says. "Why wait and get the place messy twice?"

"Good man," Evelyn says, pointing to Andrea's slack jaw. "He's a keeper. I never did understand why Silvey disliked you."

"Evelyn!" Andrea says.

Scott laughs. "Silvey didn't dislike me. She hated my best friend that came with me everywhere. And nobody is ever good enough for your best friend, right?"

Evelyn's cheeks crimson in an instant. She turns her attention back to her phone.

Andrea takes another swig of the wine from the water bottle and shakes her head. She resumes careful inspection of the itemized bid and hands it back to Scott. "I really think it's all pretty reasonable. But Silvey suggested I have Buzz look over the quotes for electrical."

"Did you say my name?" Buzz says, walking over to Andrea.

"We had a few bids for the house," Andrea says. "Can you look over the electrical on this one?" She takes the contract back from Scott and hands it to Buzz.

"Sure thing," Buzz says, pulling out a pair of glasses from his shirt pocket. He flips through the contract and reads a section. Then flips back to the first page. "Silvey's worked with these guys before. I think she said the electrician is a female too. And the numbers are spot on if not a little low."

Andrea smiles. "Thanks Buzz."

Scott points to the television. "Turn it up."

Buzz picks up the remote and adjusts the volume.

"Tonight, we bring you a live exclusive interview with New York City Good News anchor Evan Rigley and Army Air Captain Darryl Wilson, who was found during the search for survivors of the deadly tornado that hit Lawson earlier this week."

The camera turns to Captain Wilson. He's wearing a dark navy polo shirt and jeans. His salt and pepper beard is trimmed and tidy.

"Thank you for agreeing to our interview," Evan says from off camera. The captain nods and pulls at his collar. "Can you please tell our viewers your name and where you are from?"

"My name is Captain Darryl Wilson, and I had a small farm in Rayville, Missouri."

The camera stays on Wilson, but Evan asks another question, "And you served what branch of the military?"

"Army Air Defense Command was my last post." Visible beads of sweat roll down Wilson's face.

The camera cuts to Evan for the first time. He flashes a wide, bright white smile and leans forward in his chair. "And when was that?"

The camera pans back over to Captain Wilson. The beads of sweat are gone, but the man's face falls pale. "I served from 1959 to 1962."

"But sir, you are clearly not even fifty."

Captain Wilson nods. "I am thirty-nine."

Evan chuckles. "You can see why some are speculating that you are not who you say you are. How do you explain your absence for the last sixty years and without aging a day?"

Captain Wilson clears his throat. "I was born in Cameron, Missouri on September 2, 1923. My parents were Robert and Caroline Wilson. My father died in a work accident when I was twelve and my mother died two years later. The doctors said her heart gave out."

"You were an orphan by the age of fourteen," Evan asks off camera.

"Yes, sir."

"Who took you in?" Evan asks.

"My neighbors Anita and Thomas had a boy my age, Rupert. I bunked up with Rupert. I worked on their farm until I turned eighteen and could sign up for the service."

"And that's when you started your military career?" Evan asks.

"Yes, sir. Right in the middle of World War II."

"And were you part of the fight overseas?"

"No sir, I completed training two days after the Pearl Harbor invasion. I received orders to work at a command post at Camp McKinley."

"As in Hawaii, correct?" Evan asks.

"Yes, sir."

"And that is where you met your wife, Virginia?" Evan asks.

"Yes, we connected over the early death of our parents, and she became a widow due to the events of December 7th."

"Her first husband served in the US Navy," Evan says.

"Yes, sir."

"And she also died?" Evan asks.

"Yes," Captain Wilson says, adverting his eyes away from the camera. "During the birth of my daughter, Silvey. Neither made it."

Evelyn gasps.

Andrea and Scott glance at each other and Buzz shifts in his chair to hide his face.

"That is tragic," Evan says. "You survived the death of your family twice over. That is enough to drive anyone away from their duties."

Captain Wilson looks up with a frown. "What do you mean?"

"You deserted your military service," Evan says.

"I did no such thing!" Captain Wilson shouts.

The camera pans over to Evan.

"According to the service record for Darryl Wilson," Evan says, holding up a piece of paper. The camera cuts to a clear copy of a DD553 form. The camera cuts back to Captain Wilson holding and reading the piece of paper.

"No, this isn't right," Captain Wilson says, shaking his head and the paper. "Where did you get this?"

"From your second wife," Evan says.

Captain Wilson's eyes widen. "Millie's alive?"

"Yes," Evan says. "She's at a care facility in St. Joseph."

"And my son, Gabriel.

"I'm sorry," Evan says. "He died nine years ago."

Captain Wilson stands.

"Whoa," Evan says. "We've got a few more questions."

"Not anymore," Captain Wilson says, tearing off the microphone and tossing it at Evan.

The broadcast shifts back to the local anchors. "And now for this week' s forecast." The news cuts to the weather.

"Wow," Evelyn says. "That's going to be one hell of a reunion."

"That's going to keep people talking," Buzz says, shaking out a hot tamale.

"I hope that he finds his wife before the media swarms her," Andrea says.

"Um, too late," Scott says, turning his phone towards Andrea. "There's a video going viral of an old woman sitting down with Evan that they released online just before the interview with Captain Wilson."

"That's awful," Andrea says. "And such an invasion of privacy." Her own phone vibrates. She hands Scott back his phone and checks hers. "It's Rozanne. I'll be right back." She stands and swipes to answer the call. "Hi Rozanne."

"Hi Andrea," Rozanne says. "How's it going?"

"We're still waiting on an update," Andrea says. "Did you happen to watch the news just now?"

"That's kind of what I was calling about," Rozanne says. "Did Silvey get a chance to talk to you before she went back into a coma?"

"A little, why?" Andrea asks.

"Bax has a wild theory that they've shared this experience at the base while they were in a coma," Rozanne says. "Including a run in with Captain Wilson."

"Whoa, wait a minute," Andrea says. "The man that was just on the news?"

"Yep," Rozanne says. "And Bax did something really stupid after I told him that Silvey slipped back into a coma."

"Oh no," Andrea whispers.

"Silvey told him that she's gone back to the scene after she woke up because of the medication they have her on," Rozanne says and sighs. "Bax is fine and sleeping, but he took a few too many of his discharge pain medications."

"Why?" Andrea asks.

"To get back to Silvey," Rozanne says.

"Shit, seriously," Andrea says, looking over her shoulder at the volunteer at the desk. "Sorry."

"Yes," Rozanne says. "I'm not sure how much of his story is real, but Gage said the FBI stopped by here today."

"They've been in contact with me and Silvey's family," Andrea says. "I was accosted by two agents a few hours ago here at the hospital."

"I don't understand how they are connected," Rozanne says. "But keep us updated on Silvey. I don't care how late it is."

"Deal, and if Bax wakes up between now and then," Andrea says. "I want to speak with him immediately."

"Deal," Rozanne says. "Talk soon."

Andrea sighs and walks back into the waiting room to three anxious faces. "Evelyn."

"What's happened?" Evelyn asks.

"I need you to tell us everything that the FBI agent told you about Silvey and Baxton," Andrea says. "And don't leave a detail out."

"Seriously?" Buzz asks.

Andrea holds up a hand. "Not a word until she tells us what she knows."

Buzz folds his arms across his chest and leans back in the chair. "Aye captain."

"Start talking," Andrea says.

"A man by the name of Agent Carlton called me earlier today," Evelyn says. "He started the conversation off with minor questions. How long has Silvey been working at the base? Does she bring anything from the job site home? Has she ever discussed the site?"

"And your answers?" Andrea asks.

"Almost three months, not that I know of and no, Silvey barely speaks to me about work."

"What else?" Andrea asks.

"Agent Carlton spun a tale that Baxton and Silvey founds something at the base and that in order to cover up their discovery they staged the injuries."

Andrea rolls her eyes. "That's ridiculous on so many levels."

"I know," Evelyn says, holding up a hand. "But they claim to have evidence that ties Baxton and Silvey to a location on the base that is far from the vertical farm."

"Stuff was flying around and appeared miles away," Buzz says. "How do they know it's not just their work gear that got sucked up and put down somewhere else?"

"I don't know," Evelyn says. "But they were really anxious to speak to Silvey and insisted on knowing the second she woke up."

"You told them she was awake?" Buzz asks, pointing a finger at her.

"It was the FBI, Buzz!" Evelyn says.

"What the…" Buzz says, shaking his head and holding his chest. "I can't believe you would throw her to the wolves without even having a conversation with our daughter first."

Evelyn throws her hands up. "I'm not perfect. Sue me."

"Alright, let's calm down a moment," Andrea says, standing between Buzz and Evelyn.

"Why are you asking about this now?" Scott asks.

"Rozanne just called," Andrea says. "Bax believes that Silvey had an encounter with Captain Wilson while she was here in a coma."

"That's insane," Buzz says. "Hell, are you going to tell me that unicorns are real too?"

"Just the messenger," Andrea says, slumping down into the chair next to Scott. She pops the top of the water bottle and swallows the last of the wine. She frowns as she shakes it.

"It only fit half the bottle," Scott whispers. "But I did pick up a few of these." He opens up his bag and pulls out a family size red bag of peanut butter candy. "But I have a close second."

Andrea grins. "You really get me."

Scott winks and hands her the bag.

35

"Silvey?" Bax whispers, looking behind him. The swirling red light shows nothing but a long, narrow hallway. "Where did you go?"

Bax turns, runs back, and stops at the open door. "Silvey!" *Where did she go?*

Bax steps back out into the hall and runs to the right. He slows at a cracked door and listens while trying to catch his breath.

"If Captain Wilson is back," a man says. "We need to send him an update."

"Him who?" Bax whispers.

"And if she's right about her timeline," the woman says. "We have to turn off the reactor."

Bax gasps and quickly covers his mouth. He inches away from the door.

"Hey!" a man shouts from the far end of the hall. "Hands in the air!"

A man dressed in a military uniform emerges from the room close to Bax. He takes one look up at Bax and reaches for his sidearm.

Bax turns and sprints down the hall.

"Stop!"

"Get him!"

"Call all units!"

Bax ignores the shouts behind him and takes the first turn he finds. He spots a ladder midway up the wall and leaps up. He grasps a wrung and scrambles up past the flashes of the red swirling light.

A group of men turn the corner with their weapons drawn and flashlights out.

Bax hides in the shadows and holds his breath as they pass under him. He continues to climb when the men below are no longer visible. He stops at a metal cover, and he pushes against it. It creaks loudly on the second shove and flies open. He pulls up on the edge and pokes his head up. The surrounding grass is overgrown, but he spots a fence line off to his right. *Dodge and weave, Auburn. Your life depends on it.* He climbs up and kneels.

The cool night air hits his bare torso—an instant chill prickles his skin. He shakes it off and listens before moving. He moves at a slant to the right, then back to the left. He keeps as low as his tall frame allows and the fence line in clear view.

Woo, woo, woo, woo

The ground shakes.

Bax drops to his belly and covers his ears.

"Bax!"

Bax opens his eyes and stares at the grain of a wood floor. He rolls to his right and stares up at Gage. "What happened?"

"You just army crawled out of your bedroom," Gage says, squatting to his level. "Bad dream?"

"No, well, yes," Bax says, pushing himself up and leaning his back against the wall. "But I found Silvey, but then she vanished, and I was chased."

"Bax," Gage says.

"I can't believe I left her again!" Bax says, tapping the back of his head against the wall.

"Dude," Gage says, shaking Bax's shoulders. "Roz just got a call. Silvey's out of surgery and it was a success."

"Are you sure?"

"She's fine, I promise."

Bax sighs and leans forward, resting his head on his knees. "I'm sorry I took the drugs. Is Roz mad?"

"She thinks you're an idiot and she's right."

Bax looks up. "Is she here?"

"No," Gage says, standing and extending his hand towards Bax. "She's at work. We are going to the hospital."

"Wait, what?" Bax asks, taking his hand.

"Shower and get changed," Gage says, sniffing. "Silvey's friend Andrea has requested a conversation with you about this nonsense with Silvey and Captain Wilson."

If Captain Wilson is back, we need to update him.

"Earth to Bax," Gage says, waving a hand in front of his face.

Bax blinks. "Sorry I just recalled a conversation I overheard."

"Good, you can tell me about it on the way," Gage says, patting him on the shoulder. "I have to make a pit stop at the shop to check on a customer."

Bax returns to his room and looks for the shirt he was wearing. "I did have on a shirt when I climbed into bed. I swear." He tosses the covers and kneels to look under the bed. *It's gone. Did Silvey actually take my shirt?*

Bax stands and shakes his head.

"Chop, chop," Gage says, slowing outside the door. "We got things to do."

"Have you seen the shirt I was wearing?" Bax asks.

"No dude, but there are plenty more." Gage points to the dresser. "What do you want on your bagel?"

"Jam," Bax says, pulling open a drawer and selecting a shirt, a pair of socks and boxers before pushing it closed.

"Alright," Gage says.

Bax rushes through a shower and towel dries his hair while inspecting the stitches on his side.

"Any day now," Gage says, tapping on the door. "I'll be in the truck."

"Coming," Bax says, dressing quickly. He slides on a pair of shoes and closes the door. He turns the key left in the lock and takes it out. He jogs down to the truck and hands Gage the house key as he slides in.

"That's your copy," Gage says, dropping the truck in gear.

A dark sedan is pulling up the driveway.

"Twenty bucks, says that's your friend with the FBI," Gage says, roaring the truck close to the car.

"What are you doing?" Bax asks, looking down at the car as they fly by. "It's him!"

"It's private property," Gage says. "It's not like I can be pulled over for narrowly missing a trespasser."

Bax looks in the mirror. "They are turning around."

"Good, let them follow me," Gage says. He slows at the end of the drive and cuts the truck at an angle blocking the exit. "Give me two minutes."

"Gage!" Bax shouts as Gage slams the door.

Gage pulls a bat from the back of this truck and picks up a large rock. The car slows as Gage tosses the rock in the air and swings the bat. It zings over smacking the hood of the car.

The driver slams on their brakes.

"That's a warning shot!" Gage shouts. "You trespass on this private property again without an invitation. It will be more than a rock that finds your vehicle." He tosses the bat in the back of his truck and opens the door. He swings up into the truck without a glance back and pulls the truck out onto the main road.

"You're nuts," Bax says, looking back.

The sedan pulls to the end of the driveway and turns in their direction.

"They're still following," Bax says.

"It's the only way into town," Gage says, turning on the radio.

"Why in the hell are you so calm?" Bax asks.

"I didn't break any laws and know that you haven't either. What that is behind us… is a classic case of harassment." Gage hands Bax a baggy with a bagel. "Eat up."

Bax stares at Gage. "Dude."

"It's still warm," Gage says, winking.

Bax laughs and shakes his head. He slides the bagel out and finishes it in four bites. "Thanks."

Gage offers him a napkin from the center console. "There's coffee and a water here." He taps a reusable thermal mug and bottle. He shakes a pill bottle. "And Roz made me promise that you ate something before taking one of these."

Bax takes the bottle and unscrews the top. He pops out one pill and closes the lid. He swigs a bit of water with the pill and checks the mirror.

"He's still on our ass," Bax says.

"We're only stopping at the shop," Gage says, turning on to old ten highway. "Which is private property. How good is your aim?"

Bax grins. "All American, baby."

"Ha," Gage says, slowing and turning on his blinker. He waits for a few cars to pass before turning into the shop. The b in Auburn Automotive is missing.

"What happened to your sign?" Bax asks, sliding out of the truck. He watches the dark sedan slow down, but it passes the shop's entrance.

"The neon lights around the b went out two years ago after my sign guy retired," Gage says. "I forgot about it to be honest. But Dusty had a customer last week that said they could repair it for some work on his car."

"Swap shop Auburn," Bax says, laughing. "Never thought I would see the day."

"Let's just say I wasn't included on the transaction," Gage says, opening the door to the shop. "Dusty, you here?"

"Under the chevy," Dusty says.

"Did Ricky drop the alternator by?" Gage asks, squatting next to the chevy.

"I'm not under here picking my nose," Dusty says, sliding out from under the truck. "Alternator is replaced, but I had to check the coolant line. It had a drip overnight." He nods to a puddle in a bay a few feet away. "Hey Bax. How's it going?"

"Good thanks," Bax says.

"There was a guy in here asking about you about thirty minutes ago," Dusty says, pointing to his eyebrows. "I've never seen such dark, bushy eyebrows."

"Agent Carlton was here?" Bax asks, glancing at Gage. "What did you say?"

"Nothing," Dusty says. "I told him that it was private property and that if he wasn't here about his car, he can go the f... on with his day."

"Did he listen?" Gage asks.

"He didn't say another word," Dusty says. "I watched him pull out and head back towards town. His plate number is on the sticky note next to the phone."

"Alright," Gage says. "If Rita calls, let her know about the coolant line and see if she can run the plates."

Dusty shakes his head. "Already spoke with her and she said the plates are US government."

"Oops," Bax says, elbowing Gage in the side. "I wonder if the penalty for damaging government property is voided when they are on private property."

Dusty raises his eyebrows twice. "Tell me..."

"It was nothing," Gage says, checking the clock. "We need to run. You good here?"

"Yea dude," Dusty says.

"Thanks, Gage says.

"I'll tell you later," Bax says to Dusty before following Gage back to the truck.

An hour later, Gage pulls the truck into the parking garage next to the hospital.

"Bax, I believe everything you told me about the base seemed very real and honestly dude I would be freaked out." Gage shifts the truck into reverse and backs it into an open spot. "But Silvey's family may have a hard time with all of this."

"I thought I was just meeting Andrea," Bax says, rubbing his sweaty palms on his thighs.

Gage shifts the truck into park. "Did I fail to mention her parents, too?"

"Dude," Bax says, shoving Gage's shoulder.

Gage pulls the keys out of the ignition. "Well, we're here and I would rather complete the mission than turn tail and run home now."

"What mission?" Bax asks, glaring at Gage.

"A wife instructed mission," Gage says. He opens the door and hops out.

"Damn," Bax says, getting out of the truck. "I can't argue with that."

"You could, but you would lose." Gage laughs. "Roz is funny, but don't piss her off unless you are prepared to clean up the mess."

"Oh?" Bax asks, falling into step with Gage as they make their way down to the crosswalk across from the main lobby.

"She loves throwing my dirty laundry while trying to make her point," Gage says, laughing as they walk into the lobby.

"Like your literal dirty laundry?" Bax asks, pressing the up arrow at the elevator.

"Nasty habit of leaving my dirty socks and shirts on the bathroom floor came back with a vengeance."

Bax laughs. They walk into the elevator. "Do you know what floor?"

"Four," Gage says, checking his phone.

Bax presses four and the doors close. "Why am I so nervous?" He shakes out his hands and rolls his shoulders.

"You are about to meet the woman of your literal dreams best friend," Gage says.

"Wow," Bax says. "Brutal."

"Honest," Gage says as the doors open. "They should be in the waiting room."

Bax takes a step off the elevator and pushes his hair back behind his ears. "Ready."

190

"Let's hope so," Gage whispers. "That's Andrea walking towards us." He waves. "Hi Andrea, may I officially introduce Baxton Auburn."

"Hi Gage." Andrea smiles and extends her hand to Baxton. "Hi Baxton. Thanks for coming. I hope your recovery is going well."

"Hi. Bax is fine. I'm doing well, thanks."

"I have a small room reserved," Andrea says, walking past the waiting room.

Bax and Gage follow her.

"The waiting room is pretty full today and they have a meeting room down the hall." Andrea stops in front of an open door. "I just need to grab my phone and a notebook."

Bax and Gage nod and walk into the small room with five chairs and a table with a box of tissues in the corner.

"She gives off a formal vibe," Bax whispers, sitting in the blue upholstered chair.

Gage grins and sits in a matching chair. "I am pretty sure she does that intentionally."

Andrea returns and closes the door. "I hope you don't mind, but I have some very personal questions," she says, sitting across from Bax.

"Sure, but only after I hear how Silvey's doing," Bax says.

"She's been moved from recovery back to an ICU bed for close observation," Andrea says. "She's still in a coma but the doctor's assured us there isn't anything happening," she taps her temple, "up there that could prevent her from waking up soon."

"Will she have to have another surgery?" Bax asks.

"To be determined," Andrea says. "They did manage to repair her spine, hip and femur during the operation."

"That's good, right?" Bax asks.

"I think so," Andrea says. "May I ask you some questions now?"

"Sure," Bax says.

"What do you know about Captain Wilson?" Andrea asks.

Bax frowns.

Gage glances at Bax and elbows him in the side. "Go on."

"I read the article in the paper the other day and the name was familiar," Bax says. "Silvey mentioned her run in with the captain just before I found her."

"Found her where?" Andrea asks.

"Silvey didn't share anything about the base while she was awake?" Bax asks.

Andrea shakes her head. "I didn't have time with Silvey alone, but one of the consulting physicians is a childhood friend. She mentioned that Silvey had a very active coma dream but didn't share any details."

Bax nods. "I will share the entire experience starting with my own coma," he holds his hands to quote the last word, "dream. But fair warning, it will sound a bit nutty."

"I understand," Andrea says, clicking her pen. "If you don't mind, I would like to take some notes just so I can process this later and discuss this with Silvey when she wakes."

Bax nods and starts with his appearance in the guard shack near the gate and ends with his chase and his missing shirt. He sighs and holds up his hands. "That's the long version of it."

"Silvey found a nuclear reactor on base?" Andrea asks.

"She believed it," Bax says. "And from what I've researched, the name of the reactor she found on the papers in the lab checks out."

"That would be enough to have the FBI sniffing around, right?" Andrea asks.

"Oh snap," Gage says.

Andrea and Bax turn towards him.

"Sorry," Gage says. "I couldn't for the life of me make the connection between the base and Bax. I may have pissed off one agent this morning."

"They've been bothering you, too?" Andrea asks.

"They stopped by the house yesterday and again today," Bax says, pointing at Gage. "They even stopped by Gage's shop this morning."

"What did you tell them?" Andrea asks.

"Nothing about my experience or Silvey," Bax says. "I just explained our morning before the tornado, how I found Micah, and climbed out of the silo."

"Good," Andrea says, clicking the pen and closing her notebook.

"You believe me?" Bax asks.

"I'm on the fence to be honest," Andrea says. "I lean more towards facts and less towards fantasy, but the fact that the FBI has made it clear that you two know something helps cement your story."

"What are you going to do with your notes?" Gage asks.

"Wait for Silvey to wake up," Andrea says. "And do my own bit of research." She stands. "I know it's none of my business, but please don't take any more drugs."

Bax glares at Gage. "You didn't!"

"Not me," Gage says.

"Roz," Bax says, looking back at Andrea.

Andrea shrugs. "Just be smart and stay in the in here and now." She nods towards the hallway. "Her parents stepped out. You can visit with Silvey until they return."

Bax stands. "Thanks, I would really like that."

"Keep the conversation light and friendly," Andrea says, holding the door open.

"Yes, ma'am." Bax salutes and walks towards the ICU.

Gage smiles. "I'll wait across the hall in the waiting room."

36

Bax pulls up the chair next to Silvey's bed. The nurse slides the door closed.

"Hi Silvey," Bax says. "I don't know if you are still there. But I found a way out." He watches Silvey's nose scrunch up.

Bax sighs. He reaches his hand over the bed rail and gently picks up her hand.

"Bax," Silvey whispers. "You're safe?"

"Yes," Bax says.

Silvey's eyes flutter. She groans. "Everything hurts."

"Do you want me to get your nurse?" Bax asks, starting to let go of her hand.

She squeezes his hand. "Don't leave."

"I'm here," Bax says. "Did you get out before any more trouble?"

"We were running and then darkness," Silvey says, opening her eyes. She looks directly at Bax's wide eyes. "Did they do the surgery?"

"Yes," Bax says, swallowing a lump. "According to Andrea, it was a success."

"You've met Dre?" Silvey asks.

Bax nods towards the hall. "About ten minutes ago and don't be mad, but I had to tell her everything we've been going through at the base."

"Everything?" Silvey asks.

"Yes," Bax says. "Sorry, but with the FBI snooping around and Captain Wilson out and about. I didn't want to take any chances."

"Honestly," Silvey says. "I'm relieved. She may be able to help us figure some of this out."

"How so?" Bax asks.

"Her husband, Scott, is a…" Silvey says, tapping Bax's hand. "Let's call him a government contractor."

Bax raises an eyebrow and leans forward. "Like a spy?"

Silvey raises her brow twice.

Bax gasps.

"Ha, ha," Silvey says, pointing at Bax's frown. "I had you going for a moment. Scott's an engineer but he has made friends with some big dogs over the years."

Bax chuckles. "Andrea took notes while I shared the details. Maybe you're right and she can help."

Silvey winces and squeezes his hand.

"Are you sure you don't want the nurse?" Bax asks.

Silvey shakes her head. "It's coming in waves, radiating from my hip down my leg."

"The pain?" Bax asks, looking down at the length of her covered body.

"Yes," Silvey says, blowing out a breath. "It's subsiding."

"I'm sure they can make you more comfortable," Bax says, gently squeezing her hand. "You don't have to fight it."

"If they drug me again," Silvey says, tapping her head. "I'll be right back there. I want to stay here."

"You're worried about that?" Bax asks.

"Shouldn't I be?" Silvey asks.

Bax sighs. "I mean you're not wrong, but Silvey you just had major surgery. You can't expect to be awake without something to help dull the pain a bit."

"I can't risk it," Silvey says. "It's caused a ripple of fate we can't undo. I am worried if I learn anymore, it will only put you and I in more danger."

"Speaking of danger," Bax says. "I overheard a conversation between your interrogators."

Silvey frowns. "What?"

Bax holds his hand to his chest. "The short guy said something about if Captain Wilson is back we need to send him an update."

"Who's him?" Silvey asks. "Did they say a name?"

"No," Bax says, "but that was my question too. And the woman's response was if she's right about her timeline we have to turn off the reactor."

"Turn it off?" Silvey asks. "It wasn't on."

"Do you think there could be more than one lab?" Bax asks.

"Oh," Silvey says. "I mean it's possible. I was running around in the dark and I tried a few doors before the lights came back on."

"I wonder if there are still people in town that worked out there," Bax says.

Silvey nods. "I know a few that have coffee and sit up at the diner have said something about it over the years." She frowns. "But the one guy that probably knew the most passed away last year."

"Dang," Bax says. "Do you remember any other details like names or…"

Silvey snaps her fingers. "The officer outside my door let one detail slip. He said he wasn't military but secret service."

"Wow," Bax says. "Now that is a curve. I didn't see that coming."

"Right, why would a secret service agent be anywhere near a military base?" Silvey asks.

Bax pulls out his phone. "Let's see what their job was back in 1962." He types in a few keywords and taps his screen a few times. "Oh, that's interesting."

"What?" Silvey asks.

"In 1962, Congress expanded the secret service's coverage to include the Vice President without requiring his request for protection, the Vice President-elect and, at his request, the former President for a reasonable period."

"Are you saying what I think you're saying?" Silvey asks.

Bax shakes his head. "Silvey it's the JFK era. He was shot in 1963."

"Oh whoa," Silvey whispers. "We are in deep shit. You know how many conspiracy theories they've cooked up about his assassination over the years?"

"And they believe that the shooter had ties to foreign enemies, right?" Bax asks.

Silvey's skin prickles. "Hans?"

Bax nods.

The door to the room slides open.

"Knock, knock," the nurse says, looking at Bax. "Your time is up." They look at Silvey. "You're awake?"

"Yes," Silvey says, "and I would like to stay that way."

The nurse waves at Baxton. "Sir, I really need the room now. We need to call the doctor and your family."

Bax squeezes Silvey's hand. "I'll dig as fast as I can and try to connect the dots with Andrea."

Silvey nods. "I'll be here."

Bax frowns. "And take something for the pain."

Silvey glares at him.

He turns towards the nurse. "She's pretty uncomfortable."

"I can speak for myself, Bax," Silvey says.

He looks over his shoulder. "Sorry."

"On your way sir," the nurse says.

Bax nods and steps out of the room. He looks back and Silvey is still glaring at him. "So sorry." She frowns before the nurse blocks his view. He exits the unit and steps into the waiting room.

Gage and Andrea stand.

"She's awake," Bax says. "But that part about not pissing her off. I may have failed."

A petite woman stands and taps his arm. "Are you saying my Silvey's awake?"

"Yes," Bax says, looking down at the blonde woman. "Are you Silvey's mom?"

"Evelyn," Andrea says, "this is Baxton Auburn." She points to a chair beside her. "And you've already met Buzz."

Buzz nods. "How's my girl?"

"In pain," Bax says, shaking his head. "I may have said too much about that to the nurse on my exit."

Andrea smiles. "I'm sure you were only trying to help."

Evelyn frowns. "Or he's responsible for said pain."

"Evelyn," Buzz says, standing. "Enough with your accusations. Silvey's injuries are from the damn tornado!"

Every person in the waiting room turns their attention on them.

Andrea holds up her hands. "We're not treading that path again." She nods to Gage. "Thanks for bringing him. I'll walk you out." She glances at Buzz. "It may be time for a walk too."

Buzz follows Andrea, Gage, and Bax into the hall.

"I'm sorry about the old shrew," Buzz says, extending his hand out for Bax. They shake hands.

"It's ok," Bax says.

"I'm going to try to see her before Evelyn pisses her off," Buzz says, turning towards the desk.

Andrea nods and ushers them towards the elevators. "So sorry. These two are oil and water a hundred percent of the time."

Bax nods. "I have something to add to your notes."

Andrea lifts an eyebrow.

"Silvey's said the officer guarding her let it slip that he was secret service not military."

Gage lets out one loud, long whistle.

Bax continues, "And it was the year before JFK was shot."

Andrea's eyes double.

"Yea," Bax says. "We're… in it deep."

37

Silvey sighs when the nurse leaves her room.

"Finally!" Silvey says, looking under the blankets. She inspects the covered bandages along her abdomen, hip and the right leg. She wiggles her toes. She feels the tug on her hip and stops wiggling. She reaches to her back and feels the edge of the bandages. "Wonder what kind of tattoo will cover this many scars?"

"You're already considering more needles?"

Silvey drops the blanket and looks up. "Dre!"

"Hey girl," Andrea says, bolting towards Silvey. She hugs Silvey carefully. "You've been busy."

Silvey releases her and tilts her head to the side. "What can I say?" She gestures to the monitors. "Even tethered to a bed I found a way to have a little adventure."

Andrea laughs. "And mine has been playing peacekeeper."

Silvey groans. "Have they've been on their worst behavior?"

"Mind shattering," Andrea says, plopping in the chair next to Silvey's bed.

"Sorry Dre," Silvey says. "I could tell they were on edge when they came in earlier. How are you doing?"

"Minus your parents, busy. Scott and I have found a contractor and have responded to their bid. Your dad mentioned you have worked with them. It's a crew from Stanberry."

"They're amazing," Silvey says. "One of the cleanest crews I've ever worked with and their electrician, Becky, is a riot."

Andrea smiles. "That's good. Norma got a bid from them too and I think they are going to try to tackle both at once."

Silvey smiles. "Ah Norma, she's a good egg."

"Norma's extended family has really rallied the community. Between her family and the red cross, every family displaced had a warm bed and roof over their head within the first forty-eight hours."

"Considering every other household in town is related to her I'm not surprised."

Andrea laughs. "One advantage of our small town."

Silvey nods. "Have you heard from Jessica?"

"The service for Micah is tomorrow afternoon," Andrea says. "I haven't talk to Jessica directly, but I ran into her sister while fueling up." She frowns. "Jessica has had family or a friend at the house to help as she adjusts to motherhood, running a company and planning his service."

Silvey wipes a tear from her cheek. "Please tell her I'm sorry about the tampon and that I wish I could be there."

"Silvey Lynn, what are you talking about?"

Silvey sighs. "Just before the tornado hit. Midge got smacked in the face by the door and we stopped the bleeding with a tampon." She taps her nose.

Andrea laughs. "That's awful."

Silvey shrugs. "We had to improvise. There wasn't a first aid kit available."

Andrea shakes her head. "I'll be sure to pass your message along."

"Have you heard how long I'm stuck in the ICU?" Silvey asks.

"They were talking about the step-down unit tomorrow morning," Andrea says. "If you stay with us."

"What does that mean?" Silvey asks.

"You drifted off into a coma before your surgery," Andrea says.

"I didn't mean to."

Andrea smiles. "I wish Bax could say the same. It was reckless."

"He told you about his experiment with the drugs to find me?" Silvey asks.

"I heard it from his cousin's wife, Rozanne, last night. He told me this morning." Andrea checks the door and looks back at Silvey. "Do you want to share your side of this crazy adventure?"

"I do, but I don't want to pull you into it if the FBI is snooping around."

"Silvey, I already know too much," Andrea says, pulling out her notebook and pen. "I want to compare notes and see if I can find a correlation between your story and Bax's account of the events."

Silvey sighs. "It's wild, but I think it's very real."

38

Andrea slides the door to Silvey's room closed. She tucks away her notebook and pen while approaching the nurse behind the desk. "Silvey's asking about food."

"We have a tray of soft food coming," the nurse says, checking her watch. "I didn't know you were still here. I'm sorry, visiting hours have ended."

"No problem," Andrea says. "I'm on my way out."

Andrea waves back towards Silvey.

Silvey lifts her hand in response.

Andrea pushes the door open and immediately spots the agents near the elevator. She makes an abrupt turn and walks in the opposite direction. She doesn't look back but hears their footsteps follow her. She ducks into the family room she used earlier with Bax. She closes and locks the door before she digs out her phone. She dials the hospital's main line and presses zero when the automated answering prompt starts.

"Operator," a woman answers. "How may I direct your call?"

"Security to the fourth floor."

"Ma'am?"

"I need security to the fourth floor near the ICU. There is a couple here harassing me and a few others. Please send security."

"One moment," the operator says. "Can you give a description?"

"The man is less than six feet with dark bushy eyebrows and the woman has dark brown curly hair. They're wearing all black and pretending to be FBI agents."

"Security is on their way. Where are you at the moment?"

"Hiding in the family consult room down the hall," Andrea says. "I can hear the couple approaching my door."

"Security should be on the floor now," the operator says.

"Thank you!" Andrea says, stepping close to the door. She presses her ear to the door—she hears a murmur of conversation and a squawk of a radio.

"Can you two follow me?" a man asks.

"No," a woman says. "We are waiting on our sister."

"And she's in there?" a man asks.

"Yes, sir," a man answers.

Knock, knock

Andrea backs away from the door. "Who's there?"

"Hospital security," the man says.

"Please escort that couple out of the hospital," Andrea says. "They're harassing me and a few others."

"Escort these two off hospital property," the officer says.

"Now wait a minute," a man says. "We're FBI."

"Yea, yea, and that was your sister," a man says. "Let's go."

Andrea sighs and listens to the scuffle of footsteps pass the door. She unlocks the door and hesitantly cracks it open. She looks towards the elevator. Agent Carlton is glaring in her direction as the doors slide shut.

Andrea steps out into the hall and walks back towards the waiting room. She stops and looks around the room. A young couple are watching the television in the corner and an older woman looks up from her ball of yarn.

"Have you seen Buzz or Evelyn from Lawson return?" Andrea asks, pointing to the corner where they were sitting earlier.

They had each taken turns to make introductions every time someone new came to sit in the waiting room.

The woman shakes her head.

"Thanks," Andrea says, dialing Scott. It rings twice. "Scott!"

"Hey what's wrong?" Scott asks.

"The agents were waiting for me when I came out of the ICU. I had to call hospital security. Can you stay on the phone with me until I get to my car?"

"Of course," Scott says. "Are you scared?"

"No," Andrea says. "More like angry that they are hanging around here after I had them escorted off grounds once before."

"I'm guessing flashing their badges gives them access to any closed door," Scott says.

"True," Andrea says.

"How's Silvey doing?" Scott asks.

"She's awake and very aware of her pain," Andrea says, taking the steps down to the lobby. "She told me everything and it matches Bax's account of their experience." She pauses as a door opens below her. A man wearing scrubs steps into her view, and he walks down ahead of her.

"Andrea?" Scott asks.

"I'm here," Andrea says. "Almost to the lobby."

"I've made a few calls," Scott says. "My friend at the embassy is looking into the Scylla II and my buddy over at the VFW is checking for any contacts that may have worked at the nike base."

Andrea pushes open the door to the lobby. "Thanks, in the lobby." She quickly crosses to the door closest to the parking garage.

"Stay on with me until you get to the car," Scott says.

"Did you find out anything else new?" Andrea asks, waiting to cross the street.

"The last man Bax ran into may have been the secretary of defense for JFK," Scott says. "He matches Bax's description."

Andrea stops in the middle of the crosswalk. "Seriously?"

"It's possible," Scott says.

Andrea rushes into the parking garage and takes the steps two at a time. "Is he still alive?"

"Who?" Scott asks.

"The secretary of defense?" Andrea asks, unlocking her door, sliding into her car, slamming and locking her car door.

"Checking now," Scott says.

"I'm in the car," Andrea says, starting the car.

"He died like over a decade ago," Scott says. "Put me on speaker and get out of there."

"Ok," Andrea says, placing the phone on speaker mode. "If he's gone what kind of threat could Silvey and Bax be knowing he was there?"

"Great question," Scott says. "Be careful coming home."

"I'm out of the garage," Andrea says, pulling out onto the main road. "See you soon."

39

Silvey pushes some green mush around on her tray. Her stomach growls. "I know we're hungry, but this looks disgusting."

Buzz chuckles from the door. "It's a good thing I bribed the nurse." He holds up a brown paper bag with a pepper logo. "It even meets the soft diet recommendations."

"Oh!" Silvey claps. "There is a reason you're my favorite."

Buzz laughs and sits the bag on the table. He takes the tray out to the nurses and returns. "How are you feeling, kid?"

"I finally said yes to something for the pain," Silvey says, taking out the container. "It's manageable."

Buzz nods. "I promised I would deliver and leave since it is technically not visiting hours."

"Thanks dad!" Silvey says, leaning forward to peck his cheek. "Are you stopping by in the morning before heading to Micah's service?"

"Yes," Buzz says. "I even agreed to ride to the service with your mother."

Silvey makes the sign of the cross.

"I know," Buzz says, holding up a hand. "I'll need all the help I can get."

Silvey laughs and scoops up a bite. "Love you pops."

"Love you too!" Buzz says, sliding out his phone from his pocket. "It's charged and yours for the night."

"Thanks," Silvey says, taking his phone. "Any chance we've got mine replaced?"

"Your mom has that on her list," Buzz says. "Night kid."

"Night," Silvey says, watching him slide the door closed and wave to the nurse. She turns her attention to her spoon and the bowl of rice, salsa, queso, and guacamole. She finishes a little over half of the bowl in a few minutes.

Ping

She wipes her hands on a napkin and picks up the phone. She swipes the screen, and a text notification appears. "Babe? Oh yeah, nope. I'm not opening that." She swipes the notification to the right. She dials Andrea's number and hits the call icon.

"Buzz?" Andrea answers.

"Nope," Silvey says. "He gave me his phone for the evening. Are you home yet?"

"Almost," Andrea says. "I had to run a diversion leaving the ICU."

"What?" Silvey asks.

"The FBI agents were waiting by the elevator, and I had security escort them out again."

"Dang if they're not persistent," Silvey says.

"We may have a clue as to the why," Andrea says.

"I'm listening," Silvey says.

"Can you google search the keywords secretary of defense for JFK?" Andrea asks.

"Ok," Silvey says, opening a browser and types in the words. "Now what?"

"Click on the image results," Andrea says.

Silvey taps the image tab and gasps. "It's him!"

"He's the one that was leading the interrogation?" Andrea asks.

"Yes!" Silvey says, swiping through the images and pauses on one. "And the woman with the beehive is pictured with him."

"Does the caption say her name?" Andrea asks, pulling her car into the driveway.

"Jean Tremble," Silvey says, saving the image. "I'll send you the photo, but Dre this changes… everything."

"We have a few more names with faces but still don't exactly know anything for sure, right?" Andrea asks, looking at the text from Silvey.

"Right," Silvey says. "Are they still alive?"

"Not the guy, but I'll see what I can dig up on Jean."

Silvey laughs. "At least her lie about her name was close to Jane."

Andrea laughs. "I'm home. Call Bax and let him know we've made a positive id for your John and Jane."

"Yes ma'am," Silvey says, smiling. "And thanks for believing in me."

"You're the straightest arrow I know," Andrea says. "I've never once caught you in a lie and trust me your honesty is painful at times."

"Is this about your wedding again?" Silvey asks.

"No, but that's just one shining example," Andrea says. "It could be about my prom dress junior year."

Silvey laughs. "It was hideous."

"Silvey Lynn!" Andrea says.

"It's been years admit it!" Silvey says. "The yellow feathers gave straight up big bird vibes."

Andrea laughs. "Damn you. I'm hanging up now."

"Love you too."

Silvey disconnects the call and swipes back to the image she sent Andrea. "I've got your real names now."

She scrolls through a few articles about the JFK administration and pauses on one article about the Berlin Crisis. She reads the highlights about the construction of the Berlin Wall and the NATO allies' response. She googles the events of JFK's administration and finds that she's smack in the middle of Pre-Cuban Missile Crisis and post Berlin Wall era.

"That's a lot of political tension in one calendar year," Silvey says, closing the browser and opening the contacts. She finds Bax's name and clicks dial.

"Hello," Bax answers.

"Hey it's Silvey. Do you got a minute?"

"I've got days. What's up?"

"I've identified the names of my interrogators as none other than Bob and Jean," Silvey says. She forwards the image to Bax. "Take a look."

"Silvey," Bax says after reading the caption attached to the image. "That's the guy I saw. Who is he?"

"JFK's secretary of defense," Silvey says.

"No way," Bax whispers.

Silvey hears him tapping on a keyboard. "Are you looking him up?"

"Of course," Bax says. "Yea, he's the real deal, and the conversation I overheard when he referenced 'him' could be the president."

Silvey chuckles. "And now if we go back, we can ask more insightful questions."

"Whoa," Bax says. "We can't go back. Silvey, the stakes are too high."

"True," Silvey says. "But we may finally have all the pieces."

"I've done more digging on the timeline to try to connect what we know," Bax says. "The first mention of Hans Gobert was his encounter with Captain Wilson at a boy scout banquet. This was the fifth of April according to the archives. And we know that the captain's family reports him missing the following day." He pauses. Silvey hears a shuffle of papers. "But the paper in the shack was dated the following week. I confirmed the headlines with the archives."

"Captain Wilson was missing for an entire week before my encounter," Silvey says.

"Yes," Bax says. "And a week after that paper is the archive article with the sketch of Hans."

"Do you think they managed to capture and kill Hans the night you opened the gate?" Silvey asks.

"It's possible," Bax says. "Or they could have questioned him in the very room you were in."

"Or it took them that long to discover his body."

"That's dark," Bax says. "But entirely reasonable."

"I am still trying to figure out how Captain Wilson appeared here in our timeline."

"Ah yes, I've done a bit more digging on Gobert and his brother," Bax says. "His brother was a guard for a few scientists and physicists, and they were experimenting on prisoners."

"That's awful," Silvey whispers.

"It gets worse," Bax says. "They were attempting teleportation via worm holes using said prisoners."

"Whoa. Are you sure?"

"If you believe everything you read on the internet, yeah."

Silvey looks up at the ceiling. "Worm holes are science fiction, right?"

Bax chuckles. "I'm no expert on physics, but I do know one."

"Who? Sheldon Cooper?"

Bax laughs. "He's a lot like Sheldon. But my dad's best friend works for NASA."

"Oh nice," Silvey says.

"I left him a message earlier today," Bax says.

Silvey sighs. "Possible motive for Gobert was something to do with the lab?"

"I would say yes," Bax says. "But Wilson's appearance here means they figured out more than just teleportation."

Silvey chuckles. "My head is too fuzzy to contemplate time travel and teleportation."

"Can I ask you something very hypothetical?" Bax asks.

"Sure," Silvey says.

"How do you think we managed it without the lab?" Bax asks.

"If the tornado did rip a hole in the fabric of time, maybe our proximity to a worm hole gave us access," Silvey says.

"And our drugged trips back to the same spot?" Bax asks.

"Side effect of our first blip?" Silvey suggests.

"The questions and theories could go on for decades," Bax says. "Do you really think we can figure out the why and how of it all?"

"Not a chance," Silvey says. "But maybe your NASA contact has a better theory or explanation." She yawns. "Can you let me know what he has to say?"

"You'll be my first call," Bax says, fighting a yawn. "Are you fighting sleep Silvey?"

"I think my food coma just kicked in," Silvey says. "Call me before you head to Micah's service."

"Sure," Bax says. "I'm sorry you can't make it."

"It's rough not showing up for Jessica, but I know the community will show up for her and the family tomorrow."

"I bet," Bax says. "Try to stay in our time tonight."

"I'll try," Silvey says. "Have a good night."

"Good night Silvey," Bax says.

Silvey ends the call and pushes the table across her bed to the side. She pats the covers until she finds her call light. She presses the red button.

A nurse pops his head in. "Hey Silvey."

"You're back on night shift," Silvey says, recalling him from the night before.

"Yep, Geoff, at your service," he says, entering her room. "Can I put this in the fridge for you?" He picks up the bowl of rice.

"Sure," Silvey says.

"Do you need anything else?" he asks.

"A close eye on my vitals this evening," Silvey says.

Geoff's mouth falls open.

Silvey laughs.

"Are you traveling again?"

She shrugs. "Just come wake me if I am gone for too long."

Geoff smiles. "I'll be right back with your medication."

Silvey taps the phone. *Almost ten.* She notices a new message from Andrea's number. She taps the message. *A PDF attachment, Dre, really.* She opens the document. Project Rainbow is written across the top. The second author is Jean Tremble. She forwards the document to Bax as Geoff returns.

"You're white as a ghost," Geoff says, sitting down his tablet and snapping on a pair of gloves.

"I feel like they are haunting me," Silvey says. The phone pings again.

"Ah, you got some form of entertainment tonight," Geoff says. "That's great." He taps the tablet. "You're due a round of pain medication. How would you rate your pain on a scale from one to ten?"

"A seven at the moment," Silvey says, glancing at the message from Bax. It's a bug-eyed emoji. She types back a shrug emoji and turns her attention back towards Geoff. "Can you give me the minimum dose?"

Geoff frowns. "Are you sure?"

Silvey nods. "I've been numb for far too long. It's good to feel something and it only comes in waves."

Geoff nods and injects her IV. "The other two are your antibiotic and vitamin B12."

Silvey nods and checks her phone. Andrea sent another message with an image attached. She taps the image and reads the obituary for Jean Tremble. "She died over twenty years ago."

"Who did?" Geoff asks.

"Nobody important now," Silvey says, forwarding the image to Bax. "It's been a very long day. Sorry if I am being cryptic or rude."

"I'm all done here," Geoff says, picking up his tablet. "Get some rest. I promise to wake you if you travel too long." He winks.

Silvey smiles. "Let's hope I stay here." She feels a whoosh of drowsiness and fights to keep her eyes open. The door to her room slides shut and she gives in.

40

Bax pushes back from the table and stands. He stretches and walks towards the screen door. The cool night air drifts in and his mind drifts back to the same sensation stepping out of the guard shack. He squeezes his eyes closed and concentrates on every detail inside the guard's shack, the gate, Hans and his escape down the ladder. *An image of a rainbow was etched on the inside of the metal cover.* He gasps.

"Holy shit," Bax mumbles and rushes back over towards his phone. He pulls up the document for Project Rainbow. *No way.* He rushes down the hall towards the spare bedroom with a desk and printer. He turns on the printer, checks the tray for paper, and the ink levels. He taps the printer icon on the right-hand side of the document and waits. The document loads to print, 1-245 pages.

"Ugh," Bax says, thumbing the paper in the tray. "There's not even ten."

"Are you ok?" Rozanne asks from the open door.

"Sorry if I woke you?" Bax says, leaning against the desk. "I was going to print something, but it's two hundred and forty-five pages."

Rozanne frowns. "I don't think we would have enough ink for that, even if we did have the paper." She checks the closet beside the desk. "Is it important?"

"It's nothing that can't wait until morning," Bax says. "Thanks for checking on me."

Rozanne closes the closet door. "It's about Silvey, right?"

Bax nods.

"Do you want to talk about it?" Rozanne asks.

"No," Bax says, shaking his head. "I should try to get some sleep. It's late and we have a long day tomorrow.

"That's true," Rozanne says. "Good night Bax."

"Night Roz," Bax says, heading back towards the kitchen. He closes and locks the back door. He collects his notes and places the laptop back on the charger before returning to his room.

He opens the project rainbow article and starts to read as he changes for bed. He plugs in his phone and lays face down on the bed. He tries to close his eyes and slow his breathing. *Yeah, sleep is not coming until I read that thing.*

He rolls over, taps his phone, and starts to read.

Silvey pushes up the sleeves of her shirt hanging way past her hands. Once her hands are free, she pulls up the collar and sniffs a mix of dove and aftershave.

Bax. It's his shirt. But how?

"No," Silvey says, opening her eyes. A single light illuminates the small room with cinderblock walls and a cot on the side. *I'm back and so is the power.* She steps to the door and listens. *Is somebody snoring?*

She twists the knob, but it doesn't budge.

A muffled snort and a shuffle of steps makes her step away from the door. *Not alone.* She moves back towards the door.

214

"Bax?" Silvey calls.

"What do you want?" a man asks.

It's the secret service guard. Silvey paces the small room. "I'm ready to talk."

"No more jokes."

"Tell Jean."

He coughs. "You mean Jane?"

"Sure," Silvey says, grinning.

"Sir!" he shouts. "She's ready."

"Bring her," a voice shouts.

Silvey tugs on the bottom of the shirt to ensure she's covered up as the door opens and a man wearing a black jacket over a white button up fills the doorway.

She rolls to her toes to peer behind him. *No red swirling lights.*

He looks her up and down. "Where did you get that?"

Silvey falls back on her heels and tugs on the shirt. "This?"

"Yes," he says, glaring at her.

"That is a need to know, and sir you don't need to know." Silvey smirks and walks past him into the hallway. "Shall we?"

He shakes his head and steps into the room.

Silvey pulls the door shut and locks it. She slides the key out and inspects the other keys attached to the silver ring.

"Hey!" he shouts. "What are you doing?"

"Still a need to know," Silvey says, sliding the ring over her thumb and extending the longest key out between her ring and middle finger. She makes a quick right hook, punching the air, and grins. "They'll never see it coming."

He pounds on the door. "Open the door!"

Silvey walks away from the door, noting the closed doors about every five feet.

Another man dressed identical to the secret service guy shifts his posture and positions himself in the middle of the hallway. He looks past Silvey and frowns.

Silvey smiles and covers her hand with the keys. "Are they ready for me?"

"Where's your guard?" the man asks.

"He had to use the little boy's room," Silvey says, stopping in front of him. "May I?" She gestures towards the open door behind him.

He furrows his brow and folds his arms across his chest. "Wait here." He steps around her and quickly walks back toward the locked door.

Silvey steps into the room he was guarding and closes the door. Two people look up from a map covering the table. They frown.

"Who let you in here?"

"Well, Robert… or do you go by Bob?" Silvey asks, walking towards the table.

He pulls on the knot of his tie. "What did you say?"

Silvey looks down at the map. Spotting a town nearby circled in red. "What are you looking for?"

He knocks his knuckles on the table. "Answer me!"

"Bob or Robert?" Silvey asks, looking him in the eyes.

A vein bulges across his forehead.

"How do you know his name?"

"Is it Miss or Mrs. Jean Tremble?" Silvey asks, cutting her attention towards Jean's red face.

"How?" Jean and Robert say in unison.

Silvey smiles. "Now that we are all on a first name basis. I believe that we can have a real honest conversation."

The door to the room burst open.

"Sorry, sir," the agent says. "She locked the agent in the room and didn't stay put."

"Oops," Silvey says, winking at him and his snarling expression.

He charges towards Silvey, but Jean raises her hand. He stops.

"We have bigger problems to solve," Jean says, waving him away.

"Sir, ma'am." He does a perfect about face and walks out of the room.

Silvey nods. "Alrighty. Do you want to play the back-and-forth question game or get right down to business?"

"How do you know our names?" Jean asks.

"A photo published from a social event for the President," Silvey says. *Only a slight lie. I have no idea where that photo was taken.*

He clears his throat and glances at Jean. "That's impossible. We've never been seen together in public."

Silvey assesses Jean. "I'm sure you haven't yet, but that doesn't mean you won't."

"Future nonsense, again," Jean says, rolling her eyes. "She probably coerced our names from the agent guarding her. We heard reports of them chatting."

Silvey laughs. "You overestimate my skills." She taps the map. "If you are looking for Captain Wilson…"

Robert swipes her hand away from the map. "You know where he is?"

"I know when he is," Silvey says, stepping out of arm's reach.

"Explain," he says between clenched teeth.

"Sixty years from now, a massive tornado rips right through Lawson including the nike base."

Jean barks out a choked laugh. "She's insane. There is no way she could possibly know that?"

"And that you two are involved in nuclear fusion," Silvey says.

"We know that you saw the lab," Robert says. "Nice try."

"And Project Rainbow means nothing, right?" Silvey asks.

Jean sucks in an audible breath.

Silvey grins at the furrowed brows pushing Robert's glasses forward. "So, secretary…"

"You know that I am the secretary of defense for the president." Silvey nods.

"Ms. Rhoades," Robert says, wagging his finger at Silvey.

"Bob," Silvey says.

He frowns. "Think long and hard about your next statement."

Silvey points back to the map. "I can pinpoint the location for Captain Wilson's return and where you dumped the body of Hans Gobert, if that helps."

"We did no such thing," Jean says, pointing at Silvey. "Who do you think you are?"

"A simple civilian," Silvey says, clutching the keys in her hand.

"More like a traitor," Jean says.

"If you are really from the future," Robert says. "Show me what you think you know."

Silvey locates Elmira on the map and traces the road down to a blue squiggly line. "Gobert is found in an abandoned car near here."

Robert cuts Jean a look. She shrugs.

"And Captain Wilson appears in a field here," Silvey says, tapping the map just east of the nike base. "But not until April 2022." She watches the wordless exchange between Robert and Jean. "What's interesting though… teleportation is still considered science fiction sixty years from now?"

Jean's pupils double as she stares at Silvey with her mouth ajar.

Silvey hears a familiar quiet beep. "Until next time, folks." She closes her eyes and feels the air shift around her. She sighs.

"Wait!" Robert shouts.

41

Silvey listens to the familiar hum of the monitors next to her bed. She knows before opening her eyes that she's back in her hospital bed inside the ICU. She opens her eyes and stares up at the ceiling tile.

"Welcome back," Geoff says.

Silvey shifts her eyes towards Geoff standing beside her bed. "Thanks."

"You were gone for about ten minutes," Geoff says, holding up the tablet. "I had a code a few doors down. Sorry I didn't get back sooner."

"It's ok." Silvey nods towards the door. "Is your other patient, ok?"

"Stable," Geoff says. "It's almost the end of my shift. How are you feeling?"

Silvey does a mental assessment. "Still a little fuzzy, but relieved that I am here and now."

"Any pain?" Geoff asks, tapping his tablet.

"Maybe a four," Silvey says, pointing to her hips.

"Do want to hold off on pain medication until after breakfast?" Geoff asks.

"Sure," Silvey says. "Any chance I shower someday soon?"

"You have orders with the rehab team," Geoff says, looking up from the tablet. "They will have you up and out of bed soon, and that usually includes a shower along with some day-to-day tasks."

"Good," Silvey says. "Thanks for waking me up."

Geoff smiles. "You were smirking when I walked into the room. Did you see anything interesting?"

"I had a very convincing conversation with a few ghosts," Silvey says. "But I hope that I don't return."

"Did you leave anything behind?" Geoff asks.

"What do you mean?" Silvey asks.

"Just something to prove that you were actually there," Geoff says. "Tagged a wall with Silvey was here from the future."

"Ha, ha," Silvey says. "No."

"Next time," Geoff says.

"I guess I'll consider that if I return, but sadly I haven't tagged anything."

"If you need anything," Geoff says, walking to the door. "I'll be at the desk."

Silvey nods. "I'm good, thanks." She pats down the covers until she finds her dad's phone. She taps the screen and swipes away a few messages from her father's girlfriend. She taps a message from Andrea.

Found another connection! Jean Tremble was questioned during the investigation regarding the disappearance of Captain Wilson.

"Bingo!" Silvey says, tapping out of the message thread from Andrea to Bax.

Bax: I've read the entire article on Project Rainbow. I think I know how we got pulled in.

"Holy shit!" Silvey says, inspecting the timestamp. It was an hour ago. She types back immediately. *How?*

Bax answers. *I'm heading to the hospital now.*

Silvey calls Bax. He picks up after one ring.

"Hey," Bax says, clearing his throat.

"Have you slept at all?" Silvey asks.

"No," Bax says, "but I am wide awake."

"Why are you heading here?" Silvey asks. "It's only five in the morning."

"Did you go back?" Bax asks.

"Yes," Silvey says.

"I don't think we should talk about it on the phone," Bax says. "I'll be there in twenty minutes. Can you clear it with your nurse for an early visit?"

"I'll try." Silvey presses the red call light button. "Be careful."

"See you soon."

Silvey lowers the phone and waves to Geoff as he hesitates by the door. He slides the door open and steps in.

"What's up?" Geoff asks.

"Any chance you can let in a visitor in about twenty minutes?" Silvey asks, folding her hands together.

"Uh," Geoff says. "That's not really possible."

"I wouldn't ask if it wasn't super important but…" Silvey says, waving him closer. "… it's about the time jumps."

Geoff frowns.

"Please!" Silvey begs. "You can say he's here to collect blood or something, right?"

"Who's he?" Geoff asks.

"Baxton Auburn," Silvey says.

Geoff checks his watch. "If he can make it here in the next thirty minutes, maybe. But like I said my shift is ending soon and if my replacement catches him in here, I could be in big trouble."

"Thank you!" Silvey says. "He'll be here before the shift change."

Geoff raises an eyebrow. "He's the one that's there with you?"

"Not every time, but yes."

"I'll give you a buzz when he's outside the unit," Silvey says, holding up the call light.

Geoff nods and slides the door closed.

She dials Bax.

"Two exits away," Bax answers. "All clear?"

"Text me when you are outside the unit doors," Silvey says. "They're shift change is in thirty minutes. You must be out before the new shift starts."

"Got it!" Bax says.

Ten minutes later, Silvey receives a text. She presses the call light and watches Geoff rush Bax inside her room.

Geoff checks his watch. "You have eighteen minutes." He pulls the curtain covering the sliding glass door on his way out.

Silvey and Baxton nod.

Geoff steps out and slides the door closed.

"Bax," Silvey says. "Talk."

Bax sighs. "We are essentially tethered worms to the wormhole."

Silvey laughs but clamps her hand over her mouth to squash the volume.

Bax smiles. "Ok, maybe not the best opening line, but the reactor you saw is not the one tied to time travel. It's only the power source."

Silvey shakes her head and drops her hand. "You're joking?"

"No," Bax says. "The document shows the schematics for the layout of the lab. It has three chambers plus a control room. The all-white room is described as the throat where the black hole and the white hole collide. And boom, there you have it! A tunnel through space-time."

"How does that make us tethered worms?" Silvey asks.

"The research they were doing specifically in April 1962 was dubbed hooks and worms. They would tether a person aka the worm to a time aka the hook and essentially throw the line through a wormhole."

"But how did we end up as bait?" Silvey asks.

"The tornado flipped the emergency backup," Bax says. "It had its own fallout bunker safety mechanism-built in. And according to the schematic it was on the north side of the silo directly in the path of the tornado. It flipped it on before the silo was impacted and we it's only worms."

"But the dress, heels…," Silvey says, pointing at Bax. "… your uniform?"

Bax shrugs. "I haven't found any explanation in the article, but I did read something about side effects."

Silvey's eyes widen. "What do you mean?"

"The fact that we continued to go back to the initial location," Bax says.

Silvey sighs. "Ok…"

"The line doesn't break," Bax says, lowering into the chair. "Participants in the study reported going back to the same location multiple times after their first jump without access to the facility."

Silvey frowns. "For how long?"

"The longest report was a total of seven jumps."

Silvey holds up her finger and counts. "My first jump when I ran into you, my second when I woke up in the interview room, my third again in the interview room, my fourth was with you and the fifth was tonight when I confirmed the identities of Jean and Robert." Holding up her hand palm out. "I have two chances left to tell them to keep the president out of the car in Texas and that we don't blow up Cuba."

"Whoa," Bax says. "I don't think we should change the course of history."

"We don't actually blow-up Cuba," Silvey says. "And what kind of patriot would I be if I didn't try to save the guy's boss?"

"I mean yes, but…" Bax pulls out his hair tie. His auburn curls spring out and fall to his chin. "Sorry I can't think with this thing pulling on my scalp. Do you think it's really going to change anything?"

Silvey smiles and feels her cheeks slightly burn. "Um, we're running out of time. Was there anything else you learned I should know that you can't tell me over the phone?"

"I think they used Captain Wilson as the initial worm," Bax says.

"No," Silvey whispers. "Why?"

"I don't think it was on purpose," Bax says. "The first recorded use of the chamber was the night of the scout banquet."

"And that's how Wilson goes missing?"

Bax nods.

Knock, knock

Geoff pokes his head into the room. "Time to go."

Bax frowns. "Sorry. There's more, but I'll come back after Micah's service."

Silvey nods. "Thanks for coming. It helps." Her bottom lip quivers. "Please hug Jessica for me today."

"I will," Bax says.

Geoff mouths the word *sorry* to Silvey as Bax steps out of the room.

Silvey wipes away a tear. "It's ok."

42

Bax sighs as the unit doors close behind him. He walks across the hall to the waiting room and opens the message app on his phone. He types quickly. *One thing that can't wait. I know why the feds are questioning us.* His finger hovers over the send button and hits send. He looks towards the ICU door.

Silvey responds immediately. *Why?*

Our names are listed in the project document as participants. Bax sends the screenshot of the document with their names listed as participant twenty and twenty-one.

Silvey responds. *How the f... do we explain that?*

Bax types back. *We don't.*

Silvey responds. *Huh?*

We didn't break any laws... nor did we consent to any government experiment.

Silvey responds with a bug-eyed emoji. *We own them.*

Bax laughs. *You could say that. I have to get Gage's truck back before they wake up. I'll see you later this evening.*

Silvey responds with a wave emoji.

Bax stands and pockets his phone. He walks to the elevator feeling the lack of sleep slam into him. He presses the down arrow as the ICU door opens. Bax turns to look.

Geoff walks out and heads towards Bax. "Hold the elevator."

Bax steps into the elevator and holds his arm across the threshold until Geoff steps inside. "Thanks again for the early visit."

"Silvey was laughing when I left," Geoff says, pressing the one. "I guess it was worth it."

"It was," Bax says, fighting a yawn.

"Do you have to drive very far?" Geoff asks, assessing Bax's dark circles and weighted posture.

"About an hour north," Bax says, giving into a long yawn.

"Are you sure you're good to drive?" Geoff asks.

"I'll stop by the cafeteria and get a coffee," Bax says.

Geoff nods as the door opens. "I'm sure my friends can help you out."

Bax frowns and follows Geoff's extended hand to Agent Carlton. "You work for the FBI?"

Geoff shrugs. "More like consult."

"Mr. Auburn," Agent Carlton says. "Let's take a ride."

"Nah, I'm good," Bax says, reaching in his pocket and stepping out into the lobby.

"Hands up," Carlton barks.

"Whoa," Bax says, raising his hands and looking around the vacant lobby. "What did you do with the volunteers?" He points towards the welcome desk.

Agent Carlton shrugs. "They're on their break. Let's go."

"I'm not going anywhere with you," Bax says.

The agent nods towards Geoff.

Bax turns toward Geoff and faces the end of a needle and syringe. "Seriously." He takes a giant step away from Geoff.

"We are," Agent Carlton says. "Hand over your keys and phone."

"No," Bax says. "You can't do this."

"Mr. Auburn," Agent Carlton says, taking out a pair of handcuffs. "You are being detained under the suspicion of treason."

"You've got to be kidding me!" Bax shouts. "I've done nothing, and your threats are just that. If you want to speak to me, contact my lawyer."

"Take him," Agent Carlton says.

Geoff lunges towards Bax.

Bax pivots, missing the jab and shoves Geoff to the floor. He stomps on the syringe.

Something presses hard against Bax's ribs just above his sutured incision. He looks down at the weapon. "Go ahead."

"Enough with the theatrics," a woman says.

"Agent Vickers, I presume," Bax says without taking his eyes off the gun. He spots a security officer out of the corner of his eye. Bax raises his hands. "You are officially trespassing on hospital property for a third time."

A security officer with a yellow weapon pulls the trigger. Two leads extend and hit her in the back. Her body twitches as she falls and drops the weapon.

Bax kicks it towards the security officer.

A second security officer comes barreling into the lobby from a stairwell. "Hands up!"

Agent Carlton and Bax hold their hands up.

"What the hell is going on?" a third security officer says, entering the lobby from a hallway near the desk.

"These two were escorted off property twice before for harassing a patient and a few visitors," Bax says, pointing to the agents. "And this guy is a consultant for them." He says nudging Geoff with his shoe.

"And you are?" the third security officer asks.

"A visitor trying to get to their car and return home," Bax says. "I was accosted by them when I got off the elevator. I have no weapon, just a phone and keys. Feel free to search me."

The second officer pats Bax down. "He's clear." He glares at the agents. "I escorted you two off the property once and told you if you came here without a warrant, I would call the police and have you arrested for trespassing." He points to a squad car squealing to a stop outside the entrance. "And your ride has arrived."

"We've paged the emergency room and will have her checked out," the officer says, pointing to Agent Vickers as two police officers walk into the lobby.

"Am I free to go?" Bax asks.

"I'll need a statement," the first officer says. "She was pointing a gun at you when I walked in."

One of the police officers kneels and inspects the weapon. "With a bullet ready to fire. Would you like to press charges?"

Bax smirks. "Absolutely."

Agent Carlton clears his throat. "I can explain everything."

"Do you have a warrant, Neil?" the police officer asks, shaking out a bag and placing the weapon inside. "I would like to advise you that you and your partner are under arrest for trespassing plus an accomplice to attempted murder and kidnapping."

"He's wanted for treason," Agent Vickers says.

"Show me an arrest warrant," the police officer says, holding out his hand.

Carlton and Vickers glance at Bax, then back to the officer.

"Right," the police officer says, turning towards Bax. "Mister?"

"Auburn," Bax says.

"You are free to go after we get your contact details," the officer says, pointing to a second squad car pulling up. "Step outside and Officer Lee will get you squared away."

Bax nods and walks outside. "Officer Lee?"

"Here," Officer Lee says. "Can I help you?"

"They said you would take my contact information," Bax says, nodding towards the police officers escorting Geoff and the agents outside.

"And you are?" Officer Lee asks.

"Baxton Auburn," Bax says, "may I take out my wallet?"

The officer nods. "And how were you involved with this incident?"

Bax removes his wallet and takes out his driver's license. "I was here checking on a patient and was accosted by those three in the lobby on my way out."

228

Officer Lee takes his license and uses her phone to scan the front and back before she hands it back. "Is this your current address?"

"Yes," Bax says, tucking his license back into his wallet. She hands him a pen and her notepad.

"Jot down your phone number," Officer Lee says. "Sergeant, is Mr. Auburn free to go?"

"All clear."

Bax hands her the notebook and pen back. "The guy in the scrubs was working on the same floor as my friend. Posing as her nurse. Will she be safe?"

"Yes," Officer Lee says. "The three of them will be taken into custody and booked."

Bax nods. "Thanks." He turns towards the parking garage and checks for traffic before crossing the street. He enters the parking garage and jogs up one flight to Gage's truck. He takes his keys out of his pocket but drops them on the pavement. He bends and his hand tremors as he picks up the keys. He unlocks the truck and climbs into the driver's seat. He lifts his shirt and inspects the dark red outline of the muzzle on his skin. "That was really stupid Auburn."

His phone pings. He pulls out his phone and taps the screen.

Gage: Where are you and my truck?

Bax dials Gage and starts the truck. It rings once.

"Tell me you went to get breakfast?" Gage answers.

"I went to get breakfast."

"Bax," Gage says.

"Gage," Bax says.

"Did you sleep at all?" Gage asks.

"No," Bax says, backing out of the space.

"Where are you?" Gage asks.

"Heading back in a few," Bax says. "I'm sorry I took the truck in the middle of the night, but I had to talk to Silvey in person."

"Visiting hours aren't for another, what… three hours," Gage says.

"She persuaded the staff to let me in early for just a few minutes," Bax says. "But that turned out to be a trap." He exits the garage and glances back towards the entrance. The squad cars are gone.

"What do you mean?" Gage asks.

"I'll fill you and Roz in when I get back to the house." He turns on to the outer road that leads to the highway. "I'm going to stop and pick up coffee plus breakfast. Send me your order."

"Bax, are you good to drive that far?" Gage asks.

"Like I said… coffee."

Gage sighs. "See you soon."

43

A man wearing a dark navy hospital security uniform enters the ICU.

Beth stands and rounds the desk. "May I help you?"

"Hi, I'm Shane," he says, holding up his hospital identification. "Can you tell me what patient or patients Geoff Linder was assigned to during his shift?"

"Can I ask what this is about?" Beth asks, crossing her arms across her chest.

"Mr. Linder was involved in an incident this morning right after his shift, and we need to ensure the safety of the patients he worked with overnight."

Beth glances towards Silvey's room. "He had two patients in rooms one and three."

"Do you mind if I have a chat with them?" Shane asks.

"One is still in a coma," Beth says. "And let me check if my patient in three is still awake."

Shane nods.

Beth walks over to the third door and slides the door open.

"Hey," Silvey says. "You're back! How's the face?"

Beth smiles. "Healing. I have a hospital security officer outside that would like to speak with you about your night nurse Geoff."

Silvey shrugs. "It's cool. Let them in."

Beth nods and waves the officer over.

"Can I ask what happened to your face?" Shane asks, pointing to the large bandage near her left eye.

"Stitches," Beth says. "I'm sure Ms. Rhoades can tell you all about it."

Shane lifts an eyebrow and steps into Silvey's room. "Hi Ms. Rhoades."

"Silvey's fine."

"Silvey, I'm here because a visitor this morning had a rather ugly encounter with your nurse Geoff in the lobby."

Silvey sits up a little too fast and groans. "What's happened to Bax?"

Shane opens his tablet. "Baxton Auburn is a friend of yours?"

"Yes!" Silvey's heart rate monitor ticks up in volume.

"He's well," Shane says, looking at the heart rate jump into the hundreds. "Please don't panic."

Silvey glances at the monitor. "Then start talking!"

"Baxton Auburn was seen leaving the unit just before six thirty this morning and entering the elevator a few minutes before seven."

Silvey nods. "Ok."

"Geoff Linder was your nurse overnight?" Shane asks.

"Not sure I ever asked his last name, but yes, Geoff was my nurse for the second time since I've been awake."

"When the elevator reached the lobby a man," Shane says, turning his screen toward Silvey with an image of a man wearing dark clothing and his head tilted away from the camera, "was waiting for Mr. Auburn and Mr. Linder."

"I've never seen him before," Silvey says.

Shane taps the phone and shows her a picture of Geoff and Bax in profile from a distance.

"Is he holding a needle?" Silvey asks, squinting at the photo.

"Unfortunately, yes," Shane says, tapping the phone and showing her a third picture of a woman holding a gun to Bax's ribs. "Do you recognize her?"

232

"Is that Vickers?" Silvey asks, pointing at the screen.

Shane nods. "They were arrested for trespassing and attempted kidnapping since they could not provide any documentation to back up their claim that they had a warrant for Mr. Auburn."

"And Geoff was working with them?" Silvey asks, replaying her transparent conversation about her trips to the past with him.

"Yes," Shane says. "He's since been removed from hospital property with pending charges of assault and possibly medication theft. My staff did disarm Agent Vickers before she had a chance to fire."

"And Bax, where is he?" Silvey asks.

"He was free to go home," Shane says. "Did Mr. Linder ask or say anything that you would find unusual for a nurse to inquire about?"

"No, but now that I know whom he was working with I suspect that my patient rights have been violated and that the conversations we had in this room has been leaked to the agents in question." She looks around the room. "Am I safe here?"

"You're afraid?"

Silvey nods, taps her ear, and twirls her finger.

Shane sits his tablet down and moves around the room checking the monitors, bed, under the side table and pats down the chair. He plucks out a small transponder from the cushion of the chair. He holds it up for Silvey and nods before he drops it to the floor and smashes it with his boot.

"Thank you!"

"I'll request your records along with the other patient Mr. Linder was assigned to for review to be sure he has not tampered with your care during his shift."

"Ok," Silvey says. "He did mention a gap in my vital signs in my chart."

"Odd, I'll have the nursing director make sure nothing else is awry."

"Ok," Silvey says. "Will he be able to work here again?"

"No," Shane says. "He's been blacklisted from this hospital and all of them in our network. Plus, he will be criminally charged for the incident this morning."

Silvey nods. "Thank you."

Shane picks up the pieces of the transponder and leaves Silvey's room.

Silvey taps her phone and dials Bax.

"Hey," Bax answers.

"You were held at gunpoint!" Silvey says.

"Yes," Bax says, pulling forward in the drive thru.

"And you didn't think to call me?" Silvey asks.

"I think I may still be in shock," Bax says, opening the window. He holds a twenty-dollar bill out for the cashier.

"What the hell happened?" Silvey asks.

Bax takes the bag of food, coffees, and the change from the cashier. He pulls forward and into a parking spot. He recounts the elevator ride, the incident in the lobby, and his encounter with a cop outside.

"Bax," Silvey whispers.

"I'm here," Bax says.

"You're, ok?" Silvey asks.

"I'm ok," Bax says and chuckles. "Well, minus the adrenaline rush crash and the lack of sleep."

"Do you think it's safe to return to your cousin's house?" Silvey asks. "The security officer found a listening device wedged between the cushion of the chair in my room."

"They heard everything!" Bax says, slapping his palm against the steering wheel.

"I know," Silvey whispers.

"Rozanne has a scanner for such devices because of a previous situation," Bax says. "We'll sweep the house and vehicles." He backs the truck out and pulls out onto a nearly empty highway. "I'm heading back with a breakfast apology now and to try to sleep a few hours before Micah's service."

"Be careful," Silvey says. "Keep Gage and Rozanne in the loop just in case. I'll fill Andrea in too."

"I will," Bax says. "See you this evening."

"I hope so." Silvey disconnects the call and accidentally taps the red call light.

Beth taps on the door. "Are you ok?"

Silvey shakes her head. "I don't know."

"What's going on?" Beth asks, stepping inside the room and closing the door behind her.

"My privacy was invaded, my body is broken and I am stuck here with no end in sight." Silvey balls her fists. "And don't get me started on what this little encounter with a tornado has done to me financially."

Beth nods.

"Plus," Silvey says, pointing at Beth. "Your face will have a permanent reminder of my charming personality."

Beth laughs. "This is true, but I like scars." She reaches up and pats the edge of the band aid. "They give me character and a story that I once met a spunky survivor that beat all odds, including an EF5 tornado."

Silvey puffs out her cheeks and blows out all the air she can muster.

"I actually came in to give you good news," Beth says.

"Do I get to click my ruby slippers and escape this nightmare?" Silvey asks.

"If you mean the ICU, yes," Beth says. "They have a room ready for you on the step-down unit, and physical therapy will begin this afternoon."

"And that's the good news?" Silvey asks.

Beth smiles. "Silvey, it's a step in the right direction."

"Is it an open ward?" Silvey asks.

"What do you mean?" Beth asks.

"Are the hospital rooms available to any visitors?" Silvey asks, biting the inside of her cheek.

"Yes," Beth says, watching Silvey's face drain of color. "I thought that would be a good thing. Your friends and family can come and go without having to check in and out."

"Do you recall that visitor the other day that claimed she was FBI?" Silvey asks.

"Wickers or Vickers, right?"

"Michelle Vickers," Silvey says. "I'm afraid that her or one of her agent buddies will harass me like they have with my friends and family. Plus, the media will now be free to come knocking."

"I can block you from the hospital directory," Beth says. "If someone inquiries about you or your new room that is not on your list, the staff will simply say unknown."

Silvey nods. "Yes, please."

"And if it becomes a problem," Beth says. "We have security officers, like Shane that can monitor your door."

"That's comforting," Silvey says, "but hopefully not necessary."

Beth nods. "They've discontinued all but one intravenous medication. I am going to start the process of getting some of this equipment out of the way. How does that sound?"

"Good," Silvey says. "Do you mind if I text while you do it?"

"Text away," Beth says.

Silvey opens the message app, clicks on Andrea's number. The message thread is blank. "What the…"

"Is there a problem?" Beth asks, unhooking an empty bag.

"Somebody has tampered with my phone," Silvey says, tapping back to Bax's name. It's blank. "All of my recent messages have been deleted."

"Was the phone on your bed with you or over on the table?" Beth asks.

"I think I set it on the table when Geoff came in to bring my breakfast tray in right before he left," Silvey says.

"I'll step out and let security know they need to check all devices he could have come in contact with," Beth says. "I'm so sorry Silvey."

Silvey dials Andrea's number. It rings three times.

"Hello," Andrea answers.

"Dre, we have a major problem," Silvey says.

"What's wrong?" Andrea asks.

"The FBI came back and held a gun on Bax," Silvey says. "And my night nurse who knew everything was working with

236

the agents. He's tampered with my dad's phone and the security officer found a bug in my room."

"Son of a…" Andrea says. "Don't say another word. I'm calling my lawyer. This is beyond harassment. I'll be there in two hours tops."

"See you soon," Silvey says, disconnecting the call.

The door to her room slides open, and the curtain is pulled back. Four security officers enter Silvey's room.

"Ms. Rhoades, we are here to move you to a secure facility," an officer says. "I'm Officer Clark."

"Wait what?" Silvey asks, searching for Beth, hitting the call icon on the phone. She hides it under the covers. *Andrea, please pick up.* "Where's my nurse?"

"We have orders ma'am," Clark says, holding out a piece of paper.

Silvey snatches the paper from the officer, scans the bold print, and feels the embossed eagle logo. "Transfer orders to an undisclosed medical facility signed by the secretary of defense. Are you joking right now?"

"No ma'am," Clark says.

"Beth!" Silvey shouts.

"Ma'am we have to move you now," Clark says, releasing the brakes on the bed.

An officer near her head pulls the leads from the vital monitor and flops them on the bed next to her pillow.

"Seriously!" Silvey yells. "Get away from me!"

Another officer disconnects her remaining IV and fluids spew all over the floor. They push the bed forward but must backtrack and unplug the bed from the wall.

Silvey spots Beth. She's cornered by two security officers and is trying to get around them.

"Beth!" Silvey shouts.

"Silvey!" Beth shouts. "I'm sorry!"

"Call for help!" Silvey shouts, wadding up the paper order and discretely dropping it between the desk and the door as they rush her out of the unit.

"Help!" Silvey shouts as they push her bed into an awaiting elevator. "Somebody help me!"

The volunteer behind the desk stands.

"Call 911!" Silvey shouts. "I'm being kidnapped!"

An officer takes the phone away from the volunteer as the door to the elevator slides shut.

"Where are you taking me?" Silvey asks. "I have a right to know."

"To the loading bay," Clark says.

"I'm not the fucking laundry!" Silvey shouts. "You can't just unload me without my consent. I just had major surgery!"

"We're aware of your condition," Clark says as the elevator slows and the doors open. "You'll have a medic on board during transit."

"On board?" Silvey asks. "I can't fly in my condition!"

They roll her bed down to a white ambulance.

"No, you can't do this!" Silvey says. "Please, I'm begging you take me back upstairs."

"Hey!" a man shouts running towards Silvey.

Silvey turns. "Shane! Please help!"

"What's going on?" Shane asks, slowing to a stop when one of the officers turns and holds out his arm.

"We have transfer orders for Ms. Rhoades," Clark says.

"He's lying!" Silvey says. "I never consented to a transfer, nor was it ordered by anyone here."

"Where's the documentation?" Shane asks, resting his hand on his yellow taser. "Show me!"

Clark shakes his head. "Shane. Trust me you don't want to get involved."

"Clark, show me the paperwork," Shane says.

Clark nods to the guy closest to Silvey. He yanks back the covers.

"What in the hell!" Silvey screams. She slides the phone under her.

"She has a phone!" the officer says and leans forward to reach for it.

Silvey swings a left hook and hits the guy square in the jaw. He stumbles back.

"This is assault!" Silvey screams. "If another person lays a finger on me, I will sue you and your mother for everything you have!"

"Too late," Clark whispers. He lunges for her, but Shane fires the taser and it connects with Clark's side. He collapses.

The two other men rush Shane and the man Silvey just struck is glaring down at her.

"You realize this is all on camera?" Silvey asks, pointing towards a camera facing her and the officer.

He smiles and shakes his head. "It's a good thing they're off at the moment." The doors to the ambulance swing open and a medic hops out. "Let's go!" He pushes the bed towards the ambulance.

"Shane!" Silvey shouts, attempting to sit up and fight. But the pain makes her nausea. "Help!" She reaches for the medic. "I do not consent take me back inside!"

The medic shakes their head and takes her hand. "Let's make this ride as painless as possible." He places a mask over Silvey's mouth and nose.

She swats his hand away, but the officer holds her arms down.

The medic leans over her. "Deep breath."

Don't breathe! Silvey wiggles her hand free of their grasp and reaches for the officer's radio. She holds the call button down. "Help!" *Why does it smell sweet?* She turns and tries to nudge the mask off, but her body goes limp.

44

Silvey's call disconnects.

Andrea screams.

Scott slams on the brakes. "What's happening!"

"Drive!" Andrea says, fumbling the phone. "The call ended. I'm calling Evelyn. Do not stop."

Scott nods. They round the last corner, and he floors the gas. They fly up the hill towards the highway.

"What did the police say?" Andrea asks, waiting for Evelyn to answer.

"The police are already at the hospital," Scott says, taking a left on to the exit. "And they called in the county sheriff to help with the search."

"Andrea?" Evelyn answers.

"Yes," Andrea says. "I heard everything. They've taken Silvey."

"Her nurse Beth just called and said there was an emergency," Evelyn says. "Do you know what's happening?"

"Silvey was taken from the ICU to the loading bay."

"What! Hold on I'm putting you on speaker," Evelyn says. "Buzz, get over here!"

"Silvey managed to call me when the officers entered her room. They are taking her to an undisclosed secure location."

"Who is?" Buzz asks.

"Why?" Evelyn asks.

Andrea presses down on her bouncing knee. "Silvey said the transfer order was signed by the secretary of defense."

"You think the FBI agents snatched Silvey?" Buzz asks.

"Don't be ridiculous!" Evelyn shouts.

"Sorry Evelyn, but yes that's the only plausible answer after they had an agent working as Silvey's nurse," Andrea says.

"Beth?" Evelyn and Buzz ask in unison.

"No, Geoff, he was working the night shift."

"Son of a b…"

"Buzz!" Evelyn cuts him off.

"Buzz, do you have the find my phone app on your phone?" Andrea asks.

"I'm not sure," Buzz says.

"I know she had the phone up until a squeal of tires," Andrea says. "But the call disconnected shortly after."

Scott slows when he can't pass the flow of traffic ahead.

"We've hit traffic and are still north of the river," Andrea says. "Get over to the unit and find out what you can. We'll be there soon."

"Call us if you hear anything more," Buzz says.

"I will," Andrea says. She dials Rozanne. It only rings once.

"Hi Andrea," Rozanne answers.

"Hi, is Bax there?" Andrea asks.

"He just laid down," Rozanne says. "He was up all night reading an article about project rainbow and then went to the hospital to talk to Silvey this morning."

"They took her," Andrea says, her voice hiccups on the last word.

"Gage, get Bax and start the car!" Rozanne says. "When?"

"Thirty minutes ago," Andrea says, wiping the falling tears. "They yanked her out of the ICU like some kind of criminal. I overheard the whole thing."

"We're on our way!" Rozanne says. "You're on speaker. I'm handing the phone to Bax."

"Hey," Bax says.

"Bax, they took Silvey!" Andrea says.

"FBI?" Bax asks.

"The transfer order was signed by the secretary of defense," Andrea says. "Either them or someone higher up."

"Our names are listed in the project rainbow document," Bax says. "Did you read it?"

"I only got fifty pages in before I fell asleep," Andrea says, pulling up the document. She clicks in the search bar at the top and types in Silvey's name. "Participant twenty-one Silvey Lynn Rhoades." She scans the name above. *Participant twenty Baxton Auburn.* "Holy… hell. What is happening?"

"Vickers held a gun to my ribs this morning after Geoff attempted to inject me with something," Bax says. "I don't want to know what they'll do to Silvey. She's not fit to be interrogated in her condition."

"Do you have any idea of where they will take her?" Andrea asks.

"What's the closest operational military base that could have a hospital on site?" Bax asks.

"Whiteman or Leavenworth!" Scott says.

"My bet is Leavenworth," Rozanne says. "A prison is the perfect place to test new subjects if they are still experimenting."

"We're twenty minutes away from the hospital," Andrea says. "I hope they have a license plate or clear shot of the men responsible."

"Gage is driving," Bax says. "We'll be there in less than an hour."

"Bax, can you give me a play-by-play of what happened this morning?" Andrea asks.

"Sure."

45

Silvey groans and her eyelids flutter. She looks up and frowns.

"We're almost there," a man says.

"Where am I?" Silvey asks, staring at the passing ceiling tiles.

"We're almost there," a man says again.

"Who's we?" Silvey asks, looking up at the man.

He pulls off his hood exposing his face. "Captain Darryl Wilson."

Silvey frowns. "You did this to me?"

"Not directly," he says, stopping outside a large double door. He waves his badge in front of a black box on the wall and the doors swing open.

"Our team," Captain Wilson says. He points to a woman and a man dressed in identical green polo shirts. They stand shoulder to shoulder equal in height and build, but the woman has pale skin and milky blue eyes, and the man has olive skin and coal-black eyes.

"You're the owners of the vertical farm," Silvey says, pointing at the couple. "What is going on?" She attempts to sit up. "And why do I feel like a lead tank glued to this bed?"

"It's a sedative wearing off," the woman says. "We didn't want your journey here to strain your injuries." She extends her hand. "I'm Charlotte and this is my husband, Eli."

Silvey glares at her. "We've met before. Why did you snatch me from the hospital with force?"

"We intercepted the FBI," Eli says, shaking his head.

Silvey sighs. "How?"

"Chance," Eli says. "We agreed last night that we would approach you today."

"Approach me about what?" Silvey asks.

"A quicker recovery option," Charlotte says.

"You realize I had major surgery to repair my spine, hip and femur just yesterday," Silvey says.

"We weren't planning on you coming here quite so soon," Eli says. "It was only by chance like I said that we had just pulled into the parking garage when the police squad cars pulled up to the lobby of the hospital. I watched as the FBI agents were placed in the back of a squad car. Before they pulled away, a security officer was called over to the car. I saw a handover of cash, knew something was up, and followed them inside."

"We overheard the security officer recruit a few men to transfer you out of the hospital via the loading bay," Charlotte says.

"We headed them off and found the waiting ambulance," Eli says. "I found a stray wheelchair, a few blankets, draped them over Charlotte, and pushed her out onto the loading bay. The medic didn't hesitate. He threw the door open and loaded Charlotte into the ambulance."

Charlotte sighs. "I'm not proud of this, but I've carried a can of pepper spray for years. I used it for the first time on the driver and the medic."

"We did drop them off at the emergency room and made it back to the loading bay just in time to pick you up," Eli says.

"The security officer I punched got into the ambulance with me," Silvey says.

"I used a cannister of laughing gas on all of us," Eli says. "I put the mask over your face but didn't connect the line to the cannister. Charlotte had a mask on while driving, so it didn't affect her as bad." He shakes his head. "We stopped at the bottom of the hill and kicked the security officer out of the ambulance."

"And the sedative?" Silvey asks.

"The medic I sprayed had it ready," Charlotte says. "I'm sorry we didn't try a different route to intervene, but we knew that the police, security officers, and the FBI were all working together on this."

"The urgency was necessary," Captain Wilson says. "The FBI has been breathing down my neck. When I woke up, I remembered an encounter with a lady by the name Silvey Rhoades, and the rest was a bit fuzzy." He holds up his hands. "I'm sorry for turning them in your direction. The agents escorted me to the base. They were insistent that I show them where I was, but I couldn't find the entrance."

"We concealed the entrance to the passageway immediately after the tornado," Eli says.

"Why?" Silvey asks.

"Mostly for the safety of the general public," Charlotte says. "There were search parties in the area looking for the missing residents and smaller parties looking for lost possessions."

"And the FBI wants to know what is here?" Silvey asks.

"Yes," Eli says.

"The only reason I made it out of FBI custody was because of the public interest," Captain Wilson says. "And when I was leaving the care facility after visiting my wife Millie," he points to Eli and Charlotte, "they were waiting."

"We explained who we were and what we knew, plus the connection to you," Charlotte says. "And he agreed to help us understand what we have been protecting."

"And it's truly worth all the secrecy," Eli says.

"I am losing my patience," Silvey says.

"Can we show you?" Charlotte says. "It might help."

"I'm not exactly in walking form," Silvey says, waving her hand over her body.

"When we purchased the property with the silo three years ago," Charlotte says, pushing the bed further into the large space. "We discovered a section of the base that was not on the original deed." She stops pushing once they enter. The walls, ceiling and floor are all white. "We found a working nuclear fusion power lab attached to a worm hole simulator and housing bunker with a suspension chamber with our friend Captain Wilson."

"I've been here," Silvey says, pointing towards the far end of the space. "The nuclear lab is behind a mirror, and it's attached to a control room."

Charlotte points up. Silvey follows her finger to a gaping hole ripped in the center.

"That wasn't there before," Silvey says.

"The tornado sucked out a vent to this chamber," Charlotte says. "It tripped a failsafe and released Captain Wilson from suspension."

"Two questions," Silvey says, holding up her hand. "One, what is a suspension chamber and two you knew about a human trapped down here and didn't think to report it?"

Captain Wilson steps into Silvey's line of sight. "I'll answer the first question."

Charlotte and Eli nod.

"A suspension chamber holds a human in a state of stasis while their consciousness travels through time."

"Yea," Silvey says. "I'm going to need a more specific definition."

"When you and I met," Captain Wilson says. "It was not in the year 2022, right?"

"According to a friend," Silvey says. "It was 1962."

"And at any point was your body physically not in 2022?" Captain Wilson asks.

"No, but..." Silvey says.

He holds up a hand before Silvey can finish. "We travel through time in our mind and perceive our own identity with a host."

"I saw my reflection," Silvey says. "I was definitely me."

"Your mind saw you, but the men and women you interacted with saw a tall lady with tight ringlet brown curls and brown eyes."

"No!" Silvey says. "Bax saw me and recognized me and I him, plus your face is exactly how I remember."

"Who is Bax?" Eli asks.

"He worked for Micah and was working inside the silo the morning of the tornado," Silvey says.

"Ah, Baxton Auburn," Charlotte says.

"Yes," Silvey says.

"He traveled too?" Eli asks, glancing at Captain Wilson.

Silvey nods.

"That's new news to me," Captain Wilson says. "A traveler can spot another traveler's true identity."

46

Scott squeezes Andrea's hand as they ride up the elevator. Andrea finds Buzz and Evelyn in a heated argument with a man in a suit when the doors open. She sticks her thumb and finger in the corners of her lips and lets out an ear-piercing whistle.

The man in the suit turns towards Andrea and Scott.

"Who are you?" Andrea asks, marching towards Evelyn and Buzz. "And how dare you raise your voice to these people?"

"Barney Holder, I'm one of the hospital administrators and I was trying to explain that we are not at fault for the transfer of their daughter!"

"Bull shit!" Andrea says, tapping the man on the chest.

Buzz and Evelyn take a step back.

"It was four hospital security officers that took Silvey from the ICU without her consent to a loading bay where she was assaulted and then shoved into an ambulance."

Barney's face reddens. "And how would you know all of that?"

Scott holds up his phone. "Because Silvey called my wife when the men forced their way into the room, and we recorded the entire call."

"Where is Silvey's nurse, Beth?" Andrea asks, turning towards Evelyn.

"They won't let us speak to her," Evelyn says, wiping the tears running down her face.

"Sir, we have every media outlet in the metropolitan area headed here," Andrea says. "And you have less than two minutes to make this right before we make this very public."

"There is no need to make threats," Barney says.

"That is no threat," Andrea says. "My friend was assaulted and kidnapped by your security officers, and we have a witness."

A volunteer behind the desk waves. "I will back her statement. I was here."

Andrea smirks. "One minute."

Barney backs away from Andrea. "Give me five minutes."

"You have about thirty seconds," Andrea says.

Barney pulls out his phone and holds up a finger. "I need legal to fourth floor stat."

Andrea rolls her eyes and walks past Barney to the volunteer. "Ma'am. May I have your consent to record you while you give a statement?"

"Absolutely," the volunteer says.

Andrea holds up her phone. "Can you tell me your name and what you do here?"

"My name is Gretta Nichols. I am a volunteer here at the hospital. I help visitors check in here at the desk outside of the ICU."

"And can you tell me what day it is and what you saw this morning?" Andrea asks.

Barney steps in between Andrea and Gretta. "That's enough!"

"Excuse me," Gretta says, stepping around Barney. "Today is Saturday, April 23, 2022, and I witnessed five security officers enter the ICU. I overheard shouting and a few minutes later they were wheeling a patient out on a bed who was shouting for help. When I picked up the phone to call for help, a security officer came over and took the cord from the phone. He told me to mind my business. The fifth officer left the ICU and Beth stumbled out after him, shouting to call the police. A patient had been taken."

"I said enough!" Barney says, attempting to take Andrea's phone.

Buzz blocks his reach and steps between Andrea and Barney. "I dare you to lay a finger on me."

"Gretta, did you call the police?" Andrea asks.

"I did," Gretta says, pulling out her personal phone from the pink vest. "The dispatcher said they would send a unit right away."

"And did any police arrive?" Evelyn asks.

"No," Gretta says. "The security officer returned to the floor and escorted Miss Beth away from the ICU right before this couple arrived." She points to Evelyn and Buzz. "And Barney showed up a few minutes later."

"Thanks Gretta," Andrea says, turning the camera towards Barney. "Would you like to make a statement now?"

Barney's face reddens. "No comment."

Andrea ends the recording. "Let's go!" She turns to the elevator.

Gretta takes off her pink vest and drops it at Barney's feet. "I'm done here."

Evelyn points to Barney. "You and this hospital will pay for this. Let's go Buzz."

Scott holds the elevator for Evelyn and Buzz and locks eyes with Barney. "You pissed off the wrong family today."

"What are we going to do?" Evelyn asks as the elevator doors close.

"I need to track down a security officer by the name of Shane," Andrea says. "He was trying to help Silvey, and he may be able to tell us more."

Gretta nods. "I can take you down to the security office." She holds up her badge. "I need to turn this in."

The elevator slows and stops. The doors open to a cacophony of noise.

They hesitantly step into the fray of security officers and reporters shouting over each other.

"You weren't lying about calling the media," Buzz says.

"It wasn't Andrea," Scott says, shaking his head. "But I'm glad they're here."

"He's right," Andrea says. "Evelyn, can you make a statement that Silvey has been unlawfully taken from the hospital and that we need every available resource to search for her?"

Evelyn nods. "Yes, but what are you going to do?"

"Light a match on social media and watch this place burn," Andrea says, holding up her phone. "But I need to find Shane and if possible, Beth to really make this work."

Gretta nods. "It's not far. But I am not sure if there will be anyone left in the office judging by the number of officers here in the lobby."

"Scott, can you stay with Buzz and Evelyn?" Andrea asks.

"You bet," Scott says, "be careful. I'm not sure who we can trust."

Andrea nods and follows Gretta down the hall away from the crowd.

"I'll go in and ask for Shane," Gretta says, slowing down as they approach an open door.

"Ok," Andrea says, leaning her back against the wall near the door.

"Hi," Gretta says, walking into the office. "Any chance Shane's around?"

A woman behind the desk holds up a finger. She covers the receiver end of the phone. "Hey Gretta, did your badge stop working again?"

"Something like that," Gretta says.

"Come on back," the woman says. "You know where he sits, right?"

Gretta nods and walks past the desk. She takes a left and spots Beth in a room with two people in suits. She hesitates outside the door.

"Can I help you?" a man asks from behind Gretta.

"Oh!" Gretta says, holding her hand to her chest. "I was looking for Shane."

"He's in the next room," the man says. "But tied up at the moment. Can I help you?"

He's one of the four men. "No, thank you," Gretta says, backing away from him. "I'll just leave a message with the desk."

The door to the meeting room with Beth opens. The two people in suits walk out.

Gretta rushes into the room.

Beth stands.

Gretta takes Beth's hand and whispers, "Come with me."

The doorway is blocked by the security officer. "Where are you two going?"

"Beth," Gretta says. "Needs a tampon, do you mind!" She pushes past him with Beth and rushes towards the hallway.

"What's going on?" Beth whispers.

"Silvey's friend," Gretta says, pointing to Andrea. "We need your help."

Beth burst into tears.

Andrea wraps her arm around Beth and walks her away from the security office into the woman's bathroom across the hall.

"I'm so sorry," Beth says, sniffling and wiping away her tears. "I tried to stop them."

Gretta hands Beth a few tissues from the counter.

"I know," Andrea says. "Silvey managed to call me when it was happening."

"Is she ok?" Beth asks.

"We don't know," Andrea says. "Did the officer give any clue as to where they could have taken her?"

"The officer who held me back said the orders were from the government." Beth pulls out a crumpled piece of paper. "Silvey managed to drop this on her way out." She smooths out the paper and hands it to Andrea.

"Oh my god," Andrea says, reading the text. "The transfer order was signed by the secretary of defense."

Beth nods. "I didn't tell the hospital legal team that I found it. I want the officers who took Silvey to pay for what they've done."

"Thank you," Andrea says, drying a place on the counter before placing the paper down and snapping a photo of the document. She sends it to Scott. "I have one other huge favor to ask."

Beth nods. "Anything."

"Can I record you while you explain what happened this morning?" Andrea asks.

Beth turns towards the mirror and wipes her red puffy eyes. "Of course."

Andrea nods to Gretta. "Can you keep an eye out?"

"Happy too," Gretta says, patting Beth on the shoulder. "Give them hell."

Andrea presses record once Gretta steps out of the bathroom. "Can you tell me your name and what you do?"

"Beth Cartwell. I am an ICU nurse here at the hospital."

"Can you tell me what happened to a patient this morning on your unit?" Andrea asks.

"Five hospital security officers entered my unit and took my patient against her will."

"Was this patient Silvey Rhoades?" Andrea asks.

"Yes," Beth answers.

"And was she medically cleared for a transfer?" Andrea asks.

"I had a transfer order to a step-down unit on the same floor," Beth says. "But she was forcefully taken out of the hospital. I tried to fight back, but was cornered by two of the officers until they had her in the elevator."

"Do you know who gave the security officers their orders?" Andrea asks, handing her the paper from Silvey.

"No, but I found this on the floor," Beth says, holding up the paper.

Andrea pulls back and focuses the lens on the paper.

"I've never seen anything like this," Beth says.

Andrea pans back up to Beth. "Did anything else happen during your shift?"

Beth nods. "The night nurse that cared for Silvey was arrested for assaulting a visitor that had stopped by to see Ms. Rhoades. Silvey also believed that this man could have tampered with her phone."

"And who was this man?" Andrea asks.

"Geoff Linder," Beth says. "He was taken into custody by local police this morning."

"Thank you," Andrea says, putting away her phone. "I know that this has not been easy."

"I'm terrified," Beth says. "The legal team threatened my nursing license if I stepped out of line."

Gretta opens the door. "We need to hide."

"Why?" Andrea asks.

"The FBI just walked in," Gretta says. "And they're looking for Beth."

"Oh my god, why?" Beth asks.

"It's fine," Andrea says, looking her over. "Beth, go into a stall and take off your scrubs."

"What?" Beth asks.

"I'm giving you my clothes," Andrea says. "They will be looking for a woman in scrubs not a person in a hoodie and jeans." She sends the videos of Gretta and Beth to Scott and Rozanne.

Beth steps into a stall and takes off her scrub top. "I won't need your hoodie. I've got on an old college shirt." She hands her pants over the top of the stall.

Andrea steps out of her jeans and drops them over to Beth. "You good?" She slides on the scrubs and ties the waist.

"Yes," Beth says, stepping out of the stall. "They took my phone and purse."

"I've got you," Gretta says, holding up her phone. "My husband is waiting for us out front."

Andrea steps out of the stall and gestures for Gretta's phone. "Call me if you think of anything else." She saves her phone number in Gretta's phone. "And thanks for your help. If you think of anything else, let us know."

"Clark," Beth says, "he was the officer that appeared to be in charge."

47

Baxton jumps out of the car and runs for the hospital entrance.

"Bax, wait," Gage says, hopping out of the car.

"Let him go," Rozanne says. "We'll catch up with him."

Bax has to weave through the crowded lobby until he reaches the elevator. A strong hand grips his forearm. He whirls with his fist raised.

Buzz lifts a hand. "I see you are in fine swinging form today."

"I'm so sorry, Mr. Rhoades," Bax says.

Buzz shakes his head. "It's fine son, come with me."

"Have you heard anything?" Bax asks, walking with Buzz to a corner of the lobby with a few chairs and a camera crew.

"Nothing helpful," Buzz says, waving a hand towards Evelyn. "Have you met Silvey's mom, Evelyn?"

Evelyn looks Bax up and down.

"This is Baxton Auburn," Buzz says.

"Ma'am," Bax says, offering his hand.

"Do you know where they took her?" Evelyn asks.

"No ma'am," Bax says. "But I believe I know the two agents responsible for this." The camera man to Bax's right whirls around and points the lens in his direction. "Who are you?"

"We're a crew from channel five," a reporter says, extending their hand. "Heather Sanders. And you're Baxton Auburn, correct."

Rozanne and Gage step beside Bax.

"Let's give them a bit of privacy," Rozanne says, blocking the camera.

"Rozanne!" Andrea says, running up to them. "You made it!"

"Yes!" Rozanne says, hugging Andrea.

Andrea releases Rozanne and turns towards Bax. "I'm glad you're ok. Silvey told me what happened this morning."

Bax nods. "I shouldn't have left her here alone."

"None of us could have predicted what would happen," Andrea says.

"Are you wearing scrubs?" Scott asks, walking around the reporters and looking her up and down.

"Yes," Andrea says, "but only the bottoms."

"Do I want to know what happened to your jeans?" Scott asks.

"I found Beth," Andrea says. "She needed an exit."

"Ah, I've merged what we know into one video." He hands his phone to Andrea. "Take a look."

Andrea steps beside Evelyn and hits play. "Did you give a statement?"

"Yes," Evelyn says, watching the image of Silvey appear in the video. She gasps. "My girl."

"We'll find her," Andrea says, fast-forwarding through Gretta's statement. She presses play again when Beth's face appears. "Watch."

Evelyn watches Beth's statement and passes the phone back to Andrea.

"I've got the order," Andrea says, handing it to Buzz. "What do you think?"

Buzz pulls out a pair of reading glasses and slides them to the tip of his nose. He looks it over, then passes it to Scott. "I would say bogus. Because they would never put that in writing."

"I second Buzz," Scott says, passing it to Gage.

"Wow," Gage says, feeling the embossed logo at the top. "I would say this was printed on legit stationary. My guess is it was done by somebody with access to the secretary."

"Do we have what we need to expose them?" Bax asks Andrea.

"Yes," Andrea says. "Are you willing to go public with what happened this morning?"

"Yes!" Bax says.

"Heather," Scott says. "We're ready."

Heather and her crew set up a few microphones for Bax and Andrea. She records her introduction and then turns her attention towards Andrea and Bax. They spend the next fifteen minutes going over every detail of the phone call from Silvey, the video statements made by Gretta and Beth, and pause when a crew of men and women with black jackets surround them.

"I believe that's enough," a man says, pulling out his badge.

"You can take your badge and shove it," Buzz says. "Unless you are here to arrest the four officers who assaulted and abducted my daughter, move along."

Heather leans forward to read the badge. "Tell me officer, or is it agent Arnold? What does the FBI want with two civilians injured by the tragic tornado?"

"No comment," Agent Arnold says. "Our office will release a statement this afternoon."

"Unless you are here to support our search for Silvey please move along," Andrea says.

"Ma'am our priorities align," Agent Arnold says.

Bax stands and towers over the agent. "Is that what Agent Carlton and Agent Vickers priorities were this morning?"

Agent Arnold takes a step back. "We don't have agents by the names Carlton and Vickers in our field office." He turns and nods to another agent. They step away with their phone raised to their ear. "We would like to assist the family with the possible abduction of a Ms. Silvey Rhoades."

"Possible?" Andrea asks, pulling up the recording of Silvey's call. She presses play. When the recording ends, she shakes her phone. "Does that sound like a possible abduction or an actual kidnapping?"

"Can you send that recording to our tech team?" Agent Arnold asks, handing Andrea a card. "And you are?"

"Andrea Meyer," Andrea says, giving the card to Scott. "We believe that two of your agents are at fault for the abduction of Silvey. They were here in the hospital this morning, and they've harassed Mr. Auburn, Silvey's mother, Evelyn, and have attempted to corner me over the last few days."

Agent Arnold leans away from Andrea as an agent steps up to whisper in his ear. "Do you have the first names or the badge numbers for the agents in question?"

"Michelle Vickers." Andrea turns to Bax.

"Neil Carlton," Bax says.

"I'm afraid we have no record of either agent in the FBI," Agent Arnold says.

"Bull," Gage says. "I had a friend run the plates of the agent's car that stopped by to harass one of my employees at my place of business. It's registered to the US government."

Heather motions to her sound and camera guy. They nod.

"For the record," Heather says, "Agent Arnold, you claim two people are impersonating FBI agents in a vehicle registered to the US government."

"No comment," Agent Arnold says.

Buzz steps towards the agent, but collapses, holding a hand to his chest.

"Help!" Evelyn screams. The entire lobby full of people goes silent and the eyes shift towards their group. "He's having a damn heart attack. Stop your gawking and help!"

48

Silvey lays back on the pillow. "Let me attempt to summarize the plot here." She holds up a finger. "I was sucked up into a tornado and a worm hole simultaneously." She holds up a second finger. "I landed in a field a mile from here but also in a host in the year 1962." She holds up a third finger. "Where I ran into the traveling version of Captain Wilson and subsequently Baxton Auburn before waking from a coma back in 2022." She holds up a fourth finger. "I was handcuffed to a chair while interviewed by Bob, JFK's secretary of defense, and Jean Tremble about my connection to Bax."

"Whoa," Captain Wilson says, holding up a hand. "You were handcuffed and questioned?"

"Yes," Silvey says.

"What did you tell them?" Captain Wilson asks.

"Not much. They were after the identity of Bax and wanted to know what you told me after our first encounter. But once I figured out who they were, I may have let the cat out of the bag so to speak."

"They left me knowing the system was compromised," Captain Wilson says.

"You've traveled more than once?" Charlotte asks.

"Yes," Silvey says. "I am listed as participant twenty-one."

Captain Wilson's jaw falls open. "How?"

Eli and Charlotte exchange a glance and shrug.

"What are you a participant of?" Eli asks.

"Something called Project Rainbow," Silvey says, pointing to Captain Wilson. "He would know being participant number one and all."

"What is Project Rainbow?" Charlotte asks, placing her hands on her hips.

"We were testing controlled teleportation to a specific place and time," Captain Wilson says. "That was the purpose of the control room." He turns in a small circle. "All of this was just part of the research. The other was the suspension chamber."

"Ok," Silvey says. "Is this revenge? Are you going to leave me here for sixty years?"

"No Silvey," Charlotte says. "The suspension chamber can heal your injuries."

"You expect me to climb into a chamber that left him locked in for sixty years and only a tornado set him free?" Silvey asks. "Um, no thanks."

"Captain Wilson can operate the chamber and he's shown us how," Eli says. "It's remarkable, really."

"We've tested it out on each other," Charlotte says. "I had Crohn's disease, and I am completely healed. And Eli had a torn rotator cuff and a heart murmur. All healed."

"Plus, look him over," Eli says, pointing to the captain. "He'll be 101 in September."

Silvey laughs. "And this technology from the 1960s was just locked away and forgotten about?"

Captain Wilson nods. "Um, that was a classified side experiment because the nano technology inside the chamber was stolen."

Charlotte nods. "We found instructions written in Hebrew and signed by a scientist that was taken during the war and never seen again."

"What war?" Silvey asks.

"The second world war," Captain Wilson says.

"Hmm," Silvey says, tapping her chin. "And that is why Gobert attacked the base."

"He did, when?" Captain Wilson asks.

"The night I met you in the hall," Silvey says. "Bax let in a truck, and the driver was Hans Gobert."

"Who is Gobert?" Eli asks.

Silvey rolls her eyes. "A German spy with ties back to his brother who was a Nazi guard for scientist and doctors."

"The siren was a ground attack," Captain Wilson says, running a hand over his head and down his face. "I sacrificed everything for a ground attack?"

"You knew they would leave you?" Charlotte asks.

"No, but we were instructed that if we were left in for any extended period… it was due to an air assault on the base."

"The hercules missiles here were never launched," Eli says. "I did a fair bit of research about the base before we bought it. And I never found a single incident that would qualify as an air assault on the base."

Captain Wilson staggers back.

"Are you ok?" Charlotte asks, rushing towards him.

"I think I just need to sit down," Captain Wilson says, lowering himself to the floor and placing his head between his knees.

"Sorry," Silvey says, "I had no idea the truth could be so triggering."

Charlotte shakes her head. "Sixty years holds a lot of truth bombs for our friend."

"I bet," Silvey says.

"Do you want to see the suspension chamber?" Eli asks.

"Um," Silvey says, looking around the room. "Can you wheel me there?"

"Sure," Eli says. He kneels next to Captain Wilson. "Take as long as you need."

"I'll stay here with him," Charlotte says.

Eli nods and pushes the bed with Silvey towards a wall. Her reflection comes into view as he pivots the bed to the right.

"I look awful," Silvey says, reaching a hand up towards her greasy hair and down to her puffy dark eyes. "Does the chamber have a hair washing station?"

Eli laughs. "I'm afraid not, but you will be able to shower and clean up shortly after you emerge from the tank."

"Meaning I will have to submerge?" Silvey asks, looking at Eli in the reflection.

"Kind of," Eli says, pushing her and the bed around the mirror and into a grey dark room. "Have you seen the commercials for a salt water floating spa experience?"

"Weightless Wonder?" Silvey asks.

"I think that's one of them," Eli says. He pauses and flips a breaker. One by one the lights flicker on, illuminating a glass tank the size of a coffin in the middle of the cold grey space. Various lines and tubes run up along the sides of the tank.

"That looks very ominous," Silvey whispers.

"Can you imagine finding it with a man inside?" Eli says. "Charlotte screamed so long she nearly passed out."

"It's true," Charlotte says, walking in and standing beside Silvey. "I was terrified."

Silvey looks back at Captain Wilson. "Do you want to explain how it works?"

"Sure," Captain Wilson says. He walks towards the tank, reaches inside it, and scoops up a handful of white beads. "These contain millions of nanoparticles. They work in tandem with your nervous system. They map your body and identify any weakness. Once the initial map is complete, it sends a sequence of commands to the nano particles absorbed through the skin. It will continue this process until your body is back to stasis."

"And you've both tried it out?" Silvey asks, looking at Eli and Charlotte. They nod.

"Even got rid of a nasty acne scar I had along my chin." Eli says.

Silvey reaches up towards her face and taps the bridge of her nose. "Will it wipe away my freckles?"

"Captain?" Charlotte asks.

"Only the ones that are potentially cancerous," Captain Wilson says.

"I'm pretty sure I have some hardware from the surgery," Silvey says. "What happens to that?"

"It will absorb the hardware into the nanoparticles and expel it bit by bit."

"Expel it how?" Silvey asks.

"Your pores," Captain Wilson says.

"Does it hurt?" Silvey asks.

"No," Charlotte and Eli say in unison.

"It tingles at first," Charlotte says. She wraps her arms around herself. "Then it feels like a warm hug."

Silvey sighs. "For how long?"

"It varies for each person," Captain Wilson says. "And I suspect that your injuries were quite extensive based on the article in the paper."

"What article?" Silvey asks.

"It was a piece written about the survivors directly impacted by the tornado that was published yesterday," Charlotte says. "That's why we were coming to talk to you about the suspension chamber."

"I didn't speak to a reporter," Silvey says.

Eli nods. "It was the medic that found you in the field. He didn't use your name directly, but it was enough information that we put the pieces together. Plus, Captain Wilson was eager to speak to you, too."

Silvey nods. "I should at least call my family first." She pats the mattress. "Have you seen my phone? I'm sure my friend Andrea is raising hell at the hospital."

"Um, we don't have any service down here," Charlotte says. "We think the security officer pocketed the phone before we kicked him out. I'm so sorry."

"Can I text Andrea from your phone?" Silvey asks, tapping her head. "It's the only number I still know by heart."

Charlotte nods. "Will she send the FBI here?"

"No," Silvey says. "She's had a run in with both agents over the last few days. And that's the last thing she would want to do."

Charlotte pulls out her phone and hands it to Silvey after swiping the passcode in.

"Can you take me home when this is done?" Silvey asks, typing in Andrea's number.

"Yes," Eli says.

"Wait, will I be conscious while this works?" Silvey asks.

"Not exactly," Captain Wilson says. "You'll feel like you're dreaming."

"Will I travel back again?" Silvey asks, hovering her thumbs over the screen.

Captain Wilson frowns. "I only traveled twice, and it was under the guidance of the control room. I've never freely traveled without an anchor."

"And neither of you went anywhere?" Silvey asks, looking at Eli and Charlotte.

"Time wise, no," Charlotte says. "I had a dream that I was sitting down at a table with bowls of pasta and round pans of pizza."

"And my dream was all about rock climbing," Eli says.

"Things you couldn't enjoy because of your ailments?" Silvey asks.

They nod.

"I can live with that," Silvey says. "But in case I do run into the pair from 1962, do I warn them about the assassination of JFK or just let history be history?"

Charlotte gasps.

Eli's mouth falls open.

"He was assassinated?" Captain Wilson asks.

"Yes, in 1963 a year after my encounter with you," Silvey says, looking him over. "I'm sorry. I thought they would have filled you in on the history."

Charlotte nods. "We were working our way back from 2022."

"Oh, my bad," Silvey says, finishing her typed message to Andrea. "Take a look. Let me know if you want me to be any more vague."

264

Charlotte takes the phone and reviews the content of the message. "Definitely vague. Will she believe it's from you?"

"The sign off SLRP at the end is a nickname from elementary school," Silvey says. "She'll know it's from me."

"Ok," Charlotte says. "I'll walk up after we get you inside the tank."

"I would prefer it if you sent it before," Silvey says.

"I can take it up," Eli says, taking Charlotte's phone. "We should step out and give you gals some privacy."

"I'm going into that naked?" Silvey asks, pointing at the chamber.

"Yes," Captain Wilson says. "We tried it once with a pair of shorts and it dissolved them within minutes. The nanos are programed for human tissue, not polyester."

"Right," Silvey says, "and the worse that can happen is that I still have months of rehab ahead of me?"

"True," Eli says.

"Any questions?" Charlotte asks.

"Doesn't the captain need to be in here to work this thing?" Silvey asks.

"I'll step back in once you are submerged," Captain Wilson says.

Silvey nods. "Let's roll before I lose my nerve."

Charlotte rolls the bed parallel with the chamber. "I'm lucky you're small. I can barely lift my own body weight."

"And that I'm not Bax," Silvey says. "He's a literal giant." She pulls off the lead stickers stuck to her chest under her gown. "Fair warning, I have over a hundred stitches in my abdomen alone."

"You poor thing," Charlotte says.

Silvey waves her hand. "No! I do not deserve any pity. Micah's funeral is today, and I should be there to support his wife and our friends. I lived. He died."

Charlotte blinks back tears. "I'm really sorry he didn't make it. We've talked with the engineer and inspector about the installation of the spiral ramps."

"Charlotte, it was a big ass tornado. The fact that any of us made it out is a miracle."

Charlotte nods. "We are working with the insurance company and our lawyers for compensation for damages incurred by our contractors, their loss of wages, equipment and so on."

"That's great," Silvey says, taking an arm out of the gown. "Micah's wife, Jessica, could use the assistance." She takes the other arm out but holds the gown to her chest. "How do you want to do this?"

Charlotte lowers the bed rails and pushes the bed flesh with the glass. "How is your upper body strength?"

"I haven't lifted anything heavier than a glass of water since the incident," Silvey says.

"Then we'll go in stages," Charlotte says, going to the far end of the bed. "Legs first, then torso?"

"Sure," Silvey says, shimmying her body to the edge of the bed. "How deep is it?"

"You'll float on the surface for a bit before you sink in," Charlotte says. "On three." She wraps her hands around Silvey's calves. "One, two three."

"AHHHHHH!" Silvey screams.

Charlotte lets go of Silvey's legs and rushes towards her torso. She hooks her arms under Silvey's shoulders and arms.

"Stop it hurts!" Silvey cries.

Charlotte lifts the rest of Silvey's naked body onto the white particles.

"Please!" Silvey shouts.

"I'm so sorry!" Charlotte says, pressing a lever. A clear cover entraps Silvey inside as she sinks into the particles. "It's done!"

Silvey bangs on the cover. "Stop!"

Captain Wilson rushes back into the room. "Why did she scream?"

Charlotte backs away from the chamber. "I think the movement may have been too much, too soon. Is Eli back?"

"Not yet," Captain Wilson says. "Let me see what I can do to speed up the process." He taps on the console fastened to the side of the chamber.

266

Silvey pounds her hand on the cover near the captain's face. "Get me out of here!"

"She's starting to panic!" Charlotte says, looking over his shoulder at the heart rate and respiration readings.

"Give it a minute for the particles to scan and assess," Captain Wilson says, entering a command. "They'll make her comfortable soon."

49

Andrea paces the small interview room inside the security office. "Do you think Buzz could be having another heart attack?"

"We'll know something soon," Scott says. "And at least we were inside the hospital when he collapsed."

"But who knows if we can trust any of them," Andrea says, pointing towards the door. "They've split us up and have us in here like we're criminals."

"At least they didn't confiscate our phones," Scott says, leaning against the wall. He thumbs through his social media newsfeeds.

"It's gaining views," Scott says, turning his phone towards Andrea. "We're going to find her."

Andrea flips through the posts. "But if the FBI is going to block us at each step Silvey's screwed." Her phone vibrates. "I've got a text from a number I don't recognize." She swipes open the message. *Hey Dre, safe with Depp inside work. See you at home. SLRP.*

Andrea gasps. "We need to get the others."

"What is it?" Scott asks, following Andrea out of the room.

"Not here," Andrea says, swinging open the door to the next room. Bax stands knocking over the chair. Gage and Rozanne turn towards Andrea. "Let's go."

"Andrea," Scott whispers. "What about Buzz and Evelyn?"

"We can't be sure Buzz is well enough to take," Andrea says, rushing past the FBI agents and security officers. "We'll call Evelyn once we are out of earshot."

"Where are you going?" a security officer asks.

"To check on Buzz," Andrea says, forcing a smile.

Rozanne and Gage nudge Bax.

Bax shrugs.

They make it outside, cross the street to the parking garage before Andrea slows and turns towards Scott. "I know where she is."

Rozanne looks over her shoulder. "We were followed. Is your car on this level?"

Scott nods and jogs down the row. "Step inside my office." He clicks the remote to unlock the car."

They cram into the sedan and lock the doors.

"Talk quietly," Gage says. "They could be listening."

"I received a message from a number I don't recognize," Andrea whispers. "Silvey's at the base with Captain Wilson."

"You're sure?" Bax asks.

Andrea nods. "Silvey's queen of the nicknames and she signed off with one from elementary school. There's no way anyone could know to use it." She shows Bax the message. "Depp is referring to the one and only captain of all captains. The work reference is obvious to the base and see you at home meaning she's in Lawson."

Rozanne leans forward. "And she's safe?"

"We'll see," Andrea says. "Do you want to ride or follow?"

"We'll follow," Gage says. "Do you want to call in any reinforcements just in case?"

Scott starts the car. "It may not hurt to have an ambulance on standby."

"I'll work on that," Rozanne says. "I've got a friend who is a medic, and her husband is a doctor."

"Bax?" Andrea asks.

"I'll ride with you," Bax says. "If that's ok."

Andrea nods. "Of course. Gage, Rozanne be careful and if you notice a tail lead them away."

"Sure thing!" Gage says, stepping out of the car and holding the door for Rozanne.

"We'll see you soon," Andrea says.

Scott puts the car in reverse, maneuvers the car out of the spot, and speeds out of the garage.

"Do you know how she could have ended up with Captain Wilson?" Andrea asks, turning to Bax in the backseat.

"No," Bax says. "But to be honest. I'm not that surprised considering the last few days. They were sniffing around us because of something related to the base."

"Do you think there is a team camped out at the base?" Scott asks, looking at Bax's reflection in the rearview mirror.

"Highly likely," Bax says.

"Scott, does your friend still live by the old bus barn?" Andrea asks.

"Yea, why?" Scott asks, pulling on to the highway.

"There's an old railroad trail behind their place that leads out to the nike base," Andrea says.

"He's in my phone under Wayne," Scott says, checking his mirrors. "Hey Bax, does your cousin drive a dodge charger?"

"No," Bax says, looking out the back window. "Son of a…"

"Is it the agents?" Andrea asks, checking the mirror.

"I think so," Bax says.

"Scott, take the Armor Road exit after the bridge," Andrea says.

"On it," Scott says, slowing to the point of crawling across the bridge. "Oh yeah, they're passing."

"Keep it slow until they are well ahead," Andrea says. "Calling your friend. What's his real name?"

Scott frowns. "Wayne."

Andrea smiles. "Cool."

"Hello," a man answers.

"Hey Wayne, it's Scott Meyer."

"Hey dude," Wayne says. "What's going on?"

"Super odd favor," Scott says. "Are you home at the moment?"

"Yes, up in the shop working on the mower," Wayne says.

"Awesome," Scott says, "do you still have a four-wheeler?"

"Nah, I got rid of it a while ago. Why?"

"We need to get to the nike base using the trail from back behind your place," Scott says. "Is the gate locked?"

"The gates wide open," Wayne says. "It has been since the search parties were out this way. I haven't checked the path for fallen trees in a bit, but you can always go on foot."

"That's great," Scott says, pulling off the highway.

"But the roads clear out to the old base," Wayne says. "You don't need to go the long way. I've seen vans and cars with government plates running that direction for the last three days."

"Shit," Andrea mumbles.

"Any chance you still have that old drone?" Scott asks, pulling into a hotel parking lot. He backs the car into a spot between two minivans and kills the engine.

"Hell yes, even upgraded it last year," Wayne says. "I helped the search parties with it, too."

"That's great. Can you run it over towards the base and assess the situation?" Scott asks.

"Anything I should look for?" Wayne asks.

"Any people or cars around the base on the side where the old silo was being converted to the vertical farm," Scott says, looking back at Bax. He shrugs.

"You bet. Give me about twenty minutes."

"Thanks man I really appreciate it!" Scott says, disconnecting the call. "Did you see them exit or circle back around?"

Andrea shakes her head. "No, the next exit is Parvin Road. It would take them a few minutes to come back around."

"Are you ok with a slower route?" Scott asks.

Andrea nods. "Old 210?"

"Yes," Scott says, starting the engine. "Bax, can you loop Gage and Rozanne in?"

"Already on it," Bax says, sending a text message.

"I'm texting Evelyn that we left the hospital to follow a lead, but we will be in touch," Andrea says.

Bax's phone pings. "Gage said they had a tail, but lost them in Gladstone. They are just getting back on the highway."

"Dang," Scott says.

"We probably raised all kinds of red flags in my hasty exit," Andrea says, sending the message to Evelyn. "Sorry."

Scott reaches for Andrea's hand. She takes his hand. "You did the right thing getting us out of there."

"Let's hope Silvey can wait just a bit longer." Andrea says.

The traffic slows close to the exit for the interstate. They roll under the overpass and pass the casino exit.

Scott's phone vibrates. "It's Wayne." He swipes to answer. "Hey buddy."

"Hey, I got the bird close enough to see that the place is crawling with people on the south side of the road. But when I turned it around, I caught the back end of an ambulance in an old lean-to."

"That's it!" Andrea says.

Scott nods. "Thanks Wayne! We owe you one."

"No problem," Wayne says. "Swing by the shop before you hike back on foot. I'll show you the footage and where to turn when the path splits."

"You bet," Scott says. "See you soon."

"It's only a manner of time they move their search to the north side of the road," Bax says.

Scott speeds up. "Andrea, can you send Rozanne a location pin for Wayne's place?"

"Sent," Andrea says. She scrolls down to the unknown number with Silvey's message and dials the number. It goes straight to voicemail, but the greeting message is a business line. She hangs up and dials it again placing the call on speaker.

"Hi, you've reached Greening Up. Please leave us a detailed message and we'll return your call."

Andrea turns back to assess Bax. "Is that the business at the silo?"

Bax nods. "Why would they have taken Silvey?"

50

Eli runs into the room. "Big problem."

Charlotte nods. "She's still conscious and appears to be in a hell of a lot of pain."

"No!" Eli says, pointing up. "We've got eyes in the sky. I saw a drone fly over. And there are twice as many cars across the street. They'll eventually find the ambulance."

"Did you seal the entrance?" Captain Wilson asks.

"Yes, but that doesn't cover the hole in the white room," Eli says. "Is there anything down here we can use to board that up or disguise it?"

Captain Wilson looks around the space. "Create a shadow box with the mirrors in the white room."

"Brilliant," Eli says. "Any idea how long she'll take?" He gestures towards the chamber.

"She's not even completely submerged," Captain Wilson says. "We may have been better off without intercepting her. At this stage, her injuries were more severe than we accounted for."

Charlotte wipes away a falling tear. "I can't imagine the additional trauma this is causing to her mentally."

"Is there anything we can do to speed it up? Eli asks, rolling up on his toes. "Or abort?"

"No," Captain Wilson says. "She's in it until the power is cut off or Silvey reaches stasis. Otherwise, we can't open the chamber."

🚑

Scott pulls in beside Gage's car and hops out with Andrea and Bax close behind.

Rozanne waves them over to Gage and Wayne huddled around a laptop.

"We were able to pull a partial tag from the ambulance," Rozanne says. "Gage ran it by a friend of his and it's a match to one that was reported missing this morning after two of their medics showed up in the emergency room after being assaulted with pepper spray. The officer said he would wait to call it in. He gave us three hours."

Gage steps back and points to the image of the lean-to with the ambulance. "Bax, can you point out the entrance to the silo from here?"

"Um, not from this shot. Do you have another angle heading south?"

Wayne rolls back the footage.

"Stop," Bax says. "There is a person ducking behind a brush pile."

Wayne rolls it back a few frames and catches the guy looking up at the drone. "Gotcha." He zooms in on the face. "Recognize him?"

Bax leans close to the screen. "I think that's one of the owners of Greening Up, Evan or Eli."

"Why in the hell would they take Silvey?" Rozanne asks.

"We're still at a loss on the why," Andrea says, looking at the footage. "Can you roll the frame back a few more? I want to see where he came from or went to."

Wayne rolls it back until the man comes into frame. "It's like he crawled out of nowhere."

"There's hatches all over the property," Bax says. "How close is this to the lean-to?"

"Maybe twenty or thirty feet," Wayne says. "I'm recharging the battery and can fly again in about ten minutes."

"Let's wait," Andrea says. "We may have already spooked them. We need to go in with a little more stealth."

Wayne tosses Scott the keys. "Take the CJ7. You can make it pretty far in that. I'll be on standby if you need help." He tilts his head towards the drone on the tool bench.

"Thanks," Scott says. "We'll bring her back."

"Bax, ride shotgun and lookout for any down tree limbs," Andrea says, hopping in the back. "Rozanne, you good to wait here with Wayne and for your medic friend."

"Yep," Rozanne says. "Be careful." She kisses Gage and pats his cheek as he settles in the back next to Andrea. "You see any sign that you are in over your head—call me!"

"Yes, ma'am." Gage taps Scott. "Let's go!"

Gage taps Bax and leans close. "You good man, you're pale and sweating a bit."

"I'll be fine," Bax says as they roll past the open gate. The jeep rocks back and forth as they speed over the bumpy tree line path. He places a supportive hand around his ribs and winces. "Damn it, I blew a stitch."

"What was that?" Scott yells over the roar of the engine.

"We're good," Bax says, motioning forward.

Andrea glances at Gage.

Gage shrugs. "He's in pain, but won't admit it."

"Oh, damn," Andrea whispers to Gage. "I didn't even consider his injuries before pulling you guys into this mess."

"Trust me," Gage says. "Bax wants to find Silvey more than you." He waggles his eyebrows. "He's in deep with your besty."

"They just met," Andrea says, rolling her eyes. "It's just trauma bond."

"If you say so," Gage says, pointing ahead. He taps Scott. "Hang a right at the Y."

Scott follows the road to the right, but they lose cover of the trees immediately. He slows. "How far was it on foot from here?"

"Quarter mile through the pasture," Gage says, pointing ahead. "There's a creek just beyond the rise. Let's ride till there."

Scott nods and they race forward until they reach the creek. It's full and running with white rapids. He pulls the jeep around and pulls the brake. "Let's go on foot from here. I don't want to take any chances damaging the jeep or being heard."

They nod and hop out.

Bax hops the width of the creek and turns back for Andrea. He points to a large rock near the center. "Two hops." He reaches and catches her hand.

Gage and Scott hop over the creek, and they wade through thigh high tall grass towards a few buildings in the distance.

Andrea's phone pings. She checks the notification. "Shit."

"What is it?" Scott asks, leaning over her shoulder.

"They've admitted Buzz," Andrea says, showing the text from Evelyn. "He's unresponsive."

"Can this day get any worse?" Bax asks, breaking off a fistful of grass.

"Dude, you better knock on wood," Gage says, stepping towards a fence. He knocks twice on the next wooden post. "We've already passed the stage of up a creek." He points with a thumb over his shoulder.

"Let's try some positive manifestation," Andrea says. "We will find Silvey. Buzz will be perfectly fine, and we will make it to Micah's service on time."

"No, what time is it?" Bax asks.

"Almost noon," Scott says. "The service is at two, right?"

Andrea nods. "Our clock is ticking very loudly!" She stands on her toes. "How much further till we reach the ambulance?"

Bax shields his eyes and squints. "Maybe a hundred yards."

"Let's pick up the pace," Andrea says, jogging ahead of Scott.

"Yes, ma'am," Gage and Bax say in unison.

Scott salutes, and they jog at Andrea's pace for another few minutes. She slows to a stop.

"I can make out the building with the lean-to," Andrea says. "Bax, does any of this look familiar?"

Bax scans the area and shakes his head. "I never went past the parking lot, but I can see a bit of a brush pile. That could be where we saw the man attempting to hide from the drone." He points to the ground. "Keep an eye out for rusted metal covers. It could be an access hatch."

"Let's spread out and walk an arm's length apart in a line," Gage says. "We can cover more ground."

They fan out and search the ground as they walk towards the cinderblock building.

"Can anyone else hear a buzzing or humming sound?" Scott asks.

Andrea stops and squats to the ground. "It's coming from below us." She places a hand on the ground. "We've got to be close."

"Stay low," Gage says. "I can make out a few people near the road up ahead."

They stop level with the ambulance. "Gage and I will search the building."

Andrea and Scott nod.

Scott steps closer to Andrea. "How are you holding up?"

"I feel like I want to scream and vomit at the same time," Andrea says, swallowing back a sob.

Scott nods. "We're going to find Silvey."

Andrea nods. "If you were going to conceal an entrance, what would you do?" She points to the pile of green leafy limbs and brush. "This hasn't been here long enough to dry out."

Scott gets down on all fours. "There's a large metal cover."

"Bax! Gage!" Andrea whisper shouts.

Bax sticks his head out of the lean-to.

Andrea waves and points down.

Gage and Bax rush over.

"We found an entrance," Andrea says, helping Scott push the pile of brush away.

"Was this what you were expecting?" Gage asks.

"No," Bax says, "this is huge compared to the others, but I am not mad about it."

Scott and Bax lift the door. It swings open with ease.

"Somebody has greased the hinges recently," Gage says, inspecting the cover. "But why bother leaving it unlocked?"

Andrea presses the flashlight app on her phone. She holds it over the opening. "It's a ramp. Bax, watch your head. The ceiling is low for a bit."

"This looks like an old supply ramp," Gage says, pointing out the grooves in the concrete. "And we didn't find a hospital bed in the ambulance. They could have just pushed her down here bed and all."

Andrea holds the light up as she walks down the ramp and loses the natural light within a few feet. "Scott?"

"Right behind you," Scott says. "Is it just me, or did it get dark really fast?"

"Understatement," Gage whispers, pressing the flashlight app on his phone. "Can you see the bottom?"

"Not yet," Scott whispers.

"Bax, does any of this look familiar?" Andrea whispers.

Bax reaches out and runs his hand on the surface of the wall. "The texture on the walls feels the same, but it was dark when I was down here with Silvey."

Andrea turns her light towards Bax.

He raises his hand to block the glare. "What?"

"What did Silvey tell you this morning?" Andrea asks. "Did she travel here again?"

"Only that she confronted Jean Tremble and the secretary of defense with their real names before she woke up."

"Ha, she would poke the bear," Andrea says, turning her light away.

"Hey there's a hallway," Scott says. "And a light further down."

They catch up with Scott and creep down the hall.

"The humming sound is getting louder," Andrea says.

"Bax, what are the chances that reactor Silvey described is operational?" Gage asks.

"Uh, no clue," Bax says.

They stop outside a steel door with a black box.

"This looks new," Scott says, pointing to the black box. "Any harm on knocking?" He looks around. "We're kind of at a dead end."

Andrea pounds her fist on the door.

Bax steps forward and holds Andrea's arm. "Save your fist. They'll never hear you, but they can see us."

"What?" Andrea asks, yanking her arm away and glaring at Bax. He points up to a fishbowl lens with a red light. "Hello!" She waves her arms around. "If you can see me. Open this door right now!"

51

"We've got company," Eli says, tapping on a screen near the door to the white chamber.

"How many?" Captain Wilson asks.

"Four, three guys and a woman. All appear to be under thirty."

Charlotte rushes over to the monitor. "No uniforms?"

"No," Eli says. "Best guess is the cryptic text sent to Silvey's friend was enough to tip her friend off."

"And the tall one there with the curly hair," Charlotte says. "Is that Baxton Auburn?"

Eli squints at the screen. "Um, I only met him once, but it could be."

"Captain," Charlotte says. "Is it safe to let them in?"

Captain Wilson nods. "It's probably better than letting them leave and grab the uniforms on the other side of the base."

"And Silvey?" Charlotte asks.

"Submerged," Captain Wilson says.

"Ok," Charlotte says. "Let's go, Eli."

Eli nods and opens the door to the white room for Charlotte. She takes his hand, and they walk towards the door to the hallway.

Charlotte hesitates when they reach the door. "What do we tell them?"

"Start with what we witnessed this morning," Eli says, pressing a red release button parallel to the door. It clicks, and he pulls it open.

Andrea turns and charges in. "Where's Silvey? We know you have her!"

Charlotte steps back and holds up both hands. "Whoa, and you are?"

"Andrea Meyer." She points to her husband. "Scott Meyer, Bax and Gage Auburn, and you two?"

"Charlotte and Eli," Charlotte says. "We own Greening Up."

"And Silvey?" Bax asks, stepping forward and towering over the pair. "Where is she?"

"Here and safe," Eli says. "Can we tell you how?"

"After you take us to Silvey," Andrea says, looking around the room.

"She's resting," Charlotte says. "It was an eventful morning and I really want you to understand why she's here more than anything."

"Talk fast," Andrea says.

Eli nods. "We intercepted the FBI's attempt to take Silvey."

"How?" Andrea asks.

"Long story short," Charlotte says. "We watched two FBI agents and a police officer handover a payoff to a hospital security officer. We followed the officer and overheard him recruiting the others."

"Why were you at the hospital?" Bax asks.

"We wanted to speak with Silvey," Charlotte says. "We have a mutual friend."

"You mean Captain Wilson," Andrea says. "The message said she was with the captain. I presume neither of you are that rank nor any at all."

"Correct," Eli says. "We reached out to Captain Wilson because we found him down here before the tornado."

"Here in this white abyss?" Scott asks.

"No," Eli says. "In the next room."

"With the reactor?" Gage asks.

"You know about the reactor?" Eli asks.

"Yes," Bax says.

"Well, this next part might not seem so farfetched," Charlotte says, pointing to the wall behind Andrea and Scott. "When we purchased the property, we received the original deed, but when clearing the land north of the silo, we found an entrance that we didn't find on the original plans." She waves her hand around. "And discovered the ramp leading down to this room and the attached spaces. One, the fusion reactor and the other a suspension chamber with the captain."

"What is a suspension chamber?" Andrea asks.

"A stasis device that literally looks like a glass coffin," Charlotte says. "I was very startled upon first sight. We found Captain Wilson inside. He appeared to be sleeping. We searched the room high and low for instructions on how to free him beyond the note stuck to the lid. We were at a loss."

"Then the tornado," Eli says. "And we saw the captain in the viral video and rushed back. The device was open."

"Let me get this straight," Andrea says. "You found a man stuck in a coffin and didn't call the authorities?"

Eli nods. "The note attached to the suspension chamber stated that the project was classified and to trust no one."

"You leave a man trapped and kidnapped my best friend," Andrea says. "I'm not trusting you with Silvey a minute longer." She turns and marches towards the wall, finds her reflection and goes around until she finds a doorway. "Silvey!"

"Wait," Charlotte says, racing after her.

Gage steps in front of Charlotte.

Scott and Bax go after Andrea.

Andrea skids to a stop when she enters the room and spots Silvey's hair inside the glass coffin. "What the hell!"

Captain Wilson stands, extending his arms open wide. "She's safe."

"Silvey!" Andrea cries out and rushes towards the suspension chamber. "What have you done!" She bangs on the glass cover. "Release her at once!"

Scott points to the chamber. "What is going on?"

"She's perfectly safe," Captain Wilson says.

"Explain!" Bax says, poking Captain Wilson hard in the chest.

"The white particles surrounding Silvey are nano particles. They're working to repair her cell by cell. We can't interrupt the process."

Bax points to the chamber. "She's alive?"

"Oh yes," Captain Wilson says. "The door will automatically open once the process is complete."

"And you know this how?" Andrea asks, turning towards the captain. She doesn't bother to wipe her tears.

"I spent sixty years in a perfect state of stasis," Captain Wilson says, waving a hand from his head down to his feet. "It's perfectly safe."

"She's stuck for sixty years?" Scott asks.

"Oh heavens no," Captain Wilson says, walking to the side of the chamber. "She's only in for repair." He points to the screen. "And the process started thirty minutes ago. If her injuries were severe, it could take a few hours, but I promise she's perfectly safe."

"And Silvey did consent to the chamber before we placed her inside," Charlotte says from the door. "Eli and I have both tested the chamber under the supervision of Captain Wilson, and it is remarkable. I had a chronic condition that was healed with zero side effects and Eli had a bum shoulder for years that was repaired."

"Also, a minor heart arrythmia and some acne scarring all disappeared after my time inside the chamber," Eli says, stepping beside Charlotte. "That's what we wanted to talk to Silvey about this morning at the hospital."

"We read the article," Charlotte says.

"What article?" Andrea asks. "Silvey's not had any reporters at her bedside."

"A medic stated that he found a woman that was working at the base in a field a mile away and that her injuries were severe,"

Charlotte says. "We put it together that it was Silvey. And we really were just going to start the conversation today."

Andrea shakes her head. "The FBI. Do they know that this exists?"

"We don't know for sure if that's what they are after or if it's the time mechanism tied to the fusion reactor," Captain Wilson says.

"Whatever it is they've been after Silvey and I because of something you shared with them!" Bax says.

"I was very confused when the chamber opened," Captain Wilson says. "Agent Carlton found me inside the Red Cross shelter and cornered me about the last thing I remembered and all I could say was Silvey Rhoades."

"There's a paper trail a mile long about the project," Andrea says.

"The suspension chamber was never documented in project rainbow," Captain Wilson says. "It was stolen tech, and we were testing its limitations. Before the project was shut down."

"Why would they leave you down here for sixty years?" Scott asks. "And why tell your family you went AWOL and abandoned them."

"The protocol was to abandon the project if the base was under attack because of the nuclear fusion reactor," Captain Wilson says, tapping his head. "And while in the suspension chamber, I was living a conscious reality in 1962 on a loop."

"You've been reliving the same day?" Andrea asks.

"More like three days," Captain Wilson says. "The control booth set up our time with a day to adjust, a day to explore and a day to return."

"How did we get sucked into this?" Bax asks, pointing to Silvey.

"The white room sustained damage during the tornado," Captain Wilson says, pointing towards Charlotte and Eli. "That room is where the core of the wormhole was created. It would have opened a ripple and sucked anyone breathing in its path."

"Is that why Silvey saw our friend Micah?" Bax asks.

284

"If he was breathing when the hole consumed you, yes. His consciousness would have traveled like Silvey and yourself."

Scott holds up both hands. "You're telling us that time travel is possible, but only through the mind?"

Captain Wilson nods. "It's a matter of a shared experience with a host. Our consciousness attaches to a person in proximity of the jump. I physically jumped into my own body three days prior to my jump."

"Why does she keep going back?" Andrea asks.

"Her injuries rendered her unconscious making it easier to slip through the cracks. And once you've learned how to travel, it's like gravity pulling at her mind."

"Whoa," Andrea says. "Are you insinuating that anyone can travel if they learn how?"

"Essentially, yes," Captain Wilson says. "It's an art discovered over two centuries ago that people have talked plainly about in public. It's been referred to as meditation, transcending, or the opening of the third eye." He laughs at their slack jawed expressions. "The only reason we built the wormhole was to have some quantifiable data to anchor the traveler to a specific location and duration. And the suspension chamber allowed us more time to travel in a relaxed state without the body's reflex to pull us out."

"Is Silvey traveling now?" Andrea asks.

"I can't say for certain," Captain Wilson says. "Her vital signs appear normal, zero signs of distress."

"Gage," Bax says, pointing at the captain. "Do you believe any of this?"

"I don't know dude." Gage says. "This is normally Rozanne's side of weird."

The chamber hisses and the cover pops open.

Captain Wilson rushes to the control panel. "Stasis complete."

Andrea steps away and watches Silvey's body float to the top of the white particles.

Charlotte rushes forward holding a hoodie and a pair of shorts.

Bax and Scott advert their eyes as her pale, naked body appears.

"What's happening?" Gage asks, stepping forward.

Bax holds up his hand. "Stop, she's naked."

Gage abruptly turns his back to the chamber and makes eye contact with Eli.

Eli holds up his hands. "I stepped out of the room when she was placed inside to send Andrea the message. I didn't see anything."

Bax glares at Eli.

"Seriously, man!" Eli says. "I have manners."

"Silvey!" Andrea says.

Silvey's eyes fly open. "Dre?" She leans over the edge of the chamber.

"Oh thank goodness," Andrea says, rushing towards Silvey.

"Hey," Silvey says. "Glad you got my message, but can I get some clothes."

Charlotte hands over the borrowed hoodie and shorts.

Silvey looks beyond her to the men with their backs turned. "You brought the calvary?" She slides on the hoodie and shimmies her way into the shorts, trying to keep the white particles from flying out but fails. "Alright, let's see if this thing actually worked." She swings her legs over the edge and reaches for Andrea's hand. "Dre?"

"You have a broken femur and hip," Andrea says, taking Silvey's hand. "How?"

Silvey hops down and wobbles a bit.

Captain Wilson stands and claps.

The men turn around and gawk as Silvey makes a dramatic bow.

"Be careful, Silvey," Andrea says.

Charlotte smiles. "How do you feel?"

Silvey wiggles her toes, bends her knees, shakes her hips and rolls her shoulders. "Ready to go to work."

Bax walks over until he is standing in front of her. "Your actually healed?"

"Yeah," Silvey says. "You should take it for a spin. It may help your ribs and stitches heal up faster."

"Can I do that?" Bax asks.

"Whoa," Andrea says, stepping between Silvey and Bax. "Let's take a breath and process what the hell just happened."

Silvey rolls to her toes and taps her finger on Andrea's nose. "Bibbidi-Bobbidi-Boo, I am as good as new."

Andrea shakes her head. "Silvey."

"Andrea, relax," Silvey says, lifting the hoodie exposing her abdomen. "Do you see a single stitch or scar?" She turns giving her and the group a three-hundred-and-sixty-degree view of her flawless skin.

"No," Andrea says. "But how?"

Silvey takes a handful of the white particles. "Science, or maybe magic, but who cares! I've just skipped months of painful rehab and feel amazing. Please be happy!"

"I'm not mad," Andrea says, "just utterly shocked it worked."

"Same," Scott says, raising his hand.

"Me too," Gage says.

Silvey tilts her head to the side. "I'm sorry, but I don't believe I know who you are."

"Silvey," Bax says, "this is my cousin Gage."

"Ah yes," Silvey says, pointing at Gage. "Auburn Automotive, right?"

Gage nods. "It's nice to meet you."

"Does that kid Dusty still work for you?" Silvey asks.

Bax frowns.

Andrea smirks.

"He does," Gage says. "I understand he met you at the Job Corps program."

"Yep," Silvey says. "He never did work up the nerve to ask me out."

Gage laughs. "Did he stand a chance?"

Bax glares at Gage.

"He'll never know," Silvey says, stepping closer to Bax. He locks eyes with her. "Will he?"

Bax smiles ear to ear. "Not in my lifetime."

"Gross, kiss already!" Andrea says, shaking her head.

Silvey loops her hands around Bax's neck, and he leans his lips towards hers but winces. She lets go.

"What's wrong?" Silvey asks.

Bax shakes his head. "I blew a few stitches." He lifts the edge of his shirt and green puss oozes out of the incision.

"Oh yeah, you're definitely going in," Silvey says, pointing to the captain. "Get it ready."

Captain Wilson smirks. "Aye captain Silvey."

"And thanks, by the way," Silvey says, gesturing to the chamber. "I really do appreciate it."

Captain Wilson nods. "I'm happy to help."

Gage steps close to Bax. "You sure, dude?"

"It can't hurt, right?" Bax says.

Silvey turns and smiles. "It tingles and then you submerge into a dreamlike state, but you may go back…" She leans close and whispers, "… to the past."

"Did you go again?" Bax asks.

Silvey nods. "I managed to explain that we are not the enemy, not to blow up Cuba, but I didn't get to the part that may save Kennedy."

"Got it," Bax says. "And I have to go in naked?"

"If you want to keep your clothes in one piece, yes," Captain Wilson says.

"Alright people," Silvey says. "Let's give him some privacy." She waves them towards the door to the white room and loops her arm around Andrea. "Quick question. What day is it?"

"Saturday," Andrea says, glancing at her watch. "Shit!"

"What?" Silvey asks.

"Micah's service starts in an hour," Andrea says.

Silvey turns towards Gage. "Can you meet us out at the church when he's done?"

"Of course," Gage says, looking down at his dusty jeans and tee shirt.

Scott places a hand on Gage's shoulder. "I've got clothes, don't worry about running home first."

"We'll have Rozanne follow us to the house," Andrea says. "She can change and bring you two back fresh clothes."

"Wait?" Silvey asks, "Did you not park here?"

"No," Andrea says. "The feds are searching the south side of the base across the way. We came on foot from the north. It's about a fifteen-minute walk back to the jeep. Are you up for it?"

Silvey shrugs. "No time like the present to check out how well that thing glued me back together."

Charlotte walks towards the door. "Please give our best to Micah's family. We left our car in the city and probably should stay hidden until the feds are gone."

Silvey nods. "We can swing back after the service and give you a lift."

"No," Eli says. "You'll raise quite a bit of suspicion at the service. I'm sure they will have eyes there."

Andrea smiles. "Finally, an excuse to give you a quick makeover."

Silvey rolls her eyes. "We'll see. My parents will give any disguise away."

"Oh, f..." Andrea says. "Buzz and Evelyn are still at the hospital. Buzz was admitted this morning."

"Dre!" Silvey says. "You didn't think to lead with that?"

"I'm sorry," Andrea says. "There's been a lot going on!"

"We'll call them on the way," Silvey says.

"Gage, can you call us when you're top side?" Scott asks. "I'll have Wayne drive the jeep back."

"Sure," Gage says. "We'll be right behind ya."

"See you soon," Silvey says.

Charlotte releases the door and holds it open. "Straight down and then up the ramp."

Silvey extends her hand towards Charlotte.

Charlotte takes and shakes Silvey's hand.

"Thank you for risking everything to bring me here," Silvey says, releasing her hand.

"Ready?" Andrea asks.

"Race you to the top," Silvey says, running down the hallway.

"Oh, for the love of all that is holy," Andrea says, laughing and running after her.

Scott shakes his head and runs after them.

Silvey slows and looks back at Andrea. "Am I dreaming?"

Andrea huffs. "My heart rate would say no and that I need to do more cardio."

Scott catches up with them. "Hey! Let me go up first. I want to make sure we don't have any eyes turned in this direction before Silvey pops out."

Silvey pulls up her hood. "Unless they are looking for a teenager, I'm pretty sure we're safe."

Andrea laughs. "Plus, the grass as nearly as tall as her."

Scott jogs to the top and disappears from view.

Andrea bumps her hip against Silvey as they walk up the ramp. "Were you really going to kiss Bax?"

"For sure," Silvey says. "Dre."

"Silvey," Andrea says.

"I actually blushed when I first saw him," Silvey says. "And was kind of speechless."

"Shut up!" Andrea says, poking Silvey in the side.

Silvey squeals and jogs up ahead of her.

Scott appears at the top. "You're squeal just turned a few heads in this direction."

Silvey points at Andrea. "It's her fault."

Scott shakes his head. "My mother told me at our reception that I actually married two women and was the permanent third wheel. I laughed it off, but I now know that my mother wasn't wrong."

"Glad you aren't in denial any longer," Silvey says, patting his shoulder. "Let's roll." She steps up and out of sight.

Andrea pecks Scott on the cheek. "She's got an extra shot of spite today."

Scott smiles. "I'm thinking we have a case of endorphin overload. She may crash soon."

Andrea nods. "I am waiting for the high of whatever this is to wear off." She follows Scott up. "Damn, where did she go?"

Silvey holds up her hand and waves from the tall grass. "It's the perfect place to hide." She pops up. "Which way?"

Scott points towards the lean-to north of the brush pile. He glances at Andrea. "Let's hope this burst of energy gets us back to the jeep in record time."

"Fingers crossed," Andrea says, jogging after Silvey and dialing Evelyn.

"Hello!" Evelyn says before it even rings.

"We've got her, but don't make that public quite yet," Andrea says. "How's Buzz?"

"He woke up and mumbled Silvey's name, but then was back out again before I could get a nurse," Evelyn says. "Did they hurt her?"

"No," Andrea says, catching up with Silvey. "Your mom." She hands off the phone.

"Hey mom," Silvey says, slowing her pace just a bit. "How's dad?"

"That's not important," Evelyn says. "Where are you? Are you ok?"

"I'm great," Silvey says. "We're heading to Micah's service."

"How?" Evelyn asks. "They can't possibly think a funeral in your condition is a good idea."

"My condition has improved. I'll be fine."

"Silvey Lynn," Evelyn says. "You just had a major operation."

"Like I said, my condition has improved," Silvey says, rolling her eyes. "I'll come to the hospital right after, I promise. Love you." She disconnects the call. "Hey Dre."

"Yeah," Andrea says, hopping over the creek. She extends her hand for Silvey.

"I think we need to strategize a way to get my dad in the chamber," Silvey says, clearing the creek without Dre's help.

"One fire at a time, Silvey," Andrea says.

Scott starts the jeep. Andrea hops up front and Silvey hops in the back. He starts speeding back towards the tree line.

Silvey looks back at the base. "Scott, stop."

Scott slams on the brakes. "What is it?"

"Gage and Bax are sprinting this way and they're being chased by two men."

Andrea stands on the front seat. "This is bad."

Scott turns the jeep around as Gage and Bax hop over the creek. Scott slides the jeep to a stop, and they climb in the back.

Andrea sits back down.

"Go!" Bax shouts.

Scott doesn't hesitate, flooring the gas. They bounce up out of their seats. Bax grabs Silvey and pulls her back down.

Andrea turns towards Gage. "What the hell happened?"

"They found the ambulance," Gage says. "We tried to sneak around the lean-to, but we were spotted."

"And ran like hell!" Bax says, looking back. "It looks like they retreated."

Scott speeds up.

"Are you all fixed up?" Silvey asks, looking Bax over.

"Yes," Bax says, holding up his shirt. The incision is gone, and the skin is smooth. "They were going to kill the power to the room and hide out until nightfall."

"Smart," Andrea says.

"The only good news is that we don't think they saw where we came from," Gage says, holding on to the rollbar.

The jeep bounces along the narrow path.

Scott doesn't slow until they're nose to nose with Rozanne's car.

"Follow us to the house," Scott says, tossing the jeep keys to Wayne. "Thanks for your help. And if someone comes looking you never saw us. I'll explain it all later!"

Wayne smirks. "Deleting drone footage now."

"Thanks!" Andrea says, climbing into their car.

Silvey hops in the back behind Andrea.

Rozanne drops the car in gear. "Let's go, boys."

Gage and Bax climb inside Rozanne's car.

"Was Darcy coming this way?" Gage asks, holding on to the dash as she whips the car around.

"She's on duty and couldn't find a replacement," Rozanne says, turning the car right behind Scott's sedan. "She did call a medic that lives near Lawson. They were ready to head this way if I called." She looks in the rearview mirror assessing Bax. "We don't need one do we?"

"No," Bax says, looking out the back window. He spots a rise of dust near a hill from the south. "They're coming."

Rozanne takes the second left on third street staying close to Scott's car. "Who is?"

"We were spotted and chased after we found Silvey," Gage says, checking the side mirror.

"Speaking of Silvey," Rozanne says, turning left on Doniphan. "How did she run and jump out of the jeep in her condition?" She turns right and stops at the four-way intersection.

Gage points to a black SUV heading towards them. "Bax duck down. Roz go, Scott turned left. Don't lose him."

Rozanne guns the car and then turns left on Raum. "Did they follow?" She checks the mirror.

"They were still at the stop sign," Gage says, looking straight ahead. "Oh, geez."

"What?" Bax asks, sitting up and taking in the homes with missing walls and roofs along the road as they turn left on Sam Phil.

"This is worse than the pictures," Rozanne whispers, pulling into the driveway next to Scott's car.

"Let's get inside before that SUV catches up," Gage says, hopping out of the car.

"Did you see anyone following?" Andrea asks, looking down the street.

"A black SUV that could be them," Gage says, gesturing to the door. "Let's at least get Bax and Silvey out of sight."

Scott pushes open the front door. "There's a bathroom just off what used to be the kitchen and one in the basement. I'll grab a few shirts from upstairs."

"Thanks," Bax says, ducking inside "I'll take the basement."

"Rozanne come with us," Andrea says, waving her and Silvey up the steps. "I've got enough black or navy to share."

"I'm Rozanne, Gage's wife," Rozanne says, looking Silvey over. "You're, ok?"

"Hi Rozanne." Silvey smiles. "And yes, I'm ok. Which I know is confusing, but I promise we'll share the entire saga after we get back from the service and preferably with something hearty. I'm starving all the sudden."

Andrea swings open the door to the walk-in closet and hands Rozanne a black fit and flare dress and holds up a pair of black flats. "Any chance you're a size eight?"

"Actually, yes," Rozanne says. "Thanks."

"You can use the hall bathroom," Andrea says. "And Silvey, we need to hide the fact that you are… well you." She picks out a dark navy t-shirt dress and a pair of navy tights. "Any chance you can rock the boots with a heel?"

"Ugh, how high?" Silvey whines.

"Four inches," Andrea says, handing her a pair of boots. "And this." She hands Silvey a black plastic bag.

Silvey opens the bag and pulls out a wad of red hair. "Is this from our wigging out party?" She sniffs it. "Yep, still smells like bubble gum."

"We're short on time," Andrea says, pulling a black dress and a pair of heels. "Please, just make it work."

Silvey steps out of the closet and heads for the spare bedroom.

Rozanne steps out of the bathroom. "I'm done in there."

Silvey looks her up and down. "That fits you well."

Rozanne looks down at the dress. "It's not too much for a funeral, is it?"

"Not at all," Silvey says, holding the wig. "Any chance you can help me get this on after I change?"

"Sure," Rozanne says, taking it from Silvey. "Get changed. I'll try to fluff it up."

"Thanks," Silvey says, stepping inside the bathroom. She leans over the counter and inspects her face. "Freckles intact." She slides off the short sand shimmies into the tights and uses the counter to balance as she sips up the first boot and then the second. She removes the hoodie and slides on the dress. It falls mid-calf and hangs off her frame. "Might be my most unflattering outfit to date." She opens a drawer and rummages around until she finds a hair tie. She pulls up her hair and twists it in a knot, securing it with the hair tie. She opens the door. "Ready?"

Rozanne holds up the red bob with bangs. "If you are?"

Silvey nods. "Let's get this over with before I change my mind."

Rozanne steps behind her and places the wig over her hair, pulls it back and straightens it out until the bangs are centered across Silvey's forehead. "Not too bad. If you ever tire of being a blonde, you could definitely be a redhead."

Silvey laughs. "I can't believe I am wearing a wig to Midge's funeral."

Rozanne frowns. "It's better than missing it, right?"

Silvey sighs. "Yes. Let's see if the boys are ready. It's a ten-minute drive out to the church."

Andrea meets them in the hall and barks out a loud laugh. Silvey glares at her. "I'm sorry, but I can't unsee this."

"This was your stupid idea," Silvey says, stomping down the steps.

Bax gasps when Silvey enters the living room.

"Ugh, you too?" Silvey asks.

"I'm sorry," Bax says. "I wasn't prepared for the wig. You look very different."

Gage elbows Bax in the side. "Smooth. Silvey, you look nice. Are we ready?" He points towards the door. "Scott is in the car."

"Let's go," Andrea says, opening the front door.

They step out and rush towards the car.

Andrea turns and locks the front door. She pauses as a black SUV appears to slow in the reflection of the bay window. *Act natural.* She takes the key out of the door and walks towards the car. She spots only Scott. *Good, Silvey had time to hide.* She opens the car door and has one foot inside when the door to the SUV opens. "Damn!"

"Get in," Scott says, placing the car in reverse.

Andrea slides in and slams her door.

Scott waves to Gage.

Gage nods and backs out of the driveway.

A man rushes towards Scott's car holding up a hand.

Scott ignores the man until he backs his car out of the driveway.

The man waves and yells, "Wait!"

Scott rolls down his window. "We're late for a funeral." He puts the car in drive and punches it before the man can respond.

"He's pissed," Andrea says, checking the mirrors. "The SUV had government plates."

"Can I sit up?" Silvey asks.

"For now," Scott says, turning right.

"I don't see Gage's car," Andrea says.

"I gave him the location of the church and how to get out there," Scott says, watching his mirror as they slow to stop at an intersection. "Silvey, I'm sorry. But they are following. Just keep your back to the window."

"Sorry," Silvey says, slumping down in her seat. "I've been nothing but a headache for you two. Guys, after seeing your neighborhood I don't know how you've been keeping it together."

"I don't know that we've fully processed the extent of the damage and time it will take to recover," Andrea says. "You've been an excellent distraction."

Scott nods. "I can second that. And it's the first time Andrea has taken real time off since our honeymoon."

Andrea pokes Scott in the side. "I've taken time off over the last five years."

"Ha, you answered every urgent email that hit your inbox while we were on vacation last year in Peru. She even asked a tour guide to stop at an internet café in Rome."

"Dre," Silvey says. "Nothing is that urgent."

"Says the girl who doesn't have to answer to anyone but herself," Andrea says, folding her arms across her chest.

Scott turns right on three-mile lane and reaches his hand over to Andrea. She sighs and takes his hand.

Silvey smiles. "Scott, you really get her, don't you?"

Scott looks in the rearview mirror and winks.

Silvey laughs.

52

Scott slows as the flow of cars file into the church parking lot. The black SUV has tailed Scott's bumper since they reached the highway.

"How am I supposed to get out unnoticed if they are riding our ass?" Silvey asks, risking a look back.

"Is there an umbrella in the back?" Andrea asks.

"Yes," Silvey says. "But it's not raining."

"But it's super sunny and you're a fair skinned red head today," Andrea says. "Pop it open when you open the door and walk as tall as you can."

"Do you think it will actually work?" Silvey asks.

"Well, we're about to find out," Scott says, pulling into one of the few remaining spots near the playground. "

The black SUV pulls up and parks directly behind Scott, blocking them in.

"Oh, hell no," Andrea says, opening the car door and marching towards the SUV. "We're at a funeral. Get the hell out of here!"

The same man from earlier steps out of the SUV and flips open a badge. "Ma'am."

"Don't you dare start," Andrea says, pointing a finger in his face. "You have zero respect for the lives our community has lost!

What kind of self-respecting agent tailgates mourners from their home to a funeral. And harassing us in a church parking lot!" She points to the other people gawking as they get out of their cars.

Gage, Rozanne and Bax exit their car a few spaces away. They wait as Scott gets out and opens Silvey's door. She pops open the black umbrella and takes his hand as she steps out of the door.

Silvey reaches up, pats his cheek, and winks.

"Thanks, son," Silvey says, waving to Andrea. "My darling daughter, can you walk your mother in? We're running late."

"That's your mother?" the man asks, taking a step towards Silvey.

"Of course," Andrea says, blocking his view of Silvey. "I'm sorry, mother. Apparently, they weren't taught any manners."

Gage takes Rozanne's hand.

"Well played," Gage whispers to Rozanne.

"Let's hope it works," Rozanne says, falling in step with the crowd of people dispersing from the scene and they move towards the entrance with Bax.

Silvey drops the umbrella once they are under the shade of the awning near the entrance.

Andrea pats Silvey's arm. "Well played."

The line is moving slowly as people are greeted and directed to sign in.

"We'll see if it worked," Silvey says, looking back. She spots Bax and nods once.

He winks and quirks up a smile.

"I'm pretty sure it's going to be standing room only," Scott says, watching the line of people multiply.

"That's good," Silvey says. "Midge deserves a full house."

Andrea's phone buzzes. She holds it up for Silvey. "It's Evelyn."

Silvey steps to the side out of line and answers. "Hey mom, can't talk long."

"Silvey?" Evelyn asks.

"Yes, mom."

"You're father's awake," Evelyn says. Her voice shakes and her pitch is low.

"Thank goodness," Silvey says. "Tell him I'll see him soon."

"Ok," Evelyn says, "be safe."

"Mom, I love you too." Silvey disconnects the call and hands the phone back to Andrea.

"I think something is up," Silvey whispers.

Andrea lifts an eyebrow.

"Somebody was listening to the call," Silvey says, crossing the threshold into the church. She shakes hands with the greeter and picks up the pen to sign in. "Signing the Rhoades family, just in case." She hands the pen to Andrea.

Andrea nods and signs in.

They are directed towards a pew in the back.

Scott gestures to Silvey and Andrea to sit. "I'll stand in the back with them." He points to Rozanne, Gage, and Bax.

Andrea nods and squeezes his hand.

Silvey slides to the end of the red upholstered pew. She nods to a few familiar faces that turn to look her way. They frown and turn back.

"I think it's working," Silvey mumbles. "The Brain just looked right at me and frowned."

"Sarah's here?" Andrea asks, searching the pews ahead of them until she spots Sarah and a familiar blonde. "She's with Melanie from swing choir."

"Yeah," Silvey whispers, adjusting the wig to cover her face. "I see a dozen or more of our old classmates, too."

Andrea nods. "Let's hope the focus stays away from us."

The white screen towards the front flickers, and then a picture of a baby fills the screen.

"Well, that should do it," Silvey whispers. They watch the slideshow of images of Micah from diapers to his wedding day. The image freezes on Micah's smile before the video starts.

"It's a girl!" Micah yells, emerging from a cloud of pink smoke.

A few gasps and murmured words are shared with everyone watching.

"I know, I know," Micah says, holding up his hands. "We said we were going to wait, but I overheard the tech slip up. They said she's right on schedule. You were too focused on her little heartbeat and didn't hear a thing. I'm sending this to your sister with strict instructions to only share it after you deliver. But first, to my darling daughter. Your mother is the best friend you will ever have. And I know that you will absolutely be a daddy's girl, because I will love you more than any person ever will and likely spoil you beyond your wildest dreams." He pauses and looks over his shoulder. "Shoot you're home early. See you soon little women! I love you both beyond the boundaries of this life and the next."

A sob comes from the front of the church.

The next shot doesn't leave a dry eye in the church.

Micah on one knee and Jessica holding up her left hand with a ring. He picks Jessica up and twirls her around. She laughs. "I'm the luckiest man in the world." The screen fades to a photo of Micah and Jessica holding a sonagram photo.

"Today we celebrate the light and love that Micah brought to his loved ones and friends gathered here today."

Silvey and Andrea scramble for tissues.

The sniffles from the congregation make it hard to hear the speakers next few lines, but then a woman steps to the microphone and the room goes silent.

"I believe with all my heart and will to breathe that my husband is here with us today." Jessica gestures to the screen. "And thanks to my sister for keeping the hardest secret for months. I have on record that he is celebrating our beautiful baby girl." Her chin quivers. "And thank you for the vast love and outpouring of support for my family and this community. And I know that many of you sitting here today are grieving your own loss and today like the ones to come will be a step in our recovery. For generations that day will be discussed, and the tragedy that swept our small town will be news until the next major catastrophe. But know we will never forget the lives of those gravely impacted." She pauses to wipe a few tears.

"We are here for each of you, as you have been for me and Lola."

Silvey's vision blurs behind her flowing tears. They listen to Micah's family and friends speak about his legacy. The service concludes with a video of Micah standing on a cooler.

"Midge dies in two weeks," Micah says. "Get it out of your system. And Silvey…"

"Oh man," Silvey says, covering her face and sliding down in the pew.

Andrea nudges Silvey in the side.

His eyes search the crowd, but the camera stays on Micah, and he raises his red solo cup. "To Silvey and her gift of nicknames. It's been real, it's been fun, but Midge is done!" He tips back the cup. The sound of the video erupts with whoops, whistles, and claps.

Micah smiles and jumps off the cooler. The image freezes with Micah midair, arms raised and smiling from ear to ear.

Micah's dad comes to the microphone. "We ask that only immediate family attend the graveside service and please remain seated while the family steps out into the vestibule to receive you as you depart. If you would like to see Micah one last time. You can form lines on the sides. Please exit using the center aisle. And only use the west entrance to leave the church parking lot near the playground."

Jessica and Micah's family stand and walk down the center aisle. The others wait until they've left to line up near the walls and make their way towards the front.

Silvey and Andrea join the line with Scott and Bax.

They slow in front of the casket. A large spray of white roses covers one side of the casket with red ribbons that say father, son, husband, brother, and boss.

Silvey admires a picture of Lola swaddled in the tie that Micah is wearing placed on his chest. She sniffles and wipes her tears as they make their way towards the vestibule.

Bax wraps his arm around Silvey. She leans against him while they wait to shake hands with the family.

Andrea leans close to Jessica without squishing Lola and whispers, "We're here for you. Including Silvey, but don't be alarmed by her appearance."

Jessica cuts her eyes towards Bax and the redhead at his side. "Oh, my word."

"I'm so sorry," Silvey says, stepping close to her. "I'll tell you everything soon."

Jessica hands Lola to her sister and wraps Silvey in a tight hug. "I don't care how you made it here. I am just happy you're here."

Silvey nods and places a hand on top of her wig as she releases her. "Lunch next week?"

Jessica nods and hugs Baxton.

Bax ducks as they walk out onto the steps.

"Twenty bucks they're still there," Scott mumbles, walking down the steps.

"Our friends in the black SUV?" Gage asks, walking up beside them.

Scott nods.

"I'm afraid they were confronted by a few deputies," Gage says.

"How?" Silvey asks.

"It pays to have a few clients that are on the force," Gage says, walking towards their cars. "Plus, one of the deputies was already in route to escort the hearse back to the cemetery."

"Thanks!" Silvey says, reaching up to take off the wig,

"Wait!" Andrea says, stopping Silvey.

"Why?" Silvey asks.

"We told the world you were taken this morning," Andrea says. "You said yourself you think Evelyn may have somebody listening in. We don't need a million witnesses that saw you here today."

"Fine, but this thing itches and is coming off in the car," Silvey says, looking over at Bax. "Are you guys coming back to the house?"

"Just to change," Gage says, stopping by Scott's car. "We should get back to the house and make sure it's not been invaded by the FBI."

Scott unlocks the car. "We'll see you at the house."

Andrea opens the back door and Silvey climbs in and takes off the wig. She scoots over and pats the seat. Andrea climbs in beside her and lifts her arm. Silvey curls in beside her.

Scott hops into the driver's seat and looks back. "Ready?"

Andrea nods, wiping away a few tears. "I can't believe Midge is really gone."

"How many more funerals are planned?" Silvey asks.

"At least six from my block and a few more from the community," Andrea says.

"Wow," Silvey whispers.

Scott follows the slow line of cars back to town and turns up the radio.

"Hey Dre," Silvey whispers.

"Hmm?" Andrea mumbles.

"Thank you," Silvey says. "For coming to find me, twice! And playing hard ball with my parents and the agents. I really do appreciate everything you've done."

"You would have raised hell for me," Andrea says, smiling.

"And full confession, I really don't mind Scott," Silvey says, glancing at Scott. "He's grown on me. Sorry it took so long."

Andrea laughs. "He's a good egg."

Silvey nods. "And the Auburns. They're great, right?"

"Oh definitely," Andrea says. "It's great finding new friends at our age."

"And ones not in our field," Silvey says. "Bonus!"

"I look forward to many nights where the conversations don't revolve around work or children," Andrea says. "And hopefully you don't screw that up."

"What do you mean?" Silvey asks, furrowing her brow and sitting up to face her. "You think I want children right now?"

"No Silvey!" Andrea says. "I meant with you and Bax."

"Wow, I just met him Dre," Silvey says, "and you're already counting on me tossing him to the curb. We haven't even gone out on a date."

"Just saying," Andrea says. "I like Gage and Rozanne. And don't want it to be awkward."

"I don't want it to be awkward," Silvey mimics Andrea. "Give me a break. You married my ex's best friend and I had to stand there looking at his cheeky grin while you two took your vows."

"Wait?" Andrea asks. "Your memory is back?"

"Oh, yeah," Silvey says. "Better than ever. I remember the taste of our first cupcake experiment."

"Oh, yuck," Andrea says, shaking her head. "We replaced the white sugar with salt on accident."

"Yea, not our greatest bake-off moment," Silvey says. "And my brain has been on overload with my new reality. I don't have a license or any identification. I have to replace that along with my truck and the work gear I lost."

"Yes, that's a lot to think about," Andrea says. "But you can do that all after you inhale some tacos and get to Buzz."

53

Bax hesitates at Andrea's front door. "Are you sure you want to go back to the hospital?"

Silvey shrugs. "It's my dad." She gestures her head inside. "It appears I will be wearing the red wig again to get into visit."

"Are you going to try to take Buzz back to the base?" Bax asks.

"I don't know," Silvey says. "It depends on his condition and if they've cleared out of the base. According to Scott, Wayne had three different agents visit him since we left. We may have to wait until the heat dies down. And fingers crossed, the captain can stay out of sight."

Bax nods. "I know you lost your dad's phone, but I had Andrea put my number in hers until you get a replacement. Call me day or night if you need anything."

Silvey rolls up on her toes. "And I'll see you at dinner tomorrow?" Her stomach growls.

"You bet," Bax says, smiling.

Silvey places a hand over her stomach. "I am about to kill some tacos on the way to the hospital."

Bax laughs. "See you soon."

Silvey steps inside and closes the door.

"Seriously," Andrea says, "you didn't kiss him?"

"I was leaning in and then well," Silvey says, pointing to her stomach. "I need to eat and soon."

Andrea hands Silvey the wig. "We'll get something on the way."

"Is it just us?" Silvey asks.

"Yes," Scott says. "I'm on standby just in case shit goes down."

Silvey laughs. "Real positive thinking there, buddy."

"It's been a long day," Scott says, shrugging.

"Also true," Silvey says, skipping out to the car.

Andrea turns towards Scott. "Her energy breaks my brain."

"Maybe Silvey should drive?" Scott suggests. "Your wave of adrenaline and grief are probably not helping with our lack of sleep last night. Plus, the drama of this morning." He holds up his phone. "The reporter has called several times. What should I tell her?"

"Let it leak that we were followed to the church," Andrea says. "Paint the agents into the deepest, darkest corner."

"Be safe," Scott says, hugging her. "And charge your phone on the way."

Andrea laughs. "You do get me. See you later."

Silvey honks the car horn.

Andrea walks out the door and Silvey leans out the driver's side window.

"Hello. I'm starving."

"Check the center console," Andrea says, getting in the passenger side.

Silvey holds up an empty bag of chips. "Like I said starving."

Andrea rolls her eyes and pulls out a red family size bag of peanut butter candy from her purse.

"Ah yeah!" Silvey says, rubbing her hands together.

Andrea opens the bag and tilts it towards Silvey. "I called in your order. It will be ready when we roll up."

"And what is said order?" Silvey asks over a mouth full of candy. She backs the car out of the driveway.

"Four soft tacos, two with chicken, rice, cheese, and guac. Two with shredded pork, no rice, chunky salsa, queso and sour cream."

Silvey wiggles in her seat. "Oh man! That's perfect!"

Andrea connects her phone to the charger. "I'm going to send your mom a message that we are headed her way."

"Actually," Silvey says, holding up a finger. "Just say that you and Scott are coming."

"Why?" Andrea asks.

"I'm sure they'll have eyes on the parking garage," Silvey says. "And if they are expecting you and Scott maybe they won't tail us too close."

"But if the agents are already in the room with Evelyn," Andrea says.

Silvey waves her hand. "I've got a plan. Once we get close to his room, I'll step into the bathroom. Mom and I can swap clothes. I'll go in and see my dad."

"You don't think they'll notice?" Andrea asks, shaking her head. "Too risky."

"Well, it's the best I got," Silvey says, taking another handful of candy.

Andrea shakes her head. "Just stick with the red wig."

"Ugh, it seriously itches."

"Tough, we need to play it safe. And not just for your sake, but for Captain Wilson and the suspension chamber."

"True," Silvey says, taking the exit towards the interstate. "I believe that thing will change the world. And I want to pull in Sarah. She'll get the most out of it with her being a doctor, right?"

"Silvey we can't tell a soul," Andrea says.

"But it could help so many people, including my dad," Silvey argues, merging with the traffic.

"It's not ours to share," Andrea says.

"I guess," Silvey says. "But..."

"No buts, Silvey."

"Fine. Are we stopping at the one in Liberty?"

"Yes," Andrea says, typing out a message to Evelyn. She presses send and they ride in silence for a few minutes. Her eyes fall and she drifts off.

Silvey parks in a spot marked for pickup, and a uniformed staff member comes out with a bag. She nudges Andrea.

Andrea wipes the drool from her mouth and rolls down the window. She takes the bag and hands them a five-dollar tip.

"Let's switch," Andrea says. "You can eat while I drive the rest of the way."

"You didn't order anything?" Silvey asks, peeking inside the bag.

"I did, but I can eat a burrito and drive."

Silvey hops out and runs to the other side of the car as Andrea opens her door.

"Thanks!" Silvey says, taking the vacated seat and taking out the first taco. She's finished the first one before Andrea's taken her seat behind the wheel.

"Slow down, slurp," Andrea says, taking the burrito and unwrapping the top.

Silvey grins. "You haven't called me that for years."

"Midge was right you did have a skill for nicknames," Andrea says, "but your initials plus a 'p' was the best one I ever came up with that day uptown slurping up a butterscotch malt."

"They were always so thick," Silvey says. "But I could absolutely destroy one right now."

"Maybe after we leave the hospital," Andrea says, taking a bite. She backs out of the spot and merges back on the highway while they eat.

Andrea's phone vibrates.

Silvey picks up the phone and checks the notification. "It's from my mom." She swipes to open the message. "Turn around."

Andrea let's her foot off the accelerator. "Why?"

"Dad's leaving against medical advice and the hospital is on lockdown," Silvey says. "Mom is back in her hotel room across from the hospital packing her things. She'll meet us at home."

"We can work with that," Andrea says, speeding back up. She takes the next exit and turns left under the overpass, taking another left to get back on the highway. "Has she responded why they are on lockdown?"

Silvey nods. "After the news broke that the hospital security officers were part of the kidnapping. People came to the hospital armed to protect their loved ones."

"Oh, no," Andrea says.

"They've restricted all visitors from the hospital until further notice," Silvey says, turning the phone towards Andrea. "I need to tell them I'm safe."

Andrea nods. "Ok, but what do we tell?"

Silvey opens the camera app and turns the video towards her.

"Hi, I'm Silvey Rhoades, alive and well," Silvey says. "Thanks to an anonymous party that witnessed two FBI agents, Neil Carlton and Michelle Vickers, bribe a hospital security officer with the last name, Clark, to kidnap me from the ICU this morning. I was assaulted and sedated after forcibly shoved into the back of an ambulance in the hospital loading bay. The anonymous party followed the ambulance and contacted my family. I will not be returning to the hospital unless it is with a warrant to hold those accountable for their grievous actions against me and the trauma it has done to my family. Including my father who suffered a heart attack this morning due to the stress of the situation. I will not be taking any media inquiries at this time. Please respect our privacy as we heal from these tragic events."

Andrea grins. "Dropping names and taking action." She laughs. "If you ever wanted a second career, I am pretty sure public relations may be the right lane for you."

Silvey groans. "Not you too."

"Ha," Andrea says, glaring at Silvey. "I never want to be placed in the same category as Ms. Evelyn Rhoades."

"Then don't say stupid stuff like that," Silvey says. "Who should I send this to?"

"Scott," Andrea says. "He's been in contact with the reporter from this morning and it was his account that all the social media posts went out on."

"He did all of that for me?" Silvey asks.

Andrea nods.

"A very good egg," Silvey says, sending Scott the video.

A minute later, Scott calls.

Andrea swipes to answer the call. "Hey."

"Where are you?" Scott asks.

"We're headed back," Andrea says. "Buzz discharged himself before we got there."

"Good," Scott says. "I've sent the video from Silvey to the reporter and will post it online in a few."

"Everything good there?" Andrea asks.

"Not exactly home alone," Scott says. "The street is full of news vans and at least two government vehicles are parked down the street."

"Meet us at Evelyn's house," Silvey says. "I need to shower and change there, anyway."

"No, I'm good here," Scott says. "You two stay there until I call. I don't want to lead the drama in your direction." He laughs. "Plus, I'm pretty sure one of Norma's daughters just hooked up the garden hose with the spray attachment. I'll send a video if she actually sprays them off the lawn."

54

"Silvey!" Andrea shouts. "Are you ready?"

"Two more minutes," Silvey says, combing out her clean hair. She props open the bathroom door. "Is it just mom or is dad with her too?"

"They both pulled in," Andrea says, looking up the steps. "Are you ready for the twenty questions?"

"Never," Silvey says, joining Andrea in the foyer. "Let's hope this miracle doesn't give him another heart attack."

Andrea opens the door and ushers Evelyn and Buzz inside. "Hope you don't mind that we let ourselves in."

Evelyn frowns. "What do you mean?"

"I lost my keys in the tornado," Silvey says, pointing to the frog sculpture on the porch. "I used the spare."

Evelyn looks Silvey up and down. "How are you?"

"Well, thanks mom," Silvey says.

"Where's my girl?" Buzz asks, slowly walking up the front path.

"Here!" Silvey says, meeting him halfway.

Buzz hugs her close. "You scared me kid."

"It was scary," Silvey says. "How's the ticker?"

"Needed an extra shot of juice but still ticking," Buzz says, looking Silvey over. "I apparently need a sign up for whatever you're drinking."

"I hope I can make that a reality soon," Silvey says, walking him inside.

Evelyn walks to her chair in the living room and sits.

They follow her and take a seat.

"I believe we deserve an explanation with zero details withheld," Evelyn says.

Silvey nods. "I will share every detail I can recall, but mom none of what I am about to say can leave this room."

Evelyn frowns. "Why am I the only one getting that warning?"

Buzz laughs. "Because you work at the gossip hub of this town."

Evelyn huffs. "And your morning chat's uptown aren't gossip?"

"Seriously!" Andrea says. "Can you two please stop?"

Evelyn rolls her eyes. "Fine. It won't leave this room."

"Promise?" Silvey asks, turning towards Buzz.

"Yes!" Evelyn and Buzz say in unison.

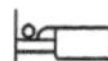

It's nearly midnight when they've exhausted all of their questions. Silvey yawns for the hundredth time. "I'm beat. If you have more questions. Write them down and I'll answer them in the morning."

Buzz leans forward in his chair. "Silvey."

"Yeah dad," Silvey says.

"I'm just happy you're safe," Buzz says, standing.

Silvey stands and hugs Buzz.

"I'm heading home," Buzz says. "Stay safe."

Evelyn walks Buzz to the door. "Do you believe any of it?"

Buzz smirks. "Our girl has been brutally honest since the day she popped out. I'm not going to doubt her explanation." He pats her on the shoulder. "Sleep on it. Don't dwell on what is hard to understand. Just be grateful you get to wake up with a kid that isn't getting dropped six feet under this week."

Evelyn nods and closes the door. She turns to Andrea. "Are you staying here?"

"If I can," Andrea says. "Scott said the street is still a bit of a circus."

"You're always welcome here," Evelyn says. "Good night."

"Night mom," Silvey says.

"Do you still have ear plugs on my side of the bed?" Andrea asks, taking a step up.

"Ha," Silvey says. "Maybe the chamber cured my snoring!"

"Oh, if that's the case I am dragging Scott there first thing tomorrow!" Andrea says, heading up to Silvey's room.

Silvey laughs. "That line might be a little long if this gets out."

Andrea holds up her hand fingers crossed. "Only if somebody can uphold their promise!"

Silvey smiles and falls face first on the mattress. "Longest day of my life."

"Night Silvey," Andrea says, clicking the lamp off.

"Night Dre," Silvey says.

"Silvey wake up!" Andrea says.

"Why?" Silvey asks, pulling the blankets over her face.

"They've actually listened," Andrea says, pulling back the blankets. "Look!" She shoves her phone in Silvey's face.

Silvey opens one eye. "What time is it?"

"Seven," Andrea says, shaking the phone. "Just read it."

Silvey takes the phone and scrolls through the article. "They arrested Clark and the other men. Wow. That's amazing. And I didn't even have to file a police report."

"I recorded the statements from your nurse and the volunteer that witnessed the entire encounter," Andrea says. "And did you read the part about the hospital security footage showing the struggle by the ambulance?"

"Oh, no," Silvey says, thumbing through the article again. "Shoot! They've linked Eli and Charlotte to the stolen ambulance."

"That part isn't so good," Andrea says. "But they did technically aid in your kidnapping, assault the driver and medic, and steal the ambulance."

"What a mess," Silvey says, handing Andrea her phone. "Priority one is getting my phone replaced today. Plus, a new one for dad."

Andrea nods. "There's one more thing you should see."

"What is it?" Silvey asks, taking her phone back.

"Wayne said his dog was barking more than usual last night," Andrea says. "He went to investigate and there was an odd light coming from the field behind his house. He flew the drone up and captured this."

Silvey presses play and watches the aerial footage pan over the building with the lean-to and hover over the metal cover flush with the ground illuminated by several field lights.

"They found it," Silvey whispers.

"Wait a few seconds," Andrea says.

Silvey studies the footage as the camera rolls left, then right and pauses on a head poking up above the tall grass. Silvey pauses and rolls back the footage. "It's Captain Wilson."

"He made it out," Andrea says, smiling.

Silvey looks up at Andrea. "What happened to Eli and Charlotte?"

Andrea shrugs. "I'm not sure if they were captured or not." She takes back her phone and flips it to her newsfeed. She gives the phone back to Silvey. "The hospital did issue a formal statement claiming that the security officers acted out on their own and not under the direction of any personnel at the hospital."

Silvey shakes her head. "No surprise there." She reads the statement. "At least the officers were terminated."

Andrea nods. "And that they apologized to the Rhoades family."

Silvey rolls her eyes. "What good is an apology if it nearly killed my dad in the process?"

Andrea sits on the bed next to Silvey. "They have to repair their reputation, and I'm sure the media will be willing to hear your side of it when you're ready."

"That will be a day after never," Silvey says, stretching her arms over her head. "How's the circus on your street?"

"Scott texted a few minutes ago with a few pictures of the street," Andrea says. "I counted at least five news crew vans."

"Any black cars with government plates?" Silvey asks.

"Yes, at least one."

Silvey nods. "Tell Scott to meet us uptown. I need a stack of pancakes and bacon stat." She rolls off the bed and pauses by the door. "My treat!"

Andrea nods and texts Scott.

"Silvey?" Evelyn calls from downstairs.

"In the bathroom," Silvey says.

Andrea walks to the top of the steps and stops when Evelyn starts up.

Evelyn is still in her clothes from the night before and her make-up is smeared across her face.

"She's here?" Evelyn asks.

"Silvey?" Andrea asks.

Evelyn nods.

"She just stepped into the bathroom," Andrea says. "Are you ok?"

"I had an awful dream that Silvey was taken," Evelyn says.

"Again?" Andrea asks.

"What do you mean?" Evelyn asks.

Silvey swings open the door and Evelyn gasps.

"You're actually here." Evelyn rushes up the final step and wraps Silvey in a hug. "It wasn't a nightmare."

"Mom," Silvey says, "I'm fine. But you are squeezing me really hard."

Evelyn releases Silvey and takes a step back. "I took something to help me sleep and my nightmares were a vivid replay of what I can see was my reality."

Silvey nods. "I suggest a long hot shower and some unmedicated sleep, mom. It's Sunday. You don't have any clients. Just rest."

"Tell me one thing first," Evelyn says.

"Sure, mom," Silvey says.

"Did you save JFK?" Evelyn asks.

Andrea laughs. "Evelyn, what are you talking about?"

Evelyn turns her phone towards Andrea. "JFK's second inauguration hit with major blizzard." She shows Andrea the old headline.

Andrea shakes her head. "Silvey."

"I didn't get a chance to warn them," Silvey says, looking at the screen. "But I did tell Bax to if he had the chance. Did JFK make it all the way through his second term?"

"No," Andrea says, turning her phone towards Evelyn and Silvey. "He died in his sleep two days after the inauguration."

"Huh," Silvey says. "That blip of reality will make a lot of people uncomfortable." She shrugs. "I'll check with Bax tonight."

Evelyn frowns. "You're seeing him again?"

"Yes," Silvey says. "We made plans this evening."

Andrea nudges Evelyn. "It's a proper date."

Evelyn nods. "Poor kid has no idea what's coming."

"Mom!" Silvey says.

Andrea laughs. "Come on Silvey, that's funny."

Silvey rolls her eyes. "Do you see me laughing?"

"Alright," Andrea says, "maybe after you eat, you'll find that somewhat entertaining."

"Fine," Silvey says, "but I'm driving."

"We can walk," Andrea says. "It's three blocks."

"Fine!" Silvey says, stepping into her room and lifting her mattress. She pulls out some cash and stuffs it in her pocket.

"What is that?" Andrea asks, pointing towards the bed.

"My rainy day fund," Silvey says, shrugging. "It's a good thing too, because my wallet is long gone."

Evelyn shakes her head. "That's Buzz behavior. I take zero credit for that."

"Ha," Silvey says. "Do you want anything?"

"No, shower and sleep for me," Evelyn says. "If you see your father remind him that he has an appointment tomorrow with his heart doctor."

"Alright," Silvey says, walking down to the front door.

"Scott has a table," Andrea says, following Silvey outside. "Are you ready for a few hundred questions?"

Silvey glances back at Andrea. "About the money?"

"No," Andrea says. "From the patrons uptown."

"I doubt anyone will even notice," Silvey says. "It's a bunch of old timers. They are usually wrapping up their coffee chat by now."

"We still have one outlying issue," Andrea says.

"The agents?" Silvey asks.

"Yes," Andrea says. "If they found the chamber, your fingerprints and DNA will be all over that thing."

"True," Silvey says. "I can always share the tech with the world if they push me for answers." She pulls out one of the white particles.

"Oh!" Andrea says. "You took one?"

"I found it in the pocket of the shorts Charlotte gave me with a note," Silvey says, handing Andrea the note.

"In case we don't make it," Andrea says, reading the note.

"It's kind of dark, right?" Silvey asks, pointing to a web address written beneath it. "She uploaded the original suspension chamber schematics."

"What are the numbers below it?" Andrea asks.

"It's the passkey to the file," Silvey says.

"When did you figure this out?"

"When we got back from the funeral," Silvey says. "I was picking up the shorts and it fell out. I showed Bax. He looked up the file and saved it just in case."

"Do you think it's safe to walk around with it?" Andrea asks, looking around.

"There were three particles," Silvey says. "I have one, Bax has one, and we agreed to hide the other."

"At my house?" Andrea asks, stopping in the middle of the sidewalk.

"Maybe," Silvey says. "It's our insurance too."

Andrea smiles. "You left that out of your very honest reveal with Buzz and Evelyn. Why?"

"Information overload," Silvey says. "Plus, it never came up."

"Sure," Andrea says. "Tell me darling daughter, are you harboring any secret government technology?"

Silvey laughs. "I know, but it was Bax and I's little secret for a minute." She waves Andrea forward. "Plus, do you know what we are calling it?"

"What? The tech?" Andrea asks.

Silvey nods.

"Healing nano bots?" Andrea asks.

"Twisting Hercules," Silvey says.

About the Author

Kim Malaj lives on a vineyard and homestead in northern Albania with her husband, Arti, author of Northern Albanian Folk Tales, Myths and Legends. Although she is a Show Me State (Missouri) lady at heart, she loves her daily life at Homestead Albania.

When she's not writing, she tends to the garden, orchard, vineyard, and livestock. She's also been known to brew up batches of raki and wine, and other sweet and savory treats made from the fruits and veggies picked fresh from the garden. She is an avid photographer, an active blogger about the homestead, and a hobbyist drone pilot, learning the art of aerial photography and filming.

Visit her blog: www.HomesteadAlbania.com
For the latest publishing news: www.KimMalaj.com